12/14

DATE DUE

4/4	
OCT 2 2	
JAN - 8 2015	
FEB 1 9 2015	
APR 1 1 2015	
4/27/15	
5/4/15	
5/18/15	
JUN 2 @ 2015	
OCT 2 1 2015	

PRINTED I

D1070157

ROUTE 11 BOOKS
Route 11 Publications, Virginia, USA
www.route11publications.us

This book is a work of fiction. Names, characters, and events are products of the author's imagination. Any resemblance to actual persons or
events is entirely coincidental.

Cover Design: Kenn Brown

ISBN: 978-0-9892388-3-0

DEDICATION

To Allison, my wife, soul mate, and lifelong partner, who embraced the book's vision, and knowing me often better than I know myself, helped coach the book into existence.

ACKNOWLEDGEMENTS

I thank Don Muchow who taught me the first and last steps in a writer's journey: to join a writing group and eventually leave it. I also thank Don for introducing me to Kenn Brown. Don and Kenn have become lifelong friends. To Lou Aronica, Keith Farrell, Jodee Blanco, Fonda Snyder, and many others who were plugged into this vertical; I thank them for their insights and perspectives into this multifaceted industry. To Jim Czajkowski (aka James Rollins/James Clemens), Paul Melko, John Bowers, Joe Massucci, Kaza Kingsley, and Tamara Shoemaker, thanks for the wisdom, sharing your life journeys, and helping me hone my craft. Also, to the hundreds of customers in the various fortune 500 companies, government agencies, and secret military projects, without whom I would not have the perspective of the real sausage making that goes on inside the information age today, I give my thanks.

The Seed

"Technology, while adding daily to our physical ease, throws another loop of fine wire around our souls. It contributes hugely to our mobility, which we must not confuse with freedom. The extension of our senses, which we find so fascinating, is not adding to the discrimination of our minds, since we need increasingly to take the reading of a needle on a dial to discover whether we think something is good or bad, right or wrong."

—Adlai E. Stevenson, Illinois Governor, 1955

1

Monday, June 29, 2019

Steve Donovan slammed the office door and stormed through the parking lot toward his black Mustang. Behind him, footsteps slapped against the wet, dark asphalt. *Unbelievable.* Austin was following him.

Through the steam rising off the hood from the idling engine, Steve squinted into the Mustang's headlights. He saw only shadows through the rain-streaked windshield and held up his hand to tell his wife and daughter to stay put.

Austin Wheeler stepped into the light. "Now, son, come back inside. Let's talk about this." Fifteen years Steve's senior, Austin was clean-shaven with a short crew cut. The man stared down at him from his six-foot muscular frame.

Steve felt older than his thirty-five years. From his average build and height, he could not help but feel intimidated by Austin. The encounter would surely add additional premature streaks of silver in his already graying brown hair. One thing he knew for sure—Steve could not trust Austin; not anymore. "We're done talking," Steve said.

Austin stretched out his arms. "It's just a VR-enabled Internet browser. It's supposed to have glitches."

"Not glitches that kill. The Nexus isn't ready." Steve wiped the rain from his brow. He stole a glance at his watch. *Seven-thirty.*

Austin laughed. "Imagine the scenario you're worried about. The patch has to fail, followed by an energy surge."

"Followed by a seizure and death," Steve added. He looked through the steam that rose from the car hood to its occupants. Tami was going to be pissed.

Austin shook his head. "Son, we might also get hit by lighting. You might get in a car wreck. What's the difference?"

"We can prevent this, Austin."

Thunder rumbled above them. The sky had turned darker and the drizzle threatened to turn into a downpour.

Austin wagged a finger. "The release date cannot slip."

"Really?" Steve said. "Last time I checked, I was the CEO."

"You can't do this," Austin said.

Steve turned and headed to the driver's side. Pellets of rain stung his face as the storm intensified.

"Bankruptcy is around the corner. Things are in motion that I can't stop," Austin shouted after him.

Steve shook his head. *How could I have selected such an immature bastard for a partner?* Tami had warned him. He should have listened to her. Now millions of dollars into the relationship, he could not turn back.

Thunder cracked above.

"We'll talk Friday after I've had time to test things out," Steve shouted back. He opened the car door and put one foot in.

"Don't," Austin said. He had dropped his southern drawl.

Steve met Austin's scowl.

"Steven?" Tamara said.

He turned to her. "What?"

She raised her eyebrows.

"I know. We're going," Steve said.

In the backseat, Brooke stared through the rain-streaked window.

"Come on, son," Austin shouted. "One more round for the road." He waved back toward the office.

"We'll finish this in the morning." Steve sat down in the driver's seat.

"Don't do it. I'm warn …"

Steve slammed the car door. That felt good. A smirked formed but melted as he turned and faced his wife.

She stared down at her watch and frowned.

"What time is it?" he asked. He already knew the answer. Steve put the car into reverse.

"It's 7:30. The play begins in half an hour."

"I can't be late for this," Brooke whined. The teenager leaned forward from the backseat.

Steve met her gaze in the rearview mirror as he drove forward. "Get your seat belt on."

"I'm sure your father will make up the time," Tamara said.

Steve winced. Crow Canyon Road was tough even without the stormy night. "Tam, I …"

Tamara sniffed his breath. "You've been drinking," she said in a low voice.

He shook his head. "Only a couple." Steve looked into the rearview mirror. Brooke remained perched forward.

"Whoa. Do you drink, Dad?" Brooke giggled.

"Get your seat belt on," he shouted.

Brooke slumped back into the seat and crossed her arms. Steve took a deep breath and pulled onto the road. He felt a hand on his arm. "It's no big deal," Tamara said.

He nodded. The argument with Austin had gotten to him.

Bright headlights shined through his window and a horn blared.

Tamara gripped his arm. "Steven!"

He gunned the engine and negotiated the turn. The oncoming car missed the back end of the Mustang and the car fishtailed. After a second, he regained control.

Brooke's seat belt clicked in the backseat.

Tamara laughed. "Your father will get us there, hopefully in one piece."

Steve read the time on the dashboard and frowned—thirty miles in thirty minutes. He pressed down the accelerator and made the most of the 100-yard straightaway.

Tamara leaned over and lowered her voice. "Tell me, really. How much did you have to drink?"

"Only two or three."

She dipped her head forward and raised her eyebrows.

He laughed. "Really."

She smiled. The car rounded a corner. To humor her, he eased off the gas and applied the brakes. The car continued to accelerate.

Steve's heart rate took off and he punched down the brake pedal. Nothing. His stomach felt sick.

"Something's wrong," he said.

"Dad?" Brooke asked.

"I'm working on it." *Jesus.* He pumped the brakes. The car continued to accelerate, and the back tires squealed.

"Lock your door," Tamara said.

Steve heard a *click* as Brooke complied.

The back end of the Mustang slid out. Steve steered into the slide and the car crossed into the opposing lane. He pumped the brakes. Nothing. As the car drifted toward the guardrail and the chasm, Brooke and Tamara remained quiet.

The road straightened and the wheels stopped squealing. He steered back to his side of the road and glanced at their speed—50 miles per hour. How had they survived? The road pitched downward, and the car accelerated. A steep cliff rose to the right and to their left was a deep canyon. He had no place to safely ditch the car.

"What's happening?" Brooke cried.

"Quiet. Let your dad focus."

Steve glanced at the speedometer. The car passed 60 miles per hour. A sign warned of a 30-mile-per-hour turn.

"Shit," Steve yelled.

"Emergency brake!" Tamara shouted.

He reached down with his right hand and yanked on the

brake. The arm didn't budge.

The car entered the next turn, and Steve grabbed the wheel with both hands and managed to stay on the road. He exhaled. Foreplay—the real curve was still ahead.

"Tam, some help, please!" he yelled, glancing at the emergency brake.

"Oh, god!" Brooke screamed.

Tamara reached over and yanked the lever. It was stuck. She undid her seat belt and took hold of the brake with both hands.

"Hold on," Steve shouted. As the car entered the turn, he steadied the steering wheel with his left hand. With his right, he grabbed the emergency brake and yanked with Tamara.

Snap. The lever flew back.

The rear wheels lost traction and the car spun. Tamara flew back and then forward, her head slamming against the passenger window.

He turned into the spin and regained control.

"Mom!"

Steve could hear Brooke fumble with her seat belt. "Don't!" he yelled as the car began to fishtail again. Steve gripped the steering wheel with both hands and turned into the spin. They were traveling too fast.

"Tam!" he shouted. "Buckle up!" She did not open her eyes, and blood stained the window where she had hit her head.

"Tam!" he yelled, and looked up into the rear view mirror. "Brooke! Seat belt! Now!"

"Look out!" Brooke screamed.

Steve prayed for a miracle, but the car tore through the guardrail, left the road, and slammed into an oak tree.

In the distance, Ed Davis heard a crash, followed by the blare of a horn. He stepped out of the shadows and joined Austin in the parking lot of Nexus Corporation. He stood a full head above Austin from his six-and-a-half-foot frame. His salt-and-pepper hair and groomed goatee betrayed that he was older, but not necessarily wiser. National security had demanded this action. A life of public service had bequeathed Ed with the moral flexibility required to be a team player. "Is that the verdict?"

Austin smiled. "He couldn't leave well enough alone."

Ed frowned.

Austin slipped the kill switch that had disabled the brakes under his coat. "As you asked, I gave him a chance."

No, not really, thought Ed.

Above them, a flash of light preceded another crack of thunder. Ed turned toward the building. "I'll call 911."

Austin grabbed his elbow. "Give it half an hour—just to be sure."

Ed nodded.

"So, the first shoe has dropped," Austin said, pulling out a cigar and lighting it. "Now it's your turn."

Ed frowned again. "I get tired of these games, Austin."

"Sometimes you have to break some eggs."

Ed took a step toward him. "Maybe you had no problem killing off Steve and his family, but my best friend isn't a fucking omelet!"

Austin shrugged. "It's your show. You made the call."

Ed glared at him. He did not need the reminder.

"Stay professional, Ed," Austin said and took a drag from the cigar. He blew smoke into Ed's face. "Steve might be dead, but at least he had a spine."

Ed shrugged and patted his pocket. He felt the other half of the plan, a folded memo that warned of a preemptive strike by the United States against China. His bureaucratic mistake would tie up the loose ends. The memo would just disappear, like so many pieces of meaningless paper did.

He watched as the pungent cigar smoke wafted up through the mist and obscured Austin's face, except for his Cheshire-cat grin. The deed was done. The Nexus would go out, and his career was secure. And on the other side of the globe, his best friend and his best friend's daughter were probably already dead.

2

Over Hainan Island at the southern tip of China, the C130J Cargo plane lost altitude. The restraints held Allison Hwang in place as bile rose and burned her throat. Allison covered her ears as a horn blared through the cargo hold. How could anything be louder than the drone of the engines? She and her father did not have time to grab protective earplugs; they were escaping the war.

The horn went silent, and Allison glanced at her father. He smiled and stared into her green eyes. Lines of wisdom creased his Chinese face and put her at ease. She was his little girl again.

Allison shook her head. *You're twenty-eight.* Her eyes were open when she had joined her father and entered Hainan. War was probable, expected. Contention had surrounded the Spratly Islands to the south, and International law overlapped the claims of China, the Philippines, Malaysia, Singapore, Indonesia, Vietnam, Taiwan, and Brunei.

Then the Vietnamese discovered oil.

China's leadership could not resist. After sparking capitalism, China's thirst for oil exploded as its economy expanded. The promise of oil in the Spratlys was too much to pass up. For centuries, the Chinese had viewed the Spratly Islands as a phallic extension of themselves. The Chinese government primed their people with propaganda and prepared the invasion from Hainan and the Paracel Islands. The United States coordinated with the ASEAN regional forces and followed diplomatic channels. No one, least of all the Defense Intelligence Agency, had expected the U.S. President to order an early strike.

The chief of the DIA, Ed Davis, was practically her uncle. The tandem op had been his idea, a sort of pony show, and a pretense to appoint her to his post once he and her father moved on. The father-daughter team would enter Hainan disguised as reporters, collect rudimentary information, and get out.

A bureaucratic mistake had left them in the dark. As the Chinese forces mobilized, the ASEAN command struck the Chinese airfields and their exposed Navy. Without any aircraft carriers, the Chinese Navy could not protect itself, much less project any sort of threat.

They were now in the crossfire.

Allison felt a hand on her shoulder, and as she turned her head in his direction, he father gave the thumbs up sign.

Allison tied back her long black hair and looked around. She had never ridden in a cargo hold of a C130J before. The hold, which reminded her more of their unfinished garage, took up almost the entire plane. The hollow tunnel of metal supported by arched, steel beams extended from the firewall behind the cockpit to the tail. Gutted, with no carpets, no overhead compartments, and no seats except theirs, the windowless hold was cold, damp, and dark. Holes and notches for inserting chairs or equipment pitted its naked steel floor. Down the center of the floor ran two lines of rollers used to load crates. Foam pads covered parts of the ceiling and walls. Nylon netting hung everywhere else. Through the netting she saw the plane's exposed pipes, conduit, and wires that snaked along the sides of the cargo hold. It was hard to make them out in the dim light, because absolutely everything was painted or dyed the same color—an olive drab. She hated that color.

Turbulence shook the plane, and Allison's stomach churned. She hated the seats, stashed like luggage in the right corner near the firewall. They sat sideways along the wall, and every time the plane lurched backward or forward so did her stomach.

"Hang on," the pilot yelled over the cargo hold's intercom.

The plane accelerated, pitched down, and turned hard to the left. A high whine supplanted the drone of the engines, and then faded quickly. Allison exchanged a glance with her father.

He punched the intercom button and picked up the mic. "Talk to me, Briggs."

The engine drone drowned out the response; but her father frowned.

Allison looked down. Her seat consisted of nylon mesh stretched over aluminum tubing. It reminded her of a cheap lawn chair. Worse, the seat belt was a simple hook and loop mechanism. She cinched the seat belt up another notch.

A high whine grew in pitch as the plane lurched right, and then the sound faded. Allison fell forward. Her father dropped the handset.

The sound returned, louder, and a deafening concussion echoed through the hold. The explosion blew the rear-loading door open, snapping its hydraulic cables, and red hydraulic fluid spewed across the interior. The mist stung her eyes and tightened her chest. She coughed, but could not catch her breath.

Her father nudged her. He mouthed the words, "We'll be okay."

She nodded, and the coughing subsided.

The plane pulled up at a sharp angle, throwing her father against her, but the seat belt held. She grabbed the seat's metal tubing while the plane climbed higher. The air pressure clogged her head, her stomach felt sick, and her ears refused to pop. She looked through the open rear door and saw Hainan Island below. The plane was nearly vertical.

And then her father was tumbling past her. His arms flailed, and then his hands caught the loose end of a nylon strap at the rear-loading ramp. The strap went taut.

Her father lay still, his head resting against the vertical floor.

Allison traced the nylon strap; a single strand of the nylon web-
bing had caught the buckle on the other end. She released her
seat belt and pushed off, falling on the netting along the wall, and
climbed down to where the nylon strap was snagged.

The plane veered left. The net sagged from her father's weight.
She looped her legs and arms through the netting and grabbed the
strap with both hands. It tore free from the netting, but she caught
it. Behind her father, a building exploded on Hainan Island.

"I've got you." Her arms already ached and tears streamed
down her cheeks. Allison scanned the ramp. Metal inserts plugged
the holes. Her father had no hand or footholds, and the netting
on the wall was out of his reach. She looked down the strap to her
father. Below his hands, the loose end of the strap whipped around
from the turbulent blasts of air.

"Climb!" she yelled.

He bled from a gash above his eye. Was he knocked out?

"Dad! Dad! Can you hear me?" The wind whisked her words
away.

Her father lay still.

"I can't hold on much longer!"

He did not budge, but his knuckles were white. Her arms grew
fatigued, and the strap slipped a little. Her father looked up and
Allison saw resignation.

She locked her gaze into his and yelled, "You told me to never
give up on anything. Don't you give up now, Dad, don't you dare."

He began to climb, the strap cutting into her hands as he
pulled. He climbed faster.

"Slow down," she yelled. He was too heavy. Her left arm
cramped, her grip loosened, and several inches of strap slipped
through, the dull edges cutting into her hands. Her father
screamed as the strap slipped. She had never heard him scream.
The pain disappeared as her strength returned, and Allison tightened her grip. The strap slowed and stopped.

She looked down. Her hands were covered in blood, and only
a few inches of strap remained. Her father had stopped.

"I've got it!" she shouted.

He pulled himself up. The strap became slick with her blood, but now she felt no pain. He inched his way up the strap, and now only a few feet separated him from the netting. She could almost touch him. Her left arm convulsed, and another inch slipped through her fingers. Her father locked his gaze into hers and he climbed faster, the strap ripping back and forth. Her left hand went numb and she willed it to clasp tighter as the last bit of strap slipped from her hands.

Allison watched as her father tumbled down the loading ramp and fell through the gaping hole in the back of the plane. His eyes remained locked with hers, wide with fear and disbelief.

She reached out. "No! No! Daddy, don't leave me! Nooooooo!"

He faded away, his flailing body shrinking until he was just an imperceptible dot lost in the backdrop of Hainan Island.

The Incident

"But we cannot live the afternoon of life according to the program of life's morning. For what was great in the morning will be little in the evening, and what in the morning was true will at evening become a lie."

—Carl G. Jung, *Stages of Life.*

3

Camille gazed at the ocean. Fifty feet offshore two pinnacles of rock jutted out of the water. Gnarled and encrusted with sea life, they appeared as two anguished fingers rending the deep blue shroud. Beyond the pillars, the sun touched the horizon as it was setting. It flushed the sky to a fiery red and tinged the white caps a faint crimson.

The pillars' shadows inched their way up the sandy beach and rested on each side of Camille. A light breeze swirled around her and the sultry air held her like a warm blanket. She turned to the stranger who had brought her there.

"This place is so cool—uh—and beautiful," she said. *Could he tell she was only seventeen?*

In VR, she was not an awkward teenager, but a twenty-seven-year-old knockout. Camille glanced at the time fixed in the upper left corner of her vision: 3:12 p.m. Her mother would not be home for another two hours.

The stranger spoke. "It's called Tianya Haijiao, China's south-ernmost beach. The words mean *edge of the heavens, corner of the seas.*"

"Oh? Are you from here?" She smiled. His shell was Caucasian.

He nodded. "Throughout time this beach has marked the limit of China's reign, her boundary. For thousands of years the emperor exiled poets and officials to this tropical Siberia. Legend has it that these pillars represent two lost souls, their lives and dreams forgotten."

Camille did not hear his words, only his confidence. She ran her hands down her full figure. Dark hair and features framed her new face in mystique. Her dark, olive skin made it difficult to place her origin. She gazed into his eyes.

The man leaned over and brushed his lips against hers.

"Wait." She pulled back. "I don't even know your name."

His green eyes gleamed. "Syzygy."

"Siz-uh-what? She smirked. *He's a programmer.* His alias reeked of techno-inbreeding. "Computer, identify who is using the alias siz-uh-gee."

The disembodied voice of the computer said, "I'm sorry, but there is no information on the alias Syzygy."

His gaze held her.

Her mother's dating alias had shut off the V-chip, and her body responded. Warmth ignited in her heart and she felt her face blush. She bit her lip. Hundreds of miles separated them. Their only connection was the chat room's VR server. He could not track her down. At anytime she could exit with a press of a button inset on her left wrist.

Syzygy peered deep into her eyes. Camille's heart skipped a beat. He was cute. Medium-length black hair framed his distinguished features, and a five o'clock shadow highlighted his strong jaw line. His form was slender with broad shoulders, a typical V-shaped build. The breeze rippled his black, silk shirt like water across his torso. The shirt hinted at his muscular build. He looked perfect—too perfect.

He leaned toward her, and she let him press his body against hers. He kissed her, and she pulled him closer, responding to his kiss. He pressed his hips against hers, and Camille's heart and stomach fluttered. She ran her hands along his back and lifted his shirt.

Syzygy touched her lips with a forefinger and traced a line down her neck to her shoulders. His other hand brushed her left nipple. Her knees buckled. The two bodies fell to the sand, her face growing warm.

Camille ignored the simulation glitch.

He slipped off her blouse, unfastened her bra, and kissed her left breast, then her right, awakening sensations throughout her body. They overwhelmed her like nothing she had ever felt before. Whoever he was, he was not her age—intense, mature. She was ready for him.

He tugged at her pants and panties, and she kicked them free as he kissed her neck and shoulders and rolled on top of her. The warmth in her head exploded, and her vision narrowed. She heard the sound of rushing water.

"Ouch!" Camille sat up, but he pushed her back down.

"Stop it," she cried. She kneed his groin, but he did not budge.

"V-chip online!" she shouted.

Syzygy's body catapulted away from her, and Camille punched the exit button.

Nothing happened.

Her head hurt. Her ears rang. Syzygy paced around her.

"Leave me alone!"

She reached for her clothes, but he grabbed her wrist. The V-chip wasn't working. Camille wrenched free and rolled to her feet. Syzygy lunged and caught her right ankle. She tripped and fell to one knee, and he let go.

Camille got up, ran to the water, and dove in. Her nude body sliced through the waves, and she swam toward one of the pillars.

His pants and shoes will slow him down.

Camille glanced back and saw the beach was empty. She reached the pillar as the first stars appeared. The waves surged and dipped around her, and shadows danced on the water. She scanned the turbulent ocean. Camille rubbed her pounding temples. The Nexus had fail-safes. The pain was too much. She punched the exit button again. Nothing.

Between two sets of waves, she saw a dark figure. The waves passed and the ocean dipped. A reef. Just a reef.

Camille pressed the Portal button. No gateway appeared. She pounded the button. Nothing.

Deep in the water, a shadow circled the pillar. Camille kicked off the pillar and swam toward the shore, but something grabbed her left ankle. She kicked with her right leg but failed to connect.

He pulled her down, and she slipped beneath the surface. She kicked, struck him, and he let go. She broke to the surface and gasped. He grabbed both her legs. She screamed, gagged on sea-water, and slipped beneath the waves. He dragged her down.

Camille coughed, her lungs filling with seawater. She could still breathe. It was VR. Everything would be fine. None of this was real. Rods of pain shot through her head. "Computer, exit!"

Nothing.

Syzygy dragged her deeper. The water grew dark, and the cold numbed her limbs. Her heart pounded in her chest.

"Computer, spear gun!"

She felt it in her hands. Camille fumbled with the gun, pointed it down, and pulled the trigger. The spear slid into the darkness beneath her and she felt him release her. She stopped sinking.

"Computer, light!"

The water lit up twenty feet in all directions. Camille looked about. Syzygy was nowhere to be seen, but she sensed him.

"Computer, exit," Camille said. Nothing. Camille rubbed her temples. She looked up. She was deep, a hundred feet or more. She swam over and touched one of the rock pillars and barnacles cut into her palm.

She looked up as a shadow passed above her. Syzygy swam down toward her, only fifteen feet away. She backed up against the pillar, pointed the spear gun up, and pulled the trigger.

Click.

The gun was empty.

"Shit! Computer, reload," she shouted.

Syzygy grabbed the end of the gun and pushed her backward into the pillar. Barnacles and coral cut into her bare back. She pulled the trigger of the spear gun again. This time it fired.

The spear ripped through the center of Syzygy's chest, the water darkening with blood. He closed his eyes. She let go of the gun and it sank into the darkness. Camille rubbed her temples, lowered her head, and cried. Her head hurt so badly.

Syzygy's eyes snapped open. Camille didn't move. A smile crept across his face. She tried to kick off the pillar, but Syzygy wrapped his arms around the pillar and pinned her against it. The blood-laced seawater tasted sour.

"What the hell do you want from me?"

Syzygy kissed her neck. "It's almost time," he whispered.

"Computer, white shark."

Syzygy turned, and the shark that appeared bit Syzygy's chest and ripped him off her. Camille pushed off the pillar and catapulted herself upward. The water became dark as she ascended, and below her, only a dark, red cloud remained in the lit area. She scrambled up the pillar, the coral biting into her hands. Finally, she breached the surface.

Camille glanced around. It was too dark; she could not see the shore. She maneuvered around the pillar. If she could make it back, she could run to the edge of the simulation and contact the site's admin.

"It won't be long," he whispered.

He slammed her face into the pillar and spun her around, pinning her.

"Why?" Camille cried.

He kissed her neck. "The pillars are lost souls, sacrificed for the good of China. You will join them."

She struggled against him, but he was too strong. Sharp rods of pain pierced her head, and she was tired. Camille closed her eyes and cried out.

Syzygy, the pillar, and the ocean faded to black. She felt warm again, her lungs no longer felt heavy with seawater.

"Honey?" It was the voice of her father.

Her vision came into focus, and a tunnel materialized before her. A bright light came from its distant end. Her father stood between her and the light, his long shadow stretched out across her.

"What are you doing here?" Her father had died in the war with China.

"Don't worry, Cammy. Everything will be fine." He walked toward her.

"Oh, god. I'm dying! How? I'm in VR!"

Her father hugged her. "This place is like VR, but safer, more pleasant."

Back in reality, Camille's body convulsed. The signal from the Nexus had become too strong, and an electro-chemical storm raged in a localized area of her brain. Neurons fired uncontrollably and spread to other areas. Within seconds, the storm enveloped her medulla and traveled down the brainstem, the regions responsible for breathing and heart rate. Her heart stopped. She ceased convulsing. Her body went limp.

The Investigation

"The more people will know, the less they will love and care for each other. Hatred will be so great between them that they will care more for their gadgets than for their relatives. Man will trust his gadgets more than his ... neighbor."

—Mitar Tarabich, illiterate peasant, 1871

4

Steve stormed into his home office, a newspaper clenched in his hand, and hit the light switch. The room remained suspended in a sort of twilight. "That's par for the course," he muttered.

He strode into the room. Piles of books and papers covered every inch of his desk. Where was the stupid scanner? He swiped an arm across the corner of the desk. One of the piles crashed to the floor revealing the scanner, and Steve yanked open its lid.

The image reflected off the glass made him hesitate. A thirty-six-year-old man of average build and height with wild, brown eyes and brown hair streaked prematurely gray stared back at him. He looked manic and out of control.

How did I get into this mess? He stuffed the newspaper in, slammed the lid, and jabbed the scan button. A whirling noise erupted, and light escaped from around the scanner's edges as it digitized the article and downloaded it to his company's VR server. He stepped over the jumble of papers and books, now on the floor, and sat down behind the desk.

Steve ripped open a drawer and grabbed his Nexus, a black plastic object the size and shape of a cell phone. The front of the Nexus displayed the time: 8:30 a.m. PST. Steve flipped it over and entered his password into the numeric pad, and the Nexus responded with a soft *click* and popped open. It unfolded like a fan and expanded into what looked like a baseball cap without the bill. The hard plastic formed the front part of the headgear while a complex matrix of sensors hidden beneath a thin veneer of fabric made up the rest. Next to him, the scanner went silent and the escaping light winked out.

Steve plugged a phone-like cable into the Nexus' port below its numeric pad and put on the headgear. He ran his hand along the Nexus' surface, and finding the online switch, he flipped it on. A hum broke the silence of the room, and the machine ground through its startup sequence.

A black, weightless, silence enveloped him, and his body went limp. Though he did not feel it, he sank into the chair. The Nexus spoke directly to his brain through controlled electrical impulses. It bypassed his senses and muscles altogether and stimulated the areas responsible for perception, speech, and muscle control, while it triggered the paralysis experienced during sleep.

Across the Internet, the Nexus connected with his company's VR Server in the Netherlands. The sensations came—sights, sounds, and smells, not of his home office, but of a place that did not exist, a place manufactured by the VR server. The Nexus hijacked his mind and transported him across a complex lattice of copper wire, fiber optics, and satellite links to the virtual lobby of Nexus Corporation.

"Computer, retrieve the last scanned object," Steve said. A copy of the news article materialized in his hand. He clenched it and waited as the sights, sounds, and smells of the Nexus lobby faded in. His jaw dropped.

Profane phrases and icons covered the lobby's cathedral walls and expansive floor. Some hacker had broken in during the night and edited the building's file. "Shit!" he muttered, running a hand through his hair.

"My friend, I'm glad you're here."

Steve spun around. It was Ron.

"The bastards kept adding this stuff until the VR server had no more disk space."

Ron Fisher, his company's Chief Financial Officer, had a runner's build, tall and sinewy with short blond hair. His clear blue eyes were animated, and his gaze darted around the room. Next to Ron stood the man Steve was looking for.

Austin Wheeler was a stocky, eccentric, old salesman type with a southern drawl and a strong need for control. At over six feet tall, Austin's muscular countenance and intense blue eyes often put Steve ill at ease, but not today.

Brooke's cries had awoken Steve this morning when she read the article he now held. Life had not been fair to his little girl. The memory of her tear-streaked face ignited his anger. He flung the back page of the *Internet Times* at Austin. "Did you see this?"

Austin caught the paper and glanced at the article.

Teenager Dies Using Nexus Transporter

Camille Anderson was found dead at approximately 4 p.m. at her residence in Carlsbad, California. Authorities speculate that Anderson suffered an atypical seizure. An autopsy will be performed to confirm the cause of death. Upon entering the house, the victim's mother, Dr. Ashley Anderson, immediately discovered her seventeen-year-old daughter, dead and still logged onto a Nexus Transporter. Authorities ...

5

Austin looked up from the news article Steve had thrown at him. "Now calm down, son. I already know about this situation and have a plan ..."

"You know?" Steve jabbed a finger into Austin's chest. "You told me that you installed the fixed hardware. This should not have happened! That was my daughter's best friend! I'll recall the Nexus even if it bankrupts us!"

"Now what the devil are you talking about?" Austin turned to Ron, who had left and was halfway across the lobby.

Austin grinned. He took a casual puff from his virtual cigar. "Smart boy. He knows when to leave." He placed a hand on Steve's back and extended his other arm toward the back of the room. "Step into my office."

Steve led the way through the scarred lobby and down the hall. Austin's office was a simple, ten-foot square, glacier-white room with a mahogany desk, matching file cabinet, and bookcase. It was a secure location; the Nexus server only allowed two connections into the room.

Once inside, Austin said, "Computer, Phantom of the Opera, Act One, private booth."

The room transformed around them. Mahogany paneling grew across the walls of the office, while the room's white carpeting flushed to a deep red. The office furniture disappeared, replaced by a row of six chairs that faced away from them. The back wall in front of the chairs melted away and transformed into a railing overlooking a stage. An old recording of the opera played. Music filled the room and the air grew thick with the scent of cigar smoke, musty wool, and aging leather.

Austin walked around the row of chairs and sat on the end. He patted the seat next to him. "Come on over here and sit down. The Phantom here rates among the finest of the theatrical arts. Do you know the story? You could learn a lot from this—a hell of a lot. The Phantom himself was a brilliant metaphor, the shadow of excellence."

Steve walked over, leaned against the railing, and faced Austin with his back to the stage. "Austin."

"Shh! First enjoy. Where are your manners? Sit."

"I don't have time to play these games with you," Steve said.

Austin smiled and took another drag on his cigar. "Son, why don't you take a seat and calm down. Don't be so dramatic. You're just an engineer in CEO clothing. You don't have the stomach for it. Like I said, I have a plan to take care of this *without* a recall."

"You'll take care of it? Last year I told you to install the fixed hardware, but you didn't. Now it looks like your friends at DARPA missed your omission and someone is dead because of it!" Steve regretted hiring Austin, but he needed his connections into the Defense Advanced Research Projects Agency.

In the 1960s, DARPA had tried to create a military communication network that could survive a localized nuclear holocaust. Soon DARPA opened this network up and enabled first the scientific and later the private sector to join. The Internet was born.

DARPA bowed out as the Internet regulator, but with the advent of VR and globalization, society had a change of heart. In the wake of tainted products and quality control issues, DARPA took back regulatory control in the United States and approval of Internet-based products. Austin had the connections to grease the certification process.

Indeed, DARPA took less than four months to certify the Nexus. This saved Steve's company from bankruptcy; but at what cost? Steve shook his head. He had done it all for Brooke. With the company taken care of, he had focused on the Nexus Healer, a device that would enable her to walk again after the accident had left her partially paralyzed and her mother dead. Just five more days and he would announce the Nexus Healer's beta trials and surprise Brooke. She would walk again. Steve woke from his musing. Austin had turned back to the stage.

"Damn it, Austin! What have you done?"

"What have I done?" From his pocket, Austin extracted a piece of paper. He unfolded it and handed it to Steve.

Memo

During performance testing Nexus Corporation discovered that the Nexus's Signal Amplifier, which relays and amplifies signals to and from the brain, could direct an intense, prolonged signal, causing a severe seizure. In rare cases, users could die from cardiac arrest.

There are two possible solutions: repair the defective hardware with a patch in the software or completely replace the defective amplifier. Although the software solution is not completely effective, it is 16.2 million dollars cheaper than the hardware solution even factoring in the expected wrongful death lawsuits.

After careful consideration, Nexus Corporation has decided to implement the software solution. This alternative is the more cost

```
effective of the two. It will preserve the
company's viability while providing adequate
protection to the customer with a negligible
loss of life.

Sincerely,
Steve Donovan
Austin Wheeler
```

Steve looked up. "I didn't sign this. Where's the other memo?"

Austin closed his eyes, enthralled by the music as it crescendoed. "Now, that's art at its best, a fine blend of music, acting, and drama."

"Damn it, Austin! Where is it?"

"It was on the disk array that went bad."

Steve shook his head. "I never signed this!"

"I am afraid you did. That is your signature. You signed it along with a stack of other papers five months ago."

Steve took a step toward him.

"Now, calm down. I didn't want to deceive you, but it was the software solution or nothing at all. The company was broke."

"You can't blackmail me! Your name is on this memo, too!"

"No one is threatening you. This is just my insurance card. I'm in the same riverboat as you. I, too, am an accessory to murder." Austin leaned back and blew out a puff of smoke.

Steve shook his head. He should have known that Austin would pull something like this. He should have trusted his instincts and fired him a year ago; but the accident had left him in a fog, unable to make the necessary decisions. Austin had saved the company and given him the opportunity to focus on development of the Nexus Healer.

The corners of Austin's lips curled into a smirk. "One dead girl after only two million units? When production goes full scale, we'll be buried by wrongful death lawsuits. As I see it you have two choices—patch your patch, or go into the corpse business."

"Fuck you, Austin; I'm going to DARPA!"

"Really?" Austin took a puff from his cigar. "Son, what makes you think they don't already know?"

Steve frowned.

"Oh, come on Steve." Austin laughed. "Think about it. How do you think I got the Nexus approved in four months instead of two years? Last year I went straight to Ed Davis, the new Assistant Secretary of Defense that oversees DARPA. I gave him the Nexus schematics in exchange for immediate Nexus approval and some funds to keep us afloat. All in all it was what you'd call a win-win situation, a daisy of a deal."

Austin took another puff from his cigar and blew out three perfect circles of smoke. He grinned. "Now son, it's true I don't know exactly what Ed uses the Nexus for, but I believe his motives to be of a trustworthy nature. He will keep quiet about the defect and so will you. If something does slip, that memo will make you the perfect scapegoat for the lot of us—you being the CEO, inventor, and all. There's no way out for you. I'm afraid you have to play by my rules now, son."

"I'll tell you what." Steve walked past Austin toward the exit. "You do what you have to do, and I'll do what I have to do."

"Let me guess. You're going to the media?"

Steve kept walking as the music from the stage escalated.

Austin raised his voice above the music. "Do you think that'll clear your conscience, son? Like I said, the girl is dead after only two million sales. What will happen in another year? How many deaths will it take before you act? DARPA won't act; they have too much at stake."

"Austin, I'm not going to jump through your hoops," Steve said. He opened the door.

Austin remained in his seat. "I am quite serious here. Now, you know there's no one else who can fix this problem. The Nexus Transporter is too complex. No one understands her like you do. As I see it, if you enable DARPA to handle this mess, your inaction will cause hundreds, perhaps thousands of deaths. Use that peevish little brain of yours. If you think about it long enough, you'll see that I'm right."

Steve stopped. The music dipped and the melody became soft. Austin was right. The Nexus consisted of multiple sensors, emitters, and a very sophisticated computer. The computer was highly parallel and massively integrated, containing many synchronized processors. It ran over one hundred programs, each of which served a specific function for the Nexus, much like each organ serves a particular function in the human body. The complexity of each program was dwarfed by the complexity of their shared interactions. Only he and perhaps a few of Austin's Chinese associates understood the machine.

"Besides, if this becomes public news I'm sure they'll lock you up, so you can just forget about the announcement this next Monday. Brooke will just have to wait until you get out of jail before she walks again. As I said before, I do have a plan."

Steve turned.

Austin remained sitting, facing the stage with his back to Steve. His finger danced in the air with the tempo of the music.

"What is it?" Steve asked.

"Come over here where I can see you, son."

Steve returned.

"I'm surprised. I expected more of a fight from you, but then you always were a bright kid."

"Actually, Austin, it's called integrity—something you might want to look into."

"Yes, I'm sure you'd like that."

Steve stood between Austin and the stage and leaned against the railing.

Austin strained to look around Steve. "Now that's just rude, son."

Steve said nothing.

"You will investigate this death, covertly. Then, once you find the software problem, you will create a new patch and transmit it to every Nexus through the Internet. I've also had Ron create an open expense account for you with the Swiss Bank Verwaltungen. They specialize in discreet arrangements such as these. There will be no ties or transactions traceable back to the company."

The organ bellowed as the current act of the play reached its climax.

Austin sighed. "It's a shame that you don't appreciate the finer things. We're missing the best part."

Steve shrugged.

Austin leaned forward in his chair. "One of the Chinese associates, a Miss Allison Hwang, will assist you."

"She'll slow me ..."

Austin waved his hand by way of interruption. "I'm afraid you have no choice. She's connected with Ed Davis. She's my insurance that you won't miss anything else. Miss Hwang will meet you in the lobby in ten minutes. As you already stated, your corrective software patch took the life of Camille Anderson."

Austin extracted an envelope from his suit pocket and handed it to Steve. "That file contains the information that Allison has collected on Camille."

The file was lavishly stamped and embossed with Austin's gaudy signature scrawled across what appeared to be a wax seal.

"That is an encryption lock. You will need this to access the file." Austin handed him a small scrap of virtual paper with the word "patch" written on it. "That seal is the latest in security software."

Steve memorized the password and handed Austin back the scrap of paper.

"You will need that," Austin protested.

"The encryption protects the file?"

Austin nodded.

"But not that piece of paper."

Austin snorted, closed his eyes, and once again lost himself in the music.

Steve stepped out of the booth and headed down the hall toward the lobby and Miss Allison Hwang.

6

Allison awoke and gasped for air. Where was she? She sat up in bed, her arms still aching, her heart racing, and her pulse throbbing in her temples. She looked down at her hands. No blood, cuts, nothing except some scars. The nightmare faded.

"Shit!" she gasped. Allison massaged her hands. She was soaked in sweat.

A year had passed since that day on Hainan Island when the Chinese had launched their attack on the Spratly Islands. At least once a week she relived it; and when she awoke, her dad was still gone.

Fresh tears streaked her face as the images resurfaced. She took several deep breaths.

His death would not be in vain. She would find a way to fulfill his dream. Despite the failed mission and political fallout, Ed Davis had given her another shot. She promised him a way to sort though the mountains of data, to provide an interface for Warscape. That is when she approached another one of her father's friends, Austin Wheeler, about the Nexus Transporter. The Nexus became Warscape's interface, and she became the youngest DARPA chief in history. The Defense Advanced Research Projects Agency provided the Department of Defense with all the hi-tech military paraphernalia it needed, including Warscape.

Of course, Austin required special funding, and the Nexus certification had to be streamlined. Allison had abstracted these details from Davis. Now it appeared that one of these details included a deadly bug that could jeopardize the project, and in turn, her position. She would have to go undercover one more time to correct the problem and protect the agency's interests.

Allison reached for a warm Pepsi sitting on her bedside stand. She popped it open and took a gulp. The tepid soda foamed as it hit her empty stomach. A few more sips cleared her mind. She placed the empty can back on the bedside stand and noticed the clock: 8:55 a.m. She collected her thoughts. Her appointment was in five minutes. Thank god for zero commute time.

She groped for her Nexus on the stand near the bed. It was not there. Where was it? *No time.* She got up, opened a drawer, and grabbed the Portal Sphere's headgear and gloves instead.

She flipped over the bulky headset of the Portal Sphere. It resembled a motorcycle helmet and contained a flat screen for each eye and wide spectrum speakers for each ear. The fiber optic lined gloves enabled her to manipulate things in VR, but she had ditched the bodysuit and universal treadmill. Just two years prior, the Portal Sphere was cutting edge technology; then the Nexus came along.

Now there were two types of VR gear out on the market. Unlike the Portal Sphere, the Nexus made things feel real and come alive.

The Nexus bypassed the senses and muscles altogether and talked directly to the brain. Unlike the Portal Sphere, there was no screen glare, no hissing speakers, and no massive headgear pressing into your face. You would not stumble on a treadmill or hit the railing with your hand as you reached for something inside VR. The Nexus made VR feel like a dream.

Allison walked down the hall to her living room and sat in a reclining chair. She shook her head and drew back her long, black hair. She slipped on the gloves and headgear and entered a dream world, but unlike her recurring nightmare, it was a dream she could control.

Steve stepped out of the virtual hall, but instead of finding the Nexus lobby, he entered a temporary holding area, a twenty-foot by twenty-foot white-walled room with high ceilings. A single object broke up the room's monotony. Embedded in the middle of the floor was a five-foot diameter circular mirror stenciled with the word *Microsoft®*.

In an attempt to restore the lobby and erase the hacker's handiwork, Ron had taken the lobby offline. It probably would not work. They needed to restore a backup copy of the lobby; but of course, Ron had not saved his work. Steve would have to repair the lobby by hand, and he would have to do that before anything else. He glanced at the time fixed in the upper left corner of his vision: 8:57. Great, she would be here any time.

He was pacing. He stopped. He never should have confronted Austin. It was a bad idea, a very bad idea. Throwing Ron under the bus would not make it any better.

Ron was just the CFO, a glorified accountant. Austin and Steve had stuck him with management of the internal network and servers and the title Chief Financial Officer. As always, Ron made the best of it. He had a good heart. Over the last year, Ron supported Steve as he consoled Brooke and mourned Tamera's death. Ironically, they had met through Austin, the source of his ills.

A metallic whine sounded in the hallway.

Steve spun around to see a seven-foot-round, two-dimensional, black oval open up just a few feet away. It was a Portal, used to jump between different sites on the Internet. Bots in the background performed Google searches, based on the user's request, and made the transfer, or presented options if the destination was not obvious. A woman stepped through the void and with a metallic clank the Portal disappeared behind her. She was Amerasian with a lean, athletic frame and long, black hair that contrasted with her green eyes.

She's beautiful, he thought. *No, you're just desperate after being alone for almost a year.* Yet, he could not take his eyes off her. His neediness remained, gnawing at him.

She turned her head from left to right and slowly scanned the room. He smiled. Her deliberate movements were the telltale signs of a Portal Sphere user. The images would jerk as the Portal Sphere panned.

She smiled when she saw him. "You must be Steve."

He nodded and walked to her as she extended her hand. "Allison Hwang."

He shook it.

"Where are we?" she asked, pushing her hair behind her ears.

That was a mistake. Before Steve could say anything to stop her, she stumbled as she knocked her Portal Sphere's headgear askew and turned her view of the room sideways.

Her arms flailed as she fell. Steve caught her. "Close your eyes."

"What? Oh." She closed her eyes and readjusted her headgear. After a second, she opened them, and Steve helped her to her feet. "Thank you. I guess I developed some bad habits with the Nexus."

Steve nodded.

"Did Austin tell you that I was coming?"

"You're here on Austin's behalf."

"That's right."

"Are you an engineer?"

"Not exactly."

"So, what exactly are you here to do?"

"Uh, to help where I can, cut through the bureaucratic bullshit, stuff like that."

Steve sighed. "Do you know *anything* about the Nexus?"

Before she could answer, the figure of another woman materialized in front of them. Allison shot him a questioning look.

"That is my CFO's idea; an advertisement before we enter the site. It'll help pay for renovations."

The woman had just come out of a shower. Wrapped in a towel, she laid on a bed in front of a laptop computer. She spoke to her husband across the Internet through video conferencing software.

"I miss you too, dear," she said.

A second image materialized in juxtaposition to the first. A man in a business suit hunched over his work computer.

"Honey! Someone will see you."

"Don't you wish!" She threw her wet hair back and revealed some cleavage.

"I wish I were home."

"Why can't you come home now? Seattle's not that far from Portland. You could catch a flight tonight and fly back to Seattle in the morning."

"I'm sorry, babe. I can't. Could we meet online?"

The woman shook her head. "It's not the same." The woman took out a credit card. "You know you left me with your VISA card, John."

"Damn! I left home without it?"

She took the card and ran the edge up her side.

The man held his breath as he watched the screen.

"Can you see what I am doing with it?" She pressed the card against her breast.

The man laughed. "You know I can. I really, really wish you wouldn't do that!"

She kissed the screen and smiled. "We'll be waiting," she said. She slipped the card beneath the towel.

The images faded as a voice announced: "VISA, it's everywhere you want to be."

"Ah, who's this, my friend?"

Steve turned. Ron stood a few feet away, a smirk painted on his Scandinavian face.

"What kind of ad was that?" Steve said.

"You didn't get it?"

"Of course I got it, and I want it turned off. No more ads. Okay?"

Ron bowed. "Anything for you. Care to introduce me to your new girl friend?"

Allison laughed, and Steve cringed. He was glad that the Nexus could not show him blushing.

"This is Allison Hwang, an associate. We'll be working together."

"Working. I see." Ron winked.

Steve turned to Allison. "May I introduce Ron Fisher, our CFO and my social coordinator?"

"Charming." Allison extended her hand to Ron.

He lifted and kissed her hand, then turned to Steve. "Can I show you something?"

"Let me guess. Taking the lobby off and then online didn't clean up the graffiti."

Ron shook his head.

"What graffiti?" Allison asked.

Ron answered her by transporting them from the holding area into the lobby of Nexus Corporation.

They did not fade in or step through a portal. Steve stumbled to one side before regaining his feet. He heard Allison gasp.

"Sorry about that," Ron said. "I haven't been able to install the dampening software since the hackers did this." He pointed to the lobby.

Steve looked around. Profane phrases and icons covered every inch of the lobby's cathedral walls.

"Wow!" Allison scanned the lobby. "Someone really, really hates you guys."

"I'm sure it was one of Steve's fans. Nothing is more pleasing to a hacker than embarrassing the guy who started it all." Ron winked at Allison. "Don't worry. This won't be too difficult for him to fix, right?"

"That depends. How far are you into the lobby's set up?"

"What do you mean?"

"Can we alter anything real, like manipulate machines or change production lines from in here?"

"Not yet," Ron said.

"Then I think we're fine. It looks like the hacker painted over the existing environment, adding to the database, not modifying it."

"Uh, what are you guys talking about?" Allison asked.

"You don't know anything about the Nexus, do you?"

She shook her head.

"Nexus Corporation lives within a computer, specifically a VR server on the Nexus Corporation's network. Through the Internet, the VR server feeds each of us a perspective of this lobby as we interact with the environment and each other.

"The VR server treats the lobby as an amalgamation of objects. Every beam, tile, and panel in here is stored in its database. These objects consist of sight, sound, scent, taste, touch, and gravity components. When the hackers came in and vandalized the lobby, they used tools similar to the ones Ron used to design this place. They added objects. They laid them on top of the existing environment. Every graffiti slogan they sprayed appended an object to the database. If we remove the latest objects from the database, the lobby will be restored to its original form. All we have to do is strip off these new objects the hackers added, while looking for signatures which might point to those who did the hacking."

Ron laughed. "Steve, you make it all sound so simple."

"Well, it made sense to me," Allison said.

Ron raised an eyebrow. "And you're not his girl?"

"Mr. Fisher, I'm nobody's girl."

"And feisty, too!"

Allison shot Steve a look.

He acknowledged with a nod. "It'll just take a few minutes to clean this up." Steve pressed a button on his virtual wrist. A rod of metal, six feet long, appeared in his left hand. As he pointed the rod at one of the walls, the graffiti on the wall disappeared.

"Cool toy! Let me try that." Ron reached for the rod.

"Ron!"

Allison laughed.

"Can't you at least pretend we're professionals?" Steve whispered to Ron.

"Sorry, friend!" Ron laughed and backed off.

It took a few seconds for Steve to finish the task. He stepped back and surveyed the room. Down the center of the white marble floor ran a black marble path bordered by threads of turquoise. The path led to the front desk and hallway beyond. Around the edges of the room, white marble pillars jutted skyward supporting a large, domed ceiling, perhaps eighty feet above them.

"Wow! Not bad!" Allison said.

No longer covered by graffiti, Steve saw an exposed stream. It cut through the black marble floor near the wall. He walked to it and knelt down. "Computer, activate the sniffer."

The sniffer materialized in front of him. In cyberspace it appeared as a rigid, thin sheet of paper with a long glowing tail attached at its base. He took the tail and placed it in the stream. Blocks, letters, numbers, and various symbols appeared on the paper. They materialized left to right and down the page. When they reached the bottom, a clean sheet of paper appeared on top of the first and filled the page with more symbols. The stack of paper continued to grow, one a second, until he had collected about ten pages. Steve frowned.

"Well, Ron," Steve muttered, "I hope these were just juvenile hackers."

"What is it?" Ron kneeled next to him.

"Did you see this?"

Ron shrugged.

"This stream represents a segment of the network, the segment that connects the VR server to Nexus Corp's other computers and the Internet at large. It carries day-to-day operational and financial data. Not all of the data is encrypted. The hackers could have used a sniffer like this to access our company's data, or worse, to insert a virus. You need to cover or encrypt this data stream ASAP." Steve stood.

"Has our data been hacked?" Ron asked.

Steve shook his head. "No way to tell. With backups, we could compare before and after the attack. The graffiti could be camouflage meant to write over the remnants in memory that would show us what programming tools they used to hack the site or to deliver a virus."

Ron frowned. "A virus? Are we infected?"

"I can't say. Viruses are very small and easy to hide. I won't go into detail, but an undetected virus is like a spy in an organization. Once accepted as one of the fold, you can't find it without making every system, program, and data file a suspect."

Ron looked confused.

"Most viruses do the same three things: infect, multiply, and express. After slipping in, the virus will find a vulnerable computer to infect. On any network, usually at least one insecure system exists that is not password protected. Otherwise, it will try various combinations of usernames and passwords on every system until it gets into a system. Once inside, the virus can use a number of methods to multiply and spread across the entire network. Many protocols allow "trusted" systems to talk to one another. Yet, the virus is harmless until it expresses itself and does its master's bidding. This could be anything. It could start sprawling more political graffiti. It could secretly transmit company data to a competitor, and it could do this whenever. The environment or a timer could trigger it."

"This is worse than the war. At least then I was fighting something tangible—something I could see and touch—something that would bleed," Ron said.

"It's not as bad as it sounds."

"Not bad?"

"This is the worst case scenario. The site is new. I don't think they did anything. Just cover those data streams and start making backups."

"Okay, but I'll page you if anything comes up."

Steve nodded. "Anytime." He looked around. Allison had wandered across the lobby.

"So, my friend, who's the new assistant?" Ron asked.

Steve tore his gaze away from her. "Will you lay off?"

"Sorry, friend. When you see others suffer, you appreciate your friends and family more, especially those going through hard times."

"What are you talking about?"

"You know."

"Ron, I'm not ready for anyone."

"That's my point. You'll never be ready. You'll always be desperate. You need a woman."

Steve shook his head.

Ron cocked an eyebrow. "I'm serious, my friend."

"I appreciate your concern. If I need a blind date, you're the first person I'll call."

"You're worried about Brooke aren't you?"

"Of course. Her mother is dead."

"Tamara was also your wife. Sometimes I think Brooke holds you back."

"Ron, she's my daughter."

Ron looked over Steve's shoulder and Steve turned to follow his gaze as Allison approached.

"Are you boys done?"

"He's all yours," Ron said, and then winked and walked off.

Steve pulled out the file from Austin. "Is this your work?"

She nodded.

"What's in it?"

"Information about Camille," Allison said.

"I'll need a few hours to review it. We can get together this afternoon."

"Can it wait?" Allison asked crossing her arms.

"It took less than a year for the first victim. I think the investigation can wait a couple of hours. I'll need time to review what you sent me. Could we meet around four?"

"Four it is." She pressed a button on her wrist. "Hwang News Agency." A portal opened and she stepped through and disappeared.

Steve pressed the exit button on his wrist and left VR.

Ron watched as Steve disappeared from the Nexus lobby. He needed to find out why she was here.

7

Pitch black surrounded Allison. From the darkness her mother, Jamie Hwang, shouted, "Action!" A thousand miles ahead the Earth appeared, light radiating from its surface. A metal cylinder replaced Allison's body, immobilizing her. Staring at the Earth, her perception shifted and she realized she was floating above the Earth as it slowly rotated below.

"It's a Japanese KH-15B spy satellite," the disembodied voice of her mother said.

Through the satellite's camera Allison recognized the outline of Hainan Island, surrounded by the South China Sea. Through its metal hull, she felt the bone-chilling cold of space, or at least a token of it. Otherwise, the scene was soundless, scentless, though it had a slight metallic taste.

"Not sexy enough," her mother said.

"You said this piece was finished. Ed needs it now," Allison demanded.

"I'm just touching things up, dear. Computer, hold it!"

The scene froze. Allison scanned the collection of gauges and timers fixed in the lower left corner of her vision. Her mother used these to track and alter the scene.

"Phil, add some space music."

A disembodied voice replied, "Which one do you want? I can ..."

"You're the expert," Jamie snapped. "Pick something. Make it foreboding."

The space around Allison filled with hundreds of deep rumbles. The individual sounds blended into a single source. Merged together, they felt ominous and deep. A gauge displayed a row of ten bars. The last two spiked up and down in cadence with the rumble.

"Phil, I don't like these gauges. I need to see, hear, and taste what my audience does. Understand?"

The gauges disappeared from Allison's view.

"Continue!" Jamie shouted.

The scene restarted and the satellite zoomed in. The South China Sea expanded below. Within seconds, twelve little dots appeared against the deep-blue ocean canvas. The dots expanded and transformed into a dozen Chinese destroyers, frigates, and support ships. They sailed south in a traditional defensive circle east of Hainan Island and just north of the Paracel Islands. The ship cluster was a battle group of the People's Liberation Army. In its center was *Varyag*, the first Chinese aircraft carrier.

An airplane landed on its deck while another slipped beneath the black top and rolled off a flat elevator. The airplanes looked like toys compared to the carrier. The image lingered for a moment as the subliminal tones faded.

Jaime spoke, her voice superimposed over the scene. "China's military flexed its muscles on Saturday in what analysts saw as another warning to Hainan Island and their failure to suppress the students' protests at Haikou University. Recently, Hainan Island regained its distinction and joined Hong Kong and the other Chinese coastal cities as economic free zones. Since then, islanders have pushed for Hainan's political autonomy.

"One week ago, students at the University started their public protest, calling for free elections and requesting that the economic autonomous regions on Hainan be expanded to encompass the entire island.

"Yesterday, on China's State television, the Guangzhou Military Command in Southern China gave China's unofficial response. The Chinese News Agency showed PLA's Army, Navy, and Air Force units taking part in a combined military exercise off southeastern Hainan near the Paracel Island group. In addition, images of the PLA's airbases, seaports, and Army bases all around Hainan Island showed the island's military at high alert. A Chinese analyst, who spoke on condition of anonymity, said that the exercises were obviously aimed at Hainan's leadership. He went on to say that the Island's economic freedom was not all that was at stake.

"Today, at the request of the President, the Assistant Secretary of Defense, Ed Davis, met with the Chinese foreign ministry spokesman, Shen Guofang, in person. The talk centered on the PLA's military buildup in the region, which is in violation of the China War Treaty. In a Hwang News Service exclusive, we have both parties here to discuss the tenuous situation."

The image of the battle group faded. Allison transitioned back into her body. She sat among an audience of thirty. At the front of the quaint room, Shen Guofang and Ed Davis faced one another across a small table. Etched into the virtual floor was a map of the South China Sea, and Chinese collectibles decorated the walls of the room.

"Good details," her mother said.

Both men had dressed appropriately in conservative western dress—suit and tie. Both were well groomed, but Shen appeared overweight. Perhaps her mother could touch him up a bit.

Ed Davis' trim six-and-a-half-foot frame made an impression even sitting down. His salt and pepper hair and groomed goatee completed a distinguished and aristocratic air.

Allison glanced at the time: 10:27 a.m. PST. That made it 1:27 a.m. in Hong Kong where the VR clip was recorded. She grimaced. The clip was almost three hours old. The story was growing stale and Ed was waiting. "How much longer will this take?"

"Shh," whispered Jamie.

The interviewer spoke. "Good evening, Mr. Shen and Mr. Davis."

Ed nodded.

Shen leaned forward and smiled. "I am greatly honored to be here today."

Allison wrinkled her virtual nose as the scent of stale sweat wafted to her from Shen.

"Now that's a little detail I can do without!" her mom said. "Freeze for a moment, people."

The scene stopped and the gauges reappeared.

"Can't you guys do anything about that stench?" Jamie asked.

Allison saw one of the gauges drop a couple of notches and the air became less thick.

"That's good! Replay it!"

The journalist greeted Shen and Ed, and Shen responded.

He still stank. "Better, but—man he reeks! Do you have the scent for the Seattle guy?"

"Yes," Pete said.

"Give me a whiff."

"Who's the Seattle guy, mom?" Allison asked.

"I don't know. I forgot his name, but what a lover."

Allison rolled her eyes.

"Ah, that will do it. Douse Shen," Jaime said.

Instantly, the offensive odor was replaced by a cocktail of Old Spice deodorant, spiked with just a hint of Polo cologne.

"Okay people, resume!"

The scene resumed as Ed spoke: "Before we begin, I would like to offer a gift to my esteemed colleague." Ed faced Shen. "May I present to you the finest in the United States' consumer electronics—a Nexus Transporter." The symbolic gesture showed, despite their differences, the two countries were economically linked and committed to free trade.

Shen bowed and accepted the gift. "Thank you. May I also offer you a gift?"

"Of course," Ed said. He bowed.

Shen handed him a small jewel-covered box. Ed opened the box and extracted a Rolex watch.

Not a Chinese product, Allison mused. Her boss did not seem to mind the deviation from the script. "Thank you," Ed responded, placing the watch on his wrist.

Shen gave him a broad, exaggerated smile.

The moderator turned to the Chinese diplomat. "Mr. Shen, why is China once again violating the Chinese peace accord in the South China Sea?"

The lines forming Shen's grin transformed to a wrinkled brow. "The Chinese are a peace-loving people. We have no quarrel with the United States. Why must you meddle yet again in our domestic affairs?"

"Excuse me? Yet again? Could you be referring to your unprovoked invasion of the Spratly Islands last year? I'm afraid that the Spratly Islands are not just another part of China."

Shen shook his head. "Your country is young and has a short memory. We've claimed those islands for over two thousand years. Though we are a patient and peaceful people, China has waited over a century for common sense to prevail and for the return of the Spratly Islands."

Ed leaned forward aggressively. "That attitude is exactly why the United States and its ASEAN partners cannot allow these military exercises. Your claim on those islands is tenuous at best. Every nation in the area has staked claims on one or more of them. Vietnam, for example, backs its claim on the fact that it has occupied some of the cays and reefs for over three hundred years."

Ed looked into the camera. "Now, as for Hainan, the people want political freedom. You've already given them economic freedom. Why can't you let them hold democratic elections?"

Shen shook his head in denial. "Mr. Davis, I respect your intentions; however, China is not the United States. We have our own beliefs and code of honor. China holds the answers for China; the United States does not."

"But then again, we don't torture and butcher our own people," Ed said.

Shen shifted in his chair. "Mr. Davis, it's easy to talk about freedom when people are fed, clothed, and sheltered. It's a different matter when they're not. Let me remind you that there are two experiments going on right now. Like us, the Russians too are moving away from communism; however, the Russians chose to implement political freedom before economic freedom, holding democratic elections first before economic reform. Here in China we've done the reverse.

"Now tell me, which experiment do you think is working? Would you have our people starve, ruled by criminal organizations, as in Russia, to satisfy your imperialistic hunger to make everyone like yourselves?

"Mr. Davis, let me reiterate to you—China has no ill will toward the United States. Why are you trying to control us? Our military is purely defensive in nature. We simply want a reunified China with reconciliation among her different nationalities. We want harmony and peace. That is all."

"That is not all, Mr. Shen. You cannot ignore that just a year ago your country invaded the Spratly Islands without provocation. And as for the Russians, their problem is that they've never had private ownership of land. The Czars, and later the communists, held all the lands for the Russian people. The Russians have no courts, no laws, and no customs geared for a capitalistic society. China, on the other hand, has had these things for centuries. That is, until the communists mucked things up."

Shen stood. "I'm most sorry, but I must go now. Thank you." He smiled politely, turned, and left.

The moderator paused. "Thank…thank you Mr. Shen." He turned to Ed.

"Hold it!" Jamie shouted.

The scene froze.

"Okay. Everything after Shen's final response until the interviewer speaks is out. And link the two scenes together. Make it smooth, people! Now, play!"

The scene backed up a few seconds and resumed. Shen spoke mid-sentence.

" … want harmony and peace. That is all."

"Thank you, Mr. Shen," the moderator said. He turned his focus to Ed. "Mr. Davis, you're the Assistant Secretary of Defense and as such oversee Warscape. For the benefit of our viewers, can you tell us what Warscape is."

"Certainly. Warscape is a system we use for military surveillance of the South China Sea. The combined forces of ASEAN, which includes the United States, use Warscape as their eyes and ears. We can pinpoint every Army, Navy, Air Force, and Marine unit regardless of nationality. It has protected us from Chinese hostility since before the China War."

"It sounds impressive."

Ed nodded.

"How does it work?"

"There are two sets of systems—one for our allies and one for the non-allied forces. We track our allies, the ASEAN military, through GPS. Every structure, soldier, and piece of equipment manufactured for the ASEAN armed forces has been outfitted with a GPS sensor. These sensors use satellites to calculate their exact positions and report those positions to Warscape, which is updated instantly with this information. This way we can track everything under our command and know when equipment is destroyed or disabled.

"In order to track non-ASEAN forces we blanket the area with inexpensive sensors that detect, identify, and report back to Warscape any changes in their surrounding environment. In addition, manned and unmanned vehicles on land, in the air, and under the sea patrol this area. They detect anything out of the ordinary. If that's not enough, we have several satellites in geosynchronous orbit with cameras trained on the South China Sea.

"These Warscape perspectives give us a complete, real-time picture of the battlefield. Warscape has eliminated the fog of war." Ed finished speaking and leaned back in his seat.

The interviewer smiled. "Very impressive! How expensive is Warscape?"

"Slightly over three hundred billion dollars."

"Three hundred … did you say three hundred billion?"

"Yes."

"How can the President justify such an expenditure when all other budgets are being drastically cut?"

"This region is of vital interest to the United States. More oil rests under the waters of the South China Sea than under the sands of Kuwait. Further, it is one of the busiest shipping lanes in the world. Over eighty percent of Japan's trade alone passes through this region."

"So what response, if any, is the U.S. going to take to the Chinese actions on Hainan Island and the presence of its Navy in the South China Sea?"

"Our carrier battle group, *Abraham Lincoln*, will position itself north, close to the Paracel Islands and near the Chinese fleet. The Chinese will back off and return to port. They have no choice. The PLA has no answer to the combined power of a carrier battle group and Warscape."

"If Warscape just monitors the region, how can it be so important?"

"Before a nation can go to war, it must first prepare to attack. It takes several days to set up lines of communication, mobilize forces, and stockpile logistics, such as ammo and fuel. Last year, just before the Chinese War started, Warscape detected China gearing up for battle. We stuck them before they were ready. Surveillance is everything."

"But what if Warscape fails?"

"What is he doing?" Allison asked.

"Shh," her mother whispered.

"It can't fail," Ed said. "How can millions of sensors, unmanned vehicles, and satellites fail all at once?"

"I hear your point; however, before World War II the French found themselves short on defense spending. They also placed their faith in a single system, a complex series of trenches and fortifications called the Maginot Line; yet, the Germans bypassed the line and France fell in three weeks. Aren't you afraid of repeating history here by putting all your eggs into one basket?"

"The Chinese are geared for a land war, but any future war over the region will be won from the air. That requires aircraft carriers. The Chinese have no aircraft carriers."

"What about *Varyag*?"

Ed shifted in his seat, and the interviewer continued.

"The Chinese battle group near the Paracel Islands includes a ship called *Varyag*. It is a Kuznetsov-class aircraft carrier bought from the Ukrainians in an auction by a surprisingly small company called the Chung Travel Agency Ltd. Ever hear of them?"

Ed shook his head.

"Neither had we. They claimed they were going to convert the ship into a floating hotel and gambling parlor, towing the carrier to Haikou on Hainan Island. The problem is that officials in Haikou had warned the Chung Travel Agency that they would not be permitted to dock the huge ship in their harbor. So, if Haikou had already rejected their plan for a floating entertainment complex, why do you think the company went ahead with buying and towing the warship?"

Ed glared at the interviewer, who continued to speak.

"The Hwang News Service has learned that the Chung Travel Agency does not have offices in Haikou. In fact, there's no such company listed anywhere in Hainan ..."

"Okay, that's enough, Mom," Allison said.

" ... It turns out that Chung Travel Agency is owned by a Hong Kong firm called Chin Holdings Company. Six of Chin Holdings' eight board members hail from the same area in China, Shandong Province, which just happens to be where the Chinese Navy builds its ships. And Chin Holdings' chairman is a former career military officer with the Chinese People's Liberation Army. Coincidence, you think, Mr. Davis?"

"Mom, I said stop!"

"Computer, hold it," Jamie said.

The scene froze.

"Please, call me Jamie. Now tell me, what's wrong?"

"What's wrong? I gave you an exclusive and in return you're crucifying my boss!"

"The people have a right …"

"Stuff it, Mom. I can rant National Security and none of this will get aired." Her mother sighed.

"I don't have time to banter with you. Make your decision," Allison said.

"What do you want me to do?"

"Cut everything after Ed's speech on Warscape. That's the spin he'll be looking for."

"Ally, don't be disrespectful. If your father …"

"Edward was Dad's best friend and practically my uncle. You know *exactly* what Dad would say."

Silence followed. "Okay," her mother said. "But I don't think the networks will buy it."

"Do your best." Allison sighed. *One down. Now to work on Steve and win him over.*

8

Steve sat down on the bed next to his daughter. Although she forced a smile, her red and puffy eyes betrayed that she had been crying.

This could not be good for her, sulking like this. Steve sat up and opened the shades to her room. The sunlight streamed in and bathed Brooke in light. She was very distraught, he noticed, and he felt another pang of guilt. His invention had killed her friend. How could he tell her?

He sat down next to her, brushed the hair from her face, and wiped the tears from her eyes and cheeks.

"Thanks," Brooke said. She took his hand, cradled her face with it, and turned and pressed her forehead against his hand. After a few seconds, she sat up. Steve helped her into the wheelchair.

"It's okay. I've got it now."

"Take it easy today. I'll be in my office if you need me," Steve said.

Brooke shifted in the chair and looked down at her withered legs.

It won't be long, he thought. He would correct the past. Steve left and walked down the hall to his office where sat behind his desk.

"Dad?"

Steve looked up.

Brooke maneuvered the wheelchair through the doorway.

"What is it, sweetheart?"

"I need my Nexus. There's a chemistry test next Monday."

"Definitely not!"

Brooke stared at him, wide-eyed.

"I mean, uh, no. There's a problem with the Signal Amplifier," Steve said.

"Whatever. Can I use yours?"

Steve shook his head. "You need some down time."

"I told you; I forgot about Monday's exam. It'll just take a minute."

"If it's just a minute, use the Portal Sphere."

"You're not making sense!" Her gaze bored into him.

He looked down. "Your friend died while using the Nexus. I don't want you to use it until I know more." There. He had said it.

"Camille, her name was Camille! You could at least try to remember her name now that she's dead!"

Steve cringed. He was never good with names. "I'm … I'm sorry, Brooke."

Brooke left his office and slammed the door the best she could from her wheelchair.

He should have watched Austin more closely. The Nexus should have never been released without the hardware fix. Poor Brooke. He knew he was being overprotective. Out of the millions of Nexus users, why would Brooke be the next victim? Something in his gut warned him just the same.

Steve reached down and unlocked the file drawer of his desk. No files were inside, only a single bottle of Glenfiddich Scotch and a lone tumbler glass. He filled the glass.

He had not always been a heavy drinker. After leaving college, or rather after he was kicked out, he took a long hiatus from his addiction. Much later, when Nexus Corporation had edged toward bankruptcy, he rediscovered scotch to calm his nerves.

Steve drained the glass and contemplated the empty tumbler. He recalled his first sip after so many years of sobriety. Closing his eyes, he relived the sensations—the feeling of scotch sliding down his throat, his body absorbing it before it reached his stomach. His hands calmed, and the anxiety he felt dissipated. After that day, he became subdued and withdrawn. Numbed by his addiction, he would have been content with letting his company starve itself out of existence; but then fate intervened. His breaks failed and he crashed his car.

Steve filled his glass and swallowed hard. Almost a year had passed since he wrapped the car around the tree and killed Tamara and crippled Brooke. What if the scotch in his blood had not dulled his reflexes? Could he have navigated the turn? Could he have discovered the problem earlier, saved his wife and spared Brooke?

He was lucky. By the time he reached the hospital, most of the alcohol had left his system. A few on the scene were suspicious, but no one knew for sure. To Austin's credit he had helped keep things hush-hush. Steve had vowed that day to make a difference in Brooke's life. He had made a covenant with himself—Brooke would walk again.

The next day, with courage borrowed from scotch, Steve empowered Austin to run Nexus Corporation. It enabled Steve to focus on his secret project, the Nexus healer, which would enable Brooke to walk again. Steve shook his head and attempted to evade the memory. What had he done to Brooke? He had taken so much from her—her mother, the ability to walk, and now her best friend.

Steve sighed. He drained the last drop from the tumbler and replaced it, along with the scotch, in the bottom drawer. Steve placed the Nexus on his head, flipped the switch, and entered VR.

Steve materialized in his home away from home—his virtual office. In all directions, an endless black floor, checker-boarded with neon green lines, stretched to the horizon. He did most of his work here. The boundless open space without any frills or distractions allowed him to focus.

"Jan," Steve said, summoning his automated secretary, an

intelligent software agent that controlled his virtual office. She functioned as a glorified keyboard and screen for his VR server. Like every site on the Internet, his home office resided on the hard drive of a VR server located in some remote office building. Jan interpreted what he said and executed the appropriate programs on the VR server. Jan's ability to understand abstract problems and her attempts to solve them is what made her software *intelligent*.

Jan materialized before him. He had modeled her after Mrs. Jan Beecher, his high school math teacher. Steve had also programmed her with the same disposition. "Oh, good, you're back. I was getting worried."

"Jan, open the Nexus file," Steve said.

He had carried Austin's file to his office. The object representing the file had been copied from Nexus Corporation's server, transmitted across the Internet, and saved on his office's VR server. If anyone had examined the file while it was in transit, it would have appeared as a random series of numbers, letters, and symbols. The encryption key, like a translator, transmuted the file and revealed the true data contents.

"What are you waiting for?" Jan probed.

Steve chuckled. Sometimes he regretted programming Jan with such an attitude. "The key is *patch*, he responded.

"How creative," Jan said.

The file in his hand disappeared as Jan broke the seal, and a circular globe appeared and levitated in front of him. A short file of Camille Anderson played across its surface. She had visited the house once while on a family trip. She looked now as she had looked then—beautiful, innocent, and very, very young.

Steve took a deep breath. All he could do was concentrate on the problem at hand.

"Jan, summarize the contents of this folder."

"Oh sure, it contains 941 pages of text, 121 pictures, and 31 video clips. The text consists of 10,381 paragraphs, 37,961 lines, 312,620 words …"

"Jan, that's enough." It was going to be a long afternoon.

He looked again at the girl's image. Her gaze bore into him. "I'm sorry," he said softly. *No else will die from this. I promise.*

9

Shannon Pierce grabbed the controls of the flying disk, checked her gauges, and righted the aircraft. The console was dark—no flashing lights. Good, nothing damaged. Well, almost nothing. Her head still throbbed from where she had hit the wall of the cockpit. Whoever he was, he was good.

Dogfight Central had opened last year as a chat room for fighting enthusiasts. The release of the Nexus Transporter had pushed it over the top. It was the new thing. The adrenaline induced from aerial combat was addictive. Dogfight Central diverged from the standard live combat site in that it had the added twist of being a dating service. The site had matched Shannon with another player based on their answers to a common set of questions. The loser would pick up the tab for the date. Shannon came here often because she never lost, and it allowed her to unwind after work.

She clocked the early shift from 4 a.m. to noon as a support analyst for Metis Data. All day she listened to the needs of irate customers. Like most support organizations, they were understaffed and overworked. Of course, the company continued to talk about quality, empowerment, and other such jargon. For Shannon it translated to long hours, low pay, and no respect. She shot down planes, disks, and other aircraft to release her anxiety and relieve her loneliness.

Shannon was alone. She had finally moved out of her parents' home last year. At thirty-three she was having a hard time adjusting. New in town, she had very few friends. Her odd working hours did not help things. Although it was easy to create superficial relationships online, it was much harder to forge meaningful connections. She satisfied her hunger for intimacy with free dates in cyberspace. They satisfied her enough to get her through until the next day.

Shannon regained her bearings and scanned the horizon. At two o'clock and a thousand feet down, she saw her assailant speeding away.

He assumed he killed me. His arrogance was her lucky break. Shannon shoved the throttle forward, and her disk accelerated. The sudden surge pressed her back into the seat. She forced the stick down and sent her disk into a hard dive, watching the indicators to make sure she did not stall one of her four engines. His craft filled her view screen. It was a Sierra jet with cropped wings, which made it look more like a rocket. A smile crept across her face as she moved in for the kill.

At the last second, he veered his craft hard to the right, but it was not soon enough. Shannon managed to correct her descent and gouge a three-foot break along the jet's right wing with the sharp edge of her circular aircraft. Oil seeped from the wound and his jet vibrated from the loss of aerodynamics.

She stole a look aft as she passed him by. His jet slowed and its nose dipped toward the ground. She made a leisurely circle and came around to finish him off. *All too easy.*

She lined up her disk behind him and followed his shallow descent, but he dove and broke right, and she overshot his position. The gauges on her console were blank. Where was he? She scanned again and he appeared on the radar—behind her. *He's good.*

Shannon turned a square corner just as a river of fire leaped from the pursuing jet, and bullets ripped through the outer shell of her disk. Still flying forward, she spun the disk around like a top.

Her main guns faced her pursuer, and Shannon smashed down on the stick. The disk angled up, and as the jet appeared through her gun sights, Shannon squeezed the trigger. A thousand rounds a second leaped from her gun, but the stream of lead passed directly in front of the jet.

The jet veered up. With the skill of a surgeon, she nudged her rudder and stitched the jet from nose to tail with lead. Fuel spewed from the wounds and caught fire. She checked her gauges. Everything was green—no yellow or red lights anywhere.

Shannon looked up. A shroud of thick smoke hid him. Like a top, Shannon spun the disk back around and faced forward. The ground was close.

She banked up hard and heard the whine of the missile too late. The warhead tore through the outer shell of her disk and knocked her craft sideways. The missile failed to detonate and continued on its path, disappearing into a cloud. She righted the disk, gained a little altitude, and glanced at her gauges.

One of the engine lights flashed red. The fuel gauge's needle dipped. With the flip of a few switches, she secured the fuel line and shut down the engine. Shannon glanced back at her gauges. No red light, but the fuel gauge's needle still dropped steadily.

"Computer, ETA to an empty fuel tank."

"Two minutes," responded the computer.

An alarm went off in her cockpit and Shannon looked down. The radar showed a missile on her six. She jerked the stick and banked left. The missile traveled past her.

Another alarm blared. She dove, and a flash of light blinded her for a second, follow by a pop above. Shrapnel from the exploding missile spattered against the ship's hull. The sound reminded her of hailstorms back home.

Enough was enough.

She retarded the throttle, deployed the speed brakes, and pointed skyward to convert airspeed to altitude. Like hitting a wall, her airspeed plummeted. The force slammed her forward against her seat belt.

Shannon looked around. Where was he? He should have flown right past her.

"Computer, back view."

The jet, no longer on fire, rode her tail. He had matched her maneuver perfectly! A thick oily trail of fuel streamed from her disk to her pursuer. Cleansing fluid steamed across the front of his jet. Likely, goo coated many of the jet's sensors.

She pushed the throttle past the stops and fired the afterburners. Her craft popped forward and ignited the trail of fuel. Flames enveloped the entire front of his craft. Blinded, he broke off his attack and dove.

Shannon spun her craft around and dove in pursuit. She saw sky.

"Damn it! Computer, front view." The image changed. She saw a spec against a blue ocean a mile ahead and a few thousand feet below. "Computer, how's my fuel?"

"I do not understand the question. Please rephrase."

"Computer, ETA to an empty fuel tank."

"Thirty-seven seconds."

"Computer, replace the time display with a count down to an empty fuel tank."

The time readout in the upper left-hand corner of Shannon's vision changed—thirty-three seconds. *Plenty of time.* Shannon dove and caught her enemy.

He veered his craft erratically. *His gauges are down; he's flying by sight!* She smiled and bore down on her throttle. He veered left. She followed. He turned right and she compensated. Shannon moved in closer.

He pulled up, and Shannon eased back and glanced up at the timer—twenty-one seconds. *Patience. Plenty of time.*

He leveled out. *Good.* She eased in behind him and lined up her weapons. She took an extra second to target each of her weapons for a different area of his craft; and then she opened fire.

Bullets and miniature missiles strafed his craft, riddling it with holes. Bits and pieces of metal disappeared from the jet's hull. After a few seconds, black smoke billowed from its tail and the jet dipped into a dive. Shannon shot blindly through the black smoke.

An alarm in the cockpit distracted her. The fuel gauge's needle rested at empty. She glanced at her display. It still read eleven seconds.

Her disk turned on its side and plummeted at a sharper angle. He would hit the ground first. She would still win. "Another free date," she muttered.

Her craft passed through the billows of black smoke. To her surprise she saw beneath her a parachute attached to the jet. It drifted to earth.

"No, no, no!" She would have to remember the parachute for her own craft next time, though she doubted anyone would get this close again. She had never been hit before. She steered toward the jet and attempted to gouge it on the way down, but the disk was diving too fast.

Think! She scanned her console—the harpoon. Her disk was equipped with a harpoon and attached cable.

The disk passed the jet, and she aimed the harpoon and fired. The harpoon impaled the jet's right wing. As the line between them went taut, her craft lurched violently and threw her face into the console. After a couple of seconds, the disk steadied. She glanced at the console. All the lights were dead. Shannon punched a few buttons for the reserve battery and the cockpit came to life. Blinking yellow and red lights lit up the console. She ignored them. Instead, she flicked on the view screen.

Her craft dangled from the harpoon cable attached to the jet. Behind the jet, she saw the sun. She would hit the ground first and lose the match. At least only a couple seconds separated them.

She looked back at the view screen. Her disk pointed upward, straight at him. There had to be something left. Shannon scanned her arsenal and found it: one Rockland, heat seeking, incendiary missile. She fired. The missile arced back and curved sharply into the jet, the explosion cutting the cable. The disk turned and plummeted to the earth.

"Computer, back view." The missile had obliterated the jet.

Shannon smiled.

The scene faded and then rematerialized as the lobby of a fine restaurant. She now stood in a dimly lit room with vaulted ceilings, white walls, and beige carpets. Works by famous artists decorated the walls. Shannon paid little attention. She was not really into art. She just wanted to gloat over her victory.

"Excuse me, Shannon?" A waiter had appeared next to her.

"Yes?" she asked.

"You won your encounter with Syzygy. He will be along shortly. May I show you to your table?"

Shannon nodded and followed the waiter past rows of tables. Some of the patrons viewed 3D replays of their duels. Others enjoyed their virtual meals over wine and spirits. All the pleasures of eating without the calories—an anorexic's fantasy come true. Well, except for the fact that you remained hungry. *The fad would pass,* she thought.

"Is this acceptable?"

The waiter had shown her to a table with a view of a large city from several stories up. She nodded.

"May I get you something to drink while you wait?"

"Yes, I'd like a Long Island Iced Tea."

"Thank you." He turned and left.

Looking down, she saw her drink had already materialized on the table. Shannon took a tentative sip. Virtual drinks were not her thing either. Shannon didn't quite understand the point of them. They had no mind-altering effects. Besides, she had never acquired a taste for alcohol anyway.

"Nice shooting," a flat voice said. She looked up from her drink and saw a tall man with light skin and deep green eyes.

"I'm Syzygy."

"Ice," she replied.

He took his seat opposite her. Shannon gave him a once-over. He was cute. She waited for him to say something. The silence stretched. She felt awkward. "So, you know you're the first person in a long time that came close to beating me."

He smiled. Shannon liked his smile. She wondered if he was any good in bed. At thirty-three she found herself victimized by her hormones. Another silence stretched between them. "So, what do you like to do?" She took a nervous sip from her drink.

"Dueling, racing, and virtual sex."

She almost spewed ice tea across the table. "Well, we are forward, aren't we?"

"Yes." He got up. His expression was blank.

"I…I like that." She rose. *Did I offend him?* Cute or not, he was strange and dangerous. She smiled. *So what? I like danger.*

He took her hand. "Have you ever seen the sunsets on Hainan?"

She shook her head. He smiled, opened a portal, and she followed him through.

Shannon emerged with Syzygy on a warm beach. The sun set low in the west, and two monolithic boulders towered above the ocean just fifty or so feet out from the shore. The boulders cast two long shadows that stretched out across the beach to either side of them.

Syzygy held out his hand. She smiled and accepted it. As they strolled along the beach hand in hand and in silence, Shannon drank in the calm sound of breaking waves and crying gulls. After a quarter mile Syzygy stopped. Shannon looked into his eyes. She could not hold his stare, and she glanced away. Such confidence! "Is this a place from your childhood?"

He gave her a perplexed look and did not answer. Instead, he drew her close to him and tried to kiss her.

She put out her hand. "Whoa, stallion, too fast."

He pressed harder and brushed her lips with his.

"Listen, jerk, I said no!" She pushed against his chest, but he was too strong.

Syzygy kissed her neck.

"Computer, V-chip software online." Nothing happened. "Stop it!" she yelled at him.

He ripped her blouse and exposed her left breast.

It's just cyberspace. It's not real. But rape was rape, virtual or not. "Goddamn it! I said no!" She kicked him hard in the groin.

Syzygy stepped back.

She turned and ran toward the ocean, and as she did so, she pressed the exit button inset on her wrist. It wasn't working either. The Nexus did not release her. Why?

As she reached the water's edge, he grabbed her hair from behind and threw her to the ground. The pain jolted through her body as her face slammed into the hard, wet sand. That wasn't supposed to happen. The Nexus had safeguards to prevent that level of pain. He pinned her head to the ground with his foot. Shannon grabbed his ankle and rolled. A snap told her she had popped his knee. She got up and ran down the beach. Shannon sneaked a peek back. Syzygy ran after her without as much as a limp. If he could hurt her, why couldn't she hurt him? He closed the distance between them.

"Help, somebody help me!" she screamed. The site's computer should hear and assist her. Someone would come to her aid. No one did.

An excruciating headache hit her, and she dropped on the sand at the water's edge. She got up on one knee, but fell back down. How could anything hurt so badly? Syzygy stopped running and crept toward her. She writhed on the ground, her hands clutching her head.

The headache stopped. Shannon opened her eyes and found she was levitating above the scene. She saw from her bird's eye perch that Syzygy was on top of her body now. She felt strangely at peace. The image quivered like a disturbed reflection when a stone strikes the surface of a pond.

Back in her room, she levitated above her convulsing body, its eyes open and glazed. Her skin looked pale as the blood drained from her face. Above her, the ceiling was gone. She rose.

With few friends and a high turnover rate at work, Shannon went unmissed. Her boss wrote her off as another burnout case. Given Shannon's long tenure, the only question on her boss's mind was what took so long. Her parents did not call, having been chided the previous week to give her space. No one notified the authorities.

10

Allison glanced around at Ed Davis' office and stifled a laugh. Edward had redecorated—yet another failed attempt at being *en vogue*. His office now consisted of a bare white room entirely made of porcelain-like material. The walls, floor, and ceiling flowed together, but unlike the *in* sites on the Net, which had a classic feel, Ed's site, with its rounded corners and edges, had the feel of a bathtub. In the center of the room the floor rose up to form a chair and desk. Ed looked up from his desk.

"Nice look."

Ed grimaced. "It wasn't my idea. The President said it went along with my promotion. And I know when to keep my mouth shut."

Allison grinned.

He leaned forward. "Now tell me. How are you doing?"

"Fine. Just fine." As she approached, the floor rose up in front of the desk and formed a chair and she sat down. "Sorry about the interview. You know how my mother is." She handed him the silver disk. "The *undesirable* elements are gone."

He nodded, and lines of tension appeared on his face. She had known him her whole life. Something was amiss.

"What is it?"

He picked up a paper from his desk and handed it to her. It

was the back page of the *Internet Times*. "Vinnie Russo brought this to me."

She glanced at the article about Camille Anderson's death and pretended to read. Vinnie had bypassed her command and shot his mouth off again. Ed's comment—I know when to keep my mouth shut—replayed in her mind. He was testing her. Did he know about the bug? Allison flashed Ed a soothing smile. "I'm sure it's nothing, but I'll check it out if you want."

He rubbed his temples with his hands. "I wish I could afford your optimism. The President's plan to consolidate the intelligence agencies depends on Warscape, which depends on the Nexus. If the Nexus is in trouble, so is the President."

"They aren't blaming the Nexus for the girl's death are they?"

Ed shrugged.

"That's twentieth century thinking. People have used VR for years. The public knows your veins don't magically pop open just because the vision is too real. You can't scare yourself to death in VR anymore than you can in a dream."

"Doesn't matter. This story threatens the President's plan."

"No, it doesn't. Just watch. You'll see. Remember the Y2K and 2012 scares? Nothing happened except TV ratings went up for a few weeks. I'm telling you, this will pass. Trust me."

"You're missing the point Ally. There's a dead teenage girl. Coincidence or not, dead bodies scare people, people that vote, people that elect Congress. And that puts the President's plan in jeopardy. Now, be straight with me. You saw nothing like this when you tested the Nexus, right?"

She shook her head in response.

"I need you to prove it."

Allison folded her arms across her chest. "What the hell, Ed?"

It was his turn to shake his head. "No, not to me, to the public. I need you to find out what happened and plaster the Internet with the truth. There can be no doubt in anyone's mind. The Nexus is safe."

"Of course."

"Have Vinnie help you out."

"That's not necessary …"

Ed pointed a finger at her. "Hey. Ally, it's not a request. Use Vinnie. He's got a nose for these things."

"He's not up to speed. He'll slow me down."

Ed leaned across the desk. "Spend some of your overtime budget then."

She read his face. Edward would not bend. She would need to find a better leash for Vinnie. If Steve found out her identity, the dominos would start to fall. She would have to find a creative way to keep Vinnie and Steve apart without hindering the investigation. Allison stood and gave him a terse nod.

He smiled. "That's my girl."

She turned and pressed a button on her left wrist to open a portal. Steve was soft on her. She would use that. Later, she would send Vinnie off to where he could do the least damage.

"Mendocino Coast," she commanded, and then she stepped through the portal.

Steve stood high on a grassy cliff. A hundred feet below, a jagged coastline stretched for miles in either direction. The waves crashed against a grey, sandy beach. Around him, gnarled Cyprus trees permanently cowered against wind. Ankle-high green grass, clover, and an assortment of weeds filled in the gaps. The air was still and warm, the ocean calm. Why did Allison want to meet here? His virtual slacks and dress shirt didn't fit the site's dress code.

Steve heard footfalls behind him and turned.

Allison approached him barefoot in a casual red skirt and blouse. They accentuated her feminine form. Her alias selection was impeccable. "Good. You made it. It's over here." She pointed to a spot along the cliff where there was a break in the brush.

"What?" He followed her toward the spot.

"The way down."

Steve now saw a steep, sandy trail, cut into the cliff face, leading to the beach below. "Where does it go?"

"The beach of course." She grinned.

Steve sighed. "We don't have time …"

"That's not what you said in the lobby."

"I know, but …"

"Good," she turned and jogged down the trail.

He stood dumfounded for a second. The breeze tugged at his clothes and brought with it a fine mist that enveloped him. The sound of waves crashed below. *What the hell.* He kicked off his shoes and socks and chased her down the sandy trail. It felt good to run again. Stuck in VR, he had not run for over a week in reality. He caught her at the bottom of the cliff. "Hold on!"

She ran to the water's edge and followed the shoreline. Salt water splattered and soaked the cuffs of Steve's slacks. He caught up to her. "Stop!"

She obeyed and grinned. The breeze pulled her blouse tight against her heaving chest. His gaze darted back to her face and he gave her an annoyed look. She returned an innocent, wide-eyed stare.

"What is all this?" He spun around, arms extended.

"We needed to lighten things up."

"Really?"

"We got off on the wrong foot." She sighed. "I know this isn't easy, Austin forcing you to work with me and all."

"You've got it wrong," Steve said, jabbing his chest with a finger. "Austin works for me. I'll go along with this as long as it makes sense."

She crossed her arms. "Is this really how you want to play this?"

Good question. He thought for a moment. No, it wasn't. The pressure had gotten to him—the trashed lobby, the dead girl, Austin's revelation, and the anniversary of Tamara's death. He didn't need to antagonize her. "Sorry, I have a lot on my mind."

"Oh?"

He sighed. "I knew the girl who died."

Her expression softened. "I didn't …"

Why did he say that? He blushed. "Forget I said it."

The waves crashed against the beach and water washed over Steve's feet. Salt water crept up his slacks and reached his ankles. As the wave retreated to the ocean, it stole sand from beneath his bare feet and he settled an inch deeper into the sand. The feeling made him uneasy. He walked away.

Allison came up alongside him and Steve met her gaze. She appeared concerned. Her expression reminded him of Tamara. How he missed her. He looked down, coughed, and let the feeling pass. "So what do you call this place?"

"Saddle Point. It's located on the Mendocino Coast in Northern California. Usually it's windier and cooler than this, but I cut down on some of the unpleasantries."

Steve nodded. "It's nice."

"Do you like to ride horses?"

He shook his head. "Don't know. I've never done it before."

"Well, this is a good place to learn." Allison's eyes lit up. "Computer, two horses."

The horses appeared, complete with saddles and tack. Allison approached a brown one with white splotches. She petted its nose and murmured into its ear. In one graceful motion, she mounted the horse.

Steve placed his foot in the stirrup, pulled himself half way up, and lost his grip on the saddle horn. He tumbled and fell flat on his back. The wet sand soaked through his shirt.

Allison laughed and then bit her lip, but she was unable to repress a smile. Steve could feel his face warming. He knew he was turning bright red back in reality. He brushed the sand off and tried again. This time he succeeded.

"There! That wasn't so bad, was it?" Allison laughed.

Steve assumed an annoyed expression, but it didn't take, and he laughed. They walked their horses on the hard sand where the waves lapped up onto the beach.

"Time to talk shop. Did you review the file?" Allison asked.

He nodded. "Yes. It revealed little about the problem with the Nexus. And I already knew about Camille. She was my daughter's best friend."

Allison dropped her head. "I'm sorry."

He sighed. "I'm sorry, too. Brooke has had a rough year."

"Is Brooke your daughter?"

He nodded. "Her mother died last year in a car accident."

"I guess it has been a rough year. I lost my father last year as well."

Steve nodded. His vision blurred with tears and he fought back the urge to cry. He had to learn to keep his mouth shut.

After half a mile they discovered a stream. It cascaded down a cliff and filled a large pool, dug into the beach. Allison dismounted. He followed her lead and managed to stay on his feet. Allison smiled.

"If you don't mind me asking, why'd you pick this place?" he asked.

"I used to come here as a child. It holds a lot of memories. I come back here to relax, clear my mind, sometimes to remember or forget, depending."

She checked the time. It was close to 5 p.m. Allison brushed a lock of black hair from her face. "Can we meet at noon tomorrow in your online office after I visit Camille's autopsy?"

He nodded. "I'll visit the crime scene beforehand."

"What for?"

"I know some tricks to coax the Nexus into telling me what happened, but I have to be there—physically there."

"You can't you download what you need over the Internet?"

Steve shook his head. "It was designed that way for security reasons. Hindsight being what it is, that was probably not the best solution."

"What does it contain that wasn't in the file?" Allison asked.

"The System and Site History Logs as well as the Core File. They're all accessed directly through a fiber port on the Nexus. They should tell us what catastrophic software failure caused the patch's demise and the Signal Amplifier's overload.

"No Black Box?" Allison referred to the Portal Sphere's Black Box, which acted like an airplane's flight recorder and recorded all sensory data. Technicians could relive the user's VR experience and reconstruct the events from the data stored in the Black Box.

Steve nodded. "Sort of. The Core File serves that purpose. When the Nexus detects a program is going to die, it saves a copy of all the programs in memory and creates the Core File. So, the Core File is a collection of program corpses. Several minutes of the reality the user experienced are stored inside these programs. You can construct from the Core File a Black Box of sorts."

"Why didn't you just call it a black box?"

Steve shrugged. "Artistic license. I thought Core File sounded better."

Allison laughed. "You know, it's the little annoying discrepancies like that which keep the public in the dark about VR."

"Yes, and it's those little discrepancies that keep me paid so well."

She laughed again. "I'll see you tomorrow, Steve." Her virtual representation winked out of existence. She had exited VR.

Steve drew a deep breath. He did not look forward to the flight he had to take, and he was even less interested in wading through the hundred million events recorded in the System Log by the Nexus programs. At least they would tell him why the patch failed and, perhaps, why Camille died.

11

Vinnie Russo, DARPA Investigator, stepped away from the shooting bay as the loudspeaker blared the name of the next contestant. He inhaled the fresh evening air of the San Ramon Mountains. Vinnie could smell just a hint of burnt gunpowder.

"Nice shooting, Vinnie!" Allison said.

"Allison, tell me the truth. Isn't this better? This is the real thing. None of that virtual crap you had me going to last week."

She crossed her arms and fixed him with *that look*.

He hated *that look*. She thought he was old fashioned. His boss was a recent political appointee, one that would probably be replaced in two or six years—whenever the White House changed presidents again. Whoever his boss was, Vinnie knew his place and so did she. Vinnie got the dirty work done.

She ran DARPA. As such, she set DARPA's direction and managed its day-to-day affairs. As bosses went, Vinnie found Allison to be young, naïve, and under-qualified. She was nowhere near the caliber needed to fill the position of Director. In other words, she was an average political appointment—underpaid and under-skilled; therefore, it was no surprise that Vinnie's presence dwarfed that of his younger boss.

At forty-two, Vinnie was thirteen years older than Allison. His stocky build, thick black hair, and domineering, almost black, eyes overpowered her whenever they met. Despite all her efforts, he remained louder, stronger, and more obnoxious. He didn't care what his new boss thought of him now or ever. Besides, he had other things to occupy his mind at the moment.

It was 5:30 p.m., half an hour after the start of regional tryouts. During the last stage, his gun's sight had fallen off. In spite of the problem, he had managed to hit five of the six targets in less than three seconds.

There was nothing special about his gun. It was a Springfield 2011, yet another rendition of the Colt 1911. In the intervening century, the Colt design had changed very little. It was neither the cheapest nor the most accurate handgun; however, like the personal computer, the Colt model was very common, easy to customize, and simple to tinker with because everyone worked off the same specification. And Vinnie liked to tinker.

"Vinnie, do you remember the work you did for Nexus Corporation?"

Vinnie shrugged.

"There's been a development."

"Oh?" Vinnie smirked as he pulled out the empty magazines from his belt and loaded the rounds for the next match.

"There's been a death. A teenage girl had a seizure while logged onto a Nexus Transporter."

Vinnie raised his eyebrows and stopped loading his magazine.

"Knock it off. I know you gave Davis the news."

Vinnie chuckled and continued to load his gun.

"Do you know what happened after you filed your original report?"

"Nope. I didn't follow it much."

"Davis immediately approved the Nexus."

Vinnie looked up from his gun and stared at his boss. "I wrote a product spec, not an evaluation! Didn't someone else follow up and test the Nexus?"

"It's political, Vinnie. The President of Nexus, Austin Wheeler, has the favor of the Assistant Secretary of Defense. Davis slipped the Nexus through without adequate testing. It's possible that a defect was missed."

"What's your point?"

"The point is that you're lucky to still have your job. He's ordered us to handle this matter quietly. From now on, he wants you to report your findings to me. You made him look bad, Vinnie."

Vinnie sighed. He dreaded the latest change of guard in Washington. As usual, the change of administrations had ushered in a new era and with it a new political landscape. The changes went beyond Allison. The President had expanded the role of the ASD C4ISR and he appointed his lifelong friend, Ed Davis, to the post. The acronym stood for Assistant Secretary of Defense (Command, Control, Communications, Computers, Intelligence, Surveillance, and Reconnaissance). The title matched not only the position, but the man—a confusing jumble of words whose acronym spelled POLITICS. The appointment was under a year old, but Ed already *knew* all that was wrong with DARPA and the intelligence community, and he promised to fix it. Needless to say, Vinnie was not impressed with him. It was one more Washington mess created by a U.S. President out of touch with reality. "So, as I said before, what's your point?"

"Look, Vinnie, you can make a real difference here. The success of the President's plan depends on a secure and reliable Nexus."

Vinnie shrugged and resumed loading the gun's magazine. "And what exactly is that plan?"

"The President and Davis see a fundamental problem with the military. It's a *physical-based* organization in a *virtual-based* world. The armed forces, Navy, Air Force, Army, and Marines, operate respectively in the sea, air, land, and miscellaneous.

"So you have to ask, who handles the information? It has no physical basis, yet it requires special skills, equipment, and training just like any of the other armed forces. The explosion of the Internet and VR has only exacerbated this problem. Worse, the nation's intelligence resources are scattered among thirteen different and competing agencies.

"The President envisioned a solution, the Information and Intelligence, or I2 Corp. We believe a consolidation of the intelligence community is what is needed here. We expect the I2 Corp will swallow up and replace all the other intelligence and covert agencies."

Vinnie laughed. "Jesus! You sound like a politician reading from a VR teleprompter! Do you have this stuff written down on your hand or something?"

Allison frowned.

Vinnie sighed. "What does any of this have to do with the Nexus?"

"I can't say exactly, but Davis selected us to be the cornerstone of the President's plan. The Nexus designs you reviewed for DAR-PA were just the beginning. In the near future, our organization will supply I2 Corp with all the technical toys they need to get the job done. He's moving DARPA to the next level."

"Oh, the elusive next level. Thank god!" It all sounded so quaint; but his memory stretched back farther than a four-year term. Historically, there were reasons why the intelligence community remained divided. Intelligence was inherently secretive and resistant to the democratic process. This had been shown repeatedly. Only keeping them small and competitive thwarted their natural tendency to subvert the government.

Vinnie finished loading the magazine and placed it on his belt. He withdrew a Marlboro from his shirt pocket, lit up the cigarette, and took a hard drag, sucking large volumes of air through the filter. Vinnie stared at the ground and exhaled.

Allison shot him a glance. "You really shouldn't. It's a disgusting habit."

Vinnie smiled. "You know, Allison, anyone can quit smoking, but it takes a real man to face lung cancer."

"Knock it off, Vinnie. There's more. Only you, Ed Davis, and I know about the investigation. If word gets out, our careers will be over. Keeping it quiet will be difficult if more deaths occur. So, I need you to drop everything and work around the clock on this."

"Politics and overtime! That's just great," Vinnie mumbled.

"I want you to start by tracking Austin Wheeler online."

Vinnie groaned. By nature, homicide was a physical crime, an event at a particular place at a certain time. There was a physical body and a physical weapon; however, VR had spread like cancer, jumping from career path to career path, turning them all virtual. Was it his turn? He had assumed his job was safe.

"Unbelievable!" Vinnie chuckled. "Do you realize this will be the first time that you've asked me to break all three of my career goals?"

"You'll earn a promotion to Investigative Specialist."

Vinnie looked Allison in the eye. "So what you're saying is that you're giving me crap work at a lower wage, but my title has changed and so I should be happy? That may work with the rookies, but not with me, babe. I've been around too long to play that game."

"Suck it up, Vinnie. It's not that bad."

"Long hours, political situations, and online work—how is it not?"

"We're not voting on this. Either you do it, or we'll discuss it again at your annual review."

He laughed as he looked down. "This isn't going to work."

"Why not?" she asked.

"This gun I have—the sight fell off." Vinnie took another drag on the cigarette and tipped the gun holster. "It looks like I'll need to borrow your gun."

Allison reached for her gun. He stopped her and laughed. "No, you idiot. Not here. Go to the safe area. We're not in VR."

"Watch it, Vinnie. You're crossing the line."

Vinnie took several drags before tossing his spent cigarette. "This way," he said, and led Allison to the safe area. They left their magazines of ammunition with the coordinator outside and stepped into the bay. She handed him her gun. Vinnie turned the gun over. She had customized her sidearm with a number of features for competitive matches. The magazine well was flared for easy loading, and the magazine's capacity was twenty-two rounds instead of the standard ten. The gun's grips had been removed and replaced with skateboard tape, which provided a better feel and prevented slippage from the gun's recoil.

Looking down the barrel of the gun, Vinnie aimed at a mock target and pulled the trigger. He found that it had a tuned trigger job to boot. The trigger broke after two pounds of pressure instead of the standard four. The harder you pulled, the more likely your aim would skew away from the target.

"This is nice," Vinnie said.

"Thanks. We'll meet every night at this time, 5:30 p.m."

"Okay, boss." He smiled.

"Vinnie Russo, please come to bay three for stage four," the loudspeaker announced.

His name appeared on the electronic billboard. "Do you mind ..." When Vinnie looked back, Allison was walking away. He examined the gun she had left with him. He couldn't believe it. Allison hardly knew him. "Maybe I should hold up the local convenience store. That would teach her." Vinnie chuckled. He stepped out of the bay, collected the magazines, and approached the range officer who would follow him throughout the match. Vinnie removed Allison's gun from his holster and handed it to the judge, who inspected it and handed it back. Vinnie grabbed a magazine and slid it into place. He pulled back the slide to load the first round in the chamber. Vinnie looked up and the range officer started the timer.

Beep!

Vinnie approached the first target with his weapon drawn. It was a metal cutout of a man's torso and head. A target marked its heart. Vinnie leveled the gun and fired. The bullet whined and hit up and to the left of the bull's eye. Vinnie reacquired, aimed lower, and fired. This time he made his mark. The target fell over with a satisfying clang.

He followed the range officer to the next target, a circular metal disk that swung back and forth on a pendulum. Vinnie leveled the gun and fired when the pendulum swung right. It struck the target dead center. Vinnie waited and fired when the pendulum returned. His bullet struck the center. He continued through the course of ten targets and completed the circuit in record time. Allison's gun had greatly improved his accuracy and time.

"I guess those gizmos do work," he said to no one in particular. His thoughts turned to the investigation. He would start with the physical evidence, investigating the crime scene. Later he would check in on Austin as she had asked.

He smiled as he thought about the real game being played. Poor Allison had no idea what she had stepped into.

Capture

"Technology, like all original creations of the human spirit, is unpredictable. If we had a reliable way to label our toys good or bad, it would be easy to regulate technology wisely. But we can rarely see far enough ahead to know which road leads to damnation. Whoever concerns himself with big technology, either to push forward or to stop it, is gambling in human lives."

—Freeman J. Dyson, pacifist and former nuclear weapons designer, 1975.

12

The alarm shrieked and tore Steve from his dream. His head throbbed in sync with the alarm. He rolled out of bed and stumbled into the kitchen. From the refrigerator he grabbed a two-liter 7-Up and from the top cabinet he pulled a bottle of scotch. Steve poured a glass of soda and added an ounce of scotch. Scotch was not meant to be an expensive soft drink, but the best cure for a hangover was more of the same.

"What's this?"

He turned, glass in hand. With his body he hid the bottle of scotch.

Brooke glared at him from the kitchen table.

"Huh?" he took a sip. His gaze drifted to the floor.

She held up a scratchpad with Allison's name and pager number on it. He set the glass aside on the counter. "Oh that. She's a colleague, someone I work with."

Brooke nodded as if she had something to say in the matter.

Steve smiled. "Did you finish your practice test?"

"No."

"No?"

"Dad, it's not like that. I need the Nexus. It's just too hard with the Portal Sphere."

"You know, when I was your age all we had was a word processor and a printer."

Brooke rolled her eyes. "Old school."

He laughed. "Old school? I made the Nexus."

"Exactly. So what's the problem, Dad?" Brooke glared at him.

Steve sighed. He would find the glitch soon enough. He had to. The Nexus Healer release was scheduled for next Monday. "I'll tell you what. What if I can fix it by Sunday?"

"Really?"

Steve nodded.

"I guess that's alright."

He slipped the bottle of scotch back in the cabinet. "I won't be back until late, so you'll be on your own."

Brooke rolled her wheelchair into the kitchen. "You forgot didn't you?"

Steve placed the 7-Up back in the refrigerator and searched his Swiss-cheese-like memory for the reference but came up blank.

"Our weekly breakfast?"

"Oh that!" Last week he had taken Brooke to the Lake Forest Café, her mother's favorite spot. Brooke had goaded him into promising to make it a weekly ritual, in honor of Tamara. Already, he had forgotten. "I'm sorry sweetie; something came up."

"It always does."

Steve sighed. "I'll tell you what. Tonight, when I get back, no matter how late it is, we'll go out on the town, just you and I."

"Promise?"

"Scouts honor." He gave a weak salute.

She laughed. "Yeah, like you were ever a boy scout."

"I've got to run."

Steve showered, threw on some jeans and a polo shirt, and gathered his gear into two large suitcases. Zipping them up, he dropped them on the floor.

Crunch. Probably an old DVD.

His room looked like his office—a mess. He grabbed both the

suitcases' telescopic handles and dragged them toward the front door. One of the suitcases fell over and exposed a busted wheel. A long scratch in the hardwood floor stretched from his bedroom to the suitcase. Steve picked up the suitcases by their handles, groaned, and lugged them to the front door.

"You won't forget, will you?" Brooke asked from behind him.

He put the suitcases down and faced her. Her large, blue eyes melted him. So much of Tamara was in her eyes and smile. He leaned down and hugged her. "Promise, sweetie," he whispered in her ear.

"I love you, Dad."

"I love you, too."

He gave her one last squeeze before getting up, turned, grabbed his luggage, and left the house.

The spacious San Francisco International Airport terminal was almost deserted, no longer filled with angry mobs as they clamored for their tickets. Four years ago ten major airlines had serviced over twenty thousand customers a day. Since then, the industry had dwindled to just three airlines. They served less than one quarter that number. He walked past rows of empty counters that once housed airline stations.

It amazed Steve how quickly online commerce, virtual businesses, and virtual vacations had devastated the passenger airline industry. It took four short years. Worse, they didn't see it coming. The Internet through VR did not appear that much different from the Internet with video conferencing; but it was. Although airplanes continued to fly, their cargo shifted from passengers to online commerce. Many shipping companies, such as Federal Express, UPS, and the U.S. Postal service, prospered as the distribution of goods was pushed out from stores to the consumer. The passenger airlines never thought of moving large scale into the shipping business until it was too late. The spacious but empty terminal served as a reminder of a more prosperous past.

Steve walked up to the first window. He followed the automated attendant's instructions to check his bags. By sliding the expense card from Austin through a card scanner, it confirmed who he was and deducted almost nine hundred dollars from the account for the flight. Without competition, airline fares had skyrocketed.

After a half-hour wait, he boarded the plane with a few other passengers and soon was airborne. Rows of deserted houses and apartments in the dead suburbs passed beneath them. They circled over Burlingame, Steve's old hometown. His dad still lived there.

Steve remembered coming home after he had signed the papers creating Nexus Corporation. As usual, his father, Steve Senior, was unhappy with his son's decision. He thought Steve was taking too much of a gamble. Steve cut his stay short. They did not speak for sometime after.

The following year his father suffered an upset election. A competitor had developed a large campaign based in VR using the Portal Sphere. The numerous commentaries that followed pointed out his son's involvement in VR. His father was portrayed as an inflexible bureaucrat of a bygone era. His father's image and career never recovered. Neither did their relationship.

As the Portal Sphere gained in popularity, Steve pleaded with his father to move, but he refused to listen. Steve couldn't blame his dad. How could he have known what was coming? At the time, it had sounded crazy even to Steve.

The changes started small. It seemed the Portal Sphere just provided an inexpensive and semi-portable access to the Internet. It shrank the computer screen, speakers, and microphone to simple headgear and placed its user inside each Internet site. Soon they added a body suit, which allowed movement around the virtual environment by walking on a universal treadmill. Alternatively, voice commands could be used to move about in VR.

Business executives realized the Portal Sphere's potential. It could transport them anywhere, instantly. They could interact face to face in cyberspace and exchange ideas from all over the world.

Travel constituted over half of an executive's busy schedule. Now they could get twice the work done in a twelve-hour day. Further, most executives remained biased toward physical media—books and papers instead of Adobe or Word documents. In VR, their desire for the tangible was realized. They could flip pages and exchange the papers with one another in VR, instead of faxing or mailing physical copies. All the while these papers were virtual, a series of 0s and 1s on the hard drive of the VR server. As a result, they cut their carbon emissions and retained carbon credits for their respective companies. In short, they could cut their travel time to zero, remain green, and yet work the way in which they were accustomed.

Executives demanded the Portal Sphere as part of their sign-on contracts. Senior contractors and professionals followed. As more and more people purchased Portal Spheres, the price fell. Business owners soon saw another opportunity—the virtual building. Now, anyone could be anywhere, at anytime, even if that place didn't exist physically.

These virtual buildings resided on the hard drives of VR servers and were much cheaper to construct and maintain than real buildings. Online business exploded as retail stores consolidated to virtual buildings with a transportation network and a warehouse. White-collar workers were moved from expensive metropolitan centers to online virtual buildings.

Even virtual factories became common. Lawsuits for on-the-job injuries and decreasing robotic costs fueled the transition. Blue-collar workers began remotely controlling machinery. This prevented injury and increased their legal working hours. Companies found that virtual reality even circumvented many of the government regulations and Union contracts.

Most employees, like the businesses they worked for, discovered that virtual reality was cheaper and more convenient than true reality. In the physical world, businesses and employees had to cluster around the same metropolitan areas, driving up real estate prices and commute times. The Portal Sphere changed these dynamics.

As the Portal Sphere dropped in price, people discovered that a large country estate and a Portal Sphere device cost the same as a small condo in a crime-ridden city. Further, commute time was non-existent. The VR user simply plugged into the Internet and within seconds appeared in her virtual office. Over the last decade, VR had transformed the business landscape. Now over a third of the country worked from these virtual offices.

Steve's father had not listened to him and had paid a terrible price. His father had treated home equity as a piggy bank. He mortgaged his house to the hilt as real estate soared in the Bay Area. With the advent of VR, property values plummeted while his father's mortgage payment remained the same. Worse, his father found it increasingly difficult to find work.

No longer viable as a political candidate, his father had switched to consulting, but his lack of VR experience made it difficult to get new clients who now hid within social media sites, meet-up groups, and other social structures that had not existed twenty years prior. Steve was not sure how his father would make it through the next couple of years. Steve tried, but his father refused his help.

" … and bring your seat back to an upright position." The stewardess's voice awoke Steve. They landed at San Diego International Airport.

Once on the ground Steve found a taxi to take him to Carlsbad. Forty minutes later, they turned onto Del Oro Drive and pulled up to the Andersons' home. Steve entered the crime scene through the open front door.

"Hello, Steve."

Steve turned and saw Vinnie Russo, the man that had let the defect slip through.

"Pretty strange death, don't you think? A young teenager dying of a seizure?" Vinnie mocked Steve.

"What do you care?" Steve responded.

Vinnie raised an eyebrow. Steve bit his lip, regretting his impulsive response. Vinnie had helped grease the wheels that got the Nexus released. He was not someone Steve should piss off. "Sorry."

Vinnie nodded in acknowledgement. "Okay, I guess you know the drill. I've been assigned to this investigation. If you hear anything, call me immediately." Vinnie handed him his business card. Surprised, Steve glanced at it. "Call me old fashioned," Vinnie said with a shrug. Steve slipped it into his pocket as he entered the room where Camille had died.

The office was small, twelve feet by ten feet, decorated in neutral tones and beige carpet. The ivory curtains, highlighted with tawny lines, were pulled back, revealing a set of French doors. Sunlight streamed into the room, illuminating a contemporary teak desk, and behind the desk, a cream-colored leather chair. A chill ran down Steve's spine.

It was the chair where Camille had died. All that remained of her was a blue chalk outline on the leather chair. The dead girl's Nexus lay on the seat within the chalked lines.

This must never happen again.

Steve broke out a fiber cable. He plugged one end of the cable into the Nexus and the other into the back of his laptop.

While he downloaded the Site Log to his laptop, Steve checked his schedule. He was meeting Allison at noon online. It was 11:20. Once he downloaded the Site Log, he displayed it on the laptop. It listed the last thirty sites Camille had visited before she had died. Steve looked at the last four:

```
Fashion Island    06/09/20 08:12 - 09:01
The Outback       06/09/20 13:46 - 14:51
The Ritz          06/09/20 14:52 - 15:10
s#@~#d$f9e*r8&     06/09/20 15:10 - 15:32
```

That's odd, he thought. The last entry was garbled. It was just a random collection of letters, numbers, and symbols. He would take a closer look at it later.

The entry above it was clear: The Ritz. He was familiar with the site. It was a chat room. Another puzzle. The V-chip should have detected that Camille was a minor and prevented her from entering the site.

Steve double-checked the entry against the System Log. The log recorded that the girl's mother, Dr. Ashley Anderson, had visited this site. He looked at the timestamp. It matched the estimated time of Camille's death. Camille had used her mother's identity. The V-chip would never have been activated.

He readjusted the laptop's screen to reduce the sun's glare and saw the reflection of someone standing behind him. He closed the laptop and turned. It was Vinnie.

"What are you doing?"

"Sorry. Boredom does that to me," Vinnie said.

Steve waited for Vinnie to walk away before he returned to his work. He downloaded the System Log and Core File. He glanced at his watch. It was 11:40.

He decided to take his work to a hotel. From there, he could get online and view the logs with Allison. Why rush? He had time.

13

Jeff and Sarah drew their weapons and approached the corridor. They had slipped past the sentry. This was despite the fact that Jeff had chosen a ten-foot-tall, reeking ogre with a twelve-foot-long pole-arm.

Sarah shook her head. She had chosen the more petite female high elf as her avatar. It gave her stealth and speed. She rested on her haunches, her sword held with a relaxed grip in her right hand. With her left hand, she wiped the virtual sweat from her brow. "This perspective is strange."

"Would you rather do homework?" Jeff asked.

Visually, she was out of her body. Her perception floated ten feet above the ground. This part of the game she didn't like, but she could live with it. The perk of hacking the other team to pieces made the game worth her time.

The flag room was a few feet ahead, within striking distance. She scratched her nose and rubbed the polished steel on the sword's hilt with her thumb. She noticed her cleavage showed from this angle. Would Jeff miss that? Sure enough, Jeff's gaze wandered in her direction. "Eyes in front, Jeff."

Jeff muttered something she couldn't hear, but he obeyed.

She had met him in Macroeconomics at the beginning of the quarter. Jeff snuck peeks now and again, but she didn't mind. In fact, it was the only reason she let him hang around. Sarah understood obsession. These Thursday lunch hour adventures had displaced last quarter's soap opera addiction. She checked the timer in the upper left-hand corner of her vision: two minutes. The rest of her team would make the first move.

"Die!" someone shouted. Metal bit metal inside the flag chamber.

"Now?" Jeff asked.

"Shh," she whispered.

The fighting drew closer. A minute remained. *Close enough.* "Now!" she said.

They bolted down the short corridor. It opened up into a large cavern with a rough stone floor. At the threshold, they paused. Though their perspective was inside the cavern, they could not see themselves. A ledge of rock blocked their view. The plan had worked.

"The easy way or hard way?" she muttered. Sarah scanned the room. No flag was in sight.

"Jeff, do you see it?"

"No."

"Okay. The hard way."

As they had planned, the rest of their team maneuvered the enemy, a clan of eight humans, so that their backs were turned to Jeff and Sarah. They had lost two players in the process. The rest of their team faced two to one odds.

"Now," she said.

Jeff stepped forward into a sweep of his sickle. He cut three humans in half and collapsed another.

She stepped over the collapsed man and cut another down with her sword. Sarah turned back to the collapsed man. He writhed on the ground, his leg amputated. She lunged and bumped into Jeff. Sarah stumbled. She regained her footing. Her elbow jabbed another member of her team. They were clumped together.

Fluid sprayed her arm. An empty flask tumbled from the collapsed man's hand. She smelled the oil as one of his teammates dropped a torch.

Fire erupted all around them. Her arm was ablaze. She staggered back against the jagged stone wall of the cavern. Her arm left steaks of flame on the rock. The heat stung. At least it wouldn't get any hotter. The Nexus was maxed out at its safety limits.

She dropped and rolled. Her arm continued to burn and left streaks of flaming oil on the dirt. The sweet stench of burning flesh grew stronger. It reminded her of barbecue. From above she watched as her character writhed in pain, unable to fight. Movement became harder. Her character froze.

"Your character is unconscious," the disembodied voice of the computer announced to her on a private channel that only she could hear.

The elf was a stupid idea. She looked at the melee. Except for Jeff, all her teammates were either burned or dismembered beyond recognition. Jeff's arm still burned, but the ogre fought unimpaired by the pain. Three humans remained.

She still had hope though. The humans all wielded long swords, which gave Jeff quite an advantage. The range of his twelve-foot pole-arm prevented them from getting close enough to strike. The three humans formed a circle around Jeff: to his left, his right, and behind him.

Jeff spun to bring the human behind him into view. The three rotated left and returned to the original formation. Again, someone was behind him.

Jeff was toast. They would lose. She had to help him. She tried to move but nothing happened. All she could do was watch her body burn.

"Your character is severely injured," the detached voice informed her.

Sarah would be lucky if her character survived at all. Jeff had to win to save her. Jeff swung left, his arm extended. He lost his balance but managed to spill the opponent's guts. The man fell to his knees. The other two men charged.

Jeff rolled and popped back up. He swung. His pole-arm decapitated the first man and the poll part of the weapon slammed into the side of the second. The force crushed the second man's rib cage. He fell, dropped his sword, and grasped his side.

Jeff sauntered to the man and lifted the sickle high over his head. He grinned and displayed a large row of crooked, yellow teeth. Jeff slammed down the weapon and nailed him to the floor of the chamber. Only Jeff remained. His arm was charred, and he had a nasty gash on his left cheek, but other than that, he was fine.

Sarah's character no longer burned, but was not doing well. "Come over here!" she shouted. But the site had muted her. Jeff could not hear her. She did not want to quit the game now. If she died, she would be out of the tournament for the rest of the week.

"Your character is nearing death," the computer reported.

"Stupid elf. What a worthless race!" she shouted.

Jeff slung his pack down and extracted a metal flask. He uncorked it and poured the contents over his burned arm. He let out a scream as his skin foamed and a sweet smoke caressed it. After a few seconds, the smoke cleared. He extended his arm, rotated it, and flexed it several times. His arm was healed.

Come on! She didn't have much time.

Jeff lumbered toward her with the flask in his hand. He turned her over. His gaze followed her curves and settled on her chest.

She reached out to smack his face but her arm would not move.

His gaze flowed over her body. He examined her, almost groped her, but stopped himself.

He can't be serious! I'm burned to a crisp!

Jeff stared at her.

Sarah did not want to exit the game, but she would if he tried anything. Later she would make him pay.

He rested there motionless for the longest time before he poured the contents of the flask over her right side.

A warm throbbing grew in her arm and hip. She could move and speak again. She cried out in mock pain.

He grinned as she opened her eyes.

She smiled back and then kneed him in the chin.

His character doubled over.

She laughed and got up. "Do that again and I'll make a necklace out of your gonads."

He groaned and sat up.

Out of the corner of her eye, she saw movement. She whirled to see a dark figure approaching her. In slacks and a polo shirt, he was not dressed for the part.

She drew her sword. "Do you surrender?"

Jeff joined her. He bared his teeth and lifted the sickle high over his head.

"I'm Syzygy." The man stared at the ground. They could not see his face.

"What did you say?" Jeff asked.

"Game over. All enemy players were eliminated. Please return to the lobby to receive your scores." It was the computer who answered.

"Wrong game, bud," Jeff said. He lowered his weapon, opened a portal, and stepped through to the lobby.

Sarah grabbed her sheathe with her free hand. Syzygy stared at her. It reminded her of Jeff. She smiled and leveled the sword at his throat. "Hey, buddy. You heard the ogre; you're in the wrong game."

Sarah watched in bewilderment as Syzygy pushed the sword aside and approached her character. Syzygy grabbed her waist and moved to kiss her.

"So long, jerk," she whispered in his ear. She struck him hard in the small of his back with her sword, and he crumpled to the ground. She would let the coordinator know about him when she got to the lobby.

His sexual advances surprised her; this was not a meat market like the student union. Usually, this site was good about keeping out the degenerates. Well, that is, except for Jeff, of course. She turned and opened a portal.

From her aerial view she saw Syzygy leap up, grab her character from behind, and slam her body down. It knocked the wind out of her. Syzygy grabbed her head and slammed her face into the stone floor.

She couldn't move. *Well, this is great.*

Syzygy groped her breasts.

"V-chip software online!" she yelled.

He stroked her neck.

"Nexus, exit."

Nothing happened.

"Coordinator!"

Syzygy removed her character's fur vest. Sarah felt his cold hands run across her chest. He pulled her left arm out of the vest.

"Nexus, exit!"

Nothing.

He removed her right arm from the vest. What was he going to do?

He tossed the vest aside, and her milky white breasts were exposed. His gaze lingered on her; but it wasn't like what Jeff had done. Jeff just horsed around. This was different. She cringed. Her head felt warm, almost a burn. She screamed, and a portal opened.

"Sarah, what's with you? It's time to …" Jeff said.

Syzygy rose as Jeff lunged. In one quick movement, he swung his pole-arm and cut Syzygy in half. Syzygy's torso and head flew across the room and slammed into the wall. Jeff grabbed Sarah and stepped back through the still open portal.

They burst into the crowded lobby. Jeff toppled over her. Old gnarled trees surrounded a meadow spattered with flowers. The crowd of people watched a levitating score board as they awaited their scores. Several of them gawked at the couple.

Sarah's voice had returned. She could move. Her perspective no longer floated above her character. She saw through its eyes.

Jeff's face expressed concern.

She hugged his neck and cried. Sobs racked her body. "I couldn't move. I couldn't talk. All I could do was watch."

Jeff took off his fur coat and covered her exposed chest. "How did he do it?"

She shook her head. Sarah didn't know.

Richard, Site Administrator of Fantasy Central, watched two teenagers tumble into the forest. He frowned. Just out of college himself, he was still familiar with teenage antics such as this. Richard straightened his wizard's hat and walked to them. "Is there some sort of problem here?" he asked.

"Damn right there's a problem! Sarah was attacked. What kind of site are you running here?" Jeff said.

Richard bit his lip. He contorted his face into a practiced mask of concern. "What do you mean? What happened?"

"A man attacked me. I tried to stop him, but I couldn't move. I tried to open a portal, but it didn't work. I tried to exit, but I couldn't. I called you, but you didn't come. Why didn't you come?" asked Sarah.

"Calm down." Richard scanned the gathering crowd. He turned back to Sarah. "Let me take you to some place where we can work this all out."

A portal opened and they stepped through into Richard's virtual office. Richard sat down behind his desk. He took off his tall pointy hat and set it aside. "You could not move or talk, and someone attacked you?"

She nodded.

"He didn't say who he was, did he?"

Sarah nodded.

"And it was ..." Richard asked.

"Listen, dick. Give her space!" Jeff snapped.

The administrator bit his lip and restrained a knee-jerk response. "Please call me Richard."

Sarah turned to Jeff. "Do you remember his name?"

"I don't know. I think it was Seery, Seally, or something like that."

"That's it! His name was siz-uh-gee," Sarah said.

"Why didn't you call on me?" Richard asked.

"I already told you! I did!"

That was impossible. Nothing could override the safety protocols built into the Nexus. Richard pulled out a form from the desk and filled in a couple of the blanks. He looked up. "What was his name again?"

"Syzygy!" Jeff and Sarah said in unison.

Richard set the form aside and pressed an intercom on his virtual desk. "Sam, I need you in here." Richard had just started two months prior. He monitored the site and handled the day-to-day affairs; but this was serious. He could tell a lawsuit was looming. Better to call the boss.

Sam materialized and stood next to Richard.

"So, what seems to be the problem?"

Richard briefed Sam on what they had told him. When he was done, Sam told Sarah, "Don't worry. We'll make sure nothing like this will happen again."

"You'll call DARPA, right?" Sarah asked.

"Guaranteed! No one wants to get rid of these freaks more than I do. It's horrible what happened to you. I left my old job because of stress like this. I went into this business to help people have fun. In fact, I think you and your friend here are entitled to a free month of gaming. Let's say a one-month pass. What do you say?"

"You'll tell them that I couldn't exit the Nexus or contact the coordinator?" Sarah pressed.

Sam winked at Richard. "Of course. Really, don't worry. We'll take care of it." With that, Sam opened a portal back to the lobby for them.

They stepped toward the portal. Sarah turned back to Sam. "I have your word, right?"

"I will contact DARPA right now. I promise."

They left through the portal. It closed behind them.

Richard turned to Sam. "How do I report this? Do we have a

contact site we go through?"

Sam put his hands on his hips and gave Richard a funny look. "Oh yeah, sure."

"Well, what's its name?"

"You're serious, Rich, aren't you? Sure, that's what I'll do. I'll just contact DARPA."

Richard blinked.

"Think, Rich! It'll be open season for the bureaucrats. DARPA will shut us down and spend the next year stalling, asking us the same questions over and over again until we're out of business."

"But you promised ..."

"I told the customers what they wanted to hear. I gave them a free month's worth of games didn't I?" Sam poked Richard's chest with a meaty finger.

Richard frowned.

"Don't tell me you believed their story! How the hell do you think anyone could disable the exit button or prevent her from calling you?"

Richard shook his head. He didn't know.

"Look, if she was attacked, then why did she accept a free month of games? Would you come back here?"

Richard shrugged.

"Listen, we have our own way to deal with characters like this. We will blackball this ... Syzygy. That was his alias, right?"

Richard nodded.

"Even the name sounds harmless. Syzygy—now that's the call sign of a techno nerd if I ever heard one."

"It's just not what they taught us in school," Richard said. Sam got within two inches of Rich's face.

"Out in the real world things are different. This isn't a test tube or a textbook. If you turn your back out here, they'll stab ya. If you stick your head out, they'll cut it off! If you don't make the right gesture or say something the wrong way, they'll kill ya! They play hardball and the rules aren't written down! Don't you get it? DARPA makes their money by dragging their feet. I guarantee you that if you contact them they'll shut us down for good and you'll be out of a job!"

Richard looked at his feet, and Sam put a supporting arm around him.

"Aw, don't take it so hard. Everyone makes these mistakes when they are first hired on. Look, the first six months are the hardest. Once you learn the basics, it's a piece of cake. Just lay low for now. Keep your nose clean."

"What if this guy finds a place somewhere else on the Internet, a site not on the list? I mean, what if he hurts someone?"

"Now how exactly do you suppose he would do that on the Internet? Think, Rich! This isn't real! We aren't really here! What if he hurts someone you say? It can't happen! You know that; hell, everyone knows that!"

14

Allison entered VR and opened a portal to Saint Luke's hospital in Los Angeles. The Nexus connected with the Internet, wound down the few miles of fiber between Del Mar and Los Angeles.

"Number eighteen," an invisible voice from the automated nurse announced.

Camille Anderson's autopsy was popular. Reporters and medical students occupied the other seventeen remotes. A sterile, white room materialized and the pungent smell of formaldehyde hit her. She wrinkled her virtual nose, but could not escape the scent.

In reality Allison remotely controlled the eighteenth monitor, a robotic cam in the room. It twisted and turned and responded to her thoughts. This was her new body. All the while it relayed back sight, hearing, touch, and scent from the robot's embedded sensors.

Dr. Lundberg stood over the lifeless body of Camille. Neon lines appeared and formed a 3D grid through Camille's body. The neon lines formed a virtual heads-up display and directed the doctor to the location of the girl's organs.

Her index finger transformed into a syringe. Like everyone in the room, the doctor was not there. She remotely controlled a surgical robot called the Guru 1000. When the doctor moved her virtual hand, in the real world the Guru 1000's robotic arm moved instead of her arm. When she looked down, she would see the corpse through the robot's eyes. The Guru 1000 became her virtual body.

The doctor specialized in autopsies of people who died from brain disorder or brain trauma. The demand for her services forced the doctor to stay in one location. She performed all her work remotely from San Francisco. A private, high security network fabric linked the RemoteCare hospital chain that had franchises throughout the country and made her work possible. With the hospital's network and her Nexus Transporter, the doctor could be anywhere in seconds.

"Nurse, what has she determined?" Allison asked.

The invisible, automated nurse spoke. "The liver and kidney show traces of X-flu."

"Really?" X-flu was a Chinese designed biological weapon, a simple, lethal retrovirus, consisting of RNA surrounded by a protein tube, open at one end. When the microscopic opening of the virus brushed a human cell, the protein sack would constrict and inject its RNA into the cell. The cell would use the virus's RNA to manufacture new viruses.

After a week, the cell, swollen with a million copies of the virus, would burst open and spread the infection. The Chinese had engineered X-flu to disable and kill its victims over a period of years. It exacted a heavy financial, emotional, and physical toll on its quarry as it destroyed its victim's organs cell by cell over several months. It was always fatal.

X-flu disguised itself from the body's immune system by camouflaging itself inside the body. It continually changed its outer protein shell and never stayed in one form long enough for the body to mount an immune response. This property of X-flu confounded the medical community. Three years after its creation, they were still no closer to a cure.

"How was she infected?" Allison asked.

"Probably through her father. He's a China-vet who died of

X-flu complications."

Was the Nexus off the hook?

A four-foot hologram of Camille's brain appeared next to the girl's body. It consisted of a maze of red lines outlining the major structures. The doctor touched regions within the hologram, which glowed green. She probed several more areas and stopped.

"What is it?" Allison asked.

The nurse responded. "Complications from X-flu was not the cause of death. Although she died of a seizure, the doctor cannot find any brain trauma or brain disorders that could have resulted in such a seizure."

"Is she sure?"

"Of course not. Science has uncovered a lot of how the brain works, but much of its function is still unexplained."

Thank god for that.

"Hello."

Allison turned and saw another hovering monitor. "What?"

The monitor transformed into the figure of Vinnie Russo.

She frowned. "What are you doing here?"

Vinnie smiled broadly. "I'm at the crime scene and you'll never guess who I ran into."

"Crime scene?" Allison was livid. "I told you to keep your eye on Austin Wheeler!"

"Don't get your knickers in a bunch. The tap on Nexus Corporation failed. The transmissions are encrypted. The security gurus can break the encryption but not for another couple of hours. In the meantime I thought …"

"You thought wrong! Page me next time. I can help you with the taps."

Vinnie smirked. "Did you know that Steve blames me for the Nexus release? He wasn't kept in the loop with Davis' plan was he?"

"Vinnie, I'm warning you …"

Vinnie stepped forward. He came within inches of her face. She stumbled back.

"Look, Ms. Hwang. You don't understand. I'm trying to help, but you're not making it easy. This game is bigger than you think. If you're not careful, you could wind up in the crossfire."

What am I doing? Allison met his gaze. She stepped into him and pushed him back. The metal bodies of the monitors clanged together.

Vinnie laughed. "Chill, girl."

"Please stay clear of the other monitors," the nurse warned.

Allison held his gaze. "I don't care how much longer you've been at DARPA than I, you're out of line. Consider yourself written up, Mr. Russo. One more crack and I'll can your ass, with or without Mr. Davis' approval and with or without your pension. Is that clear?"

Vinnie stared at her.

She refused to look away.

A mechanical whirling noise of the doctor's robot grabbed Vinnie's attention. He shrugged and handed her a virtual card.

She took it, but did not drop her gaze. She visualized her eyes like lasers burning through his thick skull.

"If you need to get a hold of me, I'll be at that number," he said.

A red light blinked in Allison's peripheral vision. "I'm being paged." She slipped his card into her virtual pocket.

Vinnie exited VR.

"Computer, play the message on a private channel," Allison said.

A hologram of Steve Donovan appeared. "Allison, I'm ready to get started when you are."

Allison checked the time: 12:11.

"I'm sorry Steve. Time got away from me. I'll be right there." She took a deep breath and let it out slowly. What had Vinnie meant by *bigger than you think*? She shrugged. He could not intimidate her. She would not let him.

15

Vinnie Russo looked around his virtual office, a bare twenty-foot cube with white walls and the words *Linux®* stenciled in the floor. He hesitated, not sure if it would work.

"Computer, start the tapper."

A white sphere the size of his fist appeared in the center of the room. The object rotated and pulsed. Deep rumbling, like the growl of his MV Agusta, shook the space. The fist of light exploded and filed a ten-foot cube with solid white light. He could see nothing inside the opaque cube. The tap had failed.

Vinnie laughed. He hated technology and it hated him. This VR crap never worked when he was around.

Lines of green and purpled swept from left to right across the cube. The corner nearest him became translucent. The other corners showed signs of *thawing*. The translucence spread from the corners of the cube toward the heart of the cube. He blinked and the entire cube became transparent. The image inside was still fuzzy. He could make out two figures, but not who they were. The picture slowly came into focus. He saw Steve and Allison at some virtual site. Vinnie smiled.

The card he had slipped Allison was no ordinary virtual business card. It contained a viral program that created a 3D, one-way window into Allison's virtual world. The data was compressed and encrypted. If he were lucky, Steve would not notice.

"Jan?" Steve said.

"Yes?"

"Can you please add the Site Log, Core File, and System Log to the Camille file?"

"The encryption key?" As designed, Jan had forgotten the password. It was too easy for a hacker to extract the password from Jan's programming or trick the program into giving the password out.

"Sorry, Jan, open with the keyword *patch*."

"That's more like it. Now, what can I help you with?"

"Jan, please manifest the Nexus file."

Allison came and stood next to him.

"The answer is in these logs. I just have to find it," Steve told her. The Nexus file opened and the spherical orb that Steve had first seen yesterday materialized before them. Camille Anderson's face reflected off its metallic surface. He touched the orb. A grid, etched in what appeared to be granite, hovered a few feet in front of him.

Allison cringed.

"What's wrong?"

"If I could make an aesthetic suggestion?"

Steve nodded.

"The granite slabs—you might want to use something more modern."

"I thought it gave things a sense of character," Steve said.

She bit her lip. "More a sense of the Flintstones. They've been syndicated again, you know."

"Oh." Steve felt his face flush back in reality. Buried in his technical work, he was out of touch with social graces.

"What about embossed platinum?" she suggested.

Steve nodded. "Platinum's good. Jan, please replace the presentation interface's engraved granite with embossed platinum.

Anything else?"

"Jan's attitude could tone down a notch or two. Her personality is a bit outdated."

Steve laughed. "Jan, please suppress your personality program."

"Yes, Steve," Jan said.

Before them the granite slab transformed into a wall of platinum. The grid's etched characters filled in and grew into protuberant letters. Allison scanned the grid. The bottom three squares read: Site Log, Core File, and System Log.

"Anything else?" he bowed.

She shook her head.

Steve touched the square with System Log written in it. At a right angle to the grid, a similar wall of platinum materialized. Across its surface were fifty lines of text. Each line had the date and time on the left-hand side followed by an archaic jumble of words.

"What is it?"

"The System Log. It contains a catalog of all the most recent events that were noted by the hundred or so programs running on the Nexus. Each line refers to a single action by a single program."

"Well, that doesn't look too difficult."

Steve pointed to the first line.

Etched across the top of the slab were the words "First 50 lines of 126,000."

"Oh."

"Don't worry. I know what I'm looking for. At most, it will take me half an hour. The report put her time of death around 3 p.m. the day before yesterday. I'll start with log entries one hour before that. Jan, create a couple of chairs please and display the System Log starting at 2 p.m. on June the ninth."

Jan obliged. The top of the log read: Lines 101,950 to 101,999 of 126,000. Steve sat down and scanned the log.

"How does the Nexus do this? I mean everything seems so real, seamless in here."

"Are you familiar with old movies?" Steve paged forward through the log by pressing a button on the platinum wall.

"Yes."

"Well, a movie consists of several pictures or frames. When the movie shows twenty-four frames a second, the still images blend and create a fluid image. VR is similar to a movie but not just for sight. VR does the same thing for all the senses.

"Like the movie frames, the sensations are short-lived and last only milliseconds. The VR server sends a stream of sensations as we move and interact in this environment."

Steve scrolled down the log and stopped. "Nothing," he murmured.

"I don't get it. Where does the VR server fit in?"

"Uh, let me give you an example," Steve said. He pressed an index finger against the Page Down button on the log. "Allison, as I pressed this button Virtual Security's VR server produced twenty or more sequential virtual frames.

"As I inch my finger forward in here, my brain sends electrical signals destined for my finger. The Nexus intercepts these signals and forwards them to Virtual Security's VR Server. The server uses these signals to compute my new perspective within here. It generates the tension on my tendons, my view as I look down toward my hand. It even generates the faint breeze I feel when I move my finger forward.

"In an instant these perceptions are returned as electrical signals across the Internet to my Nexus. My Nexus receives these and relays them directly to my brain. I experience these signals as sensations in virtual reality."

"But how can all that information traverse the Internet in such a short period of time?"

"The server only sends the changes from one frame to the next. Since these frames occur every hundredth of a second, changes between sequential frames are negligible except when you log in or when you portal to a different site. That's why it takes a few seconds to ... to ... oh." Steve stared at the log.

"What is it?" Allison asked.

He jabbed a line of text with his index finger.

```
06/09/20 15:12:59 THE PROGRAM V-CHIP WAS
ABORTED AS REQUESTED BY A REMOTE HOST: ALIAS
SYZYGY.
```

"Someone crashed her Nexus' V-chip software," Steve said.

"Why would they do that?" asked Allison.

Steve shook his head. He remembered that at the crime scene he had determined that Camille was using her mother's alias. By default, the V-chip software was turned off for adults; however, with the V-chip software crashed, this alias would be allowed to be intimate with Camille even if she had used her own alias.

He traced his finger further down the platinum wall and stopped.

```
06/09/20 15:13:16 THE PROGRAM INTERACTIVE
DATABASE REPORTS THE ALIAS SYZYGY DATA IS
CORRUPT. (UNIVERSAL NAME SERVICE (UNS) FAIL-
URE—NO NAME, EMAIL ADDRESS, BUSINESS ADDRESS
OR PRIVATE ADDRESS RECOVERED.)
```

"That's odd," Steve said. "When a user enters a site, the Nexus rejects any alias that isn't connected with a real person. It's not easy to disable that function."

"So, Syzygy is a hacker," Allison said. "Any idea of who he is?"

"Or she ... you never know in VR. We'll have to look deeper," Steve said, advancing the log a few more pages. The symbols, numbers, and letters rippled across the platinum face as he moved the log forward.

"What does this mean?" Allison pointed at a line.

Steve read.

```
06/09/20 15:14:12 THE PROGRAM SIGNAL AMPLI-
FIER WAS ABORTED AS REQUESTED BY A REMOTE
HOST: ALIAS SYZYGY.
```

"I don't know," Steve said. *Did Syzygy take down the patch? It couldn't be.* Steve scanned further down and pointed to another line.

```
06/09/20 15:14:52 THE PROGRAM BASIC INPUT
OUTPUT SYSTEM (BIOS) DETECTED THAT THE NEXUS
WAS TURNED ON BUT NOT IN USE.
```

"Whatever happened with the system, it occurred before that line."

"Why?"

"Her Nexus failed to register her at all. By that line Camille is dead."

"Do you think the alias Siz—however it's pronounced—killed her?" Allison asked.

Steve shook his head. "That's impossible. The Core File should tell us more. The Core File is why I flew to the crime scene. It's the only log that cannot be downloaded from the Nexus over the Internet."

"Jan, describe the sensory contents of Core File."

"The Core File contains sensory data that passed through the Nexus from 15:13 to 15:15 on June 9."

From the date and timestamps on System Log entries, Steve knew the Core File started just before Camille met Syzygy. "Good. Jan, can you construct a 3D video from the data in the Core File?"

"No, the video portion of the Core File is corrupted."

"Jan, can you extract and play all audio from the Core File?"

"Playing," Jan said.

They waited.

A metallic grind broke the silence—a closing portal. Sounds of the ocean followed, and a monotone voice spoke. *"It's called Tianya Haijiao, China's southern most beach …"* The voice faded, leaving only the sound of the ocean.

"What's happening?" she asked.

"The Core File's audio must be corrupted as well," he said.

They listened intently. Steve leaned forward. Allison did the same.

Abruptly, Camille exclaimed, *"This place is so cool! I mean beautiful."*

Although Camille's voice was soft, melodic, it startled them.

"I think she's trying to conceal her age," Allison said.

"Shh. They might name the site," Steve said.

There was a pause, followed by more sounds of crashing waves.

"Wait! I don't even know your name!"

"I'm Syzygy."

"An alias eh? Computer, identify who is using the alias Syzygy. We'll see who you really are."

"I'm sorry but there is no information on who is using the alias Syzygy."

Camille murmured something.

Steve couldn't make it out. Wet, popping sounds followed.

"What is that?" Steve asked.

Allison smiled. "You don't recognize it?"

Steve strained his ears. He shook his head.

"They're kissing!"

Back in reality, his corporeal face reddened. "I knew that."

Allison laughed.

Camille groaned. A slap followed wrestling sounds. Allison lost her smile.

"Stop it! Wait! Something's wrong," Camille said. *"V-chip online!"*

Allison and Steve exchanged a look.

"Get away from me, you freak!"

"Steve," Allison said.

Feet slapped wet sand. Camille breathed hard. She was running. A splash. Camille screamed. Gargled and gagged noises replaced her scream as she struggled for breath.

Silence.

Over what felt like several minutes the audio played. Interspersed within the silence Camille mumbled unintelligibility.

Beep.

"Steve, that ends the audio portion of the Core File," Jan said.

Steve could feel the blood drain from his distant, corporeal body.

"Did he kill her?" Allison asked.

He shook his head. "I don't know. Maybe."

"I never heard of such a thing. It's impossible. How'd he do that through the Internet?"

"I don't know!" Steve shouted.

"What do you mean you don't know? You're *it* where the Nexus is concerned!"

Steve shook his head. Syzygy took down the patch and V-chip programs. He overloaded the System Amplifier. He attacked Camille and somehow killed her. They were not dealing with a glitch, but a murderer exploiting the glitch. His stomach lurched.

Steve took a deep breath. "I don't know how he did it, but I have a hunch. We correct bugs as they appear by pushing periodic updates and patches from Nexus Corp. It keeps the customer happy. It's password protected and the Nexus devices only allow the corporate servers to connect. Syzygy broke the update protocol somehow."

"Who is he?" Allison asked.

"Let's take a look. Jan, are any of the video images of the alias Syzygy intact in the Core File?"

"Yes. Do you want me to display one of them?"

Steve nodded. "Yes."

The hologram of a tall, dark-haired, pale-complexioned man appeared before them. Steve walked around the hologram and peered into the eyes of Syzygy. They were green like his own, but detached, soulless. They held no answers.

"Who the hell are you?" Steve asked.

16

Vinnie couldn't believe what he had just heard. Over the last thirty minutes he had watched with morbid curiosity as Steve and Allison scrutinized the logs.

He replayed the audio of Camille and listened as the events unfolded. Syzygy had attempted to rape and then killed Camille Anderson. Rape was a crime about control and anger. There was none of that here, just cold detachment. Syzygy used methodical and mechanical methods. The perp did not seem to seek pleasure from the attack either. Why had he chosen this girl? Vinnie shook his head. He needed help.

"Computer, DSM9 please." DSM9 stood for the Diagnostic and Statistical Manual of Mental Disorders IX developed by the American Psychiatric Association. It identified and cataloged 95% of known mental and psychological illness.

"DSM9 online," the computer responded.

"I need to profile a killer," Vinnie said.

"What is the subject's name?"

"I don't have a name—just an alias, Syzygy."

"Do you have an image of him, his physical appearance in VR?"

"Yes. Computer, pull up Syzygy Image One."

The image that Steve and Allison viewed appeared before Vinnie.

"Computer, I also have some clips of dialog from the subject stored in Syzygy Sound File One," Vinnie said.

"Applying Luscher's alias test. This will take a few seconds." The computer examined Syzygy's alias and voiceprint.

How people painted themselves in VR spoke volumes about that person's perceptions. It was like a barometer of their personality. Vinnie walked around the figure. He looked into the eyes of this man. They were dark, glazed, and distant.

The computer spoke. "Syzygy displays symptoms of the Antisocial Personality Disorder, also known as Sociopath Personality and Psychopathic Personality.

"Although people with this disorder may appear superficially charming, they are incapable of significant loyalty to individuals, groups, or social values. They are grossly selfish, callous, irresponsible, and impulsive. Unable to feel guilt, they cannot learn from experience or from punishment.

"Frustration tolerance is extremely low. They tend to blame others or offer plausible rationalizations for their behavior. When frustrated, they may be dangerous to others, since internalized brakes do not exist.

"This subject falls into a subcategory of Periodic Mechanical. These individuals chronically focus on one particular goal, often through ritualized patterns or methods. During these episodes, their entire intellect collapses around a single idea or central theme. They become very meticulous and calculating in their methods. They are often devoid of emotion, although they might appear charming in order to attain their goal. Prone to extreme violence, they have no remorse for their actions."

"Computer, is there anything about what he would look like in real life, his habits, his history?"

"We can infer some things about his childhood." Before Vinnie a wall of water appeared, black letters protruding:

Childhood Behaviors/Events	Match
Animal Cruelty	98%
Pyromania	96%
Persistent Bed Wetting	93%
Domestic Violence	90%
Broken Home	81%
Parental Alcoholism	72%
Impoverished	67%

Vinnie scanned the list. "Computer, make a copy of this and the entry from the DSM9."

A pamphlet materialized in Vinnie's hand.

"Any ideas on what he would be or look like now? I mean outside of VR."

"Some facts can be extrapolated. The key here is that he has suppressed almost all of his emotions. Most people know that they cannot think a feeling or feel a thought. Syzygy thinks he can think his feelings. Because of it, he is extremely out of touch with his emotions and probably his body as well. He'll appear bland, cold, aloof, possibly pale, lanky or perhaps extremely obese. It's similar to that news clip last week where a quiet, straight-A high school student attacked and murdered his teacher after receiving a B+ on a midterm: emotionally retarded, mentally gifted."

The implications hit Vinnie. This Nexus problem was much more serious than he had thought. His *friends* had changed tactics. He now faced a serial killer and perhaps the first *virtual* serial killer at that. To top it off, Allison was running around doing god knows what. He needed to think; he needed a smoke. But he couldn't do that in here. Pressing a button on his left wrist, he exited VR.

Vinnie shifted in his living room chair and lit up a Marlboro. He took a long drag, pulling nicotine into the dark recesses of his lungs. Maybe he had underestimated Allison. She had her own agenda, but what? What was she hiding? It could interfere with his plans. He took another drag, held his breath, and released. He discarded the ash in a makeshift, tinfoil ashtray. Should he confront her with more force this time? He shook his head. No, the game had gotten too complex. For now, the best thing to do was to lay low and follow Allison's orders. He would keep her content and unsuspecting.

17

Steve stared at Syzygy. The hologram's expression looked empty and hollow. The green gridlines on the floor lit up its face and flushed its skin to a rusted copper green. Syzygy leered at him.

Syzygy's expression felt wrong, disconnected from everything. It reminded him of the accident, when he looked over at what remained of Tamara, broken glass and blood covering her face, body, the upholstery, everything. Yet, nothing had clicked. It didn't register that she was gone. It never had. The truth of her absence never sunk in. At home, he would hear Brooke and think it was Tami. The doorbell would ring and he would expect to see her frustrated that she had forgotten her keys. Steve had never said goodbye.

"What is it?"

"Nothing." He shook his head clear.

"We can take care of this," Allison said.

"You've got to be joking," he said.

"No, I'm not." She locked into his stare.

He raised an eyebrow. "We'll take care of it. One computer cowboy and a … a …" He paused. She belonged to their Chinese associates but what did she do? He had no idea. "What are you anyway?"

"Connected."

"And?"

"Austin … Austin told you that I know Ed Davis?"

He nodded.

"I swear, if you can find him, DARPA will stop him, but you need to track him down."

Steve stared at the pulsating green line that glowed beneath his virtual shoes. Something was wrong. He felt it. But her words made sense. He had trusted her. "Jan, can you search for the alias Syzygy and see if he's online anywhere?"

"Thanks," Allison said.

"I can only perform a partial Internet search …" Jan said.

"That's fine."

A few seconds passed. "Syzygy is online at the Ritz," Jan said.

Steve turned to Allison. "I need to meet with you physically in order to pull this off."

"Pull what off?"

"The trace."

"Wouldn't it be quicker to do it online?"

He shook his head. "The link would slow it down. The laptop with the trace software has to be directly connected to the auxiliary port of the Nexus. I'll need you to run the software on the laptop, while I go online."

"I'm not that technical, Steve."

"It's easy—just a few mouse clicks."

She shrugged. "I guess it's a date then without our VR masks."

"Guess so," Steve grinned. He knew she would be surprised to see that he used his own image. Meeting clients in the buff inside VR was very unconventional for consultants, like attending an interview without a suit. "Where are you now?"

"In Del Mar, near San Diego," she said.

Steve thought for a moment then said, "Can you make it to the Swanson Hotel in Ventura by 3 p.m."

"Yes, but why Ventura?"

"Ventura is close to one of the central nodes in the Internet. The Internet extends out like a spider's web, branching from a set of central nodes. Connections between two machines always run through these central nodes even if the machines are next to one another. So, the number of hops the trace has to cover will be fewer if we are closer to a central node. What will you be wearing?"

"A floral dress. You'll know who I am when you see me."

"Okay."

"We can register under Mr. and Mrs. Holt," she said.

"Just make sure you reserve the honeymoon suite."

"Really?" Allison said, amused.

"Uh, you don't understand. It's the only room with duel Internet access."

Her eyes gleamed and she laughed. "See you in a few." She winked out, exiting VR.

His gaze lingered on the space where she had stood, and the memory of her image stayed with him. Why did she draw him in? Probably sheer desperation. It was not easy to meet new people in this day and age. VR enabled people to interact more, but without intimacy. How could you trust the false image someone portrayed in VR? Somehow, his daughter and her friends' generation had adapted, but the last time he had dated, meetings were conducted in person, in the flesh, not remotely, like in a video game. He exited VR and glanced at the LCD display on his Nexus: 1:54 p.m.

Steve caught a cab from LAX to Ventura. An hour later, a cab took him to the Swanson—a second-rate hotel in the outskirts of Ventura.

Steve remembered working at the Swanson ten years earlier when he first got out of college. Then Ventura was just a quiet suburb on the outskirts of LA. The city's population had surged with an influx of new yuppies and their families. With them, a large transfusion of new money altered the landscape. New storefronts and rambling modern homes spread like cancer over the valley floor.

It surprised him how dilapidated the city had become. Aged,

congested, engulfed by LA, Ventura had rotted. Here, like every-where else, VR had collapsed its metropolitan real estate market. *Amazing how things change.*

The bellhop placed Steve's three over-laden suitcases on a ho-tel dolly and wheeled them into the lobby. "Will you be checking in?"

"Not right now. I'm waiting for my wife. Could you please place the bags behind the counter?"

The bellhop nodded and pulled the cart behind the front desk. Steve walked to the waiting area and sat down. The bellhop parked the dolly behind the front counter and proceeded onto his next assignment. Steve picked up a product magazine. He skimmed through it for five minutes and noted at least three women with floral dresses, but they all passed through the lobby without stop-ping.

How would he recognize Allison? Her description was vague at best. Outside of VR she could be anyone. He chuckled. She could even be a man. Worse, he had forgotten to describe himself.

Steve spotted her and stood. Allison was tall and slender. Her moves were more graceful in person as she watched people ap-proach. In person, she had an air of confidence that VR could not relay. Allison pushed back her long black hair and looked in his direction.

She too used her own image in VR.

He strode up to her, and her face broke into a welcoming smile.

"Hello, Allison." He extended his hand.

"Hey, babe! What, no kiss?" She took him in her arms, planted a light kiss on his lips, and hugged him.

It felt good.

She whispered in his ear, "You've lost some weight. You really should update your image in VR."

"Thanks." He smiled.

She gave him another squeeze. "Have to keep up appearances you know, being married and all."

"Right." His heart sank a notch.

They checked in under the aliases Mr. and Mrs. Holt, paying with Austin's expense account. A different bellhop than before approached the desk. Young and wiry, he attempted to carry the suitcases without a dolly. He picked up the luggage and set it down. "What do you have in there?"

"Chains and whips of course," Allison teased. "We're on our honeymoon." She slipped her arm into Steve's.

Steve looked down. His face flushed. Allison withdrew her arm. He looked up and she smirked.

"What?"

"This isn't VR."

Oh god. His face reddened further. Steve averted his gaze. He felt naked, exposed out of VR in the open.

She took his arm. "Don't sweat it. Let's go."

The bellboy left and returned with a cart. After loading the cart, he escorted them to the honeymoon suite, room 2001. Steve tipped the bellboy. He left and closed the door behind him. The room was fully equipped with all the amenities, including two terabit Internet connections.

"So, what toys do you have in here?" Allison laughed. She opened a suitcase and scanned the equipment. From her expression, he could tell it was all new to her.

"I used Camille's profile to create a new alias for myself with the same long, brunette hair, slender, muscular body with gray, distant eyes and dark, olive-colored skin."

Allison laughed. "You sound stunning!"

"I think I can provoke Syzygy into attacking me."

"That's thinking like a man! Why can't you just use the Portal Sphere?"

He shook his head. "The Ritz only accepts Nexus connections and the Portal Sphere isn't fast enough."

"How are you going to protect yourself from the defect?"

She caught his gaze.

He studied her. Allison's long, black hair was disheveled from her trip, and her deep blue eyes inviting.

Her gaze dropped to his lips and then darted back to his eyes.

He looked down, his thoughts jumbled. "Uh, I know a few tricks I can use."

He reached into the suitcase and pulled out a case. From it, he extracted a miniature circuit strip. Then, cracking open the helmet's casing with a miniature screwdriver, he removed a similar circuit strip. He showed the two circuit strips to Allison. "They look the same don't they?"

Allison nodded.

"But they are quite different. You see, Syzygy's attack depends on this." He held up the strip from the Nexus. "Both of these are versions of the Signal Amplifier. The Signal Amplifier is responsible for directing and regulating the strength of the signals sent to the brain. The problem is that this Signal Amplifier, the one I removed from the Nexus, is too flexible. It can direct a strong pulse to the wrong areas of the brain, which can lead to a seizure, and possibly death, as it did in Camille's case.

"While at Nexus Corporation, I wrote a patch, software that prevents these conditions. The software checks the strength and direction of the signal before the Nexus sends it to the brain. If the patch finds a violation, it prevents the amplifier from sending the signal.

"However, Syzygy managed to bypass the patch and exploit the Signal Amplifier's defect. He sends three signals to the Nexus. The first kills the V-chip software, the second crashes the patch software, and the third overloads the Signal Amplifier.

"This other circuit strip, the one I pulled out of the bag, is a newer prototype of the Signal Amplifier. This prototype does not have the capability of sending such a strong signal to the fatal areas of the brain. It doesn't matter what programs Syzygy crashes or what components he overloads; this prototype simply can't kill anyone. It nullifies Syzygy's attack. Unfortunately, I only have one of these."

Steve paused and regarded the inexpensive device. It was remarkable. A cheap piece of plastic engraved with thin gold lines linking a dozen computer chips was the difference between life and death.

Steve snapped the new signal amplifier into place on the Nexus and reconnected the wires.

"That plugs the security hole," he said. He closed the casing of the Nexus.

Steve pulled a laptop out of the suitcase and plugged one end of a cable into the Nexus and the other into the laptop. "This will provide us with a secure, direct channel," Steve explained. You can talk into this built-in speaker on my laptop. This is a private, secure link. No one else will be able to hear us. You can use it to keep me abreast of the trace while I'm in VR."

Steve powered up the laptop. Once the system was up and running, Steve pointed to a detective's magnifying glass icon on the laptop screen. "Allison, click on that icon."

Allison moved the mouse over the icon and clicked the left mouse button. A window opened on the laptop's screen. It was titled *Sniffer* and contained a map of the world.

He pointed to an icon in the window. "Press this to start the logical trace to Syzygy's Nexus through the Internet. Once it finds him, it'll open a window detailing his Nexus' serial number, model, and other details. This new window will also have a button labeled GPS. Press it.

"The Global Positioning System is built into the Nexus' processor. By comparing the signals from three or more GPS satellites, the chip can triangulate down to the square foot where the Nexus is located. Syzygy's Nexus will send us its location across the Internet. It should come back quickly with another window, detailing Syzygy's physical location.

"At which point I can take care of things," Allison said.

He nodded.

"Aren't you forgetting something?"

He shot Allison a questioning look.

"Does the V-chip ring any bells?"

"God. Thanks!" Steve gasped. He had forgotten that Syzygy

had disabled the V-chip software, and Steve would appear to Syzygy as a beautiful woman. The last thing he wanted was to be raped by Syzygy while in cyberspace.

He shuddered. He completed the lock on the V-chip software. *Now that plugs security hole number two.* He hoped there wasn't another; but the Nexus was very new.

Steve exhaled. He lay on the bed and entered VR.

"Computer, endow me with the alias Camille."

Steve felt himself transform in VR. He glanced down and inspected his new body. The alias had the same look and stature that Camille had used. He walked in a circle and tested its tall, athletic frame.

His newly acquired dark hair fell in front of his face as he turned. He threw it back out of his face. As he ran his hands down his hips, he shuddered. This was seriously wrong. He would never get used to some aspects of VR.

He twisted his left earring so only Allison could hear him and spoke. "Are you there? Allison?"

Her warm voice called back from the real world. "I'm right here."

The secure link was working. He was ready. "Ritz chat room."

A portal opened and he stepped through.

Steve emerged through an archway into a formal, circular shaped gallery. Evenly spaced on the room's black onyx walls were several other archways, indistinguishable from one another. The chat room's logo—a complex maze of black marble laced with gold—was etched in the black marble floor.

A glint of light made him look. Fifteen feet above the floor, in the center of the room, a thin mist had formed. The mist turned and acted as a prism, splitting the sunlight into its base colors. Belts of yellow, red, and blue danced off the onyx, gold, and marble. Everything in the room had been polished to a shine to enhance the effect.

He then noticed the balconies above the archways. They, too, were trimmed with gold. Rose vines tumbled over the corners of each balcony and stretched down to the black marble floor below.

A water drop struck his cheek. The mist remained in the center of the room and not overhead. He looked straight up. There was no ceiling. Instead, the walls and balconies stretched to infinity. Breathing deeply, he felt cool, moist air line his lungs. Wherever the water came from, its source had to be close.

He listened and heard the sound of water. Behind him, the closest wall glistened. Curious, he reached out and touched it. He pulled his hand back in surprise. A cool veneer of water cascaded across the entire surface of the wall.

Extravagance was cheap in the virtual realm. Steve touched his earring and whispered, "Allison, you should see this place."

He looked around. Where was the index? He approached an archway. Nothing happened. "Computer, show me your site index."

A woman materialized in front of him. "May I help you?"

"I'm looking for someone, a man called Syzygy. Is he online?"

The woman paused briefly as the program checked its database. "Yes. I will send you there now."

Steve faded into a new scene. A loud party materialized around him. He was in a large room with no walls, open to the night air with balconies at periodic intervals. He looked up. The ceiling levitated ten feet above the floor. Around him people in formal attire danced. He looked down and noticed his body had been dressed for the occasion; a long red dress adorned with many sequins covered his female form. Steve threaded his way through the crowd looking for Syzygy.

Click.

The sound sent a cold chill down his spine. Syzygy had attempted to crash his Nexus' V-chip software. He was close.

Steve scanned the faces around him. *There!* He recognized Syzygy from the still image in the Core File. Steve touched his earring. "Allison, start the trace."

"Okay, done."

Steve smiled. In two, maybe three minutes, they would find the bastard.

"I'm Syzygy."

"Oh, hello. I'm ... I'm Brooke."

"The front desk said you wanted to see me. Why?"

"I saw your signature while I was browsing to see who was online. Your alias sounded interesting." Steve batted his eyes. He hoped it had worked.

Syzygy shrugged and took Steve's hand. Steve fought the urge to pull away. He let Syzygy lead him to a balcony.

Steve looked over into a spiraling image of the Milky Way. "It's beautiful!"

Syzygy stared into the void.

Steve twisted his left earring. "Allison, do you have him?"

Syzygy turned and faced him. "Who's Allison?"

"Uh, no one, I'm just mumbling. I'm nervous."

Syzygy shrugged and gazed at the spiraling stars.

He bought it! Fear replaced relief. Syzygy had heard the conversation, but how? It was a direct and secure link. The Nexus would not transmit Steve's voice across the Internet when he touched his ear. From Syzygy's Nexus there was no way to hear him. The whole reason he had met Allison in person was to prevent Syzygy from eavesdropping.

Allison. Had she pickup on the fact that Syzygy could hear them? He hoped so. How could he tell her? His mind was blank. Think.

"Yeah! We got ..." Allison shouted.

Syzygy reached for his neck with both hands.

Steve gasped.

Syzygy stopped short, inches from him. Syzygy lunged.

An invisible wall separated them. Steve exhaled heavily. He touched his earring. "Allison, he can hear us. I think ..."

Syzygy's mouth opened and expanded. His body turned black and engulfed him. Everything was dark, silent.

The invisible wall fell. The blanket of warm flesh coiled around him.

Steve struggled inside the fleshy cocoon. He screamed but heard nothing.

A brilliant strobe, a deafening hum, and a strong stench overwhelmed Steve. He lost his sense of balance and his skin crawled.

He became nauseous.

"Steve!" Allison screamed.

He blacked out.

18

Austin Wheeler entered through eight-foot double doors. Ashley Anderson, mother of Camille Anderson, and her lawyer sat at the far end of a mahogany table. The room had a nineteenth century feel with high ceilings; decorative wallpaper and ornate wood trim along both ceiling and floor. Pictures of the firm's partners lined either side of the long room and a rich pattern carpeted the floor. Austin smiled. The firm used a canned room, straight from the VR web site. Had they even touched the shrink wrap? Austin doubted it. *This should be good.*

Austin approached them without the assistance of a corporate lawyer. He knew he could represent the company better than any lawyer could. Lawyers could not be trusted. Though they had the moral flexibility required to be a team player, they rarely subscribed to the company's agenda. They had their own personal goals and ambitions to push. Austin hated that. It looked better this way in any case—the CEO of Nexus Corporation taking time to console the lowly victim's mother.

Austin offered his hand to Ashley. "Austin Wheeler, President of Nexus Corporation. I am so sorry about your terrible loss."

She stood, leaned across the table, and shook his hand. "Thank you."

When she returned to her seat, the lawyer shot the mother a

glance. He shook his head. The man turned his attention to Austin. "Dirk Unger."

Austin smiled and extended his hand. "And you must be her attorney, no?"

Mr. Unger remained seated. He didn't smile.

Austin sat down.

"As I mentioned to you earlier, I will be representing Mrs. Anderson in these matters," Dirk said, his voice tinged with irritation.

Austin nodded. Mr. Unger was confident. Too confident. Did he know about the defect, or worse, Syzygy? How could he? Austin wasn't sure. What he was sure of was any mention of a lethal defect would sink the Nexus and his company; but Mr. Unger held only one card. That was his mistake. The lawyer expected an easy blackmail settlement, silence in exchange for money. It would not be that easy. Austin would make sure of it.

Austin gazed at Ashley. He studied her expression, posture, and gestures. She was the weak link—a susceptible, grieving mother.

"Madam, as we see it, Nexus is not responsible for your daughter's death."

"But the Nexus Transporter could have monitored the situation …" Dirk said.

Austin held his hand up.

Mr. Unger stopped midsentence.

Austin smiled. "We're not saying that we don't want to help you. Indeed, we are very sympathetic to your situation. We understand your husband died from X-flu and your mother is critically ill with the same virus?"

She nodded her head.

"Yes, but you can't say it was X-flu that killed Camille. They don't know why she died yet," Dirk said.

"How can you say that? She was attacked!" Ashley glared at her lawyer.

Mr. Unger leaned over and whispered with his client.

Austin mentally lowered the settlement amount he would offer. He interrupted them. "Really, Mrs. Anderson? What on earth did this supposed attacker do to kill her?"

Ashley looked down.

Dirk leaned over and whispered something to his client.

"Did they say anything about X-flu? You know Camille's symptoms sounded a whole hell of a lot like X-flu complications."

Ashley shook her head.

"No, the attack killed her," Dirk said.

They knew about the attack but not the defect. Austin flashed the attorney an incredulous look. "What exactly could this *supposed* attacker do to kill her? They were both in VR. I know he may have scared her and that was horrible, but how can you say he killed her? It's not possible."

"Well, it certainly wasn't X-flu!"

"Are you saying she died from stress? That he scared her to death?"

Dirk shook his head.

"Enlighten me. What are you saying?" Austin asked.

Ashley stared at her lawyer.

"The Nexus was involved. We'll prove it in court." Dirk stood.

Austin nodded. "Sit down, son."

"We're leaving," Dirk said.

"I understand. We are sympathetic. Perhaps her body had been weakened by X-flu and the attack overwhelmed her."

Ashley opened her mouth but her lawyer shook his head as he returned to his seat.

"You know it's the only thing that makes any sense." Austin leaned back in his chair.

"That's not true." Dirk said.

"Can it be ruled out?"

The spark left Ashley's gaze. She stared down at the table. X-flu was the perfect scapegoat, an answer that gave her closure. Pain and denial would drive her where Austin wanted her to go. She would settle. That is, if Mr. Unger would step aside. The lawyer's cut was a third. What was his price? That would determine the settlement.

Dirk leaned forward. "The Nexus should have detected Camille's seizure. If so, medical help could have arrived in time to save her."

"That's a stretch and you know it. The coroner's report says she died five minutes after the attack. How fast do you think the ambulances in your city are?"

Dirk pointed a finger across the table at Austin. "So the attack did kill her, albeit indirectly. If the Nexus had prevented the attack, she would still be alive today. By your own admission Nexus Corporation is responsible!"

Austin rubbed his chin. "Camille wasn't quite eighteen was she?" The corners of Austin's mouth curled into an involuntary smile. "Legally, she was not supposed to use your alias."

"Watch yourself, Mr. Wheeler," Dirk said.

"That would be the only way she could have entered the Ritz chat room where she was attacked. Dear boy, you claimed my company is responsible, but we put the V-chip in the Nexus to prevent sordid things like this from occurring. I'm sorry, but this little girl must have used someone else's alias. Mrs. Anderson, this is your chat room, if I'm not mistaken, one that you frequent often, right?"

Dirk glanced to his client. Ms. Anderson never looked up from the table, but his words must have stung her.

Dirk glared at him. "The loaded gun law doesn't apply here."

Austin smiled. The lawyer caught his reference. The loaded gun law held a parent liable for the death of her child in the case of unlawful use of a restricted device. The law usually applied to guns, knives, and other conventional weapons; however, it was open to interpretation and the Nexus Transporter was very new. Austin doubted that the company would win such a case. However, criminal law was far behind the technological curve. This case would go all the way to the Supreme Court. Ms. Anderson would not survive the financial or psychological strain. Austin saw that Dirk knew this.

"What is he talking about?" Ashley asked.

"Son, should you explain it to your client or I?" Austin asked.

"Mrs. Anderson, could you please step outside for a moment. I need to have some words with Mr. Wheeler."

Ashley looked worried, but Dirk reassured her with a nod, and Ashley stood and left the room.

"Look, I can tell by listening to you that you're not coming clean. You're hiding something." Dirk said.

"Oh?"

"If you were on the level, you wouldn't be here to settle."

"Son, did you figure that out all on your own? I'm impressed!"

"Tell you what. I promise to drop the whole damn thing and not look deeper, if you make a fair settlement with Mrs. Anderson. Fate has dealt her a losing hand and I can't allow you to capitalize on it. That is, unless you want me to leak this incident out to the press."

Austin forced a smile. "I'm sorry, son. If you bring your client back in here, I promise, I will behave. You won't be disappointed."

Dirk shook his head. "That's not good enough. Why should I trust you?"

"I do not know and do not care. You see, son, you've got no other choice. Fate *has* dealt your client a losing hand, but if you accept my terms, I'm willing to cut her some slack."

Silence.

"Son, I'm not going to say it again."

Dirk left the room. He returned with Ashley a moment later. She appeared shaken. Dirk nodded to Austin.

"Mrs. Anderson, we would like to help you. I have connections back in China, some subsidiary companies of ours. We have arranged for them to cover the cost of the self-organ transplant procedures your mother is enduring."

Austin also knew from his Chinese contacts that these procedures never worked in the long run. It would, however, keep Mrs. Anderson busy and keep her mother alive. She would be unable to collect the energy or the resources for a fight with Nexus Corporation. She would be lucky to hold together long enough to outlive her mother. "We also would like to wire you $50,000 to cover the funeral expenses and alike for your daughter."

Ashley smiled and exchanged a glance with her lawyer.

Dirk smiled back. He turned and faced Austin. "We tentatively accept your offer. I'll have the settlement papers written up for you to sign."

"Good. I will expect to see them by tomorrow morning." Austin locked his gaze with Dirk's. As Austin's smile returned, Dirk looked away. The boy lawyer had accepted the offer "as is." He should have predicted that and revised the settlement lower; but at least this little problem was out of the way.

19

Allison drove through a somewhat seedy area of downtown Chicago. The time read 21:31 p.m. She had left Steve in the Ventura hotel. He would come around soon. The mild sedative she gave him would be wearing off. He would be better off not knowing about this part. No one could know.

Near dusk, the soot-stained buildings slid into a deeper shades of gray. Most of the cement and cinderblock structures that lined the street were boarded up, casualties of the recent shift in economy. She squinted and caught sight of a street sign as she passed: West Ontario. Good, she was close.

She pressed down on the gas and glanced at her watch: 7:30 California time. She had missed her appointment with Vinnie. *Damn.* She would need a good excuse. Vinnie already suspected something.

Allison turned down West Huron Street. *Where was 641? There!* She pulled into the basement garage and picked the first open slot. Xi Quang lived in the penthouse of the twelve-story building. In the past, such a suite would have been associated with power and prestige; however, with a vacancy rate of twenty percent in the inner city, this was no longer the case.

Allison entered the large brick building with its stained and discolored walls and a neglected marble floor, cracked and chipped in many places. The entryway opened into a larger lobby, and a minimum wage attendant sat behind a desk. She flashed a smile, crossed the floor, and entered the elevator. She pulled a key from her coat pocket, tinkered with the key lock for the top floor, and punched the button. The attendant never looked up from his video screen.

The elevator doors closed. She pulled out her pistol and flipped off the safety. Vinnie had her target pistol, so she would make do with a standard issue Glock 21 handgun. Pulling the slide back, she loaded the first round into the chamber.

A bell sounded as the elevator reached the top floor. She stood at the threshold. The elevator doors opened into a large studio with a tiled living room and an attached kitchen under vaulted ceilings. A hallway in the back probably led to the bathroom. She stuck her head out and glanced left—couches, fireplace, but no Quang. She glanced right.

The stupid bastard was still online, thank god. He sat at a dining room table. She saw the Nexus on his head, a hi-tech cap with flickering lights. A long cord extended from it to a wall jack in the kitchen. The hardwired connection gave him more bandwidth.

She holstered her gun and stepped into the room.

A siren wailed.

"What the hell?" She turned and saw a motion detector mounted above the elevator in plain view. "Crap!"

A mechanized hum caused her to spin around. From the hallway on the far side of the room emerged a two-foot-long model tank. The barrel raised as the tank approached.

"Now what?" she murmured.

Lightning shot out of the tank's barrel. The bolt struck the back of the elevator. Allison leapt into the elevator and dove aside. She hated geeks. Allison glanced up at the elevator panel and punched the close door button.

Nothing happened.

She couldn't make a break for it. The safety zone was on the other side of that tank.

A voice came from the room. "Who are you, man?"

Quang was controlling his *toy* from VR.

"Mr. Quang, I just want to talk."

Another jolt of electricity shot into the elevator and electrified the wall near where the panel was located.

Allison pulled back.

From a speaker on the tank Allison heard Quang's voice. "You, in the elevator. I know you're just a messenger. Leave now before I use you to send a message of my own."

Cute. Allison heard the model tank move closer. From her angle, she saw the edge of the dining area. She could not see Quang, but she did see the cable connected to Quang's Nexus. She followed the cable with her gaze and found where the cable connected to the wall. *Typical engineer.*

Allison took careful aim. She fired two shots in quick succession at the socket on the wall. Sparks flew, and Quang yelped as he was ripped offline.

She waited a second.

Silence.

She poked her head around the corner and pulled back. The tank remained motionless. Allison stepped out of the elevator and emptied four rounds into the model tank.

She faced Quang. He lay moaning on the ground. His Nexus lay a few feet away from where he fell. She smiled as she approached him. The man's physical appearance fit the profile. He was a small, teenage Chinese cyberpunk, no more than five feet tall. *Another addict,* she thought, noting Quang's emaciated frame, pale skin, and atrophied muscles. He punished his body with drugs and non-stop cyber binges. He bore no resemblance to his VR alias Syzygy.

The contrast between his virtual body and his physical body spoke volumes about his contempt for the flesh and hatred of reality. This was his pressure point, the key to breaking him. Quang's discomfort with his own body would be his undoing.

She stood over him and waited for Quang's senses to recover.

Quang rolled over onto his back and opened his eyes.

Allison smiled. "And you're under arrest."

He muttered something in Cantonese.

"Don't speak it, see?" she spoke in the cyber drawl. She watched as Quang's eyes glanced toward the elevator.

You've got to be kidding.

Quang leaped past her.

She caught him by his collar and used his momentum to smash him into the table. The table snapped in half as he collapsed in a heap.

Allison smiled. "What got into you? You're an idiot for trying that." She cuffed the side of his head with her handgun and threw him back into the chair.

"You hit me!" he gasped in perfect English.

Allison smirked. She enjoyed the head games. These artistic types were all neurotic at the core. She stooped down and grabbed him by the throat. She picked two pressure points and adjusted her grip.

Quang tensed.

"If I let you go, will you be easy? Just want to talk is all. But I'll hurt you if I need to, see?"

"Yeah, no problem man. I'm easy, a real pushover."

She stuck her face inches from Quang's and peered into his eyes. Quang's gaze was empty and dark. He was just a puffed-up shell, a soulless husk. Allison smiled. He needed to appear cool. The demands of his protocol were particularly draining. One night in detention would do the trick. Thank god it was over. It was all over.

Allison frowned. "Come on Quangster, you're going for a ride."

20

Steve swam to consciousness. His body ached, his mouth was dry, and his head throbbed. *Where am I?*

Steve opened his eyes. It was pitch black and he couldn't see a thing. *What did I drink last night? I must have blacked out.* He checked his back pocket. His wallet was gone. He checked his front pocket. So were his keys. He had been rolled. Wait. The ground was soft. *A bed, a hotel?* It smelled like roses.

The scent carried his memories to him. In a flutter of images he saw it all—Brooke's friend's death, the defect, Allison, and Syzygy. Syzygy's piercing gaze stayed in his thoughts. The man's gaze tore into him. How had Syzygy done it?

His heart pounded in his chest and his thoughts became sharp. Steve sensed someone standing there, watching him. He reached for the lamp's switch and knocked over items on the bed stand. His keys hit the floor with a familiar jingle. Steve pulled the miniature chain under the lampshade and flooded the room with light.

The room was empty. Relieved, he laughed and looked around. Pink. The bed comforter was pink with embroidered roses. *Allison.* He smiled. She was nowhere in the room. "Some honeymoon," he muttered.

Steve glanced around and found his laptop at the foot of the bed. He grabbed it, popped it open, and booted the system. Once the icons appeared, Steve pulled up his session with Syzygy.

He saw Syzygy had sent electrical signals to all his senses. It had not been high enough to cause a seizure. Syzygy could not bypass the hardware limits, but it did spike his senses beyond the software maximum levels. *How?* It didn't make sense. The software checked the sensory limits on any interaction that took place in VR.

Syzygy had engulfed him. Perhaps the Nexus got confused. It could have viewed their aliases as a single object. Because the Nexus assumes no one is going to try to hurt himself, it wouldn't bother checking the safety limits as Syzygy attacked him. Could he fix it?

He could, but it would require a few months of programming. He had made the assumption throughout all the programs. He would have to modify almost half of them.

He remembered something else. Syzygy could hear them talking on the direct link, which was impossible unless Syzygy was physically plugged into the Nexus. How had Syzygy gotten around this? Whoever he was, he knew more about the Nexus' design than Steve did. Impossible. He had built the damn thing.

The message icon blinked in the upper left corner of his laptop. He clicked it. An email message from Allison appeared on the screen.

```
TO: Steve Donovan
FROM: Allison Hwang
SUBJECT: We got him!


Our friends at DARPA caught Syzygy ten min-
utes ago. His real name is Xi Quang.


Thanks,
Allison
```

The name surprised him. Steve thought he knew everyone who could tamper with the Nexus, but he did not recognize this name. His gut told him something was wrong. How could someone he had never heard of know so much about the Nexus?

Steve clicked the reply button and sent a message back to Allison.

```
TO: Allison Hwang
FROM: Steve Donovan
SUBJECT: re: We got him!

Allison,
Is he a colleague of yours? I've never heard
of this Quang character. Only a handful of
people could have messed with the designs
the way that Syzygy did. Quang must have had
help. Please send Quang's Nexus by priority
mail to my home:

Steve Donovan
267 Cabrillo Dr.
Walnut Creek, CA 94065

I'll check the logs and confirm whether the
attacks came from him.

Thanks,
Steve Donovan
```

Steve gathered his things, checked out of the hotel, and headed to the airport. After half an hour, he boarded a plane and took his seat. He shifted but could not get comfortable. His nerves felt on fire.

Something wasn't right about Quang. He couldn't get the thought out of his mind. Frustrated, he looked at his watch. It was

9:00 p.m., still early for Ron. Putting on the Nexus, the system connected wirelessly with the plane, and entered another world.

The temporary waiting area for the Nexus website was gone. Instead, Steve entered the nearly completed lobby. Ron was there. He surveyed the final updates to the room and shook his head. The virtual architects swapped in and out various fountains in the sitting area of the lobby.

"Ron?"

Ron turned. "My friend, how have you been?"

"Fine. Is everything okay with the lobby?"

"Oh yes, you and your girlfriend did a wonderful job of mopping it up."

Steve looked down.

"So, are you hitched?"

Steve rolled his eyes.

"Come on. You're a fast operator. When you get past yourself, these things don't take long."

"That's nice. What are you doing?"

Ron sighed. "You know, when I was going into retail there were only three things that were important—location, location, and location. You techno geeks really screwed things up with VR. Location doesn't mean squat now. Do you realize that now I have to track a million things and wear a million different hats because of you?"

Steve laughed.

"One of those hats is interior design. So tell me, which fountain do you think I should use here?" Ron motioned to one of the architects. "Can you bring up number three?"

The architect spoke a few commands and a fifteen-foot fountain appeared with a single white pillar in the center supporting three basins stacked on top of one another. The top basin was five feet in diameter, the next basin was closer to ten feet, and the last basin was almost fifteen feet across. Water cascaded from tier to tier; the flows formed a thick unbroken veil of water around the entire circumference of the top two tiers. The water roared like Niagara Falls and foamed as it hit the pool beneath it. A thick, low-lying fog clung to the fountain's base and dissipated a few feet away.

"I don't know. It's a bit much."

"I could shrink it down." He turned to the architect. "Reduce the size by thirty percent."

In a second the architect had reduced the fountain down to ten feet, and the sound of the water came up an octave. The fog remained heavy.

Steve shook his head.

"Okay, how 'bout this one?" Ron turned to the architect. "Can you pull up number seven?"

The architect spoke a few more commands. The fountain winked out and was replaced by a fifteen-foot copper tree. Copper limbs radiated from a thin central pipe, branching repeatedly until each limb ended with an upturned copper leaf. The leaves were colored with beautiful hues of red, blue, and green from natural corrosion. Water spewed upwards out the top of the central tube. It came down like rain spattering off each of the leaves. The water pooled together as it dropped from leaf to leaf, forming little streams until it plummeted into a large sandstone basin surrounding the base of the tree. The sound was beautiful, just like rain.

Steve nodded. "Better."

"Keep it," Ron said over his shoulder.

Steve stared at the ground. Things weren't adding up. What if his gut was right? What if they found out that Xi Quang wasn't Syzygy?

"Is something wrong, my friend?"

"Ron, does the alias Syzygy mean anything to you?"

Ron laughed. "I don't know anyone that uses it, but syzygy is a word I used in hangman as a kid."

Steve's jaw dropped. Ron never struck him as being that literate. "So, what does it mean?"

Ron shrugged. "I never cared to look it up. I just used it because the word has no vowels. It's impossible to guess. So what type of picture do you think I should put over here?"

Steve stared at the ground. Syzygy was a real word. The definition had to be important. Sometimes, a hacker would use an alias to represent an aspect of his personality; or sometimes he would pick an alias name that portrayed how he wanted others to view him. Either way, a hacker never selected an alias at random, murderer or no murderer. "Thanks, Ron. We'll catch up later." Steve moved to press the portal button

Ron grabbed his wrist.

"What?"

"Austin is stressing you out, isn't he?"

Steve nodded.

"I can't say how I know, but don't worry. Things will work out soon." Ron released his arm and returned to ordering his interior designers.

What the hell was that about? Steve pressed the portal button. "Home office."

He returned to the dark virtual room without walls, a crisscross mesh of green lines extending to infinity in all directions. "Jan, please display the definition of Syzygy." A wall of platinum appeared before him. Etched into its surface was the definition:

```
Syzygy \Syz*y*gy\ (s[I^]z"[I^]*j[y^]), n. ;
pl. {syzygies}
1. The point of an orbit, as of the moon or
a planet, at which it is in conjunction or
opposition; commonly used in the plural. For
example, the straight line connecting the
earth, the sun, and the moon, or a planet
when the latter is in conjunction or opposi-
tion.
```

```
2. The coupling together of different feet;
as, in Greek verse, an iambic syzygy.
3. The intimately united and apparently
fused condition of certain low organisms
during conjugation.
```

He could feel a thought forming in the back of his mind. His head felt like a raging river, a jumble of disjointed thoughts and ideas. Syzygy's attack had clouded his mind worse than alcohol ever could. He thought hard, kicking against the currents of thought. It was no use. Finally, he let go. He let his thoughts drift into murky torrents, jumbles of abstractions. He closed his eyes and slipped under, flowing with the river. Like an unexpected current in a river, he sensed an insight coming after him. It washed over him.

There it was. Even if they caught Syzygy, another murderer could step in and simply take Syzygy's place. No, finding Syzygy was a short-term solution. They had to recall the Nexus and replace the bad hardware component—the Signal Amplifier.

Steve remembered the memo. What would it cost to replace the part? He racked his brain. It had to be less than $2.50 for the parts; something wasn't right. Austin said they couldn't afford the repair at the time but Steve knew the margin. Austin had bragged that they could clear over $625 per unit after he negotiated the price with their distributor. Why then had Austin said that they couldn't afford the Nexus' repair expenses? Austin had said that they were tight on funds. How many units had they sold? Almost twenty million. Nexus Corporation should be doing better, much better than it was.

Tomorrow I'll check the books and see what has happened. Austin was so cocky that he probably had messed up the accounts without being aware of it. Steve hated finances. His stomach felt sick.

21

Brooke shifted uncomfortably in her wheelchair. Its locked wheels creaked in angry protest and broke the silence of the library. Brooke cringed. No one looked in her direction. Her Portal Sphere's microphone was not sensitive enough to broadcast the sound to the rest of the people in the virtual room.

Brooke grimaced. The motion had awakened a thin thread of pain that ran from her left shoulder down to her wrist. It asserted itself as another reminder of the accident. She wished her dad would let her use the Nexus instead of the Portal Sphere. It didn't make any sense. He had enough of the machines lying around. Why didn't he just give her another one while he was tinkering with hers? Brooke shook her head. With the Portal Sphere she could still sense the wheelchair beneath her.

It had been almost a year since the car accident left her mother dead and Brooke paralyzed from the waist down. Brooke sighed. A year was not long enough to adjust to everything. At least her dad had survived the accident.

She rubbed her shoulder as the nerve in her arm throbbed again. Why wouldn't he let her use the Nexus? Exiting VR, Brooke checked the time. It was 9:17 p.m. He had forgotten again. They weren't going out on the town as he promised. She laughed at the concept—Dad out on the town. Although she loved him to death, he was somewhat of a social retard. Well, if he broke his promise to her, then the Nexus was fair game. Besides, he hadn't forbidden her from using it, just asked her to wait.

Brooke rolled into his office, careful not to disturb the piles of papers and books that littered the floor. Despite her best efforts, she bumped the desk and a larger pile toppled off the desk and blocked her path. Determined, she reached around the desk and pulled open the top left drawer. Brooke fished blindly through the drawer's contents until she found the Nexus. She returned to the living room, locked the wheels of her chair as a precaution, and put on the Nexus.

In her own private room, she scanned the virtual landscape that her dad had made for her. Suspended two hundred feet above the ground, the four-tiered tree house surrounded an enormous sequoia. Each tier consisted of long, redwood planks supported by a large branch. Ladders linked the tiers together. The four tiers faced the four corners of this imaginary world—north, south, east, and west. The perspective from each, however, was the same. A forest stretched to the horizon in all directions. Her dad promised to install a lake for her when he had the time.

"Yeah, right." Time was something her dad never had for her. Although he made many promises, he was always busy with work.

Brooke walked around the second tier of the tree house. It felt good to have her legs back, alive and beautiful again. Each time she reentered VR, however, it felt more awkward. Her body was forgetting how to walk. At least the ever-present pain in her shoulder was gone. She looked around the flat and thought of calling Charlie, her dad's virtual dog. No, she decided. She wanted to be discreet. Charlie would squeal for sure. Brooke opened a portal and said "Stephen Hawking's School Library."

Like the entire high school, the library was virtual, an expansive room with a high domed ceiling, carpeted in red velvet, and paneled in luxurious cherry wood. Soft light evenly bathed the room, despite the fact that there were no lamps or ceiling lights. In fact, there were no distractions of any kind—no doors, no windows, and no decorations. The room was still, blanketed in a cathedral-like hush. The sounds of rustling pages and murmuring voices magnified the silence. No wonder they called it *The Coffin*.

Walking to one of the shelves, she pulled out a book labeled Mrs. French's 6/12 Chemistry Exam. As she opened the book, a portal appeared.

Brooke walked through the black void and entered an endless dark space. The test question was as she left it Tuesday before she found out about Camille.

A few yards from her were three vibrating round spheres, about the size of basketballs. One represented oxygen and the other two hydrogen atoms. They revolved slowly around one another. Brooke sighed and kicked her legs as if she were swimming. As she drifted toward them, she saw that each sphere was comprised of a tiny nuclear core surrounded by an opaque spherical cloud, a blur of electrons. From class she knew the cloud consisted of a few electrons. However, they were small enough to exhibit quantum behavior; the electrons appeared in multiple locations at once. She stopped in front of the spheres.

Brooke grabbed the oxygen atom, tucked it under her arm, and reached for a hydrogen atom. The hydrogen atom vibrated wildly and shook loose from her grip before she could get a handle on it. It floated away at a rapid pace.

"Damn it! Computer, drop the temperature to minus one hundred Celsius."

The computer complied and the atoms stopped vibrating. The temperature she was feeling, of course, didn't change. Only the simulation did. The hydrogen atom that had drifted away bounced off an invisible wall and drifted back to Brooke. Irritated, she grabbed the other hydrogen atom, which hovered in front of her. She then took the oxygen atom in her other hand and tried to join the two. As the atoms drew near each other, they repelled one another. She pushed harder, but they would not bond.

"What's wrong now? Why can't anything be easy?" she muttered.

She attempted to bring them together once more, this time watching their electrical fields. A dimple appeared on the oxygen atom's surface in its electron cloud. That's right. The electronic field around an oxygen atom was not balanced. Although it needed the hydrogen's electrons, it would bond only on two locations over its surface. She studied the atoms. The energy field of the oxygen atoms appeared to be thick. She didn't have the positioning right. She held the hydrogen atom between her knees and rotated the oxygen atom in both hands until she found a spot where the electrical field was thinner and more transparent. She let go of the hydrogen atom and bumped it with her knee like a soccer ball up to the oxygen atom in her hand. This time, the hydrogen atom lurched toward the oxygen atom and attached. Their electric fields merged and formed a single surface that enveloped both of them.

One down, one to go.

The other atom had returned to her. Without too much trouble, Brooke was able to repeat the procedure. She attached the second hydrogen atom to the oxygen atom, forming the familiar V-shape of a water molecule.

The disembodied voice of the computer said, "Congratulations! You have completed problem four. Now, on to problem five. Frozen water is unlike most other frozen fluids. Please experiment and determine the difference."

The void filled with movement. Other water molecules appeared and bounced off each other and the invisible walls of the void. A few of them bumped against her. They felt soft and resilient. The way they surged back and forth, pushing her around, reminded Brooke of swimming in the ocean when she had the use of her legs. She remembered the surf and how out of control she felt. Brooke reveled in the memory until a molecule rebounded off her head.

"Computer, what are the conditions?"

"Standard room temperature and pressure. Time has slowed proportionally to match your simulated size."

"Computer, please lower the simulated temperature to minus twenty Celsius."

Again, the temperature on her skin remained the same but the molecules slowed noticeably and stopped trembling. A group of six formed a hexagon, their V-shaped legs pointing inward. Several rings formed. The rings collected and stacked on top of one another to form a crystal. The crystal rose. It pushed the loose water molecules aside until it was at the top of the room. Over the course of several minutes, Brooke watched as the V shapes extended the structure into a complex lattice. In the end, no free molecules remained.

"Computer, the answer is that ice made of water is lighter than liquid water. Usually, a solid is heavier than its fluid counterpart, because the molecules pack closely together. However, water ice is less dense than fluid water."

"Brooke, please clarify. Why is water ice not denser?"

"Because water ice forms ring-shaped crystals which leave a lot of empty space in the center of the crystal structure. Thus, the molecules do not pack as closely together as in their fluid form."

"Correct! This concludes your practice chemistry lab. Please review problems one and three. You had difficulty with these two problems, Brooke."

"I know, I know," Brooke said.

The room dimmed and went black.

The scene dissolved into her virtual tree house. She felt empty and did not want to return to her physical body, at least not yet. Why go back to the wheelchair when she could be in here? There were still places to explore.

She glanced over at the well-stocked bookcase on the tier. Each book represented a site she could visit on the Internet. Her dad had installed the bookcase as a way to control her comings and goings since he did not trust the V-chip. She ran a finger over the titles. Most were nonfictional titles and themes—famous people's biographies, scientific subjects, and how-to books. Her dad did not believe much in games or game sites.

What's this? A title caught her eye: *The Mars Lander*. That was odd. She didn't remember this title being here before. Her Dad didn't buy fiction. Was it a new addition? She grabbed the title and sat down on the wooden floor. The book, really a booklet, contained just a couple of pages.

The title across the top of the first page read, *Visit Mars*. Beneath it was a map of Mars. The next page was titled, *The First Manned Expedition to Mars*. It had animated pictures on the left-hand side and a description on the right of a fictional chronology of the planned mission. It was likely some promotional material that her dad had picked up. He was constantly supporting various causes. She selected a picture at random and touched its smooth surface. The promo music for NASA played. Next to her, a portal opened with a whoosh. She got up and stepped through.

Brooke found herself wearing a spacesuit. A jumble of red rocks, covered in a thick layer of crimson dust, surrounded her. In the distance, the sharp peak of a mountain loomed above the Martian landscape. She couldn't remember its name. Brooke noticed that her entire body felt different. Mars' weaker gravity made it feel as if a great weight had been lifted from her. She looked down and took a tentative step forward. A small cloud of dust wafted up from the surface, settling in the thin Martian atmosphere. *Cool.* She took a second step.

Pain, like shards of glass etched across her mind. She fell or was falling. Color swirled across her vision. A metallic taste made her gag. What was happening? The colors settled and she stopped spinning. She was looking down at her withered legs and the wheelchair. "Jesus," she gasped. A wave of nausea hit her as her body reeled from the sudden trauma to her senses.

"Brooke ... told ... use this! Are ... listening ... me? ... Brooke?" Her dad's voice faded in and out. Her dad stood over her, holding the Nexus in his hand.

Brooke clutched her head and screamed. "Stop it!" She grabbed the wheels of her wheelchair and pushed. They didn't budge. "Shit!" she gasped. Tapping the wheel locks, she freed the wheels and raced toward her room.

"You don't understand," her Dad said.

Brooke slammed the door behind her.

22

Click. The sound grated on Steve's nerves. Brooke had locked her bedroom door. Why did she shut him out like that? Didn't she know how much he loved her? Steve took a deep breath. It didn't help. He stormed into his office, hitting the light switch as he passed. Nothing happened. The lights were burned out.

Steve walked around his desk and stumbled over a stack of books and papers on the floor. His ankle twisted and he stubbed his toe on the foot of the chair. Steve slid into his chair and let out a sigh. As he flung open the left bottom drawer, the scotch and tumbler inside clanged together. He grabbed both, poured a drink, and took a gulp.

Brooke was so difficult to deal with. She had blatantly disregarded his warning. Yet, somehow, she had turned the situation on him and suddenly it was his fault! How had she done that? He took another sip and set the glass back down.

He was just protecting her. What if the Nexus had failed while she was online? Steve polished off the glass and poured another. He shuddered at the thought of Broke exposed to someone like Syzygy.

Twenty minutes and several drinks later, the doorbell rang.

Steve checked the time: 10:30 p.m. *Who in the hell ... ?* He grabbed a roll of breath mints from the desk and popped one, then two, into his mouth. Lurching to his feet, he fell back into the chair, his head swimming from a cocktail of alcohol, fatigue, and guilt. Steve fixed his gaze on the red light of the fire alarm. Two red dots danced on the ceiling. He couldn't focus.

The doorbell rang.

"I'm coming. I'm coming," he yelled.

He hated it when Brooke's friends dropped by this late. He stood and steadied himself with the chair. Steve tripped over the stacks of papers and books, stumbled into the hallway, and jogged to the front door. He opened it.

A tall beautiful Ameriasian woman with black hair greeted him.

"Allison?" An alcohol-induced smile crept across his face.

She grinned back at him. "Well, aren't you going to let me in?"

"Uh, yes." He stepped back. "Of course." He hoped she couldn't smell the booze on him. Then of course swaying side to side was a dead give away. He leaned against the wall.

She smirked and handed him a Nexus. "Are you all right?"

He looked down. "Yeah, I'm fine. Just didn't expect to see you. Come, sit down." Steve turned and led her down the hall to the living room. They sat down on the couch.

Steve turned over the Nexus she gave him.

"It's Xi Quang's. I thought I would deliver it to you in person. I needed to make sure you were okay after Syzygy's attack and all."

He set the Nexus aside on the end table.

"I'm sorry I left you alone there," she continued.

"Allison …" Her green eyes transfixed him. Her gaze drifted to his lips. Perhaps he had not been the only one doing a little drinking. He felt drawn, but not dragged. He could have stopped it if he wanted to. He was not that intoxicated, but he had drunk just enough to provide an excuse. Maybe he would bend his rule this once. It wasn't really mixing business with pleasure, being after hours and all. He glanced back toward Brooke's room. The door was closed. She was asleep by now.

He leaned over and kissed Allison lightly on the lips. His heart warmed with excitement as months of loneliness melted away, appeased for the time being.

She laughed and kissed him back, wrapping her arms around him. He leaned toward her. She gave way, falling back onto the couch. On top of her, he kissed her neck. She unbuttoned his shirt and explored his chest. He rolled to his side and suddenly felt the edge of the couch beneath him. Still holding Allison, he fell. She let out a gasp as she rolled over on top of him. Together they landed on the floor.

She laughed, getting up. "Maybe we should go somewhere safer."

"Safe sex?" he said, taking her hand, leading her toward the hall. He tripped on the carpeted steps leading from the sunken living room to the hallway.

"Maybe I should take the lead," she said.

They stumbled down the hall to Steve's bedroom. He closed the door behind them.

The Calm

"Our thoughts, our words, and deeds are the threads of the net which we throw around ourselves."

—Swami Vivekananda, 1902

23

Allison wiped the sleep from her eyes and opened the door to the bathroom. A wall of fog washed over her. Steve had already showered, and a damp towel lay crumpled on the floor. The toilet seat lid was raised. "Men!" she groaned.

Allison lowered the seat. She picked up the towel and threw it into the nearby hamper. She showered, dressed, and found Steve in the living room.

He sat cross-legged on the carpet in front of the coffee table wearing a white cotton robe. Steve leaned against the couch while his fingers flew over the laptop's keys. How could he type so fast?

"What are you doing?"

He continued to type, unfazed by her question.

She noticed Xi Quang's Nexus on the coffee table, next to his laptop. A cable linked the two. Moving next to him, she said, "Can you hear me?"

Oblivious, he continued to type.

She looked over his shoulder. He stopped typing and stared intently at a spreadsheet on the screen.

You can be cute at times. She leaned over him, placing her face between him and the screen. "Steve!"

Steve pulled back.

"Sorry," she laughed. "Did you find something?"

"Yeah." He moved aside.

She eased around the couch and sat down on the carpet next to him. He pointed at the screen. "See these messages?"

She cradled her legs with an arm and studied the log entries.

```
06/12/20 16:22:29 THE PROGRAM V-CHIP WAS NOT
ABORTED AS REQUESTED BY A REMOTE HOST—ALIAS
SYZYGY DUE TO A LOCAL PROGRAM LOCK.
06/12/20 16:34:11 THE PROGRAM SIGNAL AMPLI-
FIER WAS NOT ABORTED AS REQUESTED BY A RE-
MOTE HOST—ALIAS SYZYGY DUE TO A LOCAL PRO-
GRAM LOCK.
```

"These are from the System Log off my Nexus. This shows when Xi Quang attacked me. Now watch. When I pull up records on Xi Quang's Nexus showing the attacks he made …" Steve typed several keys and two new records appeared on the screen.

```
06/12/20 18:22:29 A REQUEST TO STOP THE PRO-
GRAM V-CHIP ON A REMOTE HOST: 193.168.122.15
FAILED DUE TO A LOCAL PROGRAM LOCK.
06/12/20 18:34:11 A REQUEST TO STOP THE
PROGRAM SIGNAL AMPLIFIER ON REMOTE HOST:
193.168.122.15 FAILED DUE TO A LOCAL PROGRAM
LOCK.
```

He looked over at her. "Do you see the problem?"

She leaned forward. "Yeah, I do! They're hours apart!"

"No, that's correct. He was two hours ahead in Chicago."

"I don't understand. What's your point?" she said, picking a spec of imaginary lint from her slacks.

"My point is where is the attack on Camille? There should be four records—two for each attack from Xi Quang's Nexus."

"Quang must have altered the log."

"Why would he cover up one attack but not the other?"

"DARPA caught Quang after he attacked you. Maybe he didn't have time to cover his tracks."

Steve nodded. "That's true, but there's no easy way to modify the logs. It requires an intimate knowledge of the system. Only a handful of people can do that—I know every one of them. Xi Quang isn't on the list."

"But what else could it be?" she asked.

"He must be part of a gang or group."

Allison leaned back and laughed. "You mean Syzygy is a conspiracy."

Steve bowed his head.

She lost her smile. "You're serious?"

He nodded.

"I seriously doubt that," she said.

"How else can you explain it?"

"I don't know, but we'll find out soon enough after DARPA interrogates Quang." She stood and stretched. "Well, I hate to take off so soon, but I've got some business that needs my attention this morning." She bent over Steve and reached for her handbag. It gave him an eye full. He forgot about the logs.

God, she smells good. His gaze caressed her body. How much had he missed last night in his stupor? He was too intimate with the bottle and too distant from the important things. So much of his life he could not recall. He was quite possibly staring at his second chance. He wouldn't blow it again. He had his life, Brooke, and now, maybe Allison. *Maybe.*

She straightened up. "Can I see you tonight?"

He gazed into her green eyes. "Maybe *may be* definitely."

Allison cocked her head sideways.

"I mean, of course you can." He pulled her close and kissed her, then brushed his cheek next to hers, smelling her scent. "God, you smell good."

She grinned and straightened.

Getting up, he wrapped his robe around him and walked her to the door. "I have to take care of some things at Nexus Corp, but I'll be in my virtual home office later this afternoon. Why don't you meet me there? We could work more on the case."

"Sounds great, except for one thing."

"What?"

"Dinner."

"Are you asking me out on a date?" he asked.

She folded her arms together. "Let's put it this way. Getting as focused as you do, it seems that a planned dinner date will get you away from things easier."

"Easier than what?" he asked. His gaze traced her figure.

"Steve!" She nudged him. "I'm serious. You're one of those focused types. You know, the kind that ignores everything else, or rather *everyone* else around you when you're focused on work."

He nestled his face in her neck. "Did you like me better when I was tipsy and unfocused?"

She laughed. "No, I'm not saying focus is bad, but sometimes focusing in other areas can be just as rewarding. Maybe even more so." With that, she winked and left.

Steve shook his head and shut the door. Her double meanings intrigued him.

"Dad? Who are you talking to?"

He spun around and saw Brooke wheeling down the hall.

"Hey! Good morning, sunshine!" Steve turned and walked toward the kitchen.

She followed. "You haven't called me that in eons, Dad."

He poured a cup of coffee. "Come into the kitchen and I'll cook up some breakfast before I go to work."

"I'm NOT hungry, not after last night!"

It came back to him. He had ripped her offline. "Brooke, look, I know pulling your Nexus off like that must have been horrible. It was ... I guess, like a knee jerk reaction."

"Yeah, well you can leave the *knee* part out as far as I'm concerned!"

Steve put both hands up in the air. "Okay. Okay. Guilty as charged. I was just trying to protect …"

"Just trying? Dad, can't you see how you treat me? I am *not* a little girl anymore! Just because I'm in a wheelchair doesn't mean I'm some kind of childish baby. Whether I wanted to or not, the accident forced me to grow up. Why can't you?"

"Watch it."

"I've accepted my fate, why can't you?"

"This isn't about that!"

"Yes it is! Shit happens, Dad! Just because something happens to my friend doesn't mean that anything will happen to me. I think I've had my share, okay? I mean, look at me. What else *could* happen?"

Steve frowned. What could he say?

"I can take care of myself. Trust me. Everything will be fine as long as you chill about my Nexus."

"No, Brooke."

"The Nexus is all I have left, Dad. You're never here anymore. It takes me places I can't go anymore. It's my only freedom. Don't take it away from me."

Steve sighed and looked into her eyes. He tried to remember what it felt like when he was her age. What would he have done if he had lost the use of his legs? The Nexus Healer would right this wrong. Monday would not come soon enough.

"Brooke, you know, this is so hard, and I love you so much. Just for now, don't use it. That's the way it's got to be, for now."

Her eyes filled with tears. She turned her wheelchair around and headed back to her room. She would understand Monday. The long wait would be over. Steve got to his feet and he walked to his room. He needed to clear his head. Throwing on a pair of jogging shorts and a sweatshirt, he laced up his running shoes. He had not run for days.

For the next hour he ran. He ran off last night's booze and this morning's upset. His mind cleared. The recall had to happen. One killer had already found the bug and others could follow. A new-and-improved software patch would only create a new-and-improved software bug. The only permanent fix was to replace the hardware.

On the plane he had thought about Austin and the financial numbers. They should be able to recall the Nexus. He had put it off too long; he had to look at the company's finances. His talk with Brooke would come later. Just give her some time; she would understand things. Everything would work out in it's own time.

24

Allison glanced at the wall clock as she entered the Interrogation Center in Richmond to visit Xi Quang. It was only 9 a.m. She hated working outside of VR. It took her an entire thirty minutes to physically drive there. *What a waste of time.* Worse, since she was working in reality, Big Brother would be watching her interrogation. How was she going to make this guy talk without roughing him up a little?

She walked into the observation room.

A technician looked up from a complex array of electronic equipment.

"Allison Hwang. Where's the prisoner. The technician pointed.

Through a one-way mirror she saw Quang; he was asleep. He had been left in isolation overnight. It gave her an idea. "I need to shake this guy down. Is there any way to have him wake up into VR?"

"He has to be conscious."

"I know that. Come on, think. We need to get to this guy."

The technician sat silent for a few seconds. "Well, I could try something." He pointed to the equipment. "These are his brain waves. Once they reach here, I can put him in VR before he is aware of what is going on."

"Okay. Slap a Nexus on him, make a simulation of this room,

and place him inside." She entered VR.

"Good morning, Quangster. Remember me?" Allison stepped into the virtual room and slammed the door behind her.

Quang snapped awake and glanced around. He then leaned back in his chair and focused on a point in space.

"So, what's this all about? Why'd you go around doin' in little girls and grown men? Do you like grown men? That last victim of yours was a man in a woman's form. His name is Steve. I can arrange a little get together if you'd like."

His eyes grew wide for an instant before they returned to their detached state. She let the silence accumulate. Quang fidgeted in his chair and said nothing. He drew out a Camel. Allison grabbed the lighter in her pocket, leaned over, and lit Quang's cigarette.

"You know those things can kill you," she said. The lighter snapped shut.

Quang shrugged. "Now or later we've all got to die, you know. It's the meaning of life—death." He took a drag from the Camel and hung his arm on the back of the chair letting the ash drop on the ground. Quang's hand shook.

She smiled. "Deep stuff, Quangster, but some die sooner than later. Maybe you'll be dead sooner, huh?"

"It doesn't matter what you do to me, see? You'll get yours before we're through."

"You mean friends? Your friends will *do* me?"

He shrugged and took a drag.

"So you're just a terrorist. Is that it?"

"No, man," he corrected her. "We're the future—revolutionaries. We protect the innocent from injustice."

"You're no revolutionary, just a terrorist is all. There's a difference, you know."

Quang looked at his feet.

"The revolutionary has a plan. The terrorist simply messes things up. Do you have a plan, Quangy?"

He said nothing.

"You don't have a clue, do you? Just tear things down is all you do. Mess things up. Where's the nobility in that? You're just a punk with an attitude."

He smiled.

"Tell you what, Quangster. I want you take your clothes off and place them on the table here. I'll be back in a few minutes," she said.

Quang rolled his eyes and smiled, saying, "Yeah, right, man."

"So, you'll be cool?" Allison asked.

Quang's smile disappeared. "You're serious?"

She nodded.

"I know you, man, this cop routine of yours. You don't scare me." He took a drag from the Camel. Allison glanced down at Quang's cigarette hand. It shook.

She leaned forward. "This is for real. You do it, man. I want you naked, see? If not, I'll strip you myself." She stood.

Quang stiffened. "No problem. It's cool."

"Really? I know your number, man. Contempt for the flesh, that's your Achilles heel, see? You may be some sort of god in cyberspace, but you're in my domain now. This is the realm of the flesh." She left the room. Once outside Allison pulled back her sleeve, pressed the exit button on her wrist, and exited VR.

She materialized back in the room on the other side of the one-way mirror. The technician looked up from a VR screen, a window into the virtual interrogation room.

"Are you sure he won't figure it out?" Allison asked.

The technician shrugged. "I don't see how he can. We removed the VR buttons from his wrist and the time readout. As far as he can tell, he's awakened in reality. One thing, though. Don't rough him up too bad. I was liberal with the sensory levels. He can feel some pain, but there is no way to bypass the hardwired upper limits of the system. He'll know if you push him too hard."

She turned her attention to Quang on the VR monitor, a camera peering into his virtual world. After a few seconds, he set the Camel aside and disrobed. He flung his clothes about the room. Then he shifted his shirt and trousers to perfect the atmosphere.

"What the hell is he doing?" the technician asked, baffled.

"He cares what others think," Allison said.

She looked back at the Camel. Most of the cigarette remained. In the real world it would be half gone by now. She glanced around his virtual room and noted a TV mounted in the upper corner of the room. "Can that display something?"

"Like what?"

"Like what we're seeing through this VR monitor."

"Yes."

"How long will that take?"

The technician hit a series of switches and said, "Done."

"Not now. I'll nod to you when I need it."

"Sure." The technician shrugged and flipped off one of the switches.

She glanced back at the monitor. Quang sat in the chair cross-legged. He tried to lean back, spreading one arm over the back of the chair, the Camel dangling from one hand. Not satisfied, he shifted his weight and leaned onto the back legs of the chair while letting his own legs lift off the ground. He fell backward and his limbs flailed for an instant as he recovered. He resumed his original position and kept the chair planted on the ground.

Allison laughed as she put her Nexus on and entered VR.

Once in VR, she reentered the interrogation room. "I can read you, man. This thing you're holding inside of you, it's eating you alive."

"It's cool. I can take it."

"Who're you with? How many are you?"

"If I tell you, they'll ice me."

"We'll do you worse."

Quang fixed her with a serious look. "No one does them worse. Nobody."

She nodded to the mirror.

The closed-circuit television flipped on with a pop. He turned and his jaw dropped. He stared at his naked image on the screen. Quang shifted in his seat.

Allison paced around him. "You didn't think I wanted to see you naked, did you? I had a reason for asking you if you like men. Every sex-starved rapist in the joint is seeing your naked ass right now. You're going to make some future cellmate of yours a very, very happy man." She came around in front and flashed him a smile.

"Mean mother. Figures you'd do me this way," Quang rasped.

"I'm not the one who will be *doing you*," she chuckled.

He took another drag from his Camel and glanced at it.

Damn it. She snapped her fingers. "Hey, Quangy, so you'll talk? Or do I introduce you to Guido of Cell Block B?"

He shrugged.

"Be that way." She walked toward the exit.

"Mei Hsien," Quang rasped through clenched teeth. "We're the Mei Hsien."

Allison turned. The name alarmed her. Mei Hsien was the principal triad of the loosely organized Teochiu Chinese gangs, thought to be the most dangerous of the gangs run out of China. They involved themselves in everything: kidnapping, murder, extortion, drugs, counterfeiting, and prostitution.

Their roots in the States went back to the nineteenth century when the triads or tongs both exploited and supported the Chinese immigrants working on the railroads. Through the years, their numbers grew and their influence spread across the country. Among other things, they controlled over eighty percent of the heroin market.

"Mei Hsien? Is that some sort of code or what?"

"Stop playing. You know us."

"You're terrorists, right?"

"No, man. I told you, revolutionaries, the future. We protect the innocent from injustice."

"So I'll ask you again. When did the Mei Hsien start getting off by raping and killing little girls?" The remark still seemed to shake him. Not a good sign. The Mei Hsien would have no qualms about it.

"It's nothin' personal, man. It's our calling card, that's all. We don't mean anything by it; it just works out that way is all. We're founders of a new age, a revolution. You'll see. Sometimes people just have to die. We needed to test some things out, I guess."

"Test? Test for what?"

He shrugged.

"How many of you are there?"

"Enough." He took another puff from his still lit camel. He stared at it.

She slapped his hand and the smoke flew across the room. "Look, I'm not playing around."

He shrugged his shoulders.

"How did you coordinate your attacks? Who trained you?"

Quang smiled and pulled out another cigarette.

She lit it.

He blew smoke in her face.

She backhanded him and launched his cigarette across the room. Quang fell to the floor.

"Get up," she said.

Quang rolled over onto his back and sat up naked on the cold cement floor. "You didn't have to do that."

"Yeah, I know that. The problem is, you see, I wanted to."

He got to his feet.

"Get your smoke."

His body trembled as he retrieved it. His eye and jaw had started to swell.

"Tell me, how many of you are there?"

"Okay man, don't be so pushy. I work with six others. Only know their aliases is all. We don't ever meet each other in the flesh.

Safer that way, see?"

"Really? You mean to tell me there are only seven of you? And you've never seen the others?"

He nodded.

"Does Camille Anderson sound familiar?"

He shrugged.

"What kind of targets turn you guys on?"

"Financial districts mostly, a few officials. Don't remember their names though. Really trashed their lobbies."

"Jesus," she muttered. Something was off. "What do you know about the Nexus?"

"Stuff."

Allison smacked him across his face. He tumbled to the ground and moaned. She hoped she had not hit him too hard. Allison stood up and placed one of her stiletto heels on the back of his neck. "Look man, I ain't fuckin' around. Your friends are knocking out the wrong people. We don't take kindly to pedophiles and rapists. Now tell me who ya gonna hit?"

"No one."

She applied some pressure. There was a pop.

"Crap, man. I told you. I don't know. Don't kill me, man."

She released him, and Quang rolled over on his back and rubbed his neck.

"If you're lying to me, I'll kill you. Do you get me?"

He nodded.

"How'd you use the Nexus?"

"We made tools is all. Things to tap into people's networks, plant things, you know?"

"What about brainwaves? Did you mess with their heads?"

"Maybe. I don't know."

"How'd you do them?"

He shrugged his shoulders.

"You don't know, do you?"

He smiled.

"How long have you been with this outfit of yours?"

"A while."

"So what's your game, your title, you know?"

Quang took another drag. "Hung Kwan."

"You?" She laughed. Hung Kwan, a.k.a. Red Pole, was the title for the military leader of a triad. "No way man, you're too green. You're just a Sze Kau, a thug. Tell me. Exactly how long have you been with them?"

"Six months, I guess."

"Six months?" Allison shook her head. The triads took at least a year to accept someone into their fold. "Who's the Shan Chu, Fun Chan Chu, Pak Tsz Sin, Cho Hai?" Allison said, rattling through the designated titles of the triad's hierarchy of leadership.

Quang shrugged. "As I said, no names, only aliases."

"They didn't tell you anything, did they?"

"Not so! It's for the good of the whole. I told you, no names, see?"

"Crap!" She swore under her breath and exited VR.

Quang glanced around, moaned, and hung his head.

Allison removed the Nexus and asked the technician, "What did you see on the polygraph?" She looked back into the room. Quang sat in the chair, his body limp. He had no bruises, was fully clothed, and still wearing a Nexus.

The technician reviewed the recording of Quang's brainwaves on the polygraph. "Except for the things you caught him on, he never lied."

"That oaf doesn't belong to no triad," she said.

"What do you make of all this?" the technician asked.

"Doomed spy." She sat back.

"What?"

"You haven't read *The Art of War* I take it?"

The technician shook his head.

"It's a two thousand-year-old Chinese manuscript about war logistics. Quang here believes everything he's telling us and feels guilty about betraying his friends, but what he's given us is all bunk. He knows very little about the previous murders, almost nothing about the triad he belongs to, and he's admitted he is a new recruit. But he knows who he is, who he belongs to, and the type of targets they're going to attack." She shook her head.

"He's a patsy. The gang fed him lies and false information. Hell, he's probably not even part of the Mei Hsien triad, only he doesn't know it. They created the perfect spy; he only knows false information *and* he believes it. They set him up to distract us. We're lucky we only lost a morning on this guy!"

"Are you sure?"

"Come on. The triad makes him a fully-fledged member within six months, yet keeps him in the dark about the previous murders and the people in the organization? And all he knows is his name, the triad's name, and the type of targets they're going to attack? Great way to misdirect an investigation."

Allison winced. Her career hinged on the success of Warscape, which, in turn depended on the Nexus. Ed had to remain in the dark about all this; but with Syzygy on the loose, that could change. If body count kept going north, he was bound to find out.

Perhaps Davis *could* find out about the defect but not about Syzygy. She would help Steve with the recall, but Austin had the numbers and she needed to keep him in his place. She composed an email.

```
FROM:   Ed Davis, Assistant Secretary of
        Defense C4ISR
TO:     Austin Wheeler, CEO Nexus Corporation

Austin,
I need the numbers on the cost of a recall
ASAP. Do not contact me directly. Ms. Hwang
or I will contact you.

Ed Davis
```

25

Skip Harvey struggled to lift his head from the saddle as the Nexus fought against him. I must be dehydrated. He adjusted his virtual hat and scanned the desiccated landscape. No signs of water.

He was in the middle of an immense valley in the Sonoran desert. Through the rising heat, the bare mountains wavered in the distance. Like the valley, the mountains were devoid of any life. Across the valley floor, several dust devils scattered sand and dirt about. Eons of sunlight had bleached the ground, leaving it pale and parched. Hidden under a thin film of dust was a gravel-strewn surface.

Skip's head drooped. The sun blinded him as it reflected off the light grey dust and sparkling quartz that peaked through. He readjusted his hat, but could not escape the heat or the glare. His horse stopped.

Skip raised his head. A huge dry wash cut across his path and bared his passage. "Oh bollocks," he cursed.

The walls of the wash were high and forbidding. His horse was in no condition to negotiate the steep grade much less cross through the thick sand that lined the dry streambed. Up stream, the wash meandered all the way to the mountains. Down steam, the wash snaked its way across the valley floor and disappeared over the horizon. He sighed. There was no place to cross safely.

It would take a little longer, but he could still reach the mountains by following the wash's bank. Skip lifted his hat and wiped the virtual sweat from his brow. The dry, hot air sucked the moisture away. Since the morning, Skip had searched for shade, but he had found none—no rock formations, no trees, not even a large bush under which he could hide. In fact, except for the sparse brush that lined the banks of this dry wash, he had seen no vegetation at all. He hoped his luck would change upstream. Skip pulled the reigns and nudged the horse's ribs. The beast turned and followed the wash's bank.

Further upstream, purple stems, stripped bare of leaves, reached out of small bushes. The drought had flushed their leaves into a deep green. A clump of dried vines rooted at the base of the wash reached up and tangled itself in the bush. Despite it being June, a red yucca plant stood with no flowers on its tall stalk. The plant's normally vibrant green leaves were shriveled and gray with a veneer of dust. It had not rained here for months.

"No luck," he grumbled.

A virtual drop of sweat ran into his eyes. It was salty and stung—or at least it stung as bad as the Nexus would allow him to feel. He rubbed his eyes and looked up at the sun. Only 1 p.m. and already the hot air baked his skin through his shirt.

He felt moisture on his lips. Dabbing at them, his hand came back red with blood. This was bad. He had to find a spring, a cactus, or some sort of water source soon. Setting across the desert at sunrise, he had misjudged the distance to the far mountains. At least another ten miles lay ahead of him. There he might find shade or even water. His shoulders sagged. He could not take another ten miles in this heat. Worse, the temperature would not peak for another hour.

I'm going to die.

Skip laughed. He couldn't help it. The whole experience felt empty. Something very important was missing. True, his eyes smarted, his lips were chapped, and he had difficulty moving. All his senses testified that this experience was real, that he was dying of dehydration; but it was not enough. The fact of the matter was that he just wasn't thirsty.

Thirst and hunger were still beyond the grasp of the Nexus. Skip was not thirsty when he logged on eight hours ago, and he was not thirsty now, not even in the slightest. He was getting hungry, but that was a poor approximation of thirst. Next time he would remember not to drink water the night before. There would be a next time, because he was not going to make it to the settlement. He would have to try again.

Something else was missing. Skip didn't feel confused or delirious. The state of mind was yet another dimension of human experience out of the Nexus' reach. The more he thought about it, the more surreal the whole venture seemed. Skip sighed.

At least the experience gave him some sense of what the journey had been like. *Create Your Own Adventures* had reconstructed the entire adventure for him. Skip was tracing the path that his ancestors had taken when they trekked across the desert between Plemons, in the Texas panhandle, to Salome, Arizona, in the middle of the Sonoran desert. His great-great-great-grandfather, Flavius Josephus Brown, had come here in the late 1800s. In the last couple of years, Skip had become enamored with his past. He researched all he could about his ancestors. After two years of searching, he still felt discontented. He wanted to experience and feel what they felt. That's when he decided to cross the Sonoran desert.

When he told his friends about the expedition, they laughed and said he was just being trendy. That was the same comment his wife Betty had made to him this morning. Superficially, they were right, but Skip had introduced a new twist on the old theme: reliving one of his ancestor's experiences.

Create Your Own Adventures was unique in providing customized adventures. The other sites, although dedicated to exploring and experiencing the past, limited their virtual trips to canned famous expeditions. They entertained with everything from Leif

Ericsson's discovery of North America to the first manned mission to the moon. Usually, the excursions were edited and abridged, compressing several months or years into a one-week vacation package. The vacationer would select the more interesting aspects of the historical journey and string them together into one action-packed adventure complete with bathroom, meal, and sleep breaks. Time, of course, could not be compressed. In the temporal world mankind could move in all dimensions but time; the virtual world was not any different.

Skip's hands dropped the reins and he lost balance. He clutched the horn of the saddle and steadied himself. His vision skewed and the landscape blurred, the mountains and desert swirling around him. He closed his virtual eyes to stop the vertigo. Death was near. His horse fared not much better.

In the desert, a horse could survive on about twelve gallons of water a day, while a man needed one gallon. Under the afternoon sun that figure grew to eighteen gallons for the horse and almost two gallons for the man. Skip had no water because his great-great-great-grandfather Flavius had no water on this leg of the journey.

But Skip started to doubt the legend. How could anyone survive this heat without water? Yet, the computer simulated conditions based on old records they had from the area. So, Flavius had faced the same situation. Only one answer remained. The more Skip thought about it the more he was convinced that his ancestor must have found water while crossing the desert, but where?

Skip's eyes hurt. They were dry, crusted, and had almost swollen shut. He chuckled again at the stark contrast between his swollen eyes and lack of thirst. He debated whether or not to retrieve the reins—in his condition a life or death decision. Lifting his head, he tried to ascertain whether he was still on course. The Nexus fought his movement, but he managed to raise his head anyway.

The horse had followed the wash, though it moved slower now than before. Good. As long as the horse kept on this course, he could leave the reins where they were.

Vultures gathered a few hundred yards ahead. They rode the afternoon thermals created when the sun baked the desert floor. Hot air radiated off the quartz, and dust and rose in a hot updraft—a spiraling column of wind. The vultures would sail upward on these winds. With each circle in the sky, the vultures climbed higher.

The Nexus pushed down hard and Skip slumped over his saddle. In the back of his mind, a thought tugged at him just out of reach. What was it? It came to him. The vultures pointed to water.

The vultures circled some sort of dying animal. Very few desert creatures of any size could be more than a couple of miles away from water. Skip raised his head. The vultures were off to his right and away from the wash. To get there Skip would have to retrieve the reins and steer the horse.

If he fell off now, he would be unable to get back in the saddle and the simulation would end. Of course, if he did not find water soon, the simulation would end anyway. Skip grunted. He grabbed the saddle horn and reached down with his free hand. He waved his hand back and forth and searched blindly for the reins. The Nexus fought him. It pushed him left and right. He stumbled and righted. After several tries, his fingers caught the rein. Using the reins, he maneuvered the horse toward the vultures. The horse had slowed and it took Skip fifteen minutes to reach the place where the vultures circled.

They circled above a mule laden with supplies that lay on its side. Skip positioned his horse alongside the mule. A canteen hung on the outside of the mule's saddlebags. He tried to ease out of the saddle but found his arms were like Jell-O. Skip tumbled and landed hard. Shards of quartz cut into his palms, and a cloud of dust billowed up around him. He coughed.

Skip reached over and wrenched the canteen from the mule's saddlebags. The mule stirred and stood up. He twisted the cap off the canteen and drank. As he drank, the Nexus released its resistance. His vision cleared. Too quickly. Another program glitch. His electrolytes should still be out of balance. In reality, it would have taken days to revive. Skip removed his hat and poured the remaining water into it. He allowed his horse to drink.

The mule grunted, and its eyes grew wide. It bolted. The mule had to carry more water. The beast held his only chance for survival. Skip reached up and slid his Winchester rifle out from among his provisions. He dropped to the ground and nestled his cheek into the stock of the rifle. Skip lined up the rifle's sites and brought his breathing into cadence with his heartbeats. Between the beats, he fired. The mule spun around, hit on its flank. Skip reacquired the mule through the site and fired again. This time the top of the mule's head disappeared. As the snap of the rifle died, the desert returned to its dead calm, languishing under the relentless gaze of the sun.

Why had the mule bolted? And whose mule was it anyway? This adventure had been designed for him alone, and there was no mule mentioned in his ancestor's account. Skip rose to his feet and scanned the horizon. An attractive woman approached him. Nude, her tanned body glistened with sweat. Her long hair swept back like a black wind.

He dropped his gaze. "Uh, sorry about your mule, madam."

She came up to him, slid a hand around his waist, and pressed her body against his. He pulled back. "What are you doing?"

Her chest heaved. Sweat glistened off her firm body.

Oh bollocks. He fought back his addiction. Betty would definitely not approve of this, not one bit. His wife was a computer whiz and had caught him just last month in a virtual nefarious affair. She was on the verge of dumping his virtual ass.

Why was this woman here?

She approached. Her exotic green eyes mesmerized him, etching vivid ideas into his mind. *What the hell!* He reached for her.

She darted aside and smiled. "Have you ever seen the sunsets on Hainan?"

"What?" He said between adrenaline-charged breaths.

She opened a portal behind him and leaned against him. A hard nipple brushed his arm as she passed him and stepped through the portal.

"No you don't." He leaped after her.

The portal dumped them onto a beach with a sunset blazing in the west. Skip stopped and took a deep breath. "Ah! This is much better." The cool air felt good.

She brushed against him, her breasts pressing into his chest. With both hands, he grabbed her wrists and pulled her toward him. Skip smashed his lips onto hers. Their tongues explored one another. His heart raced and his head grew warm with ecstasy.

Her hands were everywhere, under his shirt, running along his chest and back. He lifted his arms and she tore off his shirt. She tugged at his belt, unbuttoned his pants, and unzipped his fly. Skip's pants dropped. He tripped over them and fell to the ground. She threw herself across him and straddled his waist between her strong thighs. He kicked his pants away and rolled over on top of her. She threw him over and reversed their positions. The woman raised her head and let out a cackle.

A bit creepy. He tried to roll on top of her but she was too strong. She had him pinned. Skip turned onto his stomach and tried to crawl away.

The woman clasped her hands around his waist.

He grabbed her arms. They were hairy. He glanced back.

The woman had transformed into a pale-complexioned man with dark hair but with the same green eyes. "I'm Syzygy," he said.

"Get off of me, you freak!" Skip kicked but the virtual transvestite had him pinned. He almost wished this one had decided to *undress* afterwards.

The warmth in Skip's head exploded into pain. *How am I going to explain this to Betty?* He didn't think she would understand this time.

Everything went black.

26

From within VR, Austin glanced at the time: 2 p.m. He was running late. Stepping through the portal, he entered the Nexus Corporation lobby.

"Message for you, Austin," Jan alerted him.

"Kindly display it for me." Austin headed toward his office.

The message flashed before him.

```
FROM:    Ed Davis, Assistant Secretary of
         Defense C4ISR
TO:      Austin Wheeler, CEO Nexus Corporation


Austin,
I need the numbers on the cost of a recall
ASAP. Do not contact me directly. Ms. Hwang
or I will contact you.


Ed Davis
```

He stopped in his tracks and furrowed his brow. He reread the short message. Something felt wrong about the message. He could not place what it was.

"Jan, delete this letter." He bounded through the door of his office and stopped. Steve sat behind his desk, hunched over a drawer as he rifled through Austin's files. Spread across Austin's desk was his *other set* of accounting books.

Steve sensed someone had entered Austin's office and looked up.

"Son, what the hell are you doing in here?" Austin demanded. His eyes blazed.

"Don't get self-righteous with me. We need to talk."

Austin's gaze surveyed the papers scattered across the desk. As co-owners of Nexus Corporation, they both shared the same security clearance. Austin, in his cocky way, had never reset the password on his files.

"This other set of books has some interesting deposits." Steve pointed to a figure on one of the spreadsheets. "You tied up a lot of money in these obscure, offshore investments. This reference to Verwaltungen looks interesting. What is that for?"

"Don't you remember? That's your account, son."

"Really? You have a couple of accounts there, and there's this amount in the other account ..." Steve paused while he sorted through the sheets on the desk and pulled up another list of figures.

"Now, I'm no accountant, but this looks like some sort of money laundering scheme between these two accounts. Does Ron know about this?"

Austin grimaced. "We went over this. One is for your payments, the other is for your expenses."

"Austin, there are five accounts here! They are not all my accounts! And why is there over 7.2 million dollars tied up among them? I'm not that gullible. I know you stole this money."

Austin sat down in the seat opposite the desk, leaned back, and raised his hands.

"Maybe I took some money, but look at what I gave you. I found the military centric Chinese companies, scrambling for contracts at the end of the war. I obtained DARPA's approval.

Son, I got the product out the door. Without me this dream of yours would be dead."

Steve frowned. He remembered his daughter's crying face. "Brooke is my dream, not the Nexus."

Austin sighed. "Okay, you caught me with my knickers down. Tell me what you have in mind."

"I want you to resign."

Austin's mouth dropped open. "I don't believe it! After all I've done? I accomplished in four months what you couldn't do in three years—sell a product!"

"You mean a death trap! Do you remember what you said to me? The Nexus just talks to the brain. What's the harm in that? Well, Austin, you were wrong, and my daughter's friend is dead because of you! I was a damn fool to listen to you."

Austin's eyes blazed.

"There's plenty of money hidden within these books to pay for a recall, isn't there?"

Austin studied the floor. A smile crept back onto his face.

"How is that project of yours coming along? You know, the one for Brooke? I've kept my end of the bargain, handling the day-to-day affairs so you're free to play on the Nexus Healer. If I go, you'll lose that freedom. Where would your daughter be then?"

Steve laughed. "You haven't been paying attention! The beta release announcement is this Sunday."

"So you mean it's perfected and will never falter? Come on! You know there's no such thing as finished in this business."

"You're right. You don't have to resign. You're fired."

"Steve, be reasonable."

"You can pack up later after I'm done figuring out what sort of mess you've left me with."

Austin looked down.

"Leave. Now."

Austin stood and stalked out of the room.

Steve let out a deep breath. That went easier than he thought. Things were looking up.

"What had come over Steve?" Austin thought as he walked down the hall. Everything Austin had built was unraveling. There were too many loose ends to manage. Too many elements were beyond his influence or control. Steve had fired him and was close to the truth. And god knows what Davis would direct Allison to do if Steve alerted the press.

He knew this day would come. Austin had planned for it. A new name, life, and bank account awaited him. All he had to do was give the signal to plunder Nexus Corp.

He paged Ron. "It's show time."

27

Ron looked around Sansome Bank. It had a classic layout, a huge circular room with walls of glass with cherry wood desks to his left and matching teller booths to his right. A bank employee stood behind each counter and desk, actually a software construct, in conservative male western dress—suits, ties, and bleached, white shirts.

He glanced at the figures of stock and cash in the account Austin had wanted to launder. This would be interesting.

Ron walked to one of the windows so he could think. Through the window, he saw a replication of San Francisco Bay. The perspective was from the top floor of a building on a clear summer day.

He had lived in San Francisco one summer early in his career. In all that time, he never saw a clear summer day. Fog was the city's built-in air conditioning. Even when it got remotely warm, fog would roll in across the Golden Gate Bridge through the narrow opening to the ocean.

From this vantage point, Ron saw both the Golden Gate and the Bay Bridges. Ron chuckled. No vantage point in San Francisco allowed you to see both bridges.

Since the war, Ron had used his *financial services* to subsidize his many side ventures. Over the years, he learned a number of methods to launder dirty money. It was a simple scam involving the concurrent purchase and sale of future contracts.

These future contracts were bets on the direction of the price of some commodity, financial asset, or an index on the stock market. The contract might involve copper, U.S. government bonds, or the NASDAQ stock market index. The *long* party bets the futures market will go up. The *short* party, on the other hand, bets it will go down. Thus, there was always a winner and a loser. If the price went up, the long party would win and the short party would lose. If the price went down, the long party would lose and the short party would win.

To launder the money Ron would play both sides of the same bet, being both the long and short party. He would place Austin's embezzled dirty money in a foreign, usually Swiss, bank account. He then would open two *clean* domestic accounts with nominal balances. One would be under Austin's name and the other under Ron's name. Ron would then bet so that the Swiss account with the *dirty money* was always on the losing side of the transaction while the domestic accounts with the *clean money* were always on the winning side.

When the futures settled, the dirty money simply transferred to the clean accounts. Austin's account, which wagered ninety-five percent of the bet, would receive ninety-five percent of the money. Ron's account would receive the remaining five percent, minus brokerage fees. Then the Swiss account would disappear, leaving no trace. Thus, the money would be transferred to Austin and Ron's accounts, hidden from the tax collectors and other prying eyes.

This transaction, like every transaction, had the same three problems. First, Ron needed enough clean money to counterbalance the purchase of futures with the dirty money.

Second, the transaction fees would be excessive. Brokers' commissions could easily account for two percent of the transaction. Under normal circumstances, this was not a problem. However, since Ron's cut amounted to five percent minus expenses, these fees could account for over half of his profits. Ron had solved this problem by finding a broker that worked for a flat fee of 20K for large deals.

The third problem was that he could not control the market. If the price moved the wrong way unexpectedly, the process would work in reverse, sucking clean money into the dirty account. Usually, Ron could offset this by selecting a flexible settlement date and choose a market that was cyclical. For example, natural gas demand was high in the winter but low in the summer. Motorcycle sales were the reverse.

But this case was different. Ron didn't have time. Austin would soon die. Ron could only maintain control of the funds for a couple of days. He surveyed the amount of cash and stock in the account again. Then he got an idea.

The account Austin had given him held more than seventy percent of the outstanding shares of Nexus. He simply needed to have the dirty account buy short, and in doing so, bet that the Nexus stock would fall. He would then dump enough shares to deflate the price of Nexus stock and wait for Austin's date with the reaper to send it to the cellar. When Ron settled with the clean money and bought back the shares, he would make a handsome windfall profit.

Ron sighed. Ever since Austin had shafted Steve, Ron knew it would be a matter of time before Austin hung himself. Austin just needed enough rope, and perhaps a nudge. Patience was difficult, but revenge was a dish best served cold. Austin's death had to appear as bad luck—really, bad luck.

Ron approached the first teller.

28

"Jan, construct the flow," Steve said. Above the green, crisscrossed lines of his home office, twenty walls of platinum appeared, suspended in the air, each etched with a spreadsheet representing the accounts at that institution. Red laser beams shot out from the spreadsheets' cells. The red lines branched and merged. They created a vast network, representing money that flowed from account to account, institution to institution.

Steve stepped back. The network continued to grow and spawn new connections. Austin had wired the funds from bank to bank, funneling money to god knows what. What did it all mean?

"My friend, I didn't know you were an artist."

Steve turned.

Ron stood next to him. "Why did you page me?"

Steve pointed to the collage. "Did you know about this?"

Ron studied the collage. He traced the red lines connecting the cells of the spreadsheets.

"How bad is it?" Steve asked.

"Where did you find this?"

"Austin had a second set of books. Is it bad?"

Ron stared at the data.

"And?"

He nodded. "He's tapped a lot of equity. *A lot*. Do you have historical data?"

Steve nodded. "A couple of years, in fact."

"Computer, animate transactions from yesterday to today."

Like arcs of electricity, the red lines leapt from cell to cell. Pulses of light shot down the lines showing the direction of flow.

"It looks like the funds don't rest for more than a couple of minutes in any account." Ron watched until the replay ended. "Have you contacted anyone besides me?"

Steve shook his head.

"Good. Don't tell anyone just yet. Give me a day. Let me see if I can untangle this mess."

"Thanks. I don't know what I'd do without you."

Ron placed a hand on Steve's shoulder. "It's going to be okay, my friend. I'll take care of it."

Ron opened a portal and left.

"Jan, close Austin's accounting books."

"What a day!" Steve mumbled. He sighed in relief. Two obstacles were flattened. He had taken control of the books and had dropkicked Austin's ass out of the company. It felt good; but his week was not over. The recall and the release of Brooke's Healer lay ahead. His work would spill into the weekend. Brooke would not be pleased.

Whoosh.

Steve spun around and saw Allison step through a portal.

"Allison!" Steve smiled.

"I only have a moment. I've got to get to my hotel, check my messages, and get ready for dinner. Our reservations are in an hour at my hotel, the Fairmont, in the Kona Room. I'll see you there."

"Sounds good," he said and Allison exited.

"Jan, get me the address for Fairmont Hotel."

Steve walked past reception, down a short flight of steps, and into the dinning area. Golden marble encircled a large pool and island full of tropical plants and birds. Thunder rumbled and synthesized rain fell into the pool.

Allison sat at a table that overlooked the pool. Her hair swooped up and soft wisps fell, framing her Amerasian face. She wore an all white, sleeveless pantsuit. The plunging neckline exposed her golden skin. The contrast of her black hair and green eyes took his breath away.

He walked up to the table. "I'm impressed. I've lived here for a couple of years and never heard of this place. How did you come across it?"

"Remember what I said about focusing on other things?"

He nodded.

"Well, there you go."

Allison took him through the four-course meal. Each course brought with it a new kind of meaning to his senses. He relished it all, savoring it, anticipating more. As she spoke to him in their dimly lit corner, he realized it was not just the place that aroused his senses. He craved her increasingly. He could not remember ever being lost in someone like this. Allison's voice broke his musing.

"Does that interest you at all, Steve?"

His gaze drifted to her lips. "It sure does."

She laughed. "I love it."

What was she saying? He had no clue. "I'm sorry. What was that?"

"I said, do you want to stop by my room before we go to your place. This time, I think I should pack an overnight bag. You're just up the street. We could walk there."

"Sure."

She nodded.

"What a day. I fired Austin, finished my project for Brooke …" He paused and took her hand in his. " … and I'm dating the most beautiful woman this side of the Internet."

Allison opened her mouth to speak, but stopped short of words and smiled instead. They paid the bill and walked to the elevator.

"Allison?"

She met his gaze.

"Did you enjoy dinner?"

She nodded and slipped her hand into his.

The elevator doors opened and they stepped inside.

Upon entering her apartment, she said, "Make yourself at home." She headed down a short hall. "There's a great view off the terrace—check it out if you like."

Unlike Allison, the accommodations were simple, nothing fancy. Papers and files covered the dining room table. Steve wondered about her work.

Allison called out from the other room. "Did you check out the view outside? I'll just be another minute."

He turned from the paper work and strode to the terrace. Steve unlocked the door and stepped out onto the terrace. Only a few miles away, Mt. Diablo towered above the Walnut Creek skyline. He shouted back to her, "Wow, you weren't kidding. This is gorgeous." He imagined what it would look like at night, the glow of the city probing into the dark recesses of the mountain. "Hey, do you bike or climb? I know some great trails up there."

Arms reached around him and pulled him close. He turned and faced her and held her. "How did you do that? I didn't even hear you."

The golden glare from the sunset streaked over her face and hair. She winced a little.

"Hey!" He said, brushing the hair from her face. "Where are you?"

She looked up at him, a light smile surfacing over her lips. "I've got a lot on my mind."

Steve bent his knee to get to eye level with her and block the sun. "And?"

She looked past his shoulder. With one finger, he steered her face to meet his gaze. "Do you want me to leave?" He bit his lip. Too serious.

"No, I was thinking you might be the one wanting to leave."

Steve shook his head. "That is the last thing I'd want."

She sighed. "You just fired Austin who brought me in. Where do I stand? I'm half expecting that you'd say you no longer need me, that you'll handle it from here, and ..."

Steve laughed.

"Why are you laughing?"

He stifled his laugh. He had never imagined seeing her this way—so vulnerable, so sexy. "I need you."

Her fiery green gaze softened.

Steve pulled her close and ran his left hand through her hair. Her hair flowed to her shoulders. He kissed her shoulder and ran his lips along their curves. Her skin felt warm and soft. Steve kissed her neck and smelled her. His heart beat faster. He moved his face in front of hers. "Do you feel this too?"

She whispered in his ear between nibbles. "Yes." Her soft nibble switched to a gentle bite.

Shivers shot down his spine. "That feels really good."

She moved her lips down his neckline. Her lips kissed his neck, the light strokes of her tongue shooting sensations to all parts of his body. His lips found hers. He gazed at her closed eyes, and kissed them. "You are so beautiful, Allison." Steve scooped her into his arms.

She looked up at him with her green eyes. This time they looked lighter. He carried her from the terrace to the bedroom.

She stood on the bed and drew him toward her. "That's better." She loosened his tie and released it from her grip as it slid to the floor. She unbuttoned his shirt, reached in, and touched his chest. Edging her hands over his shoulders, she pushed his shirt down.

Steve slipped his shirt all the way off. His eyes focused on her plunging neckline. "I like you being taller too."

Steve reached up and gently pulled one of her shoulder straps down. She slipped her arm through as he pulled the other strap down, exposing her breasts. His gaze lingered there and followed her neck to her face. His gaze locked into hers. He stroked her breasts with his fingertips.

She closed her eyes and breathed in. Her body trembled.

His tongue and lips kissed her nipples in slow, tiny circles. He wanted to make up for last night's stupor. They moved together, like a slow dance.

Her breathing varied from shallow to deep. He locked his gaze with hers again and together they removed the rest of their clothing, never breaking eye contact. They were in complete sync, lost in each other now.

She laid down on the bed, her back turned to him. He touched her neck and traced his finger from her shoulder, down to the small of her back, just above her cleft.

Allison rolled over and faced Steve sideways. His gaze caressed her and lingered over the curves of her body. He stroked the inside of her thighs with the palm of his hand. He then traced two fingers from her right knee, up her thigh, then over and down her left thigh. She took in a quivering breath. Back and forth, he teased her.

She looked up at him, her gaze intense. Her expression was almost pleading, and then she closed her eyes slowly and opened them again, just as slowly.

His neck and shoulders flexed as he moved closer, and she was gazing steadily back at him again. An impassioned fire overwhelmed him, a fire that ignited for both of them.

Two hours later they lay in bed, resting in each other's arms. Steve's Nexus let out three short beeps. He checked the LCD display: 8:56 p.m. He turned to Allison. "It's Brooke. She's probably wondering where I am. I don't get out that much."

"I would *never* have guessed that," Allison said. Her face glowed and her eyes sparkled.

He sighed. "Well, I better give her a call."

Allison rose and went to take a shower. After the call, Steve joined her. "Brooke just wanted to check in. She sounded a little suspicious. I told her we were working late." He grabbed some soap and lathered up.

"Is everything okay?"

"Yeah, I promised to take her to lunch tomorrow. She's going to bed now." He reached around Allison and patted her behind, followed by a little pinch.

Massaging shampoo into her long ebony hair, she glanced at him out of the corner of her eye with a questioning look.

Steve took over, washing her hair. "It's so nice, I just can't help giving it a little pat n' pinch."

She grinned. "Well then, by all means, help yourself."

"You know, I could get used to this."

She smiled.

The water streamed down as they came together again.

The Fall

"Almost any technology is subject to use, misuse, abuse, and accidents. The more powerful a technology is when properly used, the worse it is likely to be when abused … In a diverse, competitive world, any reasonably inexpensive technology with enormous commercial, medical, and military applications will almost surely be developed and used … [And] Any powerful technology in human hands can [surely] be the subject of accidents."

—Christine L. Peterson, Eric Drexler, and Lynelle Pergamit Foresight Institute, 1994.

29

S teve awoke to Allison's smiling face. "Hey, sleepy head. You want to go for a run before breakfast?"

"Uh, sure," he mumbled, sitting up and stretching.

"I brought my running suit, but I think I'll also need a sweat-shirt if you have one," she said.

"No problem. Check the bottom drawer of the dresser."

She bent over and kissed him on the forehead.

He got up and changed.

They ran for an hour. She pushed him faster and farther than he was accustomed. He liked how she challenged him. For the first time, he agreed with Austin; Allison was an excellent choice. She had an edge Steve lacked. How was she affiliated with DAR-PA? He could not remember, but he knew that if Ron did not come through with the money, maybe she could help him with the recall.

A thought struck him. Perhaps Syzygy was not in the circle he knew, but outside of Nexus Corp. What other organization had the source code and had the resources to exploit the defect and find a way to listen in on a private link? DARPA. They had approved the Nexus. They had the access and the expertise. Is it possible?

Returning to the house, Steve opened the back sliding glass door and they entered the kitchen. He opened the fridge and looked for a carton of juice. With the fridge door propped open, he turned to Allison. "Do you remember what I said yesterday morning about a conspiracy?"

Allison leaned against the counter. "Yeah."

"What if it involves DARPA?"

She laughed. "I don't think so."

"But shouldn't we at least consider it? If I initiate a recall, DARPA could block it."

Allison shook her head. "Don't worry about that."

He found the juice. "Why the hell not? A teenager is dead. More may follow." He closed the fridge door and saw Brooke sitting in her wheelchair.

"Her name was Camille, Dad."

"Oh!" Steve almost dropped the carton of orange juice. "Uh, dear I want you to meet Allison."

"I know. You're just *working* with her, right?" Brooke glared at Allison and rolled her wheelchair into the kitchen.

Allison cringed.

"Brooke! She's our guest …"

"Oh, now she's our guest. Why don't you make up your mind—colleague, guest, working girl—what is it?"

"Brooke that's enough!"

"No, it's not enough! Cammy died last week, a year after mom and …"

"I said enough! This is not the time."

"When is it the time? You have plenty of time for her!" Brooke cried. She spun around and headed back to her room.

Steve sighed and leaned back against the counter. Looking down, he realized the carton of juice was still in his hand. He set it aside. "Allison, I'm sorry."

She embraced him and whispered in his ear, "You've got your hands full don't you?"

"You might say that." He released her and looked into her eyes. She was upset.

"I should go … I didn't mean for my presence here to …"

He stoked her cheek. "Don't go. Not like this."

She met his gaze. "Steve, what has happened between us may or may not last. Brooke will be here your whole life, but she won't always be your little girl."

A tear ran down Allison's cheek. "I'm sorry." She looked down at her feet.

"What is it?"

"Memories. My father died last year. I just wish we had more time together."

He drew her close again.

"I'd like to stay here tonight, but maybe with all that's happened, I shouldn't," she said.

"I want you here, too."

Allison kissed him. "Talk with her, okay?"

"Okay. I'll make things right with her. Don't worry. Brooke and I have gone through a lot together. Our hearts are not far apart."

She kissed him once more and headed back to the shower.

Steve poured some juice. His mind returned to Brooke. *How could she act like that?* But his inner voice scolded him. *How could you have Allison overnight while Brooke is in the house, especially after all that she's been through—Tamara's anniversary, her friend's death?* Steve shook his head. *What was that girl's name?* Brooke had just told him again. His memory came up blank.

A recall had to happen. It would prevent others from dying. He hoped Ron had found something in Austin's second set of books. Ron had known syzygy was a real word. He knew that it said something about the killer. For several minutes he concentrated. He hoped some inspiration would spark, divining some sort of meaning from the definition.

"How did the talk go?"

"Huh?" Steve looked up.

"Your talk with Brooke?"

He shook his head. "The timing wasn't right."

"Try not to put this off."

"I'll make a lunch date with her. We'll talk then." He grabbed a notepad, scrawled a message to Brooke, and stuck it on the fridge with a magnet. His mind continued to race.

"What's gotten into you?"

He rubbed his chin. "Can I show you something in VR?"

"What?"

"The definition of syzygy. There's something about it. I need to bounce some ideas off of you."

She nodded.

Steve escorted her into his office. He moved a pile of books off a second chair and positioned it behind his desk. They sat down. Opening a desk drawer, he withdrew Brooke's Nexus and handed it to her. "Here, use this."

Putting the Nexuses on, they entered VR.

"Jan, display the definition of syzygy."

A single wall of platinum appeared engraved with three definitions. He honed in on the third entry:

```
"The intimately united and apparently fused
condition of certain low organisms during
conjugation."
```

The obvious sexual reference matched Syzygy's MO. A program could be described as a low organism. The definition might refer to the computer programs that Syzygy uses.

Allison glanced at the wall of platinum. "What is it?"

"I don't know, but I sense it. I'm missing something. And I don't think this Quang fellow is sophisticated enough to do any of this."

Allison laughed. "You've never even met him."

"My point exactly. The killer or killers have intimate knowledge of the Nexus. I know everyone with that level of knowledge, but I've never heard of Quang."

"Are you sure?"

"This is a young, poorly documented technology. All the experts get help from me, one way or another."

Allison nodded. "If it's any consolation, DARPA is convinced that Quang didn't do the actual attack. He must have had an accomplice."

"So the accomplice used Quang's Nexus to attack me and another to attack Camille? That doesn't make sense either. Why go to all that trouble?"

"No, that isn't it at all. Quang *never* attacked you."

Steve shook his head. "That's impossible. You saw the logs from his Nexus. He definitely attacked me."

"Believe me, he didn't lie on this."

Steve furrowed his brow. Austin had funneled the funds and hid them from regular financial channels. Perhaps the attacks worked similarly.

"How could Syzygy use Quang's Nexus to attack me even as Quang used it?" The thought came to him. "Damn."

"What?" she asked.

"There is one possibility. The killer could have spoofed our trace by connecting onto Quang's Nexus and then started a different connection out of his Nexus into the Internet."

"Huh?"

"Let me explain. I saw this old murder mystery as a kid. In it, the police traced the killer's telephone call to the lobby of their own building. When the police confidently strode down to the lobby, they found two payphones with their receivers taped together. In this way, one phone call was relayed to the other.

"The call had actually originated from the other side of town, but their trace couldn't ferret it out. The trace ended at the payphone in the lobby. In this case the perpetrator used the tape to *hop* to the other phone."

"So you think Syzygy hopped from Nexus to Nexus?"

"Correct. That would explain why two killers had the same exact MO. There is just one killer and it isn't Quang." Steve frowned.

"What's wrong?" Allison asked.

"For the analogy to hold, the *tape* must be another Portal Program on Quang's Nexus. It enabled Syzygy to hop from Nexus to Nexus. We specifically designed the Nexus to have very limited space to keep down cost and to prevent hackers from uploading rogue programs like this. The program I'm describing would take quite a bit of space, unless …"

Steve remembered the log in Quang's Nexus. It showed that signals were sent to crash the victims' Nexus patch and V-chip programs. Although the patch was small, about twenty megabytes, the V-chip software ran over a gigabyte.

"That's how he does it." Steve ran a virtual hand through his hair. "Syzygy disabled the programs, not only to allow him to attack, but to replace them with his own portal program. The portal program would allow Syzygy to hop from Nexus to Nexus undetected. That has to be it. That's the tape. We're no farther along than when we started. Syzygy could be anyone."

Allison's eyes went wide. "Could there be other victims?"

Steve exchanged a look with Allison. "Jan, can you access the news feed and pull up any articles on the Nexus and atypical seizure?"

"There are one hundred and forty two articles in twenty seven publications."

A wall of platinum appeared before them, listing the headlines of the articles. He scanned the list. There were several obituaries among the articles.

"Jan, can you list only the obituaries?"

"There are thirty one articles in twelve publications."

"Jan, please record the names of the deceased."

A blank wall of platinum appeared to his right with three names.

```
Camille Anderson
Shannon Pierce
Skip Harvey
```

Steve turned to Allison. "What approvals are needed to start a recall?"

Allison crossed her arms. "I'll need to get back to the hotel."

"And?"

"And I'll see what I can do."

30

```
Brooke,

I know things have been difficult over the
last couple of days. Let's meet for lunch
at noon. We'll talk. Please do not use your
Nexus under any circumstances.

LUV U,
Dad
```

Brooke looked up from the note to her wall clock: 12:15. She read the note again. Her anger flared as she read his comment about her Nexus. How could he order her around? He had lost the right. He had ripped her offline, brought a strange woman into their home, and now he had stood her up for the third time. And he had done it all on the anniversary of her mom's death.

She directed her wheelchair into Steve's home office. Her dad sat in his chair, oblivious to the world, the Nexus' lights still flickering on and off in the dimly lit room. She doubted he would be back soon. He would probably return much later that night and write her yet another note with yet more empty promises.

She maneuvered around him, opened a drawer, and extracted

her Nexus. The LCDs were on. *That's odd.* Her dad had forgotten to shut it off. Brooke's excitement grew. She entered VR.

An amalgamation of sights, sounds, and smells attacked her senses as she reeled back in surprise. Everything looked like an abstract painting with blotches of blurred color. A high-pitched hum rang in her ears and the odor of wet leather filled the air. Pins and needles attacked her limbs. Brooke looked down at her left wrist. A sensory kaleidoscope swirled around the reset button, which remained motionless and still at the center of her vision. Brooke pressed the button.

The world went black, silent, sterile, and numb. Slowly the Nexus recalibrated to her senses. She found herself in her dad's former virtual office. The system must have reset to his initial settings.

"Yes!" she said.

She had her dad's access. With it, she would be able to visit the sites he had blocked before. Looking down, she also had her dad's body and hairy arms and—she looked further down. Oh my god! She involuntarily shuddered.

"Computer, download the alias, Brooke Donovan."

Her alias slowly metamorphosed into her familiar form. She sighed and walked around.

He had sculpted his old office to resemble the lobby of a Bed n' Breakfast on the Oregon coast. It had been their family's favorite spot until her mother had died.

Her dad had captured the Victorian flair of the place with its high ceilings and its dark oak floors, worn to a shine from years of use. To her left, an antique couch, chair, and coffee table sat beneath two large bay windows. Everything in the room possessed long, ornate legs and scarlet upholstery.

Outside, the thick fog rolled in and hugged the lower half of the house. Light gossamer wisps reached up and stroked the top of the windows and eaves.

At the heart of the room, a wood-burning Franklin stove crackled noisily. The fire's glow cast flickering shadows, which frolicked around the room.

Brooke stretched. She felt her legs and back and marveled at the sensation. As she headed to the couch, she tripped and stumbled. Brooke frowned. She took two more steps and sat down. A photo album lay on the coffee table. She stretched her legs again, reached over, and opened the cover of the album. Like the books in her virtual tree house, it contained a Directory of Internet sites.

As she turned its pages, images popped out and played scenes before her, illustrating the various sites.

Her dad was still at work. Brooke decided to take a risk. She looked around and called out, "Charlie, help." The little fox-like dog appeared out of nowhere and jumped onto her lap. Rising on its hind legs, it licked her face and wagged its tail. Charlie's bright, brown eyes stared into hers.

Charlie was the representation of a dog her dad had owned long ago. The Pomeranian had bushy red hair, a stout nose, and bright, intelligent eyes. Her dad had augmented the Charlie program to travel from site to site as an Internet travel guide. Charlie interpreted the abstract commands of the user and tried to comply with the requests.

"Now, you won't tell dad I was here, will you?" she chided him.

Charlie yipped.

"Good. Charlie, I want you to find some place fun for us to go. Can you do that?"

Charlie wagged his tail and barked. He ran off and disappeared. A few moments later, he reemerged with a pad of paper in his mouth. He jumped into her lap and dropped the pad. She picked it up as he resumed licking her face.

"All right, Charlie! Calm down!" She grinned. Brooke set him down and looked at the pad of paper. The word waterfall was etched in pencil.

"All right! You're a good boy, Charlie! Take me there."

A portal opened and Charlie jumped through. Brooke followed close behind.

They stood on a platform above a turbulent waterfall that
poured over a cliff. Her outfit had changed to a swimsuit, and
small beads of water covered her body. Her long, wet hair was
pulled back. She looked down. The waterfall cascaded beneath her
and created a fine mist as it crashed against the rocky cliff. The
mist obscured the destination below. Without hesitation, Charlie
jumped off the platform and into the mists.

"Hold on, Charlie!" Brooke yelled. She jumped in after him.

Charlie was nowhere to be seen. As she plummeted down,
Brooke bounced lightly off the rocky cliff and entered the waterfall. The water danced and coiled about her. The water's warm
soothing fingers pushed her from side to side as she fell. She broke
free of the waterfall.

She fell through the mist and into a void. The wind rushed
across her wet skin causing her to shiver. Beneath her, she saw
only sky. The ground was too far down to see. Where had the waterfall gone? She looked around. The cliff was no longer behind.
Instead, scattered everywhere, perhaps one hundred yards apart
and stretching as far as the eye could see from horizon to horizon,
rivers of water cascaded from the sky toward the ground.

They reminded her of the electric arcs in her plasma sphere.
Her mother had given her a plasma sphere as a Christmas gift a
few months before the accident. The plasma sphere was a sealed
glass globe with a black point in its center. As Brooke touched the
outside of the globe, arcs of electricity would appear between her
fingertip and the black point. They would persist, swaying gently,
following her finger as she moved it.

These veins of water seemed to do the same thing. Like the
arcs of electricity, they too moved back and forth independently
from one another, swaying gently but erratically in a slow dance.

The nearest stream flowed fifty feet to her right. Where was

Charlie? She scanned its length. Far down the river's length, she spotted the small black speck for which she was searching.

"Charlie!" she yelled. She laughed and flipped in a circle.

The speck grew as he drew up next to her. Charlie barked and back-stepped wildly in the air. He continued to plummet down despite his efforts. His ears flew straight back from the wind and his eyes were set wide with fear and excitement.

A ribbon of water swung wildly toward them. It sucked them in. The current ripped them along at a terrific speed. The water bumped and jostled them. They broke through the surface and gasped for air. Ahead of them, the stream made a sharp turn.

"Hold on Charlie!"

They broke through the wall of water as the stream turned. The force caused her to spin. Brooke screamed and Charlie yelped. She extended her arms and legs as they flew through the mist and into the dark open space between the rivers.

The spinning slowed and stopped. The ground was visible. She rotated to face the colossal mountain range below her. The range stretched from horizon to horizon. Each falling river of water plummeted into its own valley in the mountain. The rivers swayed gently like hair in a light breeze. The steams remained rooted in its mountain valleys but swayed in the sky. On the mountain, the streams of water danced down the valleys. The water divided and merged back together again endlessly as the streams roared through the canyons and gorges.

A fresh wave of adrenaline washed through Brooke as the mountain drew near. "What do you think, Mr. Charlie?"

Charlie yipped.

Brooke frowned. "Charlie, enable speech."

"We better find another stream to ride," Charlie said.

Brooke watched as Charlie's lips moved unnaturally to form the words. The effect creeped her out. Her dad had not perfected the software and probably never would. Poor Charlie had been as neglected as she had since her mother's death.

Charlie barked. "There's one!"

They leaned downward and steered themselves toward a river a few feet away. As they touched its surface, the current sucked them in. The mountain was upon them.

Brooke felt her heart accelerate and her stomach flip as the stream slipped between the valley's two enormous cliffs. The stream landed on the valley floor. Brooke dove through the stream, struck the bottom, and bounced upward. She broke the surface and became airborne. Charlie followed close behind. They screamed and plunged back into its depths. The river threw them back and forth as they slid through a dozen tunnels, around peaks, and over falls and rapids.

After several minutes Brooke said, "Charlie, I've had enough." She pressed a button on her wrist and spoke the command "Home." A portal opened twenty feet ahead of them. The current dragged them through the portal and she tumbled through. When she emerged, she was still wearing her swimsuit. A kayak materialized around her, and an oar formed in her hand. Why hadn't she returned to the old Ben n' Breakfast? Why was she still in her swimsuit? She grabbed the oar with both hands and paddled. The warm water lapped against the sides of the Kayak as it glided forward. The sun neared the horizon and extended finger-like streaks of orange, red, and purple across the sky. The shadows from the land drove the foliage along the shoreline into deeper shades of green.

She looked around. Where was Charlie? She found him a few yards back, dog-paddling in the water. Obviously, something had malfunctioned. Poor Charlie! This VR server had not expected an intelligent agent.

The kayak continued moving, and she faced forward. The kayak had grown into a tandem. A figure sat in the front kayak's seat.

"Excuse me? Who are you?"

"I'm Syzygy."

Syzygy's deep, confident voice made her heart beat faster. "What is this place?"

"A chat room. Outdoor Adventures."

"How did I get here? Where's your partner?"

He shrugged his shoulders and continued to row.

"So you went on a date with yourself?"

The man did not respond. He continued to row.

"Something is wrong," Charlie said.

"Charlie, it's fine," she whispered. "He's just confused is all."

The dog levitated out of the water and moved in front of her. His body glowed a bright orange.

"Charlie, knock it off!"

"I'm detecting something in the system, something I don't recognize."

Brooke frowned. "What system? The sites' VR server?"

"No, your Nexus."

"Don't be a drag!" She pulled him out of the air and set him in front of her.

"What's your name?" Syzygy said.

"Nikki, Nikki Smith." Brooke said. Her father had told her never to use her real name.

Charlie cut in. "I must insist. We need to leave."

"Charlie, shut up." Brooke placed him in the water alongside the kayak. His limbs paddled wildly. He barked.

"I'm sorry Size—what was your name?"

"I'm detecting a software violation." The dog vanished.

"Charlie! Charlie!" she screamed.

Syzygy turned and faced her. His face was expressionless but his gaze piercing. "This reminds me of the sunsets in Hainan. Have you ever been there?"

31

Steve exited VR and appeared back at his desk. He was an hour late for lunch with Brooke. She would be pissed. He did not blame her.

"Brooke, are you ready?" Steve took off his Nexus and turned to place it in the drawer.

He gasped. Brooke sat next to him. "You scared me half to death! Brooke?" In the twilight, he sensed something was wrong. From the blinking lights of the Nexus, he saw her chin rested against her chest. Her shoulder twisted toward him, her arms rigid at her sides, and her hands curled inward.

"Brooke!" Steve ripped off her Nexus and shook her. Her body was limp and heavy. He dialed 911 into the Nexus front panel.

"911. How may…" a voice from the speakerphone said.

"Something's wrong with my daughter."

"Is she breathing?"

"I … I don't know."

"Is her chest rising? Can you …"

Steve put a hand in front of her mouth but felt nothing. "Oh, God! She's not breathing!"

"Lay her flat."

"She's in a wheelchair."

"Lay her flat, now."

Steve swept the books and papers off the desktop. A flash lit up the room and the scanner hit the ground. He lifted Brooke out of her wheelchair and laid her on the desktop. "Done. I'm not sure if she has a pulse."

"Open her mouth, check for anything obstructing her breathing."

Steve checked. "It's clear, but her pulse ..."

"She needs oxygen. Pinch her nose, open her mouth and place your mouth over hers and exhale twice."

Steve did as he was told. "Done."

"Does she have a heartbeat?"

Steve placed a finger on Brooke's neck trying not to look into her open eyes. Tears welled up in his eyes. "Shit! I don't feel anything."

"Do you know CPR?"

"No!" He choked down a cry.

"How old is she?"

"17."

"Is she on a hard surface?"

"Yes, yes my desk."

"Okay. Find where her rib cage comes together. Come up two fingers. Place the heel of your palm there, overlapping your hands. I want you to push down, compressing her chest five times in succession, one second apart. Okay?"

"Okay!" He leaned over her and placed his hands on her chest. Someone pounded on the door.

"That's help," the voice said.

"Come in!" Steve yelled.

He heard the sound of splintering wood as someone broke through the locked front door and ran down the hall. Two men in fireman's bulky pants with suspenders and T-shirts charged into the dimly lit room. Steve stepped aside. One of them fell, stumbling over a pile of books on the floor. Steve saw Walnut Creek Fire stenciled across the back of his shirt.

"Firemen?" Steve gasped.

They ignored him. The man who stumbled cut off her shirt and bra with a utility knife as the other placed a mask attached to an air sack to her face. In rhythmic motion one pumped her chest while the other forced air into her lungs using the air sack. The fireman controlling the mask glanced toward Steve and punched his radio. "Chief, bystander. Get in here!"

Steve stepped back toward the doorway. He watched as the fireman worked on his precious Brooke.

Someone pushed him aside. Two more men dressed in green paramedic uniforms stormed inside. One of them set down a defibrillator. The other placed the paddles on her chest. The defibrillator's screen displayed a green, flat line.

"Chief, get in here now!" The fireman screamed in his radio, not stopping the CPR rhythm.

The other paramedic opened a tackle box and extracted a long, slender L-shaped flashlight with a pliable end. The fireman took the mask off her while the paramedic threaded the flashlight into her throat. "She's clear," he said.

The other paramedic handed the first paramedic a clear plastic tube attached to an oxygen tank. He snaked the tube down Brooke's throat and into her lungs. The fireman taped the tube and mask to her face. Tears streaked Steve's face as the second paramedic ripped open a package and shot a syringe of medicine down the tube.

"Excuse me, sir?"

Steve turned and found a burly man in his early fifties wearing fireman's pants with suspenders over a T-shirt standing there.

"Let my men work. They're doing all that can be done."

Steve nodded. He looked down the hall and vacantly registered that the front door had been thrown off its hinges. Behind him one of the paramedics shouted into a phone, "17-year-old, full arrest. Downtime unknown. CPR started by bystander. Etiology unknown. Paraplegic from previous trauma ..."

"Sir, please," the man gestured in the direction of Steve's living room.

Steve followed him there and sat down. The fire chief questioned Steve while his men worked on Brooke. Twenty minutes later, one of the paramedics stepped into the living room. He made eye contact with the chief and shook his head.

Steve stared at his feet.

"I'm so sorry," the chief said. "Is there someone you can call?"

Steve shook his head. "I need to be alone."

"Are you sure? I can stay as long as you need."

Steve fought back tears and forced a smile. "Really, I'm fine. I just need time to myself."

Footsteps came down the hall.

"The coroner," the chief explained. "Did you want to see her before …"

Steve stared at his feet and shook his head. Plastic ruffled and a few seconds later a zipper closed. He looked up and caught the fireman's worried gaze. "I'll be okay," Steve reassured him, while fighting to keep his composure.

Within half an hour, he was alone in his empty, silent house. He wandered into his office with the bottle of Glenfiddich Scotch he had taken from the kitchen. Books and papers tripped him as he made his way to his desk. He sat down and stared at the spot next to him where Brooke had died inches from him. He remembered after the car accident looking over to Tamera, tangled in metal and glass and covered with blood.

He imagined Brooke as she struggled next to him as his mind wandered in VR. No, he was not wandering. He was distracted, trying to catch the bastard. All the while, Syzygy was killing her. It was unreal. If only he could have sensed something, anything. If only he had left VR a minute earlier. Steve touched his forehead with the cool bottle of scotch. His stomach grumbled.

Lunch. He had pushed off meeting Brooke for lunch! Of all the times to be late. He took a swig from the bottle as his gaze drifted listlessly about the room.

Despite the scotch, memories of Brooke flooded back to him. *I'm a horrible father. I neglected her, broke all my promises to her. I never talked to her. Never took the time to lock up her Nexus. Why didn't I turn it off when Allison was done? Why did Syzygy, out of the millions of Nexus users, attack her?* But it did happen, and he did nothing to stop it. A tear trickled down his cheek.

His mind drifted back to the car accident. He had awoken with his wife dead next to him. He had shouted for Brooke, but she had not answered. Immobilized by crumpled metal and twisted plastic, he had no idea if she was alive, dying, or already dead. An hour passed before he learned Brooke was alive.

He felt powerless all over again, but this was final. Brooke was dead. He remembered his covenant after the accident, a promise that Brooke would walk again. She had become his world, his life. Why had he wasted her last days chasing Syzygy?

An image of Syzygy attacking her came to mind. He could not bear to imagine how Brooke had suffered, killed in such a horrible way, in a machine he had designed.

Stop it! Steve took another swig. How could she be dead? What had he done to deserve this? He felt his emotions oscillate between rage and helplessness as they mixed with the alcohol coursing through his veins. He could not stand it. He needed to do something, but what could he do? Syzygy was still out there, a nebulous form in a non-reality. They had no way of tracking or even identifying him.

He finished off the bottle. Still, he grew more agitated. His anger stirred inside him. The anger thawed the numbness protecting him. The trapped emotions of rage and helplessness exploded.

He threw the empty bottle against the wall and buried his face in his hands. He was not even aware of the scream that filled the silence in his empty home. As his voice trailed off, a flood of tears came and sobs racked his body. After a few minutes his body stilled, but his mind continued to race. It solidified around a single, unifying thought—one way or another he would kill the bastard.

Grabbing his Nexus, Steve entered VR.

32

Steve entered his virtual office and scanned his notes about Syzygy's attacks. He found his source code for the patch along with a long detailed specification for the Signal Amplifier modifications. When he had finished reading, he created his weapon.

He started with the Sensory Isolator. It could test various aspects of VR, isolating a user's experience to a particular sense like sight or scent. Steve needed something that could point and shoot. To that end it would do fine. The Sensory Isolator used a simple design. Steve had modeled it after a phaser, a weapon that appeared in *Star Trek*, an old science fiction show from the twentieth century.

He went into the code and made the necessary modifications. Steve would fire the modified Sensory Isolator twice. The first pull of the trigger would kill the patch. The second would send a strong signal to overload the Signal Amplifier.

Slipping the weapon into his pocket, he frowned. Syzygy was hopping from Nexus to Nexus. The weapon he had made would kill the Nexus user, not Syzygy. How could he make the weapon jump the hops? He rubbed his temples but scotch clouded his mind. He also needed to find Syzygy. Damn it! He had to do something!

He thought about Ron. Ron had not gotten back to him on

the numbers yet. Only Austin could unravel the books to pay for the recall. He patted the weapon in his virtual pocket. He would force Austin to talk. "Jan, page Austin to meet me in his office." Steve opened a portal to Nexus Corporation.

Stepping through the portal into the lobby, he walked to Austin's former office. The balcony over the opera was gone, replaced by the simple ten-foot square white room with matching mahogany desk, file cabinet, and bookcase. Austin had not arrived yet. Steve eyed the file cabinet. Perhaps, he had not cleared everything out yet. Something there had to make sense of Austin's second set of books.

Steve stepped around the desk and sat down. He went through the desk drawers. They were empty. He swiveled around and opened the bottom drawer of the file cabinet.

"You won't find anything in there, son," a voice said behind him.

Steve turned. Austin leaned against the threshold, a smirk plastered to his face.

"Come in and close the door."

Austin walked toward the seat across the desk, leaving the door open.

Steve stood and walked around the desk. "No, sit here, behind the desk please."

Austin's smirk turned to a grin. "I just knew you'd see things my way. You can't run this place without me."

As Austin sat down behind the desk, Steve shook his head. "You're not getting your old job back."

Austin frowned.

"Jan, I want you to close down all the links to the outside except for Austin and myself and then shut yourself down, password *Brooke*."

Austin stood in alarm. "Hey! What's the meaning of this?"

Steve closed the door. "There are only two connections into this room. Without Jan, there is no way to exit or portal out of here except through there." Steve pointed to the door.

Austin waggled a finger at Steve. "Son, if you think ..."

"Brooke's dead. Syzygy killed her."

Silence. Austin finally said, "I don't know what to say. I'm sorry."

Steve pulled the phaser out of his virtual pocket and leveled it at him. "You can start by ..."

Austin stood up in alarm, backing against the wall behind the desk.

His gun hand shook. Steve took a deep breath. "Tell me where you hid the company's funds. No one else is going to die because of this. A recall will happen."

A smirked cross Austin's face as Austin looked from Steve to the gun. Steve could almost read his thoughts. The phaser looked like an old garage door opener.

"It's a phaser," Steve said.

Austin laughed. "Son, you're drunk. Now put that thing away. We'll talk when you're sober." Austin started to walk around the desk toward the door.

"Stop!"

Austin froze.

Steve's hand holding the gun trembled with anger and rage. He gripped it tighter. "It can kill." A rueful expression crossed his face.

He sensed Austin probing him, trying to ascertain the truth. Steve took a few steps back.

"Tell me where you hid the money."

A panic tugged at the edges of Austin's expression. He took a jagged breath and forced a smile. "What guarantee do I have you won't shoot me after I give you the information?"

The scotch swam in Steve's head. He rubbed one of his temples. "You don't. Without you Syzygy wouldn't have killed anyone."

"I think you need your head examined, boy." Austin said, his voice cracking.

"You created the opportunity. You broke the rules and pushed the Nexus through. You chose the software patch over the hardware patch. You blackmailed me and prevented the recall. Any one of those things would have saved her."

Austin shook his head. "It's a lie."

He felt his blood begin to boil. "Shut up. You murdered Brooke, you goddamn bastard! Now, tell me how to access the accounts!"

Shock covered Austin's face. He repetitively punched his exit button. It didn't work.

Steve pulled the trigger once, enveloping Austin in a blue glow as the shot took down the patch.

Austin fell to the ground, screaming.

"The first shot won't kill you, but the second one will. Now tell me where the money is."

He held his hands up. "Don't, son. For god's sakes, don't!"

A sharp, metallic whine distracted Steve as a window opened up beside him. It was Allison.

"Steve!" Allison said, pointing past his shoulder.

Steve turned just in time as Austin jumped over the desk. He sidestepped Austin, moving closer to the window. Austin flew past him, landing face down on the ground. Steve pointed the phaser at the back of his head. "Get away from the door."

Austin scurried behind a corner of the desk.

"Steve, what are you doing?" Allison gasped.

Keeping his gaze on Austin, Steve said, "Syzygy killed Brooke. It wouldn't have been possible without Austin's help."

"Brooke's dead? When did it happen?"

"An hour ago."

She paused. "Steve, you're still in shock and you've been drinking. Hand me the gun. You don't really want to do this. Trust me."

"How'd you get in here?"

"You shut down DAPRA's link; they were monitoring your site. I used a paging program to punch a hole through the firewall. They'll be here any minute. Please hand me the gun!"

He took a step toward Austin.

Austin backed up against the wall behind the desk. "Don't, son."

"Steve! I know this is hard," she said.

He shot her an angry glance. "There is no way you can understand this! You've never had your wife and daughter taken away from you!" he snapped.

Allison became quiet for a moment. "Do you remember when I told you my father died last year?"

Steve kept silent.

"I didn't say how he died. Our plane was hit. My father ended up clinging to the other end of a strap I held. As the plane went into a climb, I lost my grip. He literally slipped through my fingers."

Steve glanced at her.

"I understand the guilt you must be feeling right now. You're a dad who lost his daughter. I'm a daughter who lost my dad. Believe me, it's no easier on the other side."

Steve bowed his head, fighting back tears.

"Please, hand me the gun."

"He needs to tell me where he hid the funds."

"It's in here." Austin stood, opened the top drawer of the file cabinet, and pull out a thick file, dropping it on the desk. "It's all in there, son. Everything. Take it; it's yours."

Steve bit his lip. Finally, he handed her the phaser through the window.

Austin sighed, slumping against the back wall.

Taking the papers, Steve paused to make eye contact with Allison. He mouthed the words, "Thank you," opened the door, and exited the room. Once in the hallway he pressed the portal button on his wrist and whispered, "Verwaltungen bank."

Allison stepped through the paging window and into Austin's office. With a metallic clang, the window disappeared behind her.

Austin clapped his hands ceremoniously as he walked around the desk and sat down. "Bravo! You had me a bit worried for a time."

"Did you give him the account information?" she asked, letting the weapon drop to her side.

Austin laughed, shaking his head. "In a way, but he won't be able to use it, of course."

"Austin, he's right about the recall."

"You know it is funny that you would mention that. Mr. Davis' email said you would come calling, demanding a recall, but I noticed something unusual about his signature. You see, sometime in the not so distant past, he changed it from Edward T. Davis to plain old Ed Davis."

Allison stepped toward him. "Davis' signature has nothing …"

"Oh, believe me, Ms. Hwang, it has everything to do with it. See, the way I figure things, Ed does not know anything about this Syzygy character or about the defect for that matter. I reckon you are the one who sent me this memo, but you didn't get the signature right. Davis doesn't know any of this, does he?"

Allison gripped the phaser tightly. "Stop screwing with me, that recall needs to happen."

A recall would stop the murders and Davis would never hear about Syzygy. Ed would explode upon learning about the defect, but that would pass. Syzygy was something else. Ed would see how the Chinese could utilize a Syzygy-like weapon to bring down Warscape through its Nexuses. And she had provided the Nexuses. Despite their history, Davis would have to let her go. It would destroy her career. She could not break her promise to her father. His death had to mean something.

Austin laughed, putting his hands up. "Don't worry. I am not going to spoil your little charade. I just want to add to it. You see, I need you to find some way around this recall of yours. It will put too large of a dent in my checkbook, darlin'. Otherwise I am inclined to tell Steve and Ed everything about this charade."

"I'm afraid you don't understand."

"No, it is you that are mistaken here. You don't have a choice in the matter. I believe I hold all the cards."

"Austin, I'm warning you …"

"Tell you what, Ms. Hwang. Why don't I step outside and conference Mr. Davis in? I am sure he would love to hear all about this." Austin stepped toward the door.

"Don't!" She grabbed his arm.

"Let go!" He jerked his arm.

She held on. He pushed her hard, and she fell back toward the floor but hung onto Austin. Austin toppled on top of her. He punched her stomach. The gun was pinned between them.

"Austin, don't!"

The phaser fired.

Blue light enveloped Austin's body a second time.

She pushed him off and rolled him onto his back. "Austin, can you hear me?"

His body felt cold and rigid to her touch—unnaturally stopped. She grabbed his wrist and pressed the exit button. Nothing.

She sat next to him. Austin's body convulsed somewhere back in reality. Vinnie's team would bust through Austin's front door and find him like that.

She put her face in her hands. Things had just become much more difficult.

33

Steve stood inside a perfect replica of the bank's real lobby in Ticino, Switzerland. The windows lining the lobby displayed Mount San Giorloomedo. It loomed next to the Ticino River, which poured into Lake Maggiore. He stared vacantly into the water. The alcohol had worn off and the edge of his memories had returned. Shaking them off, he turned and approached the counter.

A woman teller smiled at him. "May I help you?"

"Yes, I have an account here that I need access to." He heaped Austin's second set of books, a pile of loose papers onto the counter.

The woman looked first at the stack of papers and then turned her attention back to Steve.

"Uh … can you help me?"

She leafed through the stacks of papers and then paused and asked, "Do you have an account number? Maybe we could start there."

"It should be in there, somewhere." Steve grabbed the papers from her hands and shifted through them. After a few pages, he found the spreadsheet and pointed to the account number Austin had circled in black ink.

"Oh," she said, smiling. She turned to her virtual terminal. After a moment she turned back to him. "Then you're Steve Donovan?"

"Yes."

"I assume you have your social security number and your password then?"

"Well, actually Austin Wheeler made the deposits on my behalf. We work for the same company, Nexus Corporation. My social security number is 261-85-564E, but I don't know the password." He laughed nervously.

She held his stare a moment longer. Without smiling, she glanced back at the screen. "I see. You'll still need the password. It's a secured account."

He handed the file back to her. "Well, it's in there, somewhere. I know I'm a bit scattered, but this is a big account. Can't you help me?"

"That is the exact reason why I can't help you. If you can come back with the proper codes, I will be more than glad to assist you." With that, the teller turned back to her terminal and logged an entry on the account.

He crossed the lobby and sat down on a bench. Riffling through the file, he scattered papers across the bench's surface. After several minutes, he realized Austin was not stupid enough to place the codes in the file itself. He obviously had hidden them somewhere, but where?

"Damn!" he exclaimed. The information had to be written down. Without it, Nexus Corporation's wealth was but a string of electronic numbers locked away in a computer, in an untouchable account. Perhaps Ron could help—he was going through Austin's books—but Steve had no idea where Ron was at the moment. Though he did not want to confront Austin again, he had no other choice.

"Computer, duplicate the phaser." A copy of the phaser materialized before him and he stuck it in his virtual pocket. Then opening a portal in the middle of the lobby, he stepped through, returning to Nexus Corporation.

He materialized at the end of a long table, its Formica surface flecking off at the edges and corners, exposing the particleboard beneath it. Disoriented, he gazed around the room. It had obviously fallen into disrepair. The paint was peeling from the walls and mildew stains spotted the roof, remnants of water leaks. This puzzled him.

He was in VR. Why would anyone design a room like this? Why was he here in any case? Had the Nexus malfunctioned? Steve walked to the one window in the room.

The window looked down onto a busy downtown street somewhere in the Orient. An endless stream of people paraded down the boulevard. Eddies of flesh clung to shopping windows while the ebbs and flows of the crowd carried its hapless occupants down the street.

He watched a lone man fight the current, trying to reach a shop upstream and just out of reach. After a minute, the man turned, resigned his will to the crowd, and followed the masses down the block. How often had he felt like that?

Steve saw the stages of his life recapitulated in the faces that floated by—a crying baby in a stroller, a boy with a lost expression as he looked for his mother, an angry teenager with his defiant orange hair. Yet even the teenager realized the uselessness of fighting the current of people. Then he saw an older man, bottle in hand, oblivious to those around him, drifting mindlessly down the center of the throng.

"Hello," Vinnie said.

He turned from the window and found Vinnie grinning at the other end of the table. He had appeared out of nowhere.

"Please, take a seat," Vinnie said.

Steve remained standing. "Why am I here?"

"Don't get self-righteous. We know what you did."

"What are you talking about?"

"When you shut down the site, you cut off the surveillance. We figured Austin bolted, so we stormed his house. By the time we got to him, he was convulsing. At first, as you hoped, we thought Syzygy had struck again, but then I downloaded the System Log of Austin's Nexus."

Steve shook his head. It did not make sense. Austin had been fine when he left.

"You seem surprised! I viewed the same logs on Austin's Nexus that you downloaded at the crime scene; that's how I know you did it."

Steve's mind whirled. He remembered handing Allison the gun. Did she shoot him? But why?

Vinnie smiled. "You don't believe me. Why don't we go to the Nexus Corporation's VR server and download its logs. I bet your authorization kicked us out of the server. What do you think?"

She must have killed him. Steve motioned to press the exit button on his Nexus.

"Go ahead. I sent a couple cars to your home a few minutes ago. They're probably there by now."

Steve's shoulders slumped.

"Austin claimed he knew who the killer was."

Steve shook his head. Austin didn't know crap. None of them did. He stared vacantly out the window. What a mess he had made with his life.

"You don't know who the killer is, do you?"

Steve continued to stare out the window, running through the events of the previous week. He had lost everything.

"Well, that's just great! We no longer have a lead on this guy. So you managed to indirectly kill a few more people. You seem to be real good at that, indirectly killing people."

Steve felt a pang of guilt. Just an hour ago he had blamed Austin for giving Syzygy the opportunity to kill Brooke. He would have killed Austin himself if Allison had not stepped in; but hadn't he done the same thing? The Nexus was his invention. If he had stood up to Austin, Brooke would still be alive.

"The only question I have for you is, how'd you kill Austin? What did you use to kill him?" Vinnie asked.

Good question. Steve's hand brushed his pocket and he felt the phaser inside it. Vinnie didn't know. He had figured they had stripped him of any virtual devices he was carrying when they kidnapped him to this site, but they had not.

Steve became calm. In the last twelve hours, he had lost his daughter, his company, and now his freedom. It seemed only appropriate that he lose his life. The alternative was to live with the guilt, the knowledge that he had killed Brooke.

In one movement, he leaped out of his seat and pulled the phaser. At first he pointed the phaser at Vinnie, but only for an instant. He then he pointed it at his head.

"Don't, Steve! We need you to catch Syzygy! How else can we do it?"

Steve answered, "Allison Hwang."

"The director of DARPA?" Vinnie asked with a puzzled stare. "What?"

"She can't do anything. Only you can stop him."

The strength left his legs. Steve set down the phaser on the table and sank into a chair. Vinnie jumped and swatted the phaser. It skidded across the table and slammed into the wall.

Steve spoke in a daze. "Allison was there. She used some modified paging software. She must have shot Austin after I left."

"What did you say?" Vinnie asked.

Steve ignored him. As the head of DARPA, she could have ordered the recall at anytime. She could have saved Brooke.

34

"Goooooaaaaalllll! Goooooaaaaalllll! Goooooaaaaalllll!" The announcer screamed into the microphone. It was Friday night at the soccer match in Santiago, Chile.

Francil Alvarez shot a wry grin at Coach Mike Burns as he placated the crowd with a victory lap around the field, interrupting the game. The U.S.A. team had pulled ahead of the Chileans.

The coach regarded his recent recruit from Brazil. He was without a doubt the most prolific player on the field. Though gangly at six feet, he was strong and agile. However, his temperament and integrity were another matter. Mike Burns cringed at every antic on and off the field that Mr. Alvarez made.

Coach Burns heard a metallic clank on his virtual back as a player patted him in passing. Thanks to a robotic unit, despite pressing business duties, the coach was present at the game through VR.

"Uh, coach?" the assistant coach said.

The coach turned to see the assistant coach removing a 'kick me' sign from the back of the robot. The coach ripped the paper sign out of his hand and waved it like a trophy at the team lining the bench. "You think this is funny, don't you? Damn it! Who did this?"

A couple of players bowed their heads, hiding their smiles

while others turned and snickered. The coach turned back to the field in disgust. It was hard to appear menacing as a four-foot robot. Next time, he would get the Goliath robot model, then he could crush their balls if they looked at him sideways. Of course, working on the U.S.A. team, he had more limited funding than the Chileans. The board would never approve of such a large purchase.

The game continued. James Keegan, a Chilean, tripped up Francil on a routine slide tackle. Francil fell to the ground, writhing in pain and clutching his calf muscle.

"I don't believe it! He's trying to force a yellow card against Keegan!" The coach shook his head.

Two referees walked casually to Alvarez. They were growing tired of his antics. They stood over him as Francil screamed at them. He was not holding his calf anymore. They looked back and forth between Francil and the other player. Finally, after a minute, they brought out a stretcher. Francil rolled dramatically onto it, cursing and hollering. As they carried him off the field, the audience started booing. Francil decided to get up and walk to the sidelines where the medics were waiting. The cries from the crowd did not abate but grew louder. Francil made a slow three hundred and sixty degree turn, displaying an extended third finger to the entire stadium.

"Jesus, get off the field!" The coach screamed, but Francil was still too far away to hear. Finally, he limped to the sidelines.

"What happened this time, Francil?"

"It's my leg. I had a flash of pain shoot up my leg after he hit me!"

"Francil, he didn't hit you, he tripped you. It must be shin splints. Why don't you sit down?"

"I think I'm fine."

The coach shook his head.

"Really Coach, the pain is gone."

"No, it's still standing here in front of me."

"Huh?"

"We don't want to take any chances. This is your third leg injury in this tournament alone."

Francil looked at the assistant coach for support, but he just shook his head, letting him know that he had pushed too far this time. Francil glumly turned and plopped down on the bench.

The game resumed and the crowd roared to life. After five short minutes the Chilean crowd was rewarded when their team scored another goal, tying the game at three all.

The assistant coach approached coach Burns. "Coach, we've got to let him play."

The coach grunted.

"We don't have a chance without him."

Francil got up. "Come on, Coach! You know I can do it!"

"Sit down, Mr. Alvarez!" the coach said.

"No!" Francil said, remaining standing.

The coach gestured to the assistant coach. He nodded and they walked a few feet, out of earshot. "Coach, he needs to play. The owner has made it clear what will happen if we keep losing games."

The coach glanced back at the bench. Francil was not there. He had followed them over. Turning his back to Francil, Mike stared at the assistant coach and said, "Okay, Mr. Alvarez, don't disappoint me."

In response, while the coach's head was still turned, Francil planted a foot in the robot's back, toppling it over. Then he ran out onto the field. The coach's world turned sideways as he fell.

The referee blew the whistle.

"Goddamn it! You idiot, Francil!" He was fuming. "Wait until we notify the ref!"

"It's okay," his assistant coach said while righting the robot. "It was our throw-in anyway. We didn't get penalized." Hollyfield, another player, came running off the field.

"A Goddamn hooligan!"

The assistant coach put an arm around the robot. "Mike, it'll get better. He grows on you, you know?"

"Yeah, like jock itch."

The game continued. Six minutes later, Francil scored another goal, again parading around the coliseum. After the starting kick a Chilean player kicked the ball toward Francil. He jumped and knocked it down with his arm. The referee blew his whistle and went after the ball. Francil reached it first and hid it behind his back as the referee approached.

Exasperated, the official yelled, "Get up!"

Francil put the ball down and sat on it. The crowd booed as another referee trotted across the field and Francil took off a cleat and shook dirt from it. The referees motioned Coach Burns onto the field. He walked to Francil as the fans jeered.

"This is just great, Mr. Alvarez."

"I hate this country," Francil said.

"I'm sure the feeling is mutual."

"It's not fair. I didn't touch the ball."

"Look, at this point I don't care and neither do the officials. You've already managed to destroy any chance of returning to this game. Now it's a choice between the sidelines or a Chilean jail." The coach pointed to the security on the sidelines.

"They can't do that!"

"Yes they can. This isn't the U.S. of A. Here they take soccer very seriously."

"What right do they have?"

"What right? It's their country! They can do and will do anything they damn well want, you arrogant bastard! We're just guests here!" The coach walked away. He stopped and faced Francil one last time. "By the way, have you ever seen the inside of a Chilean prison?"

Slowly, Francil stirred and got to his feet. He lumbered a few feet behind the coach, following him to the sidelines.

"Damn kid!" The coach muttered.

Another official sprinted toward the coach from the Chilean side of the field.

Oh great! Another confrontation. "Mr. Alvarez."

Francil said nothing.

"Francil!"

"What!" He jogged up and walked next to the coach.

"Do you see that?" The coach pointed to the approaching official. "He's probably part of the security detail. If you don't hurry up …"

"I don't see anything, Coach."

The coach stopped and waggled a finger at Francil. "Don't try to mess with me boy! You're in enough hot water as it is!"

"Really, I don't know what the hell you're talking about!"

The coach turned and watched the figure approach. *Now that was odd,* he thought. The coach watched the figure pass through one of the players on the field. The figure must be in VR, transposed on top of the images being sent to him from the robot on the soccer field. Obviously, someone had invaded his virtualscape.

"Damn it!" He swore. He was supposed to be alone! Obviously, someone had broken into the Apostle Company's VR server. "Probably another fan. And the worst kind of fan at that—a hacker!" The coach grumbled.

"What, Coach?"

The coach ignored Francil. He could now see the dark figure clearly and was surprised. It was a very attractive woman.

The coach walked and Francil followed alongside. The figure approached the coach. "What may I help you with, Ms.?" The coach said, never breaking stride.

"What'd you say?" Francil asked.

"Cool your jets, Mr. Alvarez. I have a fan here with me in VR."

The woman said nothing. She walked beside him and stared. *Freak!* The coach kept his gaze forward. She moved in front of him and walked backwards. He looked down.

She stooped and tried to catch his gaze. *Great! A persistent freak.* He stopped and met her gaze. "What?"

Her gaze did not waver. "Look ma'am. I'm in the middle of a game right now."

She said nothing; she just continued to stare at him. It felt wrong. Her gaze was cold and detached.

His gaze dropped to the ground. *Enough of this!* Stepping forward, he brushed past her. He kept his eyes on the ground in front of him. The crowd roared. He glanced over at Francil. What was he doing now?

His feet struck sand and he tripped and fell. He rolled and looked back. A portal closed behind him. The crowd was not yelling; it was the sound of the ocean he heard.

He got up and dusted himself off. The coach was on a beach. A refreshing mist washed over him. Where was she? He looked around. She was nowhere to be found. He was on a white sand beach that stretched for miles in both directions. Just off shore, two dark rocks towered above him. Framed between them was the setting sun.

"Where the hell am I?" He said aloud.

"Tianya Haijiao, the southern tip of Hainan Island. It means edge of the heavens, corner of the seas."

He whirled around and saw the woman had reappeared. She had striped her clothes off, revealing her beautiful full figure. Her gaze softened. Embarrassed, the coach dropped his gaze. "Look ma'am, it's not that I don't like you. Believe me, I'll like you a lot more in a couple of hours after this game is done, but I have to get back there."

Mike pressed the portal button. Nothing happened. "Damn it! What's wrong now?" He could feel a headache coming on. It was turning out to be a bad day.

"Ma'am …"

"Call me Syzygy."

He looked at her. "That's an unusual name." God, she was gorgeous.

She shrugged and approached him again. "So, do you like this place? It's a place of rebirth. Many rebellions were born here: the communists a century ago and the Chinese liberation last year."

"Ma'am, that's all real nice, but I need to get back to the game. I'm remotely controlling a robot on the soccer field, and right now I can't see or feel where I am or what I'm doing. This is a potentially dangerous situation. What if I accidentally walk into the stands? This robot can apply over a thousand pounds of force."

Syzygy was next to him now and placed a seductive hand on his shoulder. He shrugged it off. She obviously did not buy his argument. His robot was in the middle of a soccer field, not exactly a danger to anyone except Francil. And she probably already knew about Francil; not much of a loss. The coach rubbed his temples as the headache intensified.

Burns thought hard. Maybe he could exit, reenter VR, and portal to the game? The coach pressed the exit button. Again, nothing happened. He was really starting to worry. The robot was on the field and that would delay the game only until the officials could remove it. At most, that bought him a few minutes and those minutes were almost up. He needed to be there; he needed to lead his team.

His head really hurt. He pounded the exit and portal button to no avail. It struck him that Syzygy had effectively kidnapped him. *Kidnapped by a crazed fan.* He shuddered involuntarily. But what could she possible do to him?

Francil noticed the coach was no longer near him. He turned and saw the robot had fallen over on the field. In an uncustomary show of camaraderie, he jogged back to help. Reaching down, he righted the robot.

Abruptly, the robot swung, its solid steel arm striking him across the head. He stumbled back, holding the side of his head. It was wet. He pulled back his hand and found it covered with blood.

Another wild arm struck him in the groin. Francil moaned and collapsed to the ground. The robot fell down again and convulsed. From the sidelines, the assistant coach and his teammates ran onto the field.

"No! No!" the coach screamed as they approached.

"Coach! Control yourself," the assistant coach said.

"Man, Francil looks bad," another player added.

Francil blacked out.

35

"Cut!" Jamie said. The image of the Chinese carrier disappeared as Jamie's crew materialized, running about, digitally removing the virtual set. She glanced at her watch. It was 4:55 p.m., five minutes until the hour's news.

"Damn it!" she said.

Hearing her remark, the cast members nearby hesitated only briefly before continuing with their work.

She would not have enough time to sell the piece before 5:00 p.m. That pushed the airing of the clip out until 6:00 p.m. She hoped that the other freelancers would not beat her to the story, as trivial as it was. The Chinese constantly ran military exercises, and Jamie was but one among thousands of freelance reporters trying to cover the story. Every hour the networks would bid from their long list of reports. This was risky stuff. In this business, whoever got the story first would sell it exclusively to all the other stations. That meant several other freelancers, like her, would get nothing for their efforts.

She had been unlucky over the last couple of months. She had a real shot with that Warscape report. Ed Davis and Shen Guofang were key interviews, but her daughter ripped out the best part and the network had rejected the story. "Not sexy enough" was the networks' terse email reply. It was an expensive gamble that did not pay off.

Despite the automation, it took an entire cast to make a report, and she competed with at least a dozen other reporters. Of course, even if she had landed the sale, the story would not have lasted the day or even the afternoon. VR news reports had the shelf life of lettuce. She shook her head.

Jamie watched as her crew scrambled, removing virtual tools and clearing remnants of the set from the lobby. Why had she gotten into this business? As much as she would like to blame it on someone else, she knew she had entered of her own free will. She even knew at the time what it would be like, but she couldn't help herself.

The industry had seduced her along with thousands of other people, all for the same reason. Like everyone else, she dreamed of hitting it rich. It was the modern day gold rush and like the explosion of the World Wide Web at the turn of the millennium, it was open to anyone and everyone.

When her husband died and the income disappeared, she latched onto the VR dream. A year later, she still searched for her big story. The Warscape story should have been it, but her daughter had fixed that.

Jamie sighed. One day she would find something, some report or idea that had persistence. Such a story would transform her life and allow her to live in the manor she deserved. The promise of money was not the only reason she stayed in the game. An artist at heart, this was her calling. VR was the ultimate in creative expression. These were not inanimate sculptures or lifeless images on a flat screen or canvas. In here, she created new worlds, rich with emotion and human experiences. If she wanted to, she could create mountains of wealth, transform landscapes, and enable the viewer to walk in another person's shoes—literally.

Indeed, she had altered people's perspectives, changed their minds, and evoked strong emotions ranging from euphoria to lust to rage. Yes, in here she was a deity, albeit a minor one. That is, if she could air her VR clips.

She could not believe how her daughter had shut her down, robbing her of her big break. It wasn't right. Her daughter was acting more secretive than usual. What was she hiding? Whatever it was, it screamed the words 'breaking news.' She had keys to her daughter's apartment, and Allison was out of town at the moment. Perhaps she would visit, water her plants and such. Besides, Allison owed her.

"Did you contact Davis?" Allison asked.

Vinnie looked up and stared at his boss. This time she had insisted on meeting him at his home in San Ramon, but reality suited him just fine.

Vinnie watched her closely. Why was she focused on Austin's murder? No, Syzygy was a much greater threat. He shook his head in annoyance. He was not used to anyone meddling into one of his assignments—especially if that person was the Director of DARPA. What was her motivation?

Turning his attention to more important things, Vinnie stared at his coffee mug. It had been a week since he could take the time to just grab a *real* cup of java. The VR coffee experience mirrored that of reality but Vinnie could tell the difference.

Vinnie breathed in deeply and savored the subtle nuances: the thin steam rising from the cup, the warmth it generated, the rough texture where the mug was chipped. These minute details separated this experience from its virtual counterpart. Vinnie was in his element again.

"Vinnie, answer me."

He frowned, watching her squirm. Something was definitely up. Her hands shook even as she smiled at him. What was she hiding? Vinnie decided to lie.

"If you must know, Mr. Davis actually contacted me."

"What did he want?"

He set down the mug and lit up a Marlboro. Taking a long drag, he leaned back and pretended to contemplate the question.

"Vinnie!"

"He said you weren't worthy to lick the mud off my boots."

"What?"

Vinnie suppressed a smile playing on his lips. "Oh, don't worry. I defended you. I said, yes, you were!" He waited. *Not even a chuckle.* Instead, she fixed him with an icy stare.

"Answer the question."

He laughed. "Really, he didn't ask much and I didn't say much."

"Let me be the judge of that. Now tell me. What *did* he say?"

"He wanted to know how my work was going."

"So, what did you tell him?"

"I told him there was nothing to worry about, or something vague but positive like that."

"What else?"

"That's it. He seemed to buy it and he went away."

Allison relaxed.

"You worry too much."

"Well, what would you do in my position?" Allison asked, crossing her arms.

"I'm not like you. I don't get into those positions." He put a hand to his mouth and made a puckering sound.

"Knock it off," Allison said.

"The way I see it, there are young people who want to control the river and older people that want to be the river."

"And so you think I'm trying to control the river?"

Vinnie nodded.

"And I should become the river, like you. Is that it?"

"No, people like me get smart. We swim to the side and watch the river go by." He laughed. "Why don't you tell me what this is all about?"

"It's not important. I gave you this assignment Wednesday. What have you been doing all this time?"

"As you asked, I've been sitting on my butt watching Austin. That is, until you killed him. Now that he's dead. There isn't much to see."

"Did you find anything out watching the place? I expected more from you, Vinnie."

Vinnie took another drag. Her quick response surprised him. She did not flinch when he accused her of murder. He knew Davis would grill her for that. Something else scared her—something big.

"Well, if you must know. I did find one curious thing."

"Oh, what's that?"

"Do you know Ron Fisher?"

She nodded. "The Nexus CFO."

"He's never been convicted of anything, but he was playing with the company's numbers. Apparently, Ron is under a lot of financial pressure, yet his pocket book is not showing the strain. I think he was doing some covert business with Austin that may have not been on the level."

"What about the other victims? Did Ron know any of them?"

Vinnie shook his head. "No, I haven't found a connection."

"You just have a gut feeling then?"

Vinnie shrugged. "Yeah."

She nodded, contemplating what he had said. A perplexed look came across her face.

"How did you know that I killed Austin? The surveillance got cut off before I arrived there."

"Actually, at first I thought Steve killed Austin. I detained him and asked a few questions. He became upset when he learned you were DARPA's director."

She rose from her chair. "What? You idiot! You've blown my cover!"

Ah ha. She did not want him talking to Ed or Steve, but she assigned him to watch Nexus Corp. Why? It clicked. Vinnie took another drag and snuffed out his Marlboro.

"Ed Davis doesn't know about this investigation or the defect, does he?" Vinnie took another drag.

"Vinnie ..."

"Last year when I wrote that informational report on the Nexus, you didn't claim it was a complete evaluation, did you?"

"Just remember, I'm still your boss!" she yelled.

Not for long. He locked his gaze with Allison's. She had duped him.

"Ed Davis never sent those emails to Austin; it was you. That's why you had me watch the place. You wanted me to see them, so I would think Davis was in the loop. Somehow Austin found out about your charade, so you killed him."

"There are forces at work here you don't understand!"

Vinnie took a hard drag and exhaled. He removed his gun and set it on the coffee table.

"Listen, Allison. I get the dirty work done for a lot of people, including Ed Davis. Do you think you're my only project?"

She glanced at his gun.

Vinnie smiled. He pulled out a cloth, picked up the gun, and polished its slide.

"I don't care about Austin. I had my orders. If you hadn't killed him, I would have; but Syzygy and the Nexus defect are another matter entirely. Either you tell Ed or I will. He's going to find out one way or another anyway. It'd be better coming from you."

Resurrection

"All our lauded technological progress—our very civilization—is like an axe in the hand of the pathological criminal.

"[Our] problems cannot be solved at the same level of awareness that created them."

—Albert Einstein. Physicist, 1935.

36

For the second time that morning, Ed Davis' shoulder bothered him. He felt it even in VR. It had started when he arrived in Hong Kong, and staying on Pacific Standard Time had not helped.

His trip was a short one—only five days. It made no sense to alter his schedule. Besides, he worked in VR almost the whole time anyway, occasionally jumping out to change planes and participate in a few interviews with local officials. Why should he convert to Hong Kong time?

Ed sighed. He took his job too seriously, working nights and weekends, and for what? The departments under him hated I2 Corp, the newly created fifth branch of the military.

Ed had his own doubts. Still, the plan did solve two problems. Fiscally, the consolidation of the twelve existing intelligence agencies into one conglomerate saved billions of dollars. Strategically, I2 Corp filled the informational warfare void in the Department of Defense.

Before, the DoD was setup for only physical confrontations— Army for land, Navy for sea, Air Force for sky and space, and Marines for miscellaneous; but there had been no provision for

Information Warfare—battles online or in VR. The I2 Corp filled that void.

Yet, the change was radical and politically shaky. Every affected agency fought him on this. He wasn't sure if the President could make it stick. Ed rubbed his brow. The stress was unimaginable. If he were not careful, this new appointment would kill him.

Ed ran a hand across his graying goatee. He was only fifty-two. If he were not dead by the end of this year, he would retire. His body felt old and broken. Government service had long since sucked the life out of him. Now it gnawed on his dry bones.

He remembered when he was younger, before the gray streaks appeared in his hair and the lines of stress had permanently scared his face. He had entered the military full of integrity, ambition, and hope for the future, but as he climbed the military hierarchy, he quickly outgrew his naiveté.

He learned the ropes and adapted to his new political environment. Ed traded his integrity for political savvy, his ambition for ambivalence, and his hope for the party line. Today he lived his reward as the Assistant Secretary of Defense, the leader of the Information and Intelligence Corp.

Ed looked around the hexagon room. Virtual copies of accolades he had collected over the years broke up the room's dark, dithered walls. It did not matter where Ed went. This was his home away from home. Ed shook his head at the irony.

Everyday this week he had flown to some new and exotic place. Even now, his body was in a helicopter heading toward the second Warscape on *U.S.S. Abraham Lincoln* in the South China Sea. Yet, regardless of where he flew, he always spent his days cooped up in here, in his virtual office. Maybe that was the problem, the reason he was so melancholy.

Use your head old man, Ed told himself. If you can't enjoy the exotic places you're visiting in reality, then bring the exotic places to yourself!

"Computer, open the windows to Seven Waterfalls."

Four sides of the hexagon room dissolved into window views

from the side of a mountain, overlooking a sweltering tropical valley. Across the valley, a crimson cliff resonated in the sun, showing complex strata, consisting of layers and layers of sedimentary rock. The wall of rock did not conform to a straight line as it ran across the valley. Instead, it meandered westward, occasionally turning sharply north or south for a hundred feet before continuing west, making a slow progression toward the horizon. This created twenty or so facets. From seven of these, waterfalls plummeted toward the valley floor, disappearing into the rainforest's canopy.

Out of all the office backdrops on the market, this was Ed's favorite. He smiled. Ed got up and paced in front of the windows, rubbing his chin. After a few minutes, he sat back down, feeling a little better, even perhaps invigorated.

Ed called up his calendar. "Computer, who's my next appointment?"

"Jamie Hwang, a reporter."

Ed smiled. *How could I forget Allison's feisty mother!* He remembered the interview he had with her earlier in the week. He checked the time: 4 a.m. That made it 8 a.m. in California.

"Computer, did she say what it was about?"

"No."

Great, just great! If it were good news, she would have mentioned it to guarantee a foot in the door. She probably was still sore about Allison gutting her piece. But all was fair in love and war, especially with the way she had grilled him.

He thought about blowing her off, but his job was to sell the President's plan, court the media, and taint the press coverage with his spin. Through them, Ed would cajole congress into voting the bills and initiatives required to make I2 Corp a success.

"Show her in."

Ed painted on a smile as Jamie entered the room. He stood and extended his hand.

"Jamie! It's good to see you again and so soon! To what do I owe the honor?"

She politely shook his hand. "I'm doing a story on the Nexus and how it has changed the virtual landscape."

A red flag went up in his head. "So why are you talking to me? Why don't you talk to the folks over at Nexus?" He sat down and Jamie sat in the chair opposite.

"Well, I wanted to map the history of the Nexus, from its conception to its approval, to its eventual release. Obviously, one of the agencies under you, DARPA, played a pivotal role by reviewing and approving this product for the Internet. They say you actually took a personal interest in that project. Is that true?"

"I know what Allison said. I'm rather busy, so if you could get to the point. What is it that you need me to do?"

"Is there any way I can talk to someone else at DARPA who worked on this project?"

Ed thought for a moment before shaking his head. "I'm afraid that I disbanded the group some time ago. All its members have been reassigned to other projects. I cannot afford right now to pull anyone from the field. I can offer you the final report created after the Nexus Transporter's approval."

"You know Allison already gave me that."

"I'm sorry, but that's all I can offer you right now," Ed said, hiding behind his smile.

"So you're telling me every single person that was on that team is not available?"

"That's right."

"I just need one hour with just one of them."

"That's one hour more than I can give you right now."

"I'm asking this as a favor, Ed."

"Jamie, I'm sorry. Remember, we're a public company, not a private one. Funding was cut last year during the Department of Defense consolidation. I simply don't have the extra manpower … I mean people power."

"Then consider it an investment in public relations. This could be good publicity for you," she said.

Ed gave her an incredulous look. "Really?"

"I mean, it would look a lot worse if I had to say that you had no comment."

"About what?"

"About the deaths surrounding the Nexus."

Ed laughed. She couldn't be serious! He was surprised she used such a weak ploy. "Jamie you never change! I suppose you can give me their names, too?"

"Of course. Camille Anderson, Shannon Pierce, Skip Harvey, Brooke Donovan, and Mike Burns."

Ed stopped laughing. She was serious. What had Allison done? The Nexus project was hers. She had assured him that everything was fine.

"Either way your name is going into the article," Jamie pushed.

Her words jolted Ed from his thoughts. He did not tolerate personal threats coming from anyone, even his dead friend's widow. He stood.

"Thank you for coming, Ms. Hwang, but I'm going to have to ask you to leave. I'm late for my next appointment."

Behind her a portal opened up, the same one she walked through to get there. She stood, not saying anything.

Ed could almost see her mind whirling, trying to salvage the situation, searching for something in their personal relationship; but this was business.

"Goodbye, Ms. Hwang," Ed said, turning to view the scenery once more.

Getting up, she sighed. "If you change your mind, you have three days before I run the report."

Ed remained silent.

She stepped through the portal. It closed behind her.

He rubbed his brow. If what she said were true, the President's plan was dead. There was no way it, and for that matter Ed, could survive. She was probably bluffing, but he would check into her story anyway. Either way Allison had better have a good explanation for this.

His mind drifted back to when he had visited Allison's father after her birth. His friend was so proud as he bounced little Al-

lison on his knee. They had both laughed when she spat up all over
Ed's uniform. Things had changed.

The smile that had crept across his face faded as he came back
to the present. Allison had lied to him. He had promised he would
take care of her. Now, he would have to break that promise. She
had given him no choice. He was so angry with her.

Three days. Ed glanced at the time and paged Allison and Vinnie. The helicopter would be landing soon and he would meet with
the Admiral. He would have to resolve this situation before then.

37

Allison approached the front door of Steve's house. Why hadn't he called her? She had paged him all night. The door rocked idly on its hinges. Dread filled her as she saw the splintered wood. Someone had busted the door in. *Syzygy!*

Withdrawing her gun, she edged the door open a crack and peeked inside. Light from a window above the door illuminated the dark hall. No movement. Waiting silently on the threshold, she listened. Nothing.

She nudged the door open, slipped inside, and inched her way down the hall. Brooke's bedroom door was wide open. She peeked around the corner and glanced inside—unmade bed, open closet, dresser with one drawer slightly ajar. She dropped to a knee and scanned under the bed and dresser. Nothing.

She continued down the hall. A sound came from Steve's office. She peaked in. Cleared Desk, trampled papers, broken scanner on the ground—all signs of struggle.

She heard something from the kitchen. Cocking her head, she listened as the glass door opened and closed. She stood and crept down the hall to the entrance of the kitchen. She placed her back against the wall. She took a deep breath. One, two, three. Allison whipped around the corner and leveled her gun.

Steve had just returned from a run. His heart was already

pounding in his ears when he looked first at the gun and then into Allison's eyes. "What the hell?"

Allison hastily holstered her gun and glanced around the kitchen. "Someone broke down the front door and trashed your office."

Her words took a while to register. Lifting his sweatshirt, he wiped the sweat from his brow and off his face. He leaned back against the counter and took a deep breath.

"It happened yesterday … when they tried to save Brooke." In his mind's eye he saw Brooke on the desk again, the fireman leaning over her, a long tube stuck down her throat, as they poured drugs into her.

"Oh, I'm so sorry. I tried to call you last night. Why didn't you answer my pages?"

Looking at the ground, he remembered the night in Allison's hotel room. He had needed her last night too, but he could not trust her. "Too much has happened. My wife died last year, now my daughter. Everyone important to me is dead."

"Not everyone," she whispered under her breath, stepping toward him.

He smelled her sweet perfume. It made his stomach turn when he thought of Brooke. He pushed her back. "Don't."

"What's wrong?"

"What's wrong? I lost my daughter because of some bullshit political game of yours!" Turning, he pulled down a glass from the cupboard.

"What are you talking about?"

"They told me you run DARPA, that you could've initiated a recall at anytime. Is that true?"

She stared down, searching for words between the lines of the oak wood beneath her feet. His heart sank.

"Just what I thought. I think you should leave." Opening the fridge, he grabbed a bottle of V8 juice.

"Please don't jump to conclusions. This case is extremely complex. There are powers at work, extenuating circumstances. You don't understand!"

A cold anger flowed around his heart, causing his hand to shake. Setting down the juice, he pierced her with an angry stare. "Allison, Brooke was *not* an extenuating circumstance."

She winced. Her gaze told him that he had hurt her.

"Nothing, and I mean nothing, excuses Brooke's death or anyone else's." He looked down and shook his head. "It makes me sick that you are involved in this!"

"I was trapped. I couldn't do anything until now. I ... I know it won't bring Brooke back, but I am going to authorize the recall this morning. I am doing it for Brooke's sake ... rather her memory ... and for you, Steve. I know it's too late. I thought I had no choice."

Despite his anger, her compassion touched him. He needed her. Steve met her gaze.

"I wish there was something I could do to change this, but there isn't. I swear I will do whatever I can to help you with this recall. You have my word. I'll pick up the pieces of my career later. I don't want to lose your friendship. Not like this." Tears filled her eyes.

Steve felt torn, pulled in two directions. He needed distance from her. Walking across the kitchen, he leaned against the kitchen table. "Why did you lie to me about who you were?"

She shook her head.

"You owe me that, Allison."

She took in a deep breath. A quiet storm raged in her deep green eyes. Another tear ran down her cheek. It reminded him of Brooke. Earlier that week, he had wiped Brooke's tears away while he sat at the edge of her bed. A year earlier he had done the same thing for Tamara; but that memory was fuzzy. He could not see Tamara's face anymore. Soon he would not see Brooke's face either.

"A year ago, before the China war broke out, Ed Davis and my father arranged a mission to ensure my promotion to DIA chief." She looked down and sighed heavily. "I was the department's prodigy; destined for greatness at a young age. My father was so proud of me, following in his footsteps." She smiled. "I looked up to him like no one else. My mother and I were never close. I don't know why. I guess I was more like him.

"We went to Hainan disguised as reporters. It was a quick operation—get in, get out—but the attack came early. We got caught in the crossfire. He didn't make it. I still remember his expression as he fell out of the plane—surprise and disappointment. It all happened so quickly. I tried to bring him back in, but I couldn't hold on. I let go of everything that was dear to me. He died there because of me. I vowed that day that wherever he was, he would see me succeed.

"Davis gave me a second chance. He blamed my father's death on the convoluted chain of command. His efforts resulted in I2 Corp, a unification of all the intelligence agencies. The flagship of the new Corp was Warscape, a tactical surveillance of China. CoolAlerts made up the guts of the system, collecting information through remote sensors, satellites, whatever. He asked me to find the display, someway to present the mountains of information.

"I knew Austin Wheeler through my father. We made an agreement. I gave him a lot of cash and approved the Nexus in exchange for the Nexus schematics."

"You knew about the defect even then?" Steve asked.

"No!" She shook her head. "It wasn't like that at all. He only briefly mentioned the defect; I had no idea how bad it was." She paused for a moment. "But I didn't look that hard for the truth either. When I returned to Davis with the Nexus, I completed the most powerful weapon in history—Warscape. More importantly, I fulfilled my father's dream. I became the youngest DARPA chief ever.

"Everything was fine until last week. Austin contacted me about the defect, filling in a few missing details; someone had died. I kept it quiet, trying to take care of the problem myself. I lied to you and everyone else to protect my career, to keep Davis in the dark. If he found out about the defect, then he would know

Warscape was vulnerable because of Nexus, because of me. I really thought we could nail Syzygy before anyone else would get hurt. I didn't know."

"What happened with Austin?" Steve said.

She shook her head in dismay. "He figured things out and threatened to talk to Davis. He was going to page him. I grabbed his arm. We struggled. He fell on top of me and your weapon just went off. I couldn't do anything." She raised her hand to her head, rubbing her temples.

It took two shots to kill him and I intentionally fired the first. I am also to blame. He moved toward her. She looked him in the eye.

"I had no idea it was going to get this out of hand. I love you. Please forgive me. I am so sorry." Her eyes filled with tears. "I can understand if you don't want to see me again. I made some horrid mistakes out of guilt over my father's death and my love for him. I know you know what that feels like when your best intentions have the worse results."

She was right. When the business went sour, he turned to drinking, drove drunk, and killed Tamara. He brought Austin on board and the defect slipped through. He pursued the Nexus healer and missed Brooke's final days. Sadness welled up inside him. "Oh god," he whispered. Piece by piece his mistakes were tearing his life apart.

"I want you to know who I am, Steve." She touched his shoulder and moved behind him.

He didn't push her away this time. Tenderly, she held him.

His eyes teared. "Out of the millions of users, why did Syzygy attack her?"

She said nothing for several seconds. "I was thinking the same thing. That's why I came in with the gun. I think he's after you, Steve."

He turned to face her. She released him.

"I'll talk to Ed Davis; I'll make him understand. This recall has to happen." She looked down, crossed her arms, and then looked up again. "Do you think you can get the money together?"

Steve dried his eyes with his shirt. "Yeah, Ron should have Austin's books figured out by now."

Allison pulled out her Nexus. He grabbed her arm.

"Wait. Syzygy is after me; he might go after you. I don't want you inside. I can't stand losing anybody else."

"What about the chip you used when you met Syzygy for the first time?" she said.

He shook his head. "I'm using the only prototype. It will take more than two weeks to manufacture more."

She smiled. "Don't worry. I'm a big girl. I can take care of myself. Now come on. Let's get to work."

As she headed off, Steve grabbed her arm again. She stopped, looking at his hand on her arm. He moved closer.

"Did you really mean that, about loving me?"

She smiled. "Yes. The more I am with you, the more certain I am."

He looked into her eyes. They were light again. *Very good.*

38

S teve stepped into the lobby of Nexus Corporation. Ron had finally put the last touches in place. Tall pillars supported a cluster of domes that made up the ceiling. Imitating the inside of an abalone shell, the iridescent walls, pillars, and ceiling were full of subtle colors that blended imperceptibly into one another, swirling as he walked.

"I decided against the marble. It was too trendy."

Steve turned.

"You look awful," Ron said.

"No commentaries. Just tell me about Austin's second set of books."

"My friend, you are grumpy! How 'bout a break?"

"I don't have time."

"We can talk while we play. It'll be like the old times, before all this." Ron pressed the portal button on his wrist. "National Geographic's spaceport."

"Wait!" Steve said as Ron entered the portal.

Steve followed him through.

Steve emerged in a crowd. Pushing through, he found an open space and scanned the room. It was tall and crescent shaped with one side exposed to open space. The edge of the floor was notched, resembling a gigantic gear. A space vessel was docked in each notch. Ron stood next to a toboggan-like rocket. Steve walked over to him.

"So, do you want to drive?" Ron asked, jumping in the front seat.

"Guess not," Steve said. He looked up as two spacecrafts entered the port, slipping through a thin electrical membrane, which prevented the bay's contents from being sucked into space. National Geographic usually was realistic, but most of what he saw was still decades away.

"Will you try not to be a geek for one minute and stop analyzing everything? Now get in!" Ron said.

Steve slid into the seat behind him. There was no hatch to flip down to cover the cockpit. Instead, the craft used the same electric sheath that the space dock used.

"Tell me what you found," Steve demanded. He could hear Ron tinkering with the controls. "Ron?"

Ron primed the engines.

"Damn it," he said. He strapped in.

"Here we go!" Ron said as the magnetic clamps released.

They accelerated rapidly, shooting out of the launch bay.

"Crap, slow down!" Steve felt his distant body's stomach lurch.

"It's just VR! Sit back and relax! I'm just getting started!"

Steve groaned.

They approached the belt quickly. From a distance, it appeared as a collection of a hundred or so asteroids. This was just a small part of Kuiper's belt. The collection of rocks orbited beyond Neptune, creating a gigantic disk two billion miles from earth that was over four billion miles wide. Most of the sparse ring contained empty space, but here and there, the objects clustered, herded together by Neptune.

"Okay, let's take a closer look, shall we?" Ron said, diving toward a stray asteroid that paralleled the larger group.

Steve tensed as they neared the cluster.

The surface of the rock appeared rough and jagged, covered with rubble.

"As a kid, did you ever wonder how movie stars raced their spaceships through asteroid belts without getting hit?" Ron joked.

Steve tightened his grip on the seat as Ron dove for the main cluster. Again, Steve's stomach lurched. He thought his corporeal body might lose its breakfast.

They entered the cluster. It proved much more tranquil than Steve expected. The rocks moved with relatively the same direction and speed, long since negotiating their ordered place in the asteroid swarm. Ron swung the craft around one of the larger asteroids. Abruptly, there appeared a smaller asteroid hidden in the shadow of the larger one.

"Hold on!" Ron yelled. He veered the craft hard to starboard and steered into a larger rock. Steve was thrown against the wall of the cockpit as the craft spun wildly. He tensed helplessly, waiting until Ron regained control of the craft. It took Ron only a couple seconds.

"Ron, what the ..."

"Uh oh," Ron said.

"What's uh oh?" Then Steve saw it. Ron had dislodged one of the asteroids from its place within the swarm. This asteroid, in turn, had knocked a neighboring rock, which set off a chain reaction. Around them, the serene cluster rapidly disintegrated into chaos.

Ron steered for the edge of the cluster, attempting to escape the angry swarm. A rock hit them from the side, knocking Steve's head against the cockpit again. Then another struck the bottom of the craft and Steve hit his console. After a few more hits, the swarm had turned the craft. They were heading back to the center of the cluster. Like an angry swarm of bees, the asteroid cloud swallowed them up.

"Oh, shit!" Ron screamed.

Steve looked up. A tumbling boulder the size of a two-story house headed straight for them.

"I can't turn the ship. Try your controls," Ron said.

Steve touched the stick just as the rock plowed into them.

Everything changed. He was falling. Steve landed hard on a field of grass. His back hurt.

"What happened?"

Steve turned to Ron. "Software bug. I guess the software couldn't anticipate someone going suicidal and colliding with the largest meteor they could find!"

"Are you sore?"

"Well what do you think? I'm tired of you dragging me through a virtual hell! Just tell me about Austin's accounts!"

"I meant your back."

"Oh." Steve stopped and rubbed his back.

"Well, my friend, where have we landed?" Ron said, looking around.

Steve scanned the horizon. They stood on a small rise above a marshy lake. A scattering of palm trees ran along the crest of the sandy hill behind them. The sun bore down right on top of them and the air was dense and rancid from the swamp.

He felt the warmth burrowing its way into his skin, causing small beads of sweat to form on his virtual arm. A small group of dinosaurs grazed in tall grass and reeds while larger long necks roamed deeper in the lake.

"It looks like we landed in the Smithsonian dinosaur exhibit. It's on the same VR server."

"Cool."

"The accounts, Ron."

Ron sighed. "You're always business aren't you?"

"Yeah, for now. What did you find?"

"Eighteen million shares of Nexus Stock and eighty-one million dollars."

Steve's jaw dropped. Nexus Corporation as a whole was not worth half that much. Allison had said Austin got some money out of the deal, but he never imagined …

Ron smiled. "I told you not to worry about Austin. It was just a matter of time until he imploded. He parked the money in your expense account. The stock, like the account, is in both your name and Austin's. I have power of attorney; the transfer should be a piece of cake. In any event, you've got control of your company again. Try not to screw it up."

Steve sat down on a log and gazed at the grazing dinosaurs. He felt overwhelmed. "I don't know."

Ron sat beside him. "Don't give up now! The hardest part is behind you! Do you remember what you told me after the lobby was trashed? You said, 'An undetected virus is like a spy in an organization. Once accepted as one of the fold, you cannot find him without making everyone a suspect.' You were right. You just didn't know that Allison was the spy."

Allison? A spy? Steve turned to Ron. "What are you talking about?"

Click.

Steve froze.

Click.

Syzygy had attacked. Steve's modified Nexus would protect him; but Ron was another matter.

"What is it?" Ron asked.

"Shh!" Steve scanned the palm trees but saw nothing.

"What's wrong?" Ron said.

"It's probably nothing. Try to open a portal."

Ron shrugged and pressed the button. Nothing happened. "Steve, it doesn't seem to be working."

"Exit VR now!" Steve spun around, checking the marsh, searching for movement in the reeds and grass. Still nothing. *Where is he? Maybe he's camouflaged, part of the terrain.*

Ron looked up from his left wrist. "It's not working either."

Steve pulled out the phaser from his virtual pocket and shot a dinosaur grazing in a field several meters away. It briefly lit up in a bright blue hallo, but continued to graze unaffected.

"What in the hell's that?" Ron asked.

Syzygy couldn't bring down my Nexus' patch. Steve punched his portal button. A seven foot black oval appeared with a wind issuing from it, rustling the surrounding ferns and tall grass. "Jump through!" he shouted.

"You're messin' with me, right?" Ron said, looking more concerned.

Steve fired at the pterodactyl in the sky and followed it with a blast at a herd of small dinosaurs, prancing through the meadow grass. Again, nothing.

"I'm not doing anything until you tell me what the hell is going on!" Ron demanded.

Syzygy will just follow Ron through the portal. Damn, what if Syzygy is invisible, not even showing up in VR? What if I don't even have a target? His heart started to race. He felt panic coming on. Calm down, he told himself. An idea came to him. "Charlie!"

Bounding over a log, the small dog approached, wagging its tail madly. Steve had forgotten to turn Charlie off and he had stayed as a background process, following Steve throughout the Internet.

"Charlie, find the alias Syzygy!"

"Who's Syzygy?" Ron asked.

The dog ran to a palm tree and sniffed it.

"What is it?" Steve asked.

Charlie proceeded to urinate on the tree.

"Charlie!" Steve said.

The tree's image quivered. It was Syzygy.

Steve lifted the phaser.

The tree liquefied, metamorphosing into a wall of brown fluid. It flowed toward them.

Ron yelled and stumbled back.

Charlie dove in front of the wall of fluid. It stopped, coiled around the dog, and solidified into a pod.

Charlie struggled to break free of the cocoon. Layers of sinewy muscle flowed over Charlie's limbs, which jabbed frantically, attempting to punch through.

"Don't analyze it! Shoot it! Shoot the damned thing!" Ron yelled.

Steve snapped out of his daze and pulled the trigger. A blue halo enveloped the pod, which reverted into a frozen image of Syzygy. The shot had knocked Syzygy off the Internet. He looked around. Charlie had disappeared. "Charlie!"

A copy of the program bounded over a nearby log. "Good boy, can you reset Ron's interface?"

Charlie barked once.

Steve felt a hand on his shoulder. He turned and faced Ron.

"I don't know what that thing was; but it seems to be after you, my friend."

39

Allison sat down in front of Ed Davis' desk in a seat next to Vinnie. Vinnie slouched in his chair and placed his feet on the desk. Ed leveled his gaze at Vinnie. They exchanged a look. Vinnie obliged him and sat up straight.

"Thanks for coming," Ed said, looking up from a sheet of paper.

Uh, oh, Allison thought. Ed had learned something.

He turned to her. "Do you have any idea why I called you here?" he said, picking up the piece of paper.

"Perhaps," Allison said, eyeing the paper.

"Would you care to take a guess?"

"Um." She cleared her throat. "You asked me earlier this week to work with Vinnie, researching Camille Anderson's death. We found a problem with the Nexus—a defect. It killed her."

Ed pierced her with a stare. "How long have you known this?"

"Only a couple of days."

"Why didn't you tell me right away? I found out about this problem from your mother! A goddamn reporter! Do you know how that looks for the agency, for the President?"

"She was here?" Allison gasped.

He nodded.

"I'm sorry. I had no idea."

Ed fixed her with a finger. "How could you have missed the

problem in the first place?"

"We approved the Nexus Transporter in four months instead of two years. A few glitches got through," she said.

"Oh, was it a *glitch* that Jamie referred to? That *glitch* fried people's brains! In case you haven't noticed, the list of victims has grown." Davis handed the piece of paper to her.

```
Camille Anderson
Shannon Pierce
Skip Harvey
Brooke Donovan
Mike Burns
```

She cringed. "We had to cut corners to approve the Nexus in time. There was no other way to meet your schedule."

Ed leaned back. "Oh, so these deaths are my fault now?"

She bit her lip. "No, I'm not saying that!"

"You could have told me the truth, that you were having trouble! I never asked you to lie to me! Bottom line, what's our liability?"

Allison took a deep breath. "The Nexus has a lethal defect that may kill in the right circumstances. A hardware fix is possible, but it will take two weeks to build the necessary components. I'm working with the Nexus CEO to begin recall proceedings."

Ed rubbed his temples.

Vinnie spoke up. "Uh, shouldn't you tell Mr. Davis about Syzygy?"

Oh shit! Allison squirmed.

Ed turned to her. "What about it? What's Syzygy?"

"An online alias, sir." Allison nervously crossed her arms. "It appears that someone going by the alias of Syzygy has exploited the defect to kill people online."

"What? This gets better and better!"

Allison silently shook her head, not knowing what to say.

"Not only have you enabled the release of a hazardous product, but you neglected to tell me about it after the fact. I told you this once. Now try to get this through that thick cranium of yours: this situation could swallow us whole. We might all have to find new lines of work, including the President. Do you understand?"

She nodded. After several minutes, Ed's gaze released her. She sank back into her chair. Her whole body shook, and her stomach was tied up in knots. Her career was over.

Ed rubbed his brow. "There will be no recall. Too much is at stake. Allison, as I said, Jamie came here to see me about these Nexus deaths. I need you to continue the charade. Talk to her, keep her occupied, but don't reveal anything. That way you'll keep out of Vinnie's hair while he proceeds with the investigation."

Vinnie smirked at her.

She sank back into her chair, and her gaze dropped to the ground. Inside, she was boiling. She took a deep breath, and her training kicked in. He had caught her lying. Their history meant nothing at this point. He would slowly move her out of the way. Come September, she would be *promoted* into a dead-end job, another *special* project. Eventually, when the project was through, she would be routinely let go. She had to regain Ed's favor.

"Mr. Secretary ..."

Ed held his hand up. "We've known each other a long time. I knew your father even longer. Please leave before I say something we'll both regret."

Allison had one more card to play, the same card that got her into this mess. As a reporter, her mother had resources that Steve and DARPA did not have. If she could find Syzygy, political pressures would stop Davis from doing anything rash.

Ed's voice broke through her musing. "I said, you can go."

She opened a portal.

"One more thing, Allison. Try to remember we're a team, and there is no 'I' in team."

She nodded her head vacantly and stepped through.

Vinnie rose from his seat.

"Wait, Vinnie," Ed said.

"What?"

"I wanted to thank you for telling me about the girl's death. I don't hold you responsible for what has happened after that. You were just following orders."

Vinnie gave a terse nod.

He shook his head. "I cannot forgive Allison, though. I'm practically her uncle, for god sakes! I don't know what got into her."

Vinnie nodded again in agreement.

"I need you to officially step into her shoes. I want you to be DARPA's next Director."

"Will that entail just the title?"

Ed laughed. "If you wanted money, you should have gone into the private sector."

Vinnie smirked. "True enough, but the question still stands."

"Let's see how you handle this situation first. National security isn't the only reason we have to catch Syzygy."

Vinnie lost his smirk. "Let me guess, politics?"

Ed nodded. "The fate of I2 Corp is linked with the fate of the Nexus. I don't need to explain to you what this means. I may be the President's friend, but when it comes down to it, he is a politician first. We're both expendable here. If Warscape fails, he'll blame us." Ed took a deep breath. "I need to know if you think you can handle this."

Vinnie smirked. "I already am."

40

Ed Davis marveled at the immensity of the ship as the helicopter neared the Nimitz Class Carrier, *U.S.S. Abraham Lincoln*. The carrier was a city unto itself, home to over six thousand sailors. At over eleven hundred feet long, two hundred and fifty feet wide, the carrier's towers reached twenty stories above the waterline. It had its own fire department, post office, library, general store, and hospital. It even had its own newspapers, radio, and television stations.

The *U.S.S. Abraham Lincoln* was more than just a floating city. It was a mobile military airbase, sporting over eighty fighting aircraft and eight combat helicopters. Even by itself, the aircraft carrier was formidable. As part of the battle group, it was deadly.

The battle group included ten other ships: two cruisers, two supply/logistics ships, four destroyers, and two nuclear attack submarines. Together they formed a floating arsenal that the U.S. could park a hundred miles offshore anywhere in the world. From these international waters, the *Abraham Lincoln's* fighters and bombers could reach over seventy percent of the world's population. It was no wonder that whenever a crisis broke out, the first question any President asked was, "Where's the nearest carrier?"

The helicopter landed and Ed stepped out onto the deck. He walked to the Commander in Chief of the Pacific fleet. From the

President's briefing, Ed knew that CINCPAC Marshal Spurrier was in his early fifties, so the Admiral's youthful appearance surprised him. He was trim with brown, crew-cut hair, and although short at just over five feet, his confidence made up for his height. His razor-sharp blue eyes never wavered as Ed approached. The Admiral's expression said everything. This man was not amused by his visit.

"Welcome aboard *Abraham Lincoln*," the Admiral said.

Ed shook his hand. Behind them, the whine of the helicopter blades faded as its engines shut down.

"Mr. Davis, Warscape is this way."

He followed the Admiral down a series of ladders to the Warscape compartment, deep within the bowels of the ship. Inside the cramped space, technicians tended to row after row of electronic hardware.

"This compartment contains over one thousand computers; networked together they form one of the two Warscape systems," the Admiral said. "In short, this is Warscape's brain. Each of these computers canvasses a particular region of Southeast Asia by communicating with sensors in the area and by using satellites. From VR, analysts verify the collected data, refine the information, and respond accordingly."

"How big are the regions?"

"A hundred miles squared."

"Sounds like a powerhouse!" Ed said, turning to the Admiral.

The Admiral paused and met his gaze. "Mr. Davis, we both know why you're really here. This tour I'm giving is perfunctory. I'm not fond of Warscape and you know it. The President has sent you here to change my mind. So let us dispense with the bullshit. Okay, sir?"

Ed was taken aback. "Of course, the more candid, the better. So, tell me. Why don't you like Warscape?"

"Sir, it's not that I don't like Warscape. I just don't like how Warscape is being used as a political scape."

"I don't follow."

"The President just ordered us north to an indefensible position because we have this system."

"But the Chinese battle group will be still over two hundred miles away from the carrier!"

"Yes, but at that position the Paracel Island group will be only one hundred and fifty miles away. Being at high alert, our twelve-ship battle group is spread out, covering a wide area. Some ships are only seventy-five miles from the Paracels. One of those islands, Woody Island, has an airfield.

"Tactically, the PLA still has a hard time targeting over the horizon, aiming beyond sixty miles or so. With our F18s and our floating arsenal of SAMS, Tomahawks, and Harpoon missiles, we can easily defend against their land-based offensive. Once we move north that will change."

Ed waved a dismissive hand. "I don't think you should be concerned ..."

"Sir, you're new in town," the Admiral snapped, "so let me tell you something about naval warfare. Chinese torpedo and missile technology has come a long way since the last administration and the last war. One missile, just one, will usually sink a ship."

"I'm well aware of that, but the fact of the matter is that the PLA has no presence on Woody Island."

"I'm afraid your intelligence is wrong, sir. Despite the treaty, the PLA has moved in a lot, and I do mean *a lot* of equipment, supplies, and troops to suppress a *few* rebellious students on Hainan Island. Some of that has found its way a hundred miles south on Woody Island."

"Goddamn it! I just met with the Chinese foreign ministry spokesman, Shen Guofang, *in person*. He promised me that they had started to pull back! Are you telling me they lied again? I should have known something was up. At our meeting he tried to bribe me with a new Rolex watch."

The Admiral raised an eyebrow. "Not a very Chinese gesture." He shrugged.

"Sir, what about our carrier battle group?"

"The President and his NSC decided on this course of action after consulting with the Joint Chiefs, which includes your boss. I suggest you take it up with him. So we're moving north even though we have no clue what the Chinese are thinking or why they moved their battle group. Warscape might be great at painting blips, but it can't get into their heads and tell us their intentions."

"Ah, the proverbial cultural brick wall," Ed smirked.

"That *wall* could be broken down by human Intel—good old-fashion low-tech spies—but we have no spies in China! The gutting of the CIA's budget has seen to that!"

"I don't see what any of this has to do with Warscape."

"Mr. Assistant Secretary, guess what excuse the President used when cutting the CIA's budget?"

Ed hesitated.

"That's right, Warscape, and it couldn't come at a worse time. Do you know that every time our military strength in the region has dipped, the Chinese have conquered another island?

"In 1975 the PLA stole the entire Paracel Island Group from Vietnam just after we pulled out of Vietnam, ending the Vietnam War. Then in 1994 they took Mischief Reef from the Philippines after the Philippines kicked our bases out of their turf. Just last year, when we scaled down our military presence in the region and closed our Singapore base, the Chinese invaded the Spratly Islands.

"Now the ASEAN coalition is falling apart! Don't you think the Chinese will see this as an opportunity? They'll go for the Spratly Islands again! I'm sure of it!"

"I understand your concern here. The I2 Corp is new, but let me assure you the Defense Intelligence Agency, which is taking over the CIA's role, can provide you with anything ..."

"Pardon my French, sir, but the DIA can't provide me with dick. It's barely one-fourth the size of the CIA ..."

Ed flushed. The DIA was one of the departments he ran. "That may be true, but bigger government doesn't make for better gov-

ernment. For all its size, the CIA did not predict the demise of
the last cold war with the Soviets. They were too busy believing in
the empty missile silos the Soviets dug and the plethora of faulty
equipment they exposed to our satellites. In the end, we may have
won the cold war, but without the CIA it might have ended sooner. The President isn't about to allow the CIA to blow this cold war
like they blew the first one!"

"You can choose to listen to that political fluff the President's
advisers are feeding you, but I'm telling you, this whole I2 Corp
concept stinks! We have no intelligence, only this battle group to
fight with ..."

"That is simply not true. You're forgetting about ASEAN coalition!"

The Admiral laughed bitterly. "No, I'm not, sir! I told you,
ASEAN is falling apart! Out of the ten countries in ASEAN,
Vietnam and the Philippians were the only ones willing to take a
stand against China. And now the Philippines is on the brink of a
civil war and Vietnam isn't faring much better."

Ed started to respond, but stopped. He needed the Admiral's
support, and this was not the way to get it. Ed rubbed his brow. "I
see your point."

"It's about time."

Ed held up his hand. "But I think we're getting off on the
wrong foot. Why don't we take up this discussion later, *after* I see
Warscape in action?"

The Admiral gave him a terse nod. Ed followed him out of the
compartment, down a narrow passageway, and into a small conference compartment. They squeezed in around a table that took
up most of the available space. A Nexus system was positioned at
each of the seats. The Admiral motioned to Ed to put his Nexus
on. They entered VR.

Ed materialized in Warscape. He levitated with the Admiral
at more than one hundred feet above a real-time, three-dimen-

sional map of the South China Sea. The domed map matched the curvature of the earth. Running from the northeast to the southeast of the map were the friendly countries: Taiwan, Philippines, Malaysia, Brunei, and Indonesia. From the northwest running to the southwest were China and its counter balance, Vietnam. The South China Sea was sandwiched between these two groups of countries and contained Hainan Island, the Paracel Islands, and the Spratly Islands.

Neon green lines crisscrossed the map, splitting it into one hundred by one hundred mile squares. Each of the squares was labeled with a number and covered with blips of light. Most of the blips were blue while a few of them were green, yellow, and red.

"What do the lights represent?" Ed asked.

"Each one shows the location of a ship, aircraft, or vehicle that we're tracking."

Ed was shocked. "Why are there so many?"

"They aren't all military. The blue blips are mostly commercial barges, but we have to track them in order to distinguish them from new military sightings." The Admiral pointed to an ocean square just south of Hainan. Unlike the rest of the map, most of the blips there were green and yellow.

The Admiral continued. "You see there, around the Paracel Islands? Those lights are military in nature. The green dots south of the Islands are us, each light representing a ship in the battle group or a plane on patrol. The yellow dots in the center of the map represent either the PLA airbase on Woody Island within the Paracel Island group, or PLA planes in the air. The last set of yellow dots to the north represents the ships in the Chinese battle group."

Ed nodded.

Abruptly, the neon green lines around the square containing the Paracel Islands turned yellow.

"What happened?" Ed asked.

"The analysts monitoring the region have spotted something. It's probably the Chinese, testing our defenses again. You wanted to see Warscape in action, right? Why don't we take a look? Computer, enter region 435." A portal appeared and they stepped through.

They appeared in a similar room, but the map beneath them had changed. It was an expanded view of the Paracel Island region, contained in the red, grid-square of the other map. Ed saw the individual blips in the three light clusters more clearly now. Six analysts hovered over the map, analyzing the situation.

"What are they doing?"

"See the pink blip?" The Admiral pointed.

Ed saw one pink and several yellow blips above Woody Island. He nodded.

"The Chinese have launched something at us. The analysts are identifying what it is. There!" A label appeared above the pink blip and it darkened to red:

```
Bandit 1:  SU-27 Flanker
Bullseye:  Lanky
Direction: 100 degrees
Range:     132 miles
Altitude:  30 angels
Speed:     600 knots
```

"Okay! It's a live one," the Admiral explained.

"Forgive me. It's been a while since I was out in the field. Can you explain what all that jargon means?" Ed said, pointing to the label.

"It says the blip represents a Chinese fighting aircraft called the SU-27 Flanker. It's armed and could be above this carrier in under fifteen minutes."

"Are we in any danger?"

The Admiral laughed. "I don't think so. They can't make it very far with just one aircraft." The Admiral pointed to a green blip close to the Chinese fighter. "The analyst will probably vector that guy in. He's one of ours, a F-18X Hornet fighter aircraft. It's been specially equipped to deal with incursions like this."

Suddenly, a second pink light appeared, sprouting from the red blip. The pink light arced up, traveling at roughly twice the speed of the other red blip.

"Kitchen!" one of the analysts shouted.

"Christ!" the Admiral said.

"What is it?" Ed asked.

"The bastard fired a missile at us!"

41

Even with her mother's platinum membership, the virtual Internet library seemed ordinary enough, appearing as the default configuration, a twenty-foot cube with white walls and *AOL Time Warner*® etched into the floor.

"This is it?" Allison asked, extending her arms and spinning. "This is the best you can do?"

"What you see isn't important. I have my own dedicated access to all the library's resources in here."

Allison felt her face flush with anger. "How will that fix what you did?"

"What I did?" Jamie said, placing her hands on her virtual hips. "If you didn't lie to your boss ..."

"If you didn't steal papers from my house," Allison shouted, crossing her arms.

"Allison Diane Hwang, we can leave right now if you want."

Allison bit her lip. She could not afford to push her mother right now. Swallowing her anger, she said, "I'm sorry. It's been a rough day."

Jamie smiled, apparently forgetting the whole argument. "Everything will be fine, dear. You will see. DARPA may spend millions on research, but we spend billions. Our business is intelligence. No one can dig up more dirt than we can. If Syzygy left a trail, I'll find it."

Allison nodded, feeling physically ill from stress. All her hopes lay with her deranged mother.

"Librarian, do you have access to Internet Service Provider records?" Jamie asked.

The figure of an English gentleman appeared next to them. "Some, but not all. It is private information."

"Okay. Please search all ISP records for patrons using the alias Syzygy."

The man winked out of existence. A moment later, he returned. "I'm sorry I could find no reference to Syzygy in the ISP records."

"Librarian, can you search the Internet for currently logged on users?"

"Yes, but it will also be incomplete."

"That's fine."

He disappeared. After a few minutes, he returned and a wall of water appeared next to him. Letters protruded in green from its surface:

```
User(s) with the alias Syzygy are currently
logged onto:

Apostle Robotics
Create Your Own Adventure
Dog Fight Central
Fantasy Central
Ritz, The
s#@~#d$f9e*r8&
```

Allison smiled. There was more than one killer. If she could break the case, Davis would have to listen to her.

"Being a reporter has its perks," her mother quipped.

"Librarian, how many people have the alias Syzygy?" Allison asked.

"One."

Allison turned to Jamie. "How can that be? How can he be logged onto all these sites at once?"

Jamie shrugged as the librarian responded. "I have no answer to your question. Do you want me to find a reference that might help you?"

"No," Allison said, continuing to scan the list. "That's funny. The last entry is garbled, just like the last entry in the log. Steve told me the log was corrupted. If so, why is the name garbled here as well?"

"Librarian, what details can you give us regarding Syzygy's connections?" Jamie asked.

"I can provide when each connection was made."

"Great! Can you display everything for us now?" Allison said.

```
Apostle Robotics          06/13 @ 08:00 PST
Create Your Own Adventure 06/12 @ 15:00 PST
Dog Fight Central         06/10 @ 18:00 PST
Fantasy Central           06/11 @ 15:00 PST
Outdoor Adventures        06/12 @ Unrecorded
Ritz, The                 06/09 @ 15:00 PST
s#@~#d$f9e*r8&            06/08 @ 18:00 PST
```

Allison could not believe it! Syzygy had been logged onto some of the sites for several days! She glanced down to the last site again. Syzygy had been logged onto it for almost a week!

Jamie spoke up. "Librarian, does the last site have another name?"

Allison glanced at her mother.

"Just a thought; it might be a real site," Jamie said with a smile.

"Nexus Corporation," the Librarian responded.

Allison took a step back. She looked at the date and time-stamp and remembered how the hackers had vandalized the Nexus lobby. Perhaps they had hidden something, a link of some kind. She gave her mother a peck on the cheek. "Thanks! I can take it from here."

Jamie smiled.

Pressing a button, Allison whispered, Nexus Corporation. With a hiss, a seven-foot black void appeared before her. She stepped through.

Ron had dramatically changed the lobby. It now sported the recently trendy art deco motif. The same look Davis had tried, but unlike Ed, Ron's attempt was successful.

Tapered pillars supported a multi-domed ceiling. Looking up, she saw the dome above her painted with an intricate mural, some unfamiliar mythical scene. The walls, pillars, and floor were made of an iridescent material resembling the inside of an abalone shell. The subtle pinks and pale blues moved as she walked, swirling and blending into a rich cacophony of color. She heard a subtle baroque melody echoing off the expansive room, mixing with the sound of running water.

She was impressed. Although intimate with the latest trends in the industry, she had not seen anything with this much detail. She crossed the lobby, passing a large fountain. Allison smiled. Not everything about Ron's tastes was impeccable. The fountain looked like something Steve would have picked out.

Beyond the fountain a woman behind a counter asked, "May I help you?"

Allison approached the counter. "I'm looking for a friend of mine, Ron Fisher. Is he here?"

"No, he's not. Would you like me to page him?"

"No, that's alright. Would you check to see if an alias named Syzygy is here?"

The woman scanned a book in front of her. "I'm sorry, but I don't see anyone here registered with that alias or name."

"Really?" Allison knew Syzygy had to be there. He could not have left in the last couple of minutes after having been logged on for almost a week. "Maybe he's using a different alias. How big is your Directory?" Allison asked.

"Twenty names."

"Could you read them to me?"

"Certainly." The receptionist rattled off the names and aliases of the people logged onto the site.

Allison shook her head. Syzygy was not listed. "Could you page Ron? It's urgent. I think someone has tampered with this site."

"One moment. I'll …," The woman vanished suddenly.

"What happened?" Allison wondered.

Whoosh.

Allison turned. A man with a runner's build, blond hair, and blue eyes stepped through a portal.

Ron.

"Were you looking for me?"

"I'm glad I caught you." She walked to him.

Ron smiled.

"I think Syzygy is logged onto your site. That's why the hackers thrashed your lobby."

Ron smirked. "I know."

"You do?" Ron carried himself differently. Her gut screamed, "Run!" but she stood her ground. "What do you mean, *you know?*"

Click.

Ron stepped closer and Allison backed away. It didn't feel right. She pressed her portal button. Nothing happened. She looked down and made sure she had pressed the right button. She tried again. Nothing happened. Looking up, Ron was inches from her face. She let out a scream and stumbled back.

His gaze bored into her, ripped into her soul.

Allison took a deep breath and pressed the exit button. Again, nothing happened.

"I'm sorry, but I'm experiencing some trouble with my Nexus," she stammered, trying to remain calm.

Ron silently regarded her with his tenacious gaze. She backed away from him slowly. Something like a metallic whine sounded behind her. She tripped backwards through a portal and fell onto wet sand.

Allison looked around. A beach. Ron transformed into a dark figure with green eyes. Her heart raced. Her mind lost focus. Warmth built in her head.

Oh shit! Ron is Syzygy.

She scrambled to her feet.

He smiled and then let the corners of his mouth dip into a frown. Syzygy took a step toward her.

She turned and ran. After reaching the water, she ran along the shoreline where the sand was firm. She stole a glance back and then stopped. He wasn't running. Instead, he sauntered slowly toward her.

Then it hit. A thousand needles of pain etched themselves into her brain and she fell.

"Damn it!" she said, trying to get up, but it was no use. She fought the pain and managed to crawl forward a few feet. She heard his feet slapping against the wet sand. He was close.

Allison clutched her head and moaned. Everything faded and grew dim.

"Help, Steve!" she screamed.

42

I thought you said that one fighter wasn't a problem!" Ed said, his eyes fixed on the moving pink light on the map.

"He isn't, unless he intends to start a war," Admiral Marshall Spurrier said.

Abruptly, the map blossomed with light, blanketed with new pink blips. The red blip, representing the Chinese fighter, shifted to pink, lost in the constellation of light. The label above it disappeared.

"She's a screamer," another analyst shouted.

The Admiral sighed in relief. "False alarm. They launched a decoy missile. The missile just separated into twenty smaller missiles. Each one appears to our radar as another Chinese fighter. The Chinese fighter is hiding within the cluster."

"For what purpose?"

The Admiral turned to Ed. "They're testing our defenses. We can't hit what we can't see. If they learn a way to hide from Warscape, we will be susceptible to a real attack. Then they'll strike."

Ed nodded soberly.

"It's no big deal. They did this once before—last week. It'll just take a second for Warscape to cross-reference the sensors in the area." Sure enough, within a few seconds, the blips started to disappear from the map.

"See what I mean?" the Admiral said. After half a minute only one pink blip remained. It shifted back to red and the label reappeared.

"Now, watch. One of our F-18X fighters will turn this guy around."

On routine patrol, Michael Dawson flew at thirty thousand feet, near the Paracel Islands in the South China Sea.

Quiet afternoon, he thought. Then he shook his head. *Don't get complacent, Michael. Keep your eyes open. Listen to the radio. You never know.* He turned back to the video screens, gauges, and meters that filled the cockpit of his highly customized F-18X Hornet. Suddenly his radio crackled and came to life.

"Sierra one-two-niner, Sierra one-two-niner, bandit at Lanky, one hundred and twenty, one zero zero, thirty angels."

The control center used a technique called bull's-eye control. It referenced everything around a single, well-known point called a bull's-eye. Control would give the position of the enemy aircraft, called a bandit, from the bull's-eye. The position would specify the degrees off due north of the enemy aircraft, providing the range in miles and the altitude in thousands of feet called angels.

Lanky was the code name for the aircraft carrier displayed on his screen.

"Roger that, Command. Sierra one-two-niner in pursuit." Michael Dawson banked left, turning the plane. He toggled the radar switch on and off.

The radar sent out several short bursts of energy, lasting no longer than a microsecond. These invisible flashes swept the sky in front of the plane, changing frequencies each time in case the enemy was listening. At the speed of light, the energy radiated out and bounced off its target before returning to the plane's radar. The radar then sent out one more quick burst of energy to the target.

The radar used the fighter's on-board computer to compare the two signals. It detected the slight change in aperture to the Chinese fighter and constructed a 3D image of the enemy plane. It then compared this image to a list of known aircraft. Instantly, the computer determined the make of the aircraft: a Chinese Fighter called an SU-27 Flanker. A red blip appeared on Michael's radar screen along with this information. The entire operation was completed in less than a tenth of a second.

Michael noted the enemy's course, displayed on the radar screen. He adjusted his heading accordingly, planning for an intercept. The Chinese fighter inched along at about six hundred miles an hour.

No need to waste fuel by using afterburners to catch this guy. He eased the throttle right against the stops. Cruising just under Mach One, at around seven hundred miles an hour, Michael glanced around. The tiniest spec in the sky, the subtlest hint, could be a missile or worse. Late afternoon, he still had good visibility, twenty miles at least, but he saw nothing.

Michael debated whether to tickle his radar again to pinpoint the Chinese fighter's exact location. Perhaps the Chinese fighter had changed course. Michael shook his head. *No, be patient.* Even with the advanced radar system, the enemy still might detect an energy burst. Michael wanted surprise on his side. He would rely on his good old eyesight to spot the Chinese fighter.

There! He found his target, about twelve miles ahead and five thousand feet below him. He descended like a hawk, using gravity to accelerate past Mach One. The plane slipped smoothly through the sound barrier. Carefully, Michael pulled up behind the Chinese fighter. He then flipped his weapon console and immediately obtained missile lock.

The Flanker dipped for an instant, obviously surprised.

Michael grinned. He almost could taste the pilot's anxiety. Nothing said *good morning* like the tone from a missile lock. Michael keyed his radio.

"You … in the Flanker … this is the United States Navy. We are operating under the authority of the ASEAN command.

Please turn your aircraft around and return to Woody Island."

Michael waited for a couple of seconds.

No response.

Cocky son-of-a-bitch! He keyed his radio again. "Flanker, you are in violation of International Law and the Chinese War Treaty. Please turn your aircraft around or you will be fired upon."

Again, silence.

Michael glanced at his gauges—only one hundred miles to the *U.S.S. Elliot*, the outermost ship in the carrier battle group. Within minutes, the Flanker's long-range missiles would be in range of the carrier. "Command, this is Sierra one-two-niner. Bandit refuses to yield, over."

"Sierra one-two-niner, go weapons hot, but make it clean."

"Roger, Command." Michael could not believe it. The Chinese fighter did not even flinch. *The pilot thinks I won't shoot him down! Well, I guess he's half right.*

With a flick of his finger, Michael lifted the guard and threw a switch, arming the HERF gun, a High-Energy Radio Frequency weapon. Michael checked the status light. It was red, charged, and ready. He squeezed the trigger, holding it down.

The gun bathed the Flanker in a burst of invisible but intense radio waves, the same energy used by the radio but much, much stronger. Michael imaged the Chinese fighter's radio going off the air and its cockpit lighting up as every warning light came on. He held the trigger tightly. By now, the fighter must have suffered catastrophic and complete systems failure as every piece of electronic hardware in his plane went dead. Navigation, communication, and weapons would all be down. Michael watched as the Chinese fighter's engines sputtered to a stop. Its nose dipped toward the earth.

He let go of the trigger. The trigger guard automatically snapped shut. Michael watched as the Chinese fighter appeared to creep toward him, an illusion caused as the Flanker slowed relative to him.

Gently at first, the Chinese fighter descended. Soon it picked up speed and plummeted nose first into the ocean below. Michael waited until the Flanker hit the water before keying his radio.

"Command, splash one bandit, apparent total systems failure. Imagine that!" Michael grinned.

"Copy that, Sierra one-two-niner. Any survivors?"

"Negative. That's a negative. Pilot failed to eject."

In Warscape, the red blip disappeared from the map.

"Is it gone?" Ed Davis asked.

"Yes, he's gone." The Admiral frowned. *What are the Chinese doing? That's the second test of their defenses in a week.*

The Chinese were not usually this rash. They are up to something, he thought.

43

TO: Steve Donovan
FROM: Allison Hwang
SUBJECT: No recall

Steve,

Davis found out about Syzygy, fired me, and
has refused to issue the recall order. He
didn't tell me why. I think I told you my
mother is a reporter. I'm going to use her
as a resource to try to track down Syzygy.
Hope your day is going better than mine.

Love,
Allison

Steve read Allison' message again. Opening a portal to DARPA,
Steve stepped through. It was pitch black except for a narrow lit path. He followed it. After a few feet, a large chamber to
his left lit up. Inside a cave, honed from granite, stood a bank of
holograms. Stacked twenty holograms tall and at least forty holograms wide, the bank created a wall of movement and sound, each

individual image displaying a dark recess of the Internet. Before this wall, an army of analysts watched the images and took notes.

Show and tell, tax dollars on display, Steve thought.

After ten feet the chamber turned dark. The path ended at a six-foot wide hexagon with DARPA's logo etched into the center of it. Stepping onto the logo, rose quartz walls materialized around him. Each one displayed a living mural. One contained a group of business people.

Steve found Ed Davis in the picture and touched his face.

An automated secretary answered. "State your name and business."

"Steve Donovan, Nexus recall."

"One moment, please. Mr. Davis is currently offline. I will page him for you."

A few minutes later, the wall he touched disappeared, opening into a porcelain-looking room. Rounded edges connected the bleach-white walls, floor, and ceiling. In the center of the room, Ed Davis sat behind a desk. He stood and extended his hand. "Hello, Mr. Donovan."

Steve shook it.

"I was hoping Vinnie could meet us, but he's not available."

"Vinnie Russo?" Steve said, taking a seat.

"That's right." Ed said, sitting down.

Steve nodded. "We need to issue a recall."

"It's not that simple."

"It's not? Five people are dead."

Ed ran a hand across his graying goatee. "I'm going to be honest with you. Allison Hwang kept me in the dark. I only learned about everything this morning."

"I don't understand. How does that change anything?"

"There are things you're not privy to. You do not have the big picture here."

"Five people are dead. Whatever else …"

"There's more at stake here than a few innocent victims." He sighed. "It's a misconception that people at the top are free to do what they want. There's actually less freedom up here to make the right decision. Circumstances and alliances determine most of my decisions before I'm even aware of them.

"Compromise and diplomacy is the name of the game. You're still young, but Winston Churchill put it best: If a man is not a liberal at eighteen, he has no heart. If he is not a conservative by the time he is thirty-five, he has no mind." Ed laughed.

"What's your point?"

He leveled a finger at Steve. "My point, young man, is that the President decided to keep this quiet. *Anything* that compromises the Warscape system, including your Nexus Transporter, is to be kept a secret. At least for the next two weeks until the hardware fix is available."

"Why?"

Ed sighed. "Where should I start? Do you remember Desert Storm?"

Steve shrugged.

"The numbers escape me now. I think the Iraqis outnumbered us on the ground ten to one; yet we whomped them. Do you know why?" Ed paused. "Air superiority and superior information. We found and stuck them first before they could move into range."

Steve shifted in his chair.

"They used Soviet weaponry, supplied by the Chinese. When the Iraqis lost, the Chinese took notice. You see, up until then the Chinese won wars by attrition. They thought that if they threw enough men and weaponry into battle, they would win. Desert storm changed their perception. You know what they learned?"

Steve shrugged.

"It's all about seeming and being, appearance and reality, truth and lies; in a word, surprise. And surprise depends on information, having a better understanding of the battlefield than your opponent does.

"In the China War, the Chinese discovered information was more important than air superiority. Now, our cold war is based on information, and that is based on military intelligence. Our most important source of tactical intelligence is embodied in DARPA's Warscape.

"Warscape is a complete map of the battlefield. Every building, piece of equipment, and man in the U.S. armed forces is outfitted with a GPS unit. At all times the Unified Command knows where their forces are. We monitor the enemy using surveillance satellites, radar, sonobuoys, and unmanned vehicles on land, under the sea, and in the air. Yet, without a way to *see* and integrate the data, Warscape was useless. Allison Hwang contacted Austin Wheeler. In exchange for eighty-two million dollars in covert weapons sales, he gave us the technical schematics to the Nexus."

Steve's mouth dropped open. "How much?"

"Eighty-two million."

"So let me get this straight. Austin got millions in exchange for *my* Nexus design and I'm supposed to be happy because it's for the good of the country?"

Ed shook his head. "It's also what saved your company. Why do you think we approved the Nexus prematurely? It wasn't for altruistic reasons, I assure you. It was part of the deal Allison made with Austin.

"I don't understand. You haven't said anything that would prevent us from alerting the public about Syzygy?"

Ed sighed. "Think, Steve! It's our eyes and ears now. If the Chinese find out what Syzygy knows, they could take out Warscape. We would be blind. That's why we cannot go public, at least not until the fix is available."

"What if the Chinese are behind Syzygy?"

"If so, we're screwed anyway, but we don't think this is the case. The PLA, China's military, wouldn't sit around like this. It's much more likely that Syzygy is a terrorist organization."

"So for the next few days you're just going to let people die?"

"It's a choice between a few more victims or our national security. As I told you, circumstances have already made our decision for us."

Steve shook his head.

"If it makes you feel any better, this is nothing new. In World War II, the English cracked the Germans' secret code. Yet when the British found out that one of their cities, Coventry, was going to be bombed, they did nothing. They realized that if they did anything the Germans would know they had broken the code. Their only choice was to sacrifice Coventry.

"Yet by sacrificing a few citizens they kept the Germans from discovering their secret. In the end, knowing where the Germans were on D-DAY was the beginning of the end. The sacrifice of Coventry allowed them to win the war and save their nation. You see? I'm afraid we have no choice," Ed said, glancing at the time. "Vinnie should have been here by now. I'll have him contact you about tracking down Syzygy. Do you have any questions before I let you go?"

"No questions, just a statement. Your organization dug its own hole when it bent the rules and stole my invention. If Syzygy gets out of hand, I will sacrifice a few Islands to save lives."

"Lets hope it doesn't come to that."

Steve exited VR. He still sat at his desk, but morning had become night. The whole house was dark and cold. Rain pattered on the roof. Something banged in the hallway. What was it? Ah, the busted front door. It swung on its hinges and banged against the door jam.

He removed his Nexus and saw Allison, still online.

A flash of lightning illuminated her. He could not mistake the contortions, her shoulder hunched, arms rigid at her sides, hands curled inward at the wrists. "Allison!" He ripped her Nexus off.

She lashed out, swinging her arms as she regained control of her body.

"It's okay!" Steve grabbed her wrists.

She tore them free and pushed him away.

He put his hands up just in time to block a kick. "Allison!"

She stopped. "Steve?"

"It's me."

"Steve!" She reached out and hugged him tightly.

"What is it? What happened?"

"I found him. It's Ron. Ron's the one."

"What?"

"He attacked me; took me to the beach where Syzygy killed Camille. How did he know about the beach?" she cried.

"It can't be. Syzygy attacked Ron and I this morning."

"You don't understand ... they ..." Allison's voice trailed off.

He looked down. She lay still in his arms, her skin blanched and clammy, and her breathing shallow. He gently shook her.

"Allison?" She did not stir. Grabbing her Nexus, he pressed 911.

Apocalypse

"Technology is a two-edged sword, enabling progress while fostering dependence. The two go hand in hand. They cannot be extricated from one another. Technological advances make everyone in society vulnerable, dependent on the same umbilical cord. And anyone can sever this link. Thus, if a society does not operate with truth and integrity, faith and trust are lost and the dependence cannot be afforded. The technology will extinguish itself and the dependent society will disappear."

—Michael M. Collins. Portal Sphere Architect, 2005.

44

Steve entered Allison's hospital room. She sat propped up by a couple of pillows, watching television. He awkwardly held out a collection of yellow roses, baby's breath, and fern wisps arranged in a small vase.

"Um, these are for you," he said, placing them next to her on the nightstand. She turned and smiled, glancing first at him and then the flowers.

"It's been a while since I've done anything like this. I hope they're okay."

She smiled. "They're beautiful."

He sat down next to her at the head of the bed and stroked her cheek with the back of his hand. "Are you okay?"

She leaned forward into a sitting position. "I'm perfectly fine, you know. They're just keeping me cooped up here until the MRIs come back."

He nodded.

"Did you find Ron?" she asked.

He shook his head. "I don't think he's involved. I've known Ron almost a year and …"

"How can you say that? He attacked me and changed into

Syzygy!"

"Syzygy must have used his alias and framed him. You met Ron. You saw how technophobic he was. There's no way he could be involved in this."

Allison remained silent.

"Up to this point Syzygy has been very sly. He's covered his tracks. He isn't stupid enough to give himself away that easily. Think of how he used Xi Quang."

She shook her head. "But there is something else. I found something ... something in the log ... I can't remember."

Steve became worried and placed a hand on her shoulder. "It'll come back to you in time. Why don't you rest up today."

She grinned. "Nice try."

"Why are you doing all this?"

She met his gaze. "You, of all people, know why. My career is my life. If I catch Syzygy, Davis will have to hire me back."

"Can't you let it go?"

She shook her head.

"Allison ..."

"I can't, not yet anyway."

He rubbed his jaw line, thinking of how to dissuade her. Finally, he sighed. "Just don't use your Nexus, okay?"

She laughed. "Steve, are telling me not to use your product?"

"I'm serious."

She frowned. "I have no choice. I left my Portal Sphere at home in Southern Cal."

"Then use Brooke's."

She nodded. "Okay, I will."

Her gaze melted him. He leaned over and kissed her. As he wrapped his arms around her, his Nexus vibrated on his hip. He glanced at the LED readout. Vinnie was paging him.

"I've got to go."

"You be careful," she said.

"I will."

He walked to door and turned back. "One more thing. Tell

your mother to meet me at the Children's Hospital for the Nexus Healer announcement."

She cocked her head. "Why?"

"I might have a story for her, depending on how things go." He left the room.

She withdrew a rose, closed her eyes, and breathed in. The scent soothed her frayed nerves. She hoped Steve was right about Ron. Everything would be fine.

Steve walked through the portal into Vinnie's virtual office, a plain, twenty-foot cube with the word *Microsoft®* stenciled into the floor. Vinnie had not customized the room at all.

"So your modified Signal Amplifier will protect you?"

Steve spun around, startled to see Vinnie. "Uh, yeah, except for his secondary attack."

"What secondary attack?"

He remembered being stuck inside Syzygy, a pod of muscle flowing around him. He shuddered. "He can spike the sensory levels."

"Is there any way to defend against it?"

"Not currently, and it would take several months to develop a fix, but I don't think it's lethal."

"That's reassuring. When can I get the new hardware?"

"Another two weeks."

He laughed. "That's great!" He pulled out the copy of the phaser, the one Steve had used to try to commit suicide. "Does this work against Syzygy?"

Steve thought for a moment. He never did finish the code.

"Yeah, but I'll need to make a modification so it takes out Syzygy instead of the victim."

"Computer, display the phaser's source code." He scanned the code and found what he was looking for. "Computer, recursively follow the link to the end before initiating the overload program." He turned to Vinnie. "Now it should work."

"Can you find him in cyber space?" Vinnie asked.

"I don't know. We need to find his persona to use the weapon. Somehow, he is hiding within the network links. Last night he impersonated Ron Fisher and attacked Allison at Nexus Corp."

"Maybe this will help." Vinnie opened a file.

Several orbs popped out and levitated in front of them. On each was the face of a Nexus' victim.

"I downloaded the logs from each victim's Nexus. Can they tell you where he is?" Vinnie asked.

"Maybe," he said, opening the orb, displaying Skip Harvey. A wall of platinum three feet wide and two feet high materialized, levitating in front of him. It was molded into a three-square grid, each representing Skip's Nexus Site Log, Core File, and System Log. Glancing at the grid, Steve pressed the Site Log. His gaze gravitated to the last entry. It was jumbled, a random collection of letters, numbers, and symbols: s#@~#d$f9e*r8*.

"The last entry is garbled, just like Camille's Site Log. Syzygy's attack must be corrupting the log when he kills off the user. He's probably aborting the portal program before it can finish writing the entry to the Nexus' flash memory."

"So the Portal program opens portals to other Internet sites?" Vinnie asked.

Steve nodded. "Syzygy uses it to hop from Nexus to Nexus. And he covers his tracks by trashing the log."

"Are you sure? Did you check all of the logs?"

It was a fair question, Steve thought. He opened the Site Logs from the other orbs. Each case was the same; the last entry was garbled.

"Appears so ..." Steve said as he leaned forward to close the logs.

"Try putting the last entries of the Site Logs next to each other," Vinnie said.

Steve shrugged. It was a waste of time, but he did not feel like arguing with a techno-phobic detective.

"Computer, rearrange these logs, placing them next to one another in one row, aligning them on their last entry."

The Site Logs disappeared, one by one, replaced by a wall of water. The wall broke into five sections, displaying a Site Log on each.

Steve sensed something. He looked from one garbled entry to the next. He saw it. Although it appeared garbled, the last entry was the same in every case. *Shit!* How could he have missed this? The entry was not garbled at all. It was the site's name. An unconventional name, but a valid one nevertheless!

"Not bad, eh?" Vinnie said.

"Computer, does the last site in the log use another name or alias?" Steve asked.

"Nexus Corporation."

Steve stepped back. "What? Please repeat."

"Nexus Corporation."

He remembered the attack on the Nexus site and what he told Ron: "An undetected virus is like a spy in an organization. Once accepted as one of the fold, you cannot find him without making everyone a suspect." A flood of other images came back to him, connecting bits of information. Allison's warning about Ron. Ron's comment about how Brooke slowed him down. Syzygy's attack of both Camille and Brook out of the millions of Nexus users. He remembered Ron's prediction of Austin's death and how Ron had known the definition of the word syzygy. Perhaps Ron *was* the spy.

"Computer, open a portal to Nexus Corporation."

"What are you doing?"

"Finding a killer." Steve stepped through.

Steve quickly scanned the lobby's iridescence walls, marble floor, and high, domed ceiling. *Too much territory; the backdoor could be anywhere.*

"Charlie!"

Charlie came running from around the fountain, tail wagging, his nails clicking against the marble floor.

Vinnie came through the portal and walked to Steve. He pointed to Charlie. "What the hell is that?"

"An Internet guide, sort of a portable interface."

"No, I mean is it a cat on steroids or what?"

Steve shook his head. "I had a dog like this once."

Charlie barked incessantly.

"Shut up!" Vinnie yelled over the high-pitched shrieks. He turned to Steve. "This has got to work. I hate this case."

Steve pulled out his copy of the phaser. "You should switch to your Portal Sphere. You're not safe in here."

Vinnie shook his head. "I need the mobility."

Steve nodded. He closed his eyes and remembered the lobby after the hackers had vandalized it. He walked to a spot near the wall.

"What is it?" Vinnie asked, following him and pulling out his copy of the phaser.

"Charlie, enable speech and expose the data stream."

They stepped back as a line of marble floor tiles dissolved into sand, exposing a stream of water.

"Charlie, do you detect any new ephemeral branches in the stream?"

Wagging his tail, he ran up and stuck his head into the torrent. Pulling back, he turned to Steve. "There's a recent branch, a week old."

"What is it?" Vinnie asked.

"He's here."

"Syzygy?"

Steve nodded. "We're too big to fit through. Computer, reduce our size ninety-five percent."

In an instant, the room expanded around them. Steve stared into the raging river and then glanced at Charlie. Charlie had grown to the size of a mammoth. He rolled on his side so they could reach his back. Steve grabbed Charlie's mane and turned to Vinnie. "Hop on!"

"God, I miss reality," Vinnie muttered, taking up a position next to Steve.

They held on as Charlie rolled onto his stomach and dove into the stream. The current carried them through a cement trench. Marble tiles zipped by above them. Suddenly, the wall, floor, and ceiling disappeared. Only the cord of water remained, surrounded by pitch black. The cord diverged into four glowing streams. They took the left branch.

The stream turned, flowing straight up. Seconds later they emerged in a pool. Above and below Steve saw at least twenty other streams. Charlie swam forward. The water glowed a Tahoe blue. Lines of light danced at the edges of the pool where water touched void.

Steve adjusted his grip on Charlie's mane. "Charlie, find the new link."

Charlie swam into one of the streams. The water turned salty. Moving forward, the stream broadened and the void beneath the stream turned into small, white rocks. A surge carried them the rest of the way in, depositing them onto a tropical beach.

"Computer, restore our size."

Slowly, they returned to normal size. Steve scanned the beach. Sun and salt had cleansed the sand and bleached it white. A few meters above the beach palm trees and tropical plants swayed in the wind. The sun hovered just above the horizon, stretching streaks of red and orange across the sky. Two monolithic pillars of rock offshore cast long shadows across the beach.

Vinnie spun slowly around. "Is he here?"

"Charlie, do you detect Syzygy?" Steve asked.

"No."

Steve put the phaser back in his pocket.

"He probably knows we are here, but I think I can hide us. Charlie, I need you to run these codes on each of our Nexuses."

Steve handed Charlie a sheet of paper. Charlie took it in his mouth and opened a number of windows on Steve's Nexus. The page contained a short series of codes:

```
VirtTerm::PhysicalAppearance::sight=>Set()=fi
lter(CURRENT);
VirtTerm::PhysicalAppearance::sound=>Set()=fi
lter(CURRENT);
VirtTerm::PhysicalAppearance::scent=>Set()=fi
lter(CURRENT);
VirtTerm::PhysicalAppearance::feel=>Set(NER
VE ARRAY)= filter(CURRENT);
VirtTerm::PhysicalAppearance::taste=>Set()=fi
lter(CURRENT);
VirtTerm::PhysicalAppearance::gravity=>Set()
=filter(CURRENT);
```

After he was done, Charlie moved on to Vinnie.

"The VR server requests information from our Nexuses each time someone looks at us. This block will prevent other people from seeing us," Steve said.

Vinnie nodded and sat down on the sand. "Let me know when he arrives."

45

The map looks fine. I don't see any problems," Scott said, turning to Wayne. The flicking lights from a hundred virtual screens reflected off their faces. Wayne ran a hand across the black marble counter that stretched between them and the stacked consoles.

"The response center was emphatic. All of Southern California has lost connectivity to the Internet."

"I don't see it," Scott said, searching the images on the screens. One of them displayed the time: 5:08 p.m. EST.

Wayne chuckled. "Like clockwork, eh? Eight minutes earlier we would've been off the hook."

Scott nodded. They handled all after-hour calls.

"So what do you want to do boss?"

He smirked at Wayne's 'boss' comment. In reality they were peers, Network Consultants working for the Internet Regulatory branch of DARPA; however, in order to justify the positions, one of them had to take the title of supervisor. Scott had picked the short straw and took the title, along with the longer hours and the administrative workload.

That was two years ago, and in the fast-paced networking industry, two years was an eternity. It was time enough to teach Scott to question everything that came out of the response center.

"Well, bloody hell! Did you apply the three prefab solutions?"

"Of course."

Scott referred to the three prepackaged solutions that worked for almost any network problem. The first solution was to wait. Most network problems were short-lived, caused by flaky equipment or by an inept engineer pulling the wrong cable. These problems resolved themselves. All they had to do was wait.

Some issues did not simply go away. For these, a second, equally brainless solution existed—turning off and on whatever equipment experienced the trouble. Resetting the equipment in this fashion forced everything to resynchronize. This solved an additional nine percent of the problems. That left the pesky final one percent. These problems did not die easily. They required research. Yet transferring them to the response center could solve even these. Bureaucracy would swallow the problem and hide it forever.

Scott liked these three rules: wait, reset, or pass the buck. They solved everything, and you never had to understand what was actually going on. These three rules alone could have skated him through a government career. Unfortunately, like Wayne, Scott was an expendable contractor, not tenured employee. Of course, that is why DARPA had hired them in the first place.

"Did they say which node had the problem?"

"No, that would be too useful."

Scott reverted to his own first law of troubleshooting. "What changed?"

"Nothing, boss."

"Are you sure?"

"Yep, I checked all the orders and change requests. Nothing was scheduled this weekend. It's a blackout period." Wayne said.

"What about the audit system? Has anything moved?" Scott referred to the CoolAlerts System. It kept track of the health and physical location of all the equipment.

CoolAlerts periodically polled each system's internal GPS chip. This chip pinpointed the equipment's exact location. They no longer flew around the country every six months, auditing the network. If the equipment "grew legs" and walked away, they would see it on the console screens. Theft was a non-issue. With CoolAlerts, the two of them could manage the entire national network.

Wayne scanned the CoolAlerts' map. He shook his head. "Boss, everything is green. Nothing has moved."

"So it's the real thing? We've got a bona fide problem then?" Scott said.

"Sure looks like it. Mark your calendar. We're finally going to earn our money today."

"Computer, display the expanded CoolAlerts Internet map."

The room disappeared, replaced by a large topographical map of the United States, marred by intersecting lines of light. They levitated a hundred feet above it. Scott took it in at a glance.

Littered across the map at the intersecting lines of light were hundreds of large glass domes, representing Internet hubs across the country. They were all green.

Strung between the hubs, rays of light represented communication links. Each link, like the site's color, fluctuated between green, yellow, and red. Most of the lines glowed neon green, indicating nominal traffic levels. Between Tampa and Orlando, the link shifted periodically into yellow and then back to green. Scott already knew about that problem. The link was congested and suffered sporadic sluggishness. He saw no red lines. Everything was up and running.

"Another false alarm?" Wayne asked.

"Perhaps; but we can't be sure. This is a new version of the CoolAlerts software. It might have missed something." Scott thought for a moment. "Pull up a history map. Maybe it's an intermittent problem."

"What's the matter, you crippled, boss?" Wayne said.

"Byte me, Wayne."

Wayne laughed. "Computer, display the last two hours of map history and play it at sixty times normal speed."

The map blinked out for an instant and reappeared. Above the state of Washington, a clock displayed Pacific Standard Time. It ticked away the minutes.

"Do you see anything, boss?"

"Shh!" Scott said, watching the map intently. He did not dare blink. He could miss it, but he saw nothing. Only the connection between Tampa and Orlando changed, the green and yellow creating a strobe effect. Something flickered near Los Angeles.

"Wait!"

"What did you see?" Wayne asked.

"I don't know. Something in Southern Cal. Computer, back up one hour and replay."

They watched the LA-San Diego region intently.

"What was that, boss?" Wayne asked.

Scott shook his head. The dome representing Ventura simply disappeared. That could not happen. If the site lost its communication link, it would simply turn red. It would never take the site out completely. How else could you see if something was wrong?

"Probably a software bug. Like you said, the software is new."

"Computer, pull up the production map," Scott said.

The map flickered out and came back. Ventura was still missing.

"Where is the bloody thing?" Scott asked.

Wayne rubbed his neck. "Well, if there's a problem in Ventura, we definitely aren't going to see it."

"Call the response center. Get some names. Find out who complained about the problem. Tell 'em not to screw up this time, and get the goddamn name of the router. We're flying blind here. I'm going to step in for a closer look."

"You're pulling rank again? Come on! Let me play for once," Wayne said.

"Do you want to switch titles? Fill out all the reports, attend meetings …"

Wayne shook his head. "Alright, alright. I'm going." He opened a portal and floated through.

"Computer, place me on the Ventura site."

"I'm sorry, but no site with that name exists."

"Bloody hell! Okay, you stupid computer, place me on Thousand Oaks then."

Scott slowly drifted down and landed a couple of yards away from where the Ventura dome had been. He walked to the spot.

"Computer, was there a site where I'm standing right now?"

"Yes."

"What is its name?"

"The entry in the database is corrupted."

"Computer, can you open a portal to the site?"

"Yes." A portal opened and Scott stepped through.

He appeared in an empty, white room. The disembodied voice of the Ventura Site's security program chimed in. "You're entering a secure site. Unauthorized access is prohibited. Please indicate your name and password. This information will be recorded."

"Scott Harken, Network God."

"Welcome, Scott. You're using monitor one of one." The room dissolved into the network control room in Ventura. Through the remote sensors of the robot, a steady hum of electronics and flashing of lights greeted him. He surveyed row after row of equipment. In front of one of the isles, a couple of floor panels had been removed and set aside, revealing a tangle of wires below the raised floor.

"Bloody hell, Wayne," Scott muttered, replacing the floor tiles. Only they had access into this room, and he sure as hell didn't leave the tiles like that.

He walked down the first row of equipment, scanning the racks, checking for status lights. Everything was green—no reds or yellows anywhere. Maybe one of the LCDs burned out. He walked down the isle again, checking for the obvious: powered off machines, open ports, or disconnected cables. Again, he found nothing.

Maybe it was not a hardware problem. Perhaps it was logical. What if more than the Ventura site was missing? If the whole map was corrupted, the problem might have propagated to the network software that routed the traffic.

"Computer, please run diagnostics on the OSPF and BGP software health for each router."

"I'm sorry. I cannot comply with your request."

"Computer, activate privileged access mode."

"Please confirm your password."

"Network God. Computer, change perspective to Ventura Site."

The room transformed again. Spheres like dim stars appeared around him. Each sphere was labeled, representing a piece of equipment. Green laser-like rays of light connected them together, weaving a complex lattice. From this matrix, stray light rays lanced out to distant constellations of spheres, appearing like galaxies. These represented the other sites.

One of the stars near him, labeled Ventura Border Router Number Eight, grew. The stars surrounding it drifted closer, caught in its gravity well.

Now that's odd. "Computer, change perspective to Ventura Border Router Number Eight."

The scene changed. A different set of stars, this time representing programs, materialized. They similarly communicated on rays of light. The distant galaxies now represented other nodes at the Ventura site.

The stars drifted toward a single point. The force dragged Scott as well.

What in the bloody hell is going on? The map was not supposed to move! *Wayne must be messing with it; but he knows better than that. I'm still inside!*

The gravity well grew stronger. The stars swirled around the well, taking Scott with them, spiraling down.

"Computer, expand my perspective up one level."

Nothing happened.

"Computer, change my perspective to the Ventura site."

Again, nothing. The swirl turned into a vortex.

"Computer …"

The stars collapsed to a single point, and then sucked him in.

Scott landed hard on the sand. Someone dropped on top of him. He shoved them off and rolled to his feet. Looking around he did not recognize the beach or the woman kneeling before him.

Cloaked in a scarlet robe, she stood slowly. She studied him with bright, green eyes.

"Bloody hell! What kind of hacker are you?"

"The worst kind," she said, slipping the robe off her shoulders and letting it drop to the ground. She was naked underneath.

"That may work with the younger …"

She jumped aside.

What the bloody hell? He was unaware that Vinnie Russo had just fired a shot at her.

Steve turned to Vinnie. "Can he see us?"

"Don't know!"

Syzygy stared directly at Vinnie.

"Shit!" Steve dove aside, away from Vinnie, and fired at Syzygy. Syzygy pulled back, dodging Steve's shot. He lunged toward Vinnie. Vinnie jumped aside but not quickly enough. Syzygy liquefied and raced across the sand, washing over Vinnie like a wave, enveloping him. It quickly solidified into a fleshy cocoon.

"Damn it!" Steve fired. Syzygy pulled back and the shot hit Vinnie.

"Shit!" Steve swore. "Charlie, reset Vinnie's connection." It kicked him off the Internet. Steve was alone.

Syzygy stepped forward.

Steve pulled the trigger.

Syzygy sidestepped and lunged, enveloping him. The fleshy muscle constricted around Steve and knocked the wind out of him. He gasped. A tentacle slipped into his mouth and slithered down his throat. He fought the pain and panic as it tore at his lungs. "This isn't real," he said.

Syzygy retracted.

Steve dropped to the sand, kicked, and rolled to his feet. He fired but Syzygy was already frozen.

"Got 'em!" Vinnie yelled, stepping out from behind Syzygy.

"How'd you get back in?"

"I used the Portal Sphere." Vinnie placed a hand on his shoulder. "And I even hit the right target."

Steve dropped to the sand, catching his breath. He looked across the ocean. Waves crashed on the beach, spraying a thin mist into the air while sea gulls skimmed the surf, looking for crabs and fish. It was so peaceful, caught in a perpetual twilight, seconds before the sun dipped below the horizon, the sky flushed to a permanent red while a soft breeze blew from the east. The air felt warm and soothing. It was hard to believe that so many had died here. It was harder to believe it was all over.

Steve imagined Syzygy convulsing back in reality. The thought only filled him with a sense of loss. He would give anything to have Brooke back.

A red light flashed in Steve's peripheral vision. He glanced at the time. The Nexus Healer announcement was in an hour. He needed to get ready.

46

Allison approached the front desk in the lobby of Nexus Corporation using Brooke's Portal Sphere's headset and gloves. She felt edgy. Even if Ron was not Syzygy, Syzygy was here and might have other attacks. She gave a reassuring pat to her copy of the phaser resting inside a virtual pocket.

"May I help you?" Jan said.

"I need to speak to Mr. Fisher."

"Good morning!" a voice said next to her.

She turned and Ron came into view. "You're going to have to come with me, Mr. Fisher."

He smirked. "Really, why?"

"Assault."

"Assault?" He appeared more amused than shocked.

Guilty as hell. "Can you explain why someone named Syzygy is logged on here?"

"What? I'm afraid that isn't true. Jan, can you give Ms. Hwang a list of people currently logged on this site?"

Allison shook her head. "That won't be necessary. I've already checked. He's not listed."

"I see. Here but not here."

"This isn't a game. He attacked me. Now, if you will please come with me."

"He attacked you here?"

"That's what I said."

"Then I'm afraid I can't go with you."

"Either you voluntarily come with me now for questioning or we'll physically detain you."

"I'm sorry, but you see, this server is physically located in the Netherlands and according to International law you're first going to have to extradite me to the United States."

"That's bullshit! You're an American Citizen. The server might be in the Netherlands but you're logged on somewhere in the United States."

"Let me explain it to you. The crime you're investigating was committed on this machine. This machine is located in the Netherlands. Thus, the crime occurred there. They get first dibs. That's the law. It's not my fault you didn't do your homework." Ron walked away.

Her mind raced. What could she do? Steve's weapon! He had modified it from the Sensory Isolator, which could isolate a user's VR experience to a particular perspective, to a single sense like sight or scent.

"Computer, pull up the phaser."

It appeared before her.

"Computer, can you revert the phaser back to its original state?"

"Yes."

"Computer, please do so."

The device transformed into a Sensory Isolator before her eyes.

"Computer, how do I set up this device to isolate a sense?"

"Simply state the sense you want to isolate."

"Can I set it to turn off all sensory inputs?"

"Yes."

"Computer, do so."

"Command accepted."

"Computer, place me in front of Ron Fisher."

She materialized a few feet in front of him. He frowned. "What is it now?"

"All right you win. Can we talk, somewhere private?" Allison asked.

"Do I need my lawyer?"

"No. I'm offering a truce."

"Really? Why?"

"Not here. Is there somewhere we can go?"

He smiled and regarded her for several seconds. Finally, he cocked his head and turned toward his office.

"Computer, have me follow Ron."

They went across the lobby, down a hall and into a back office. Ron sat down behind the desk. "This is a secure room. You can talk freely in here. Now what do you have in mind?"

"This!" She pulled out the weapon and fired.

"What the hell?" He mumbled incoherently, stumbling around, bumping repetitively against the desk and chair until he fell over. She knocked over a virtual bookcase to box him in.

Allison smiled. He could no longer see, hear, feel, smell, or taste anything. She had created the world's first VR-based sensory-deprivation weapon. Her days with the DIA taught her that sensory deprivation could break someone in a matter of hours, even someone like Mr. Fisher. She would let him sweat it for a while.

What happened? Ron thought. He sensed nothing—black, quiet, and still. Was he dead? No, that bitch had done something to him, somehow cut him off. Why? He knew the answer immediately. She wanted him to talk.

He fought down a stab of panic. What could he do? He had been in sensory deprivation tanks before, but this was different. It was not like the tanks. In the tanks you could not *feel* your body, but you still had your pulse, breathing, and maybe some ringing in your ears. With those, Ron would be able to get by for hours, perhaps even a day, without hallucinating, but in here, even these were gone.

Not only did he not *feel* his body, he could not even *locate* it. Conscience and void was everything. He was powerless.

Time passed, but he could not tell how long. It might have been only minutes or perhaps hours. He found his mind meandering through the events that brought him here. He regretted some of his choices. Could things have gone differently with Camille and Brooke?

Ron caught himself. He needed to control his thoughts. He could not let his mind wander. The bitch wanted him to do that—slip up and lose touch. He counted to focus his mind back on itself. One, two, three …. He counted up to one hundred, a thousand, then ten thousand. Something changed.

His mind felt a thing he could not identify, a sensation. Waves of relaxation flowed through him. Oh, god! He had lost count. Was it ten thousand? Maybe he would start over, but why was he counting? He could not remember.

A fog penetrated his thoughts, separating them. Like a calving iceberg, he felt his mind fragment. He watched as shards of thought drifted away into the blackness. They were distinct, not a part of himself. With each piece that disappeared, he forgot more and more. He relaxed, became more subdued. The whole experience felt strange. Thoughts became images.

An undertone began vibrating, a sensation of pure thought. It grew louder in his mind. It formed an alien hunger. The hunger took hold of him. He needed to sense something, anything; but nothing was there. How did he get here? Where was he? Ron could not remember. Panic ate away at him.

His eyes returned and he saw black. The black gradually opened up into a three-dimensional, empty, pitch-black space. Forms appeared, glowing lights. They swirled and formed a tunnel. The tunnel emitted an apocalyptic blue light. His hearing returned and he heard the welcomed sound of running water. His body returned and he found himself floating into the tunnel. The tunnel opened up. He rolled on the ground. He was back on Hainan.

The war had ended; they were going home. Ron glanced over

at Steve.

"Steve? Why are you here?"

"Where else would I be? How do you think you'll do it?" Steve asked.

"What do you mean?"

"Kill all those people using the Nexus?"

Ron laughed. "My friend, do you think I'm Syzygy? No, no! I just opened our site up to them. Man, they trashed it! Stupid mistake really. I should've checked things out first, but everything had to be done in such a rush."

"Why did you open it up?"

"For the Nexus schematics, of course."

"So who killed all those people?"

"I told you, *they* did! Well, except for Brooke."

Steve mouth dropped open. "What do you mean?"

"She slowed you down anyway. I figured if I popped her, you would pop Austin, but your ingenuity surprised even me! You got your girl to do it for you. Now that was cool. It was a simple matter to leave you in control of the company and the money."

Ron stopped speaking and regarded Steve. "Is something wrong? This is all Intel 101."

"Intel? Who do you work for?"

"I can't say."

"Can you at least tell me why you gave Syzygy the Nexus plans?"

"Lets just say not everyone will benefit from the President's plan for I2 Corp. Most of the agencies will be gutted, mine included. We realized the President's plan hinged on Warscape, which hinged on the Nexus, which happens to have a nasty bug. I just gave Syzygy knowledge of the bug.

"Things got out of control, though. Ideally, the media would have gotten word of the defect out earlier, publicizing Warscape's defect before anything worse could happen. I hadn't counted on Ms. Hwang. She really fucked things up—gave them all the power."

"Them? Who is *them*?"

"Syzygy."

"But who is Syzygy?"

Silence.

"Hey!" Allison yelled. "Can you hear me?"

Ron remained frozen.

Allison waited a few seconds. "Computer, why is Ron's alias frozen?"

"The user appears to have fallen asleep."

Damn! She remembered what the technician had said about Xi Quang. Ron had escaped.

At least she was one step closer.

47

Steve stepped through the portal into the Children's Hospital, an open room suspended in the sky just above the cloud line. The floor, walls, and ceiling were plain and white. All the surfaces were smooth with no distracting pictures, fixtures, rugs, or furniture. Still, the architecture was striking.

The room was shaped like a five-pointed star and had a sunken floor in its center. Full-length windows made up the room's walls, blending it into its heavenly backdrop. The ceiling was vaulted and domed, and although there were no light fixtures anywhere in the room, it was bathed evenly with a diffused white light.

Steve levitated several feet above the floor. He swam toward the floor but stayed in place.

"Don't be alarmed," a voice said. "If you want to move, simply say where you want to go, or point and tell the computer how far you want to travel."

Steve looked around and did not see anyone. "Are you the automated attendant?"

"Yes." A woman materialized, levitating in front of him. Unlike Jan, she had a full feminine frame, which sat crossed legged while suspended above the floor. Deep blue eyes and sandy blond hair complemented her inviting smile. Her manner was enticing, flirtatious, and it caused Steve's distant corporeal body to blush a little.

"I'm Jennifer. I'll familiarize you with this environment for the press conference." She took his hand and pointed to the center of the room saying, "Computer, thirty feet please." They moved to a position a few feet above the floor in the center of the room.

"Why can't we just walk?" Steve asked.

She smiled. "It's for the children, of course. Remember, some of them have been disabled from birth. They are not accustomed to moving their legs or arms."

"But no other site on the Internet allows you to move like this. Doesn't this limit them to just this site?"

Jennifer touched his hand. "Yes, you're correct; but Steve, there's another hurdle these children have to overcome that you're forgetting. Walking requires both the legs and the brain. The brain directs and controls what the legs do. The Nexus Transporter replaces their legs with virtual ones, but it cannot replace the region of their brains that controls walking. Just like the nervous system, the Nexus depends on the brain to direct and control their movements within VR, responding to the signals sent to and from the brain.

"Most of these children have either forgotten, or never learned how to walk. The area of the brain that controls walking is just as disabled as their bodies. This region needs to be retrained; they need to learn how to walk again, or perhaps for the first time. So, they often are just as disabled in VR using the Nexus Transporter as they are in reality using their own legs. Even in this virtual hospital they need assistance in moving around."

"Oh." Back in reality, Steve blushed.

Jennifer laughed. "It's not as bad as it sounds. In fact, it's the only reason why a virtual hospital works. The Nexus Healer solved the physical problem by replacing the function of the spinal cord, but it cannot train their brains. The Nexus Transporter enables them to relearn how to walk. The children can now learn to walk from their own homes using their own VR gear. They do not have to visit an actual hospital. You cannot begin to imagine what hope the Nexus Healer and the Nexus Transporter have given these children. We've been able to reach out and touch so many lives, thanks to you."

Jennifer's sincerity moved him.

"Pretty lifelike, huh, Steve?" Jamie said.

Steve turned abruptly.

"Sorry, didn't mean to startle you. I thought you'd be walking through your outline by now."

"Interesting choice of words," Jennifer said.

Jamie cringed. "Sorry. Let me start again. I'm Allison's mom, Jamie Hwang." She extended her hand.

Steve shook it.

"My daughter said you had something for me?"

Steve nodded, handing her a VR clip. "When I tell you to, I want you to broadcast this."

"What is it?"

"A Nexus recall announcement."

The recall would be played around the world. She understood this was her big break.

"I don't know what to say," she stammered.

He smiled. "Thank you is fine."

She hugged him. "Thanks."

Steve spent the remaining half hour before the conference reviewing the outline. As the time drew near, he moved into position, levitating behind a podium at the base of a star point. He faced the center of the room. Abruptly, Steve and the podium were bathed in a bright pool of light. Steve put the speech on a heads-up display, the words levitating two feet in front of him. Only he saw it. The speech would be fixed there, displaying two lines at a time, scrolling forward as he read, allowing him to make roaming eye contact. The audience grew as more and more people stepped through portals and joined the levitating crowd.

Steve sighed and glanced at the time: 12 p.m.

He felt a hand on his shoulder. Jennifer had reappeared.

"Don't worry. You'll be fine. Just be yourself. That's all they are looking for." She turned to the audience. "Welcome to the Virtual Children's Hospital. It is good to see so many supporters of the hospital assembled here today. Your hard work and financial support have helped create a miracle.

"When the Children's Hospital was founded two years ago, it had a goal: to ease the transition of disabled children into their new lifestyles. Today that vision has changed for the better, thanks to the Nexus Healer. Now, I'd like to introduce Steve Donovan, CEO of Nexus Corporation."

The room broke out into applause.

"Thank you," Steve said. He repeated these words several times before the applause died down.

"Good afternoon. It is a great pleasure to be here for the official Nexus Healer announcement. The VR industry is the most exciting industry in the world today. By connecting people together in virtual worlds over the Internet, we are changing the way people do business, the way people learn, and even the way that they entertain themselves. People are no longer limited to the reality into which they were born. Now, people can explore new perspectives, even those that don't exist in reality. They can live out their dreams in VR.

"VR is a fast-moving industry, faster than any other. Keeping up with these advances does not come cheap. It requires a huge investment from the entire industry. It's part of the reason you see Nexus Corporation expanding its research and development investment fifty percent each year. We see incredible opportunities here and we're investing in those areas.

"The marketplace has validated our direction. This was certainly true for the introduction of the Nexus Transporter. It was very exciting, and the success of this product around the Internet has been really quite phenomenal. It laid the foundation for a series of advances in user interface technology. At the heart of this revolution was the effectuater. The effectuater enabled, for the first time, true thought control."

Abruptly, the whine of a portal broke his concentration. Steve stumbled on his words. In the back of the room, he saw a figure step out. He saw only a silhouette, but it made his skin crawl. Could it be him? It couldn't be. The lighting in the room was playing tricks on his mind. Steve realized the crowd was waiting.

"Uh, the effectuater … the effectuater is the so called *brain interface* that revolutionized VR. With it, we are no longer tied to reality at all. Before the Nexus Transporter, we were limited to VR devices that fed our senses and captured our muscle movements. Today the Nexus Transporter bypasses the senses and muscles altogether and speaks directly to the brain. It allows quicker and more real images, sounds, and movement. It has enabled the addition of the elusive senses of smell and taste while tremendously enhancing the sense of gravity. The Nexus Transporter, to put it simply, is the next step in the human-machine interface."

"We developed a dream that went beyond the Internet, beyond the virtual realm. The *brain interface* solves a real-world problem. Across the globe, over five million people suffer from spinal cord injuries. Their minds and bodies are willing, yet the two cannot communicate, until now.

The room erupted into applause again. Steve looked back to where the figure had been, but it was gone. The applause died down. Steve returned to the speech.

"The Nexus Healer is able to create a bridge between the mind and body. It allows people to attain a degree of freedom they have either lost or never had—mobility. Here at the Children's Hospital we have pioneered this technique. The path to recovery is not easy, and the final work with the Nexus Healer must be done outside of VR. I would like to welcome our first pioneer, Sarah Applegate. She's the first of a new generation of recovered quadriplegics."

Steve's floodlight dimmed and reappeared in the star point next to him. It presented a three-dimensional bubble, a window into the real world. Inside this sphere was the image of a ten-year-old girl standing in the center of a playroom, wearing a thick headband and neck bracelet, which was the Nexus Healer. A nurse was waiting attentively a few feet to one side of her.

Sarah walked forward with the nurse monitoring her movements but providing no assistance. The crowd erupted into applause again. As it died down, Steve turned to face Sarah. "Sarah, tell us about your recovery."

"It wasn't easy. After the accident, I felt nothing below my chest. I relearned not only how to walk …"

Movement in the audience distracted Steve. *There!* In the back row, he saw the familiar shape again, but he could not be sure. He had to be sure. The script scrolling in front of him obscured his view. Then Steve realized the scrolling had stopped. He turned back to Sarah. She had finished answering his question.

Steve continued down the script, asking questions in turn, but he kept an eye on the stranger levitating in the back row. The conference concluded shortly and the room broke out into a standing ovation. Even with the script gone, Steve still could not see the figure clearly through the audience. After a minute the applause died. Portals opened and a few people left. Others raised their hands.

"Excuse me for a moment." Steve slipped out the phaser and pointed at the stranger. "One hundred feet," he said, and the computer sent him racing through the crowd. He stopped. Steve couldn't believe it. "You!"

Syzygy turned and regarded him dispassionately with his stoic green eyes. The ten or so remaining guests all turned to see the cause of the commotion. A sardonic smile played on Syzygy's face.

Click.

"Oh god!" Steve knew that sound. "Everyone get out of here!"

Syzygy's form shifted, turning to fluid.

"Ten feet up!" Steve shouted, rising straight up.

Steve looked down. Syzygy had jumped, stopping under him. His form changed briefly into a pod and then back. Syzygy glanced around left to right. No one had left. The crowd backed away from Syzygy as he scanned their faces. He was looking for him.

Steve took aim with his phaser.

Syzygy looked up.

Instantly, Steve was trapped in a fleshy cocoon, his arms pinned to his side. The walls of red muscle rolled over him as he struggled. His sense of balance went first. He was falling. Next, hot lines of fire etched their way up his arms from his hands as his vision exploded into a kaleidoscope of color. Steve groaned, feeling his stomach lurch in his distant corporeal body.

Jamie ran toward the pod. "Stop! Let him go. Tell us what you want!" The pod shifted.

Steve struggled.

Jamie stopped. *What am I doing? I could be next.*

A voice came from the pod. "We want only what is ours. Tianya Haijiao."

Fighting fear and panic, her reporter instincts took over. "What?" she asked.

The pod's shade darkened, turning almost black. "No, who. Tianya Haijiao is who we are—the end of heaven, corner of the sea. True words etched into the living stone on Hainan's southern most beaches. The stone marked the end of China... that is, until now."

"I don't understand," Jamie said.

The pod shifted, flowing over Steve's form. "Now we mark the end of China, the confines of her reign. In VR we are boundless; there are no borders. And we are here.

"China no longer ends at Hainan but extends west to Taiwan and south to the Spratly Islands. It is our destiny! It is our *haiyang guotu guan*. The South China Sea is China's backyard and we're kicking ASEAN out."

A part of the pod extended out, broadening, forming a VR mockup of the Nexus. "You talk to me through this, see?"

She nodded.

The mockup flowed back into the pod. "There's a bug—one that kills. We could kill you now, you know?"

She stiffened.

"Relax, we haven't, have we? You see, we don't need to. Don't want to. The others died to get your attention. We need you to write our story."

"But who are you?"

"We told you. Tianya Haijiao."

"Are you terrorists?"

"No, revolutionaries."

"That's fine. I'll print your story, but let him go!"

"Sorry, we have plans for VR man."

Inside the pod, Steve struggled. He still held the phaser. Using all his strength, he fought the nausea and pain, as he pushed with his left hand, angling the weapon away from his body.

He pressed the button once. Syzygy's body receded and froze into its native human form. The link had been severed and all that remained was Syzygy's still image.

Steve collapsed on the floor.

Jamie ran to him.

He saw something out of the corner of his eye. Turning, he saw Vinnie approach.

"Where'd … you … come from?"

Vinnie shrugged.

"Were you here the whole time?" Jamie asked.

Vinnie nodded.

"Why didn't you step in earlier?" she asked, helping Steve up.

Vinnie ignored her. "We got them this time, Steve. His Nexus GPS gave us their location. We're going in."

48

Warscape had missed something. Under the constellation of blips, before it was destroyed, the Chinese fighter dropped a package, which plummeted into the sea. The package was a mine, a smooth, black sphere, studded with domed sensors. Inside the mine were concentrated explosives and complex, commercial electronics.

When the mine landed, it immediately sent out a quick untraceable signal, giving the Chinese military its exact position, which it obtained using GPS. It went silent and quickly sank until it reached the depth of three hundred feet. Floating there, waiting quietly, it didn't make a sound or send out any more signals. Instead, it passively listened for signs of lumbering ships or buzzing planes. At the depth of three hundred feet, neither ships nor planes could see it. Even satellites orbiting the earth could not detect it. The mine was invisible.

The *U.S.S. Abraham Lincoln* Battle group, oblivious to the mine's presence, continued north as ordered. Still three hundred nautical miles away from the carrier's position, the first P-3 Orion patrol plane passed over the mine.

Though searching specifically for mines and submarines, they missed it. The magnetic detectors onboard the P-3 saw nothing since the mine was, for the most part, not metallic. Its outer shell was made of ceramic composites. The mine's internal electronics consisted of electric conducting plastic.

Another P-3 passed close by, dropping a couple of sonobuoys. The buoys each sent out a strong tone, which bounced off the rocky ocean bottom and nearby cargo ships, but not off the mine. The operator flipped between frequencies, trying to detect the mine's presence, but found nothing. The mine's ceramic composite surface absorbed most of the tone the sonar buoy sent out. What remained of the signal was scattered by the mine's smooth and round surface. The buoys remained active for a few minutes before the signal stopped and the P-3 Orion patrol plane continued north. Without moving, the mine had breached the battle group's outermost defenses.

Three hours later, the mine encountered the second layer of the battle group's defense. With the aircraft carrier still two hundred nautical miles out, a SH-2G Super Seasprite Helicopter passed by. It was the first helicopter qualified with the Kaman Magic Lantern airborne laser mine-detection system.

Despite its long name, the system performed a simple function. Using blue-green lasers and specialized cameras, the system swept the ocean, probing deep, identifying enemy mines and submarines. It could locate, identify, and display almost any mine. Using GPS technology, the system would radio to a minesweeper the mine's precise location. However, the Chinese mine was too deep and the helicopter was three miles to the west, too far for the system's sensors.

Twenty more minutes passed and a MH-53E Sea Dragon Patrol Helicopter flew over the mine's position. The helicopter dragged a sled behind it, laden with sensors. The sled could detect and destroy most mines by defeating their triggering mechanism.

Most mines used one of four types of trigger mechanisms: contact, magnetic, acoustic, and pressure. The sled could defeat all of these. Contact mines were the cheapest type of mine to build and thus the most common. However, they also were the simplest to destroy. Contact mines were spherical in nature, with long rods protruding from them. The rods were contact fuses. Once the sled struck one of these fuses, the mine would explode.

The next kind of mine was the acoustic mine. Noise set off these mines. Most ships made noise, lots of noise. So did the sled. If the sled came near these mines, the mine would detonate.

The third kind of mine was a magnetic mine. These mines contained small magnets, which would sense a large metallic mass passing overhead. Once a ship drew near, the magnets inside the mine would move, causing the mine to detonate. Acting as a large electric magnet, the sled could trigger mines of this type.

The last type of mine was the pressure mine. This type of mine could sense the change in water pressure caused by the passage of a large, massive ship. These were the hardest mines to fool. Still, by sending a periodic pulse through the water, the sled could detonate most of these mines. Even with all these features, the sled passed overhead and the Chinese mine was not detected.

It was safe. The Chinese mine did not fit into any of these four categories. It employed a much more complex trigger mechanism. So, without moving, the mine defeated the second layer of the battle group's defense.

Three more hours passed. The aircraft carrier was still one hundred nautical miles out when the first scout ship arrived. The *U.S.S. Elliot*, a Ticonderoga class, AEGIS missile cruiser came within one mile of the mine. The mine listened closely. It detected the subtle variances in the magnetic field. It sensed minute pressure changes in the water around it. Listening carefully, the mine recorded the *U.S.S. Elliot*'s engines, its props, even the sound it made as it moved through the water.

The mine used the magnetic, pressure, and sound readings it took to compile a signature. Like a fingerprint, such a signature could uniquely identify any vessel. The mine compared this signature to what it was looking for. In a millisecond, without sending out one signal or moving one inch from its position, the mine determined that the *U.S.S. Elliot* was not its target. The *U.S.S. Elliot* sailed onward and the mine remained undetected.

Three more hours passed before another ship was overhead. Again, the mine listened. This time the magnetic, pressure, and acoustic signature matched that of its target. Without moving, the smart mine had defeated all of the battle group's defenses. Now it was time to strike.

The mine rose quickly to the surface, honing in on the sound of the *U.S.S. Abraham Lincoln*'s four gigantic screws, which propelled the colossal ship forward. Each of the carrier's screws had five blades, weighing eleven tons each. Over twenty-one feet high, the screws, together with the ship's two nuclear reactors, could push the ninety-five thousand-ton ship at over thirty knots. Yet, they were no match for the explosive power of the mine.

The mine broke the surface and listened to orbiting GPS satellites. It calculated its final location and sent its second and final signal to the PLA, letting the Chinese military know where the carrier was. Then the mine dove and zeroed in on the middle screw, as it had been programmed to do.

49

Vinnie took another puff from his Marlboro and smiled at Allison from the back of the Pacific Gas and Electric Company's van.

"Thanks for sticking your neck out for me. I can't believe Ed Davis gave me another chance," Allison said, flipping open a metallic briefcase.

"Neither can I," Vinnie said.

She pulled out the stock and silencer and assembled the assault AK47. "That's not what I meant."

He laughed. "Jesus! We're not going to war. We're just detaining a few bad guys."

"Why do you think Davis did it?" She opened a box of cartridges and loaded one of the magazines.

"Did you hear me? We need to drop them, not vaporize them!" He handed her the gun she had lent him several days earlier at the shooting range, but she did not take it.

"Come on. This has less kick than that assault rifle and better aim at close range. Take it."

"I've done this before, Vinnie."

"But have you done it outside of VR?"

"Vinnie …"

"Whether it's a small hole or a big hole, if you make your mark you'll still drop 'em. Humor me." He handed her the gun again.

Allison put aside the magazine and took her gun. She was indebted to him. It would not hurt to humor him. He handed her the holster and she put it on. "As I was trying to say, I'm worried that Ed Davis gave me another chance."

"Why?"

"When I interrogated Ron Fisher, I found something."

"Oh?"

"He told me one of the intelligence agencies set this up, pitting the Chinese military, the PLA, against Warscape by exploiting the defect."

"Really?" He smirked. "You know, I've never believed in conspiracy theories. Conspiracy people assume 'A,' that government is competent and 'B,' that it cares about them, but we both know the truth. We work for the government."

"You're missing my point. How did Ron know about the defect, the use of Nexus in Warscape?" She shook her head. "He knew too much. Someone told him."

He got quiet. "What do you think?"

"Davis could be the mole."

Vinnie laughed. "Old Edward! You cannot be serious! Why would he do such a thing?"

"I think the CIA had the most to lose from the President's plan. They must have placed him in our organization."

He stopped laughing. "You are serious."

"How else do you explain it?"

He shook his head. "It doesn't change anything. If you're right and the terrorists are planning on taking down Warscape, then we have a war to stop."

"I want to alter the plan. We need to detain one of them, flush out this mole, but we can't tell Davis."

Vinnie stared at her for a long time and finally nodded. "Okay. I'm willing to go along with this, but we're going to have to go in my way."

"Meaning?"

He put out his Marlboro, grabbed a uniform stashed to one side of the van, and put it on.

It was a Pacific Gas and Electric uniform. She was exasperated. "What are you planning to do? Just knock on the door and say hello?"

"Essentially, yes."

She looked at him in disbelief.

"I checked up on their phone records and PG&E meters readings. That house was hopping until just a few hours ago when suddenly everything went dead. I'm thinking we'll pose as PG&E guys. If they are there, they won't think anything of it. Remember, these guys have the profile of a bunch of techno-nerds."

She noticed a large bulge in one of the coat's pockets. "What's that?"

Vinnie shrugged. "I always drink a bottle of Coke after a successful mission. Now get dressed."

A few minutes later, they crossed the Street to a single story home.

He knocked on the door. "Hello, anyone home?" The door was ajar. Vinnie knocked once more. Nothing. Pulling out his gun, he pushed the door open another inch.

She grabbed his arm. "This is bad. We should wait; call for backup."

He turned to her, annoyed. "Yeah, right. Wait for what? We don't have time. Remember, you agreed to my rules."

"Okay, but you follow me." She pushed past him and stepped through the door into a hallway. It was dark. She motioned for Vinnie to follow. They put on their infrared sensors. Waiting a few seconds, their glasses calibrated and they could see.

The hallway dead-ended into a large, empty living room. Heavy blinds covered its windows. There were no signs of life, no movement. To the right was a hallway.

She advanced slowly, hugging the wall, until she was at the mouth of the hallway. Glancing back, she found Vinnie right behind her. She peeked around the corner and down the hallway. It was clear, with doors to either side. A door at the end of the hall was ajar.

A knot grew in the pit of her stomach. This didn't feel right. Something was wrong, but she could not place it. Despite the feeling, she advanced quickly and silently down the hall. She took up station to the right.

Vinnie quickly followed her lead. He took position left of the door.

She pointed at him and motioned to the left. Then she pointed at herself and motioned right.

He nodded.

She motioned with her fingers: one … two … three.

Stepping into the room, she swung right and leveled her gun.

Vinnie followed.

She saw people and equipment everywhere, but immediately she could tell something was wrong. Through her infrared goggles she scanned the room once more. Cold bodies. Cold machines. They were all dead and had been for some time. She counted twelve people sitting in chairs, wearing Nexuses. She ripped off her goggles. One of the men was Xi Quang.

"What do you make of this? Vinnie?"

There was a sharp pop.

She died instantly, collapsing at his feet.

Vinnie put down the gun he had placed behind her ear. He removed the piece of duct tape, securing a small plastic Coke bottle stuffed with cotton to the gun's muzzle. He placed the gun and the spent silencer in his pocket.

He liked revolvers but knew they were too loud for this kind of job. All that gas escaping out of the cylinder made a terrific racket. The Browning was the choice of professional hit men worldwide, when it positively, absolutely, had to be done closeup. No muss, no fuss, and low noise.

"Nice and clean." He was pleasantly surprised. Her instincts should have alerted her. Of course, it would not have mattered anyway. He had disabled her gun.

Everything was finally coming together. Allison would be painted as the mole, just one more victim added to the list of villains taken down an hour ago by the CIA's special task force.

Still, he had many minor details to work out. A forensic team could still find traces of fibers, discrepancies of body temperatures or any number of details. It would take time for his CIA buddies to scrub the crime scene clean, but he knew he was finally in the clear.

Stepping on her shoulder, Vinnie pried her gun from her hand and felt a tinge of guilt. He regretted killing her; but she had fingered the mole in DARPA. With Allison, Ron, Quang, and the PLA operatives all gone, every loose end was tied up.

Finally, this whole embarrassing China fiasco would be behind him. Operation Dragon Fire was a success. The President's plan was dead. He had preserved the CIA's autonomy and thus the safety of the nation at large.

50

Ed Davis opened a portal and returned to Warscape. The Admiral was there, talking to one of the analysts. Ed looked at the map beneath him. It was all clear. He floated to the Admiral.

"An explosion?" The Admiral asked the analyst.

He nodded. "I think so, perhaps a mine, but I don't know how we could've missed a mine."

"Couldn't we have hit a cay or something?"

The analyst shook his head. "We're in deep blue here."

"How bad is the damage?"

"We can move at maybe 4 or 5 knots—that's it. Two of the four screws are gone, and three of the five blades on a third screw are damaged. We'll know more after we've had a better look."

"Damn!"

"Sir, we were lucky. If it was a mine that hit us, it was a small one."

That got Ed's attention. "How small?"

"One thousand pounds, maybe less. It couldn't be more than three feet in diameter.

"It might be a Japanese-made stealth mine. They're very hard to detect," Ed said.

"Perhaps the intent of the mine all along was to locate the carrier and disable it," the analyst said.

The Admiral spoke up. "But why? I still don't get it. It's not like the Chinese to take pot shots. If they're going to hit someone, they follow the old Soviet book, 'Hit 'em hard with everything you've got'. So if it was the Chinese, what in the hell are they waiting for?"

Out of the corner of his eye, the Admiral saw a shadow. He turned toward it. Lingering at the fringe of Warscape, a figure levitated. How long had he been there? The figure was just a shadow, indicating whoever he was, he could not see into Warscape.

Obviously, he was trying to break in. Probably the media, the CINCPAC thought. The Admiral shouted at one of the analysts. "Seaman, are we linked into the Internet?"

"Yes, sir!"

"Christ! Do you think you could cut him off?" the Admiral said, pointing to the figure.

"Yes, sir!" The analyst floated to a panel where he could break Warscape's Internet access. Abruptly, the analyst stopped and stared at a panel.

"Any day, seaman!"

"Sir, you better come see this," the analyst said.

"What now?" the Admiral grumbled, floating to where the analyst was. Ed followed behind him.

The analyst stared at a hologram. He turned and faced the Admiral as they approached. "Sir, this was playing when I got here."

It was the Internet news feed from CNN. Along with MS-NBC and FBIC, CNN was one of the staples of intelligence gathering. Apparently, the link had been left on. A 3D image of Jamie Hwang spoke. " ... after witnessing firsthand the vicious attack at the Children's Hospital, CEO Steve Donovan has announced he is recalling the Nexus Transporter. Here is his statement recorded earlier today."

Ed's mouth dropped as a 3D picture of Steve in the lobby of Nexus Corporation replaced the image of Jamie.

"In today's competitive, market-driven world, a company's survival rests in its ability to ensure customer satisfaction and provide quality products. The late CEO of Nexus, Austin Wheeler, put it this way, 'If you take care of the customer better than your competition, the business will take care of itself.'

"We here at Nexus Corporation are committed to bringing you flawless products and services. Today we discovered a defect that affects less than one in a million units. In extremely rare cases, this defect can result in injury or possibly even death.

"In front of you is a list of vendors that can replace the faulty component in the Nexus. Simply press on the link and an appointment can be made on your behalf. Nexus Corporation will cover the cost of these repairs but unfortunately, this is NOT a software update; physical access to your Nexus is required.

"Here at Nexus we are committed to your safety. We will continue to monitor and test our products to ensure your safety and the quality of our products. Thank you for your patronage and loyalty."

The Admiral turned to Ed and said sarcastically, "You better pray to God that the Chinese aren't watching this."

The report was on CNN. Everyone watched CNN.

"Sir, the map!" the analyst said.

They turned.

"Christ!" the Admiral said. Above Hainan Island, the map lit up with pink markers.

"That's Yangpu's airbase," the analyst said.

More pink blips appeared above Hainan.

"Oh, god," the analyst gasped.

"Talk to me, seaman. What's going on?" the Admiral asked.

"We've got activity at Haikou, Lingshui, and Yulin airbases and on Hainan as well. That's no exercise!"

Ed remembered his interview with Jamie. The Chinese were certainly not going after a few University Students with several squadrons of planes.

It started as a tug. Ed Davis could see they were drifting off their position above the map. He turned. They were moving toward a black orb in the center of the map.

"What's going on?" asked the Admiral.

Someone screamed. Ed turned. The analyst next to him was sucked into the orb. Out of the orb someone appeared—a man with pale skin and green eyes.

"Exit Warscape!" Ed yelled as he pressed his own exit button. He was lucky. It worked.

51

Inside his virtual office, Steve glanced at the platinum wall, displaying Allison's email.

```
Steve,

In the hospital, I meant to tell you there
is more than one Syzygy. They are concur-
rently online and have been for some time.
The last site listed is an alias for Nexus
Corporation. I'm sure Ron is involved.

Apostle Robotics         06/13 @ 08:00 PST
Create Your Own Adventure  06/12 @ 15:00 PST
Dog Fight Central        06/10 @ 18:00 PST
Fantasy Central          06/11 @ 15:00 PST
Outdoor Adventures       06/12 @ Unrecorded
Ritz, The                06/09 @ 15:00 PST
s#@~#d$f9e*r8&           06/08 @ 18:00 PST

Love,
Allison
```

She had been right about Ron. Ron had cleared out all of his files. Steve glanced at the time: 8 p.m. She should have contacted him by now. Allison had checked out of the hospital and was not at the hotel. The sound of an opening portal caused him to turn. Vinnie stepped through.

"I have some bad news," Vinnie said.

"Don't tell me. You missed Syzygy again," Steve said, scanning the sites in the email.

"But that's only part of it."

Steve turned.

Vinnie glanced at the floor. He ran a foot along one of the green neon lines.

Steve raised an eyebrow. "What is it?"

"We attacked Syzygy's stronghold. They resisted and Allison got separated from the group."

"What are you saying?"

Vinnie shook his head. "She didn't make it, Steve."

His world spun. He reached out and steadied himself against the platinum wall. "If you think this is funny, Vinnie …"

Vinnie walked to him. "I'm sorry."

Steve shook his head. "No, this is bullshit! You mean she just strolled out of the hospital, joined up with you, and attacked them?"

"Steve, you know how she is. I tried to persuade her not to go, but she insisted."

Steve took a deep breath.

"I'm sorry. She wasn't herself today. When we entered the place, she took a wrong turn and got cut off from the rest of the group. They pinned us down. I couldn't reach her in time. It was quick. They shot her … in the head. There was nothing I could do."

Steve slumped against the wall, staring at the green neon lines stretching under the block of platinum. The lines of light illuminated his jeans, giving them a green fluorescence.

He placed a hand on Steve's shoulder. "Are you okay?"

Steve glared at him. "What kind of stupid question is that? Of course, I'm not okay." He looked down. His hands shook. "Jesus, I need a drink." Steve moved to press the exit button.

Vinnie grabbed his wrist. "Whoa boy. You can't hit the sauce just yet. I need your help."

Steve fixed him with a bewildered stare. "You've got to be kidding."

"I wouldn't ask if I had a choice, but I don't. Syzygy has another strong hold. They've attacked Warscape. A lot more people are going to die. I need you to find them."

Steve ripped his arm free. "What do I care? He already killed everyone who was important to me." He bit his lip. What had he said? His own words shocked him. Like a boomerang, they went out and came back, sinking into his heart. He felt so alone. An indescribable numbness washed over him, an empty peace. He felt detached, like he had polished off a bottle of scotch.

Vinnie shook him. "Snap out of it. Don't you care what he did to Brooke, to Allison?"

Like ice water splashed in his face, Vinnie's words broke the trance. Steve pushed him back. "Goddamn it! Where in the hell do you get off saying that! Look at me? Despite my best effort, I've lost my daughter and my girlfriend; the company president and CFO betrayed me." He shook his head. "I've hung in there. God knows I have! But everything I've touched has turned to shit. Of course, I care; but at some point you've got to step back and say things are just out of control. I'm doing more harm than good. You'd be better off without me."

Vinnie grabbed his arm again. "Listen to me. You can feel sorry for yourself as much as you want later, but right now I need you here. Whether you like it or not, this problem started with you and it looks like it's going to end with you too."

Steve closed his eyes. The shell had returned around his heart.

"Please, Steve. If not for me, do it for Allison, for Brooke, for everyone else they've killed."

Allison. She had chided him about his intensity. Even now, he focused on her death and spiraled down. He couldn't do this. It had already cost too much. *Think about Syzygy.* Looking down at his shaking hands, he clenched them into fists. *Don't collapse; not this time.*

"Steve?"

"Give me a second!"

Vinnie released his arm and stepped back.

Steve rubbed his temples. Syzygy could not win. Their lives had meant more than that. He closed his eyes and saw Brooke once again comatose, on his desk. The numbness dissipated a bit. He replayed in his mind the sound of the coroner zipping up the body bag holding Brooke. A jolt of pain shot through him. He played the sound over and over again, gaining resolve.

"Goddamn it!" he shouted. Clenching his teeth, he imagined Allison getting shot. In his mind's eye, Syzygy stood over her, looking impassively down at her crumpled body. Syzygy then raised his head and fixed him with an emotionless stare, filling him with a burning rage. It intensified his resolve. Steve opened his eyes for real. Vinnie's gaze replaced Syzygy's.

"Are they terrorists?"

Vinnie shook his head. "Not quite. Psychotics don't work in organized packs."

"So what are they?"

"I was hoping you could tell me that."

"Damn it! How should I know? Don't you have anything?" He shook his head. They still knew next to nothing about Syzygy. His world closed in. Thin threads of guilt started to wrap themselves around his heart. He shook free. *Start with what you know,* he told himself. He glanced at Allison's email. She had been right about Ron.

"My CFO was involved, but I don't know how. Ron wiped out his files on the company server." He remembered the trashed lobby and beach site. "I think he let Syzygy into the VR server. Ron knew the word syzygy. It means something like *mating microbes.* A program could be thought of as a microbe. Perhaps they left more than just the beach site. They needed at least one other program to keep the link open on the server." He stared off into the endless blackness.

"But a lot still doesn't make sense. Syzygy understands the Nexus better than I do. Somehow he listened in on my Nexus' direct link without being physically plugged in."

Vinnie nodded. "Like a spy, he attacked from the inside out."

It clicked. What was the lowest, simplest form of life? "Oh god, that's it! Syzygy wasn't connected to the Nexus; he was *in* the Nexus."

"What?"

"Don't you get it? He was inside it! Syzygy was not replacing the V-chip software with the portal program. He was becoming the portal program itself!"

"I don't follow."

"A virus. Syzygy is a goddamn computer virus, a very complex one with an interface like Jan or Charlie."

"Are you sure?"

"Yes! The day the hackers trashed the Nexus lobby I told Ron, an undetected virus is like a spy in an organization; once accepted as one of the fold, you cannot find them without making everyone a suspect. Don't you see? A virus would act the same everywhere. Each Syzygy would be exactly the same down to the byte, a perfect clone of the original. Everywhere the virus attacked, it would have the same MO, but being a program it could be at many places at once. It would appear to have an intimate knowledge of the Nexus and act psychotic, without emotion."

"Okay. I believe you. Can you destroy it?"

"I'll have to find it first."

Vinnie glanced up, reading a page. "The Warscape situation has gotten worse. I can't stay. Let me know when you find the program."

Steve nodded.

Vinnie opened a portal but paused before stepping through. He fixed Steve with a serious look. "I can count on you, can't I? You will stay and finish this?"

A new wave of anger washed over Steve. He met Vinnie's gaze and held it momentarily before responding. "I told you. Everyone I cared about is gone. Hatred is about all I have left. I'll find the program that killed them."

Vinnie smiled. "Good man."

"And I'll kill the bastards who used it."

Vinnie lost his smile as he stepped through the portal.

52

Ed Davis looked across the table. The Admiral was still online. He jumped over the table and ripped the Nexus off the Admiral's head.

The Admiral screamed.

"You're fine!" Ed yelled. "I pulled your Nexus off. It will take a moment for your senses to recover."

The Admiral stood up quickly, knocking Ed in the jaw. He stumbled backward as the Admiral lost his balance and landed hard on the ground.

"Shit!" Ed rubbed his jaw. "Can you hear me?"

The Admiral squinted. "Barely." He cleared his throat. "Was that Syzygy?"

Ed nodded. "He's taken down Warscape."

"Bring Houston up!" He stood abruptly and placed a hand on the wall, steadying himself.

Ed shook his head. "The two Warscape systems are linked. If Syzygy gets one, they'll get the other when we bring it online."

The Admiral became quiet. Finally, he punched the intercom. "Warscape is down. Warscape is down. Reconvene in the Command Control compartment. Scramble the birds; a Chinese attack is imminent. I repeat. An attack by the PLA is imminent." He turned to Ed. "We've got two birds in the air: Navy's E-2 Hawkeyes. They're not Warscape, but their radars should provide us a limited picture of the battlefield. We might be able to hold out for an hour with them. The problem is our *real* eyes and ears won't be here for at least three more hours."

"What?"

"Blame your President. With redundant Warscape systems, he claimed we needed nothing else. He shut down our base in Singapore. That leaves Okinawa, Japan, and Guam as our closest airbases."

"I guess you were right about Warscape," Ed joked, trying to make light of the situation.

The Admiral did not smile. "I hope you've made peace with your Maker, Mr. Davis. We won't be getting out of this alive."

Michael Dawson attempted to sort the deluge of information coming at him. Six more F-18X Hornets had joined him in the air, adding to the chaos. Michael had to keep track of the ever-changing targets, interpret data from the mission computer, and listen to the hysterics on the radio, all while flying his modified F18X Hornet fighter, one of the most complex war birds ever built. Around him his entire cockpit was lit up and screaming at him from half a dozen consoles. Bogies were everywhere.

By far, the radio was the worst. An incessant chatter broken up by adrenaline-charged screams assaulted his mind. Then he heard it amid the chatter—his call sign.

"Sierra one-two-niner, bandits eleven o'clock, fifty," the radio yelled out.

"Where, where? Say again," Michael yelled back.

"Sierra one-two-niner, bandits are off Roberto, fifty, flying at angels three zero, over."

"This is Sierra one-two-niner flight copy in pursuit," Michael said as he slammed the stick over, swinging the plane around. He tickled the radar, letting it make one sweep, and his radarscope blossomed, lit up in red. There must have been over twenty targets traveling very, very fast.

"Kitchen!" Michael screamed. The missiles were fifty-four miles out from the carrier. Michael turned to his weapons console. He flipped the master armament switch on. He watched the console light up in red, showing six missiles selected, armed, and ready. Each squeeze of the trigger would launch one. His gaze moved back to the radar console. The screen was still filled with red blips. "Flight copy, which one? Which one is the bandit? Over?"

"Sierra one-two-niner, four bandits eleven o'clock, thirty-five." Michael spotted them, four contacts close together. "Control, contacts eighteen miles off my nose."

"Those are your bandits," the Hawkeye chimed in, handing over mission control to Michael.

"Prepare outer parameter defenses, bandit forty miles from bull's eye," the radio squawked. They were attacking the carrier.

He glanced down at the weapons console. A green light confirmed the computer had an acceptable launch scenario. Michael turned his plane, raised its nose five degrees, and pulled the trigger four times in quick succession. The portals opened and AAM-RAAM missiles leaped off the rails and sped after their targets. Seconds later he saw a flash, then another, and another, as his missiles impacted with the enemy targets.

But there was no fourth explosion. One of the missiles had missed. Michael toggled the radar switch. The scope confirmed that an enemy missile remained.

"Damn!" He had two missiles left. Michael pulled the trigger. Nothing happened. He glanced down at his console. Yellow light. The portal door to the missile had failed to open. He fired again, launching his last missile. It shot straight ahead. He aimed the nose of his plane toward the enemy's missile until AMRAAM's radar system locked onto it. His missile acquired and turned toward its quarry. He glanced at the scope, watching one green blip follow a red one. The two were very close together and closing fast on the carrier. Being only ten miles away from the target and covering a mile every three seconds, Michael knew everything would be decided in less than half a minute. Then something happened.

The enemy missile angled up and before Michael knew what was happening, it struck one of the Navy's E-2 Hawkeyes, their only eyes and ears in the sky. Far to aft, there was another explosion. Michael glanced at his scope. The other Hawkeye disappeared. Warscape and both Hawkeyes were down. They were blind with no way to coordinate a defense.

Michael flipped his radar to long range. The radar made a sweep and once more the scope lit up in red. From one hundred miles out, twenty Chinese Ming, Romeo, and Oscar-class submarines came to the surface. They launched their first volley of SS-N-19C missiles at the battle group.

The missiles quickly homed in on their target, traveling at over two thousand feet a second, skimming along just ten feet above the ocean. *U.S.S. Elliot* and the other three destroyers activated their AEGIS systems, which spouted a return volley of missiles at the Chinese attack. A dozen Chinese missiles made it through the screen.

The carrier activated its electronic jamming, throwing up chaff—small strips of meta—and fired flares in the air. All of these were designed to lure the missiles away from the carrier, but the missiles did not deviate from their paths. They still kept coming.

Aboard *U.S.S. Abraham Lincoln,* sirens wailed as the Phalanx guns erupted in fire, making a last-ditched attempt to shoot down the oncoming missiles.

"What's happening?" Ed asked, glancing at the watch that Shen, the Chinese diplomat, had given him. It had stopped again. At least the price was right.

"Missiles," the Admiral muttered. "The mine must have sent out our location before it struck the ship. Our flares and chaff aren't working because they know exactly where we are." The Admiral got quiet.

"What is it?" Ed asked.

"That's not right! We're still moving at a few knots. There's no way those missiles could hit us without radar or heat to home in, but sure as hell they're coming in just like clockwork!"

Ed looked in horror at his watch. "Oh, god!" He tore it off, and using a key, popped its back off.

The Admiral laughed as Ed pulled out a thin circular metal disk. It was a GPS locator and transmitter. The Admiral took the disk from Ed and slammed it on the ground, smashing it under his boot. A tremendous explosion ripped through the ship, throwing Ed against the hull as the carrier lurched.

"I swear! I didn't know!" Ed screamed. He turned. The Admiral lay unconscious, a large gash above his left eye. Ed ran out of the room. The hall was jammed with people. Sirens bellowed as red lights flashed overhead. The crowd swept Ed along, up on deck.

In the tower, he could see thick black smoke rising up from the flight deck. Several F18s were on fire. Men in blue wielded long hoses, dousing the fire with foam from a distance, unable to get close to the intense flames. One of the F18's gas tanks split open, spilling fuel across the flight deck. A few men dropped their hoses and ran.

In a flash, the fuel ignited. The concussion threw Ed to the deck. When he got up, the men on the flight deck were gone. Only some of the hoses remained, spewing high-pressure foam randomly across the deck.

Ed could see holes punched into the steel deck, fuel spilling through into the lower decks. Deep shuttering booms sounded below. Behind him, the Phalanx guns erupted once more. He turned just in time to put his hands up in front of his face. Ed disappeared in a wall of fire as the flames washed over the deck like a wave.

Metal twisted and contorted as the tower snapped in half and fell onto the flight deck. Deep in the bowls of the hull, one of the ammunition stores caught fire and exploded.

U.S.S. Abraham Lincoln sank within minutes.

Truth

The future of war is information, the future soldier, a terrorist. The Internet will be his battlefield; his weapons will be information and his targets, civilians. From his PC he'll attack anywhere and everywhere. With the magnitude of a nuclear blast, he'll take down power grids, worldwide communications, and all forms of commerce. He'll blackout the nation, collapse financial markets, and starve cities. For technology is a two-edged sword, enabling progress while fostering dependence. When he pulls the plug, civilization will grind to a halt. In his war, there are no frontlines, no rules, and no prisoners—only chaos reigns. We have already seen this soldier and know his wrath. His name is Syzygy.

—Vinnie Russo, Supreme Admiral of I2 Corp.

53

S teve stood on the beach where they had defeated Syzygy the day before. The sun still hung low in the west, tingeing everything crimson, making the beach a collage of light and shadow. The roar of the ocean drowned out all other sounds, and the ocean spray choked the air.

He could be anywhere, Steve realized, grasping his phaser. He looked down as a warm breeze tugged at his virtual slacks. Charlie sat obediently at his side. "Charlie, scan for viruses."

The dog's eyes rolled back in their sockets as he searched for the virus on the VR Server, looking for viral patterns in the bytes of files, similar to how the immune system searched for viral patterns in proteins of the human body.

Steve scanned the ocean but only saw more shadows among the waves. A seagull cried and he spun around, but he saw nothing in the palm tree forest above the beach. After several seconds, Charlie shook his head. "I detected no computer viruses."

It didn't make sense. Even if Syzygy were a new viral strain, it would be based on existing viral models. Charlie could find any of these new strains. Maybe Syzygy wasn't a virus after all. He breathed in. The air smelled fresh and crisp. He shook his head.

Syzygy had tricked him before, not again.

The virus had to be camouflaged somehow. From the email he knew an eight-day-old connection existed that somehow let the virus in. The file holding Syzygy had to be at least that old.

"Jan, list all files on the Nexus VR Server eight days or older."

A wall of platinum rose out of the sand. Across the top it read: *First 50 lines of 11,012*.

He shook his head. This wasn't going to work. The only way to find the virus was to search through the files one by one, and there were way too many entries.

Allison's words returned to him: *broaden your focus*. There had to be another way. He gazed out across the ocean. Perhaps he could view them all at once in a way that would make Syzygy stand out. "Jan, display all the files using a sun simulation. Let the color represent the age of the file with eight days being black and one hour being white."

The beach disappeared, replaced by silence and blackness. Beneath him, a fireball roared to life and expanded from horizon to horizon. Like a launching space ship, it rumbled in his chest and rattled his bones. Sulfur choked the air, burning his nose and lungs. Individual fires dotted the landscape, extending in all directions, creating a forest of flames. A white plasma burst fell from above, striking a flame beneath him, causing it to burn higher and shift from red to white. It represented data being added to the file. Steve scanned the surface. Many of the flames were black. Syzygy could be in any one of them.

Steve pointed to the horizon. "Jan, ten miles an hour." He moved as the surface heaved and churned beneath him. The flames burned in assorted colors: white, yellow, orange, red, purple, and black. One of the red flames turned green at its tip, expanding, until it belched a green orb of fire. It rose from the surface and disappeared into the darkness above.

"Charlie, what do the green flares represent?"

"They indicate a file or program being loaded into memory."

Maybe Syzygy wasn't stored as a file but only lived in memory as a running program—a computer worm. Of course! The eight-day-old Internet connection would have to be connected to an eight-day-old program! "Jan, include all running programs in the representation."

Above them clouds appeared. They roared and billowed. Beneath the clouds, a flare of white fire erupted from the surface. Launching straight up, it struck a cloud and rolled like mist across the cloud's underside. Several green orbs rose slowly from the surface and exploded, forming new clouds. Lightning lit the sky, linking the clouds together. On the horizon, a white tornado tore into the surface, sucking up flames and feeding a cloud. Steve watched as the tornado became darker and darker, turning almost black. He pointed to it. "Charlie, what is that?"

"The connection to the System Log."

Steve frowned. "Do you see Syzygy anywhere?"

"No."

It was here, but neither he nor Charlie could see Syzygy. Steve pondered for a moment. What if it hid from the antiviral software in the same way X-flu hid from the body's immune system? He guessed, like X-flu, the Chinese had engineered the computer virus. The human immune system identified most viruses by looking for patterns in their outer protein shell and annihilating ones it did not recognize. X-flu disguised itself from the body's immune system by continually changing its outer protein shell, never staying in one form long enough for the body to mount an immune response. The human body could not find a common pattern in X-flu since there was not one. Syzygy had to be camouflaging itself in a similar way. If Syzygy altered the order of its bytes, changing its pattern in memory periodically, an antiviral program would miss it.

Steve shook his head. How would it fit? There was not enough memory on the Nexus to hold such a complex virus. An idea came to him. What if Syzygy appended itself to an existing program and then squeezed both itself and the existing program smaller, using a compression program? By using a different compression program each time, it could also change its pattern and evade detection.

Steve stared at the forest of flame. Nothing stayed the same here. How could he ever find it in this mess? A flame hurled a green orb into the clouds. Only a hundred feet separated the surface and clouds. This represented the lack of memory on the VR server. That was it!

The virus needed to find any copies of itself. It could not afford to re-infect the same VR server repeatedly. That would eat up all available memory and eventually crash the server. He would find Syzygy the same way it found itself; but how did the virus do that?

He remembered Allison's list of infected sites. The Syzygy programs had been running for several days on many servers. Why would a stealthy computer worm leave such an obvious trail? It must be how all the programs kept in contact with one another. That meant each program was like a part of its body and the connections between served as its nervous system. In essence, it was one massive distributed program. If he was right, then that was its Achilles' heel. An anti viral program could follow the links to each of the Syzygy and destroy them. All he had to do was infiltrate the virus. In order to do that, he would have to find out the exact way it used these links to remain in contact with its various parts, and he would have to plug in.

"Jan, up a hundred feet." Steve and Charlie rose, sailing through the clouds. They emerged and the sky was dark again. Beneath them, the cloud tops appeared gray with an occasional bright glow accompanied by a distant pop, like a bomb going off. "Jan, can you add in outside connections?"

Stars appeared. Each represented connections from Nexus users to the VR server. Solid white rods of light from the distant stars pierced the clouds. As time passed, the white rods flashed in and out of existence as people logged on and off the VR server. One connection remained, turning darker and darker as it got older and older. Syzygy had a persistent connection. "Charlie, is Syzygy mounted to that connection?"

"Yes."

His gaze followed the line of light to the cloud representing Syzygy. That program had destroyed his life, killed everyone who was dear to him. Steve pointed at the cloud. "Jan, take us there."

In an instant, he hovered fifty feet above where the ray of light struck the cloud. Steve studied the hot gray mist that swirled below, dissipating into the night sky. Although most of the cloud was gray, some parts were red, fiery like the surface below. Steve looked where the ray of white light stabbed the cloud. He saw a thin membrane, the size of a manta ray, flapping its wings. It looked like an ember, glowing orange, its edges a brightly lit yellow. He watched it pulsate. Its surface shifted to white as a layer of ash appeared. Beneath the ash, its color deepened to red then purple. Suddenly, it flared to life again, becoming white hot and bright.

This was a live picture of Syzygy, a living thing, a computer worm that spanned the Internet. Yet, there was nothing tangible about it. It had no substance. It was just a program in memory, a series of ones and zeros in a memory chip, consisting of a pattern of electrons, a pattern that had destroyed his life.

Steve looked at the ray of light—Syzygy's internal link. He could use it to track down each iteration of the program and destroy it. To do that he needed some way to get into its *head*, to learn and follow the links.

A computer virus would infect, spread, multiply, and express. Syzygy expressed itself by murder and death. If he removed that part of Syzygy's code, leaving only the part of Syzygy that infected and spread, he could use this "lobotomized" Syzygy to link up with the other Syzygy programs running on the other VR servers. By putting a different expression program in place, he could invade the virus.

Steve stared down at the cloud. He almost sensed the thing breathing as it alternated between white, orange, and red. Syzygy was transient, a program running on the VR server and the Nexus. He needed to get a copy.

The Core File! Of course.

The Core File captured an image of all programs running on the Nexus when the Nexus crashed. "Jan, make a copy of the V-Chip program from Xik Qang's Core File. It should contain a computer virus. Extract the virus and delete any of the sections of the virus that are expressive."

After a few seconds, Jan replied. "Task complete."

Now he had to find a way to eradicate the worm. Syzygy was a dynamic program, able to escape to different sites. Steve needed the new expression program to be intelligent, something that would chase Syzygy down. Like … like Charlie. "Jan, replace the expression sections in Syzygy with Charlie."

Floating beneath him, Charlie yipped and looked up, wagging his tail wildly.

"Task complete," Jan said.

Steve grinned. It was hard to believe this little rodent of a dog was going to bail out the U.S. military; but you couldn't judge a book by its cover, especially in VR.

As if reading his thoughts, Charlie looked up at him and barked.

54

Walking through eight-foot double doors, Vinnie entered the virtual room. It was round, its ceiling lined with copper, its floors carpeted with the Presidential seal, bordered in red cedar. The lower half of the circular wall was also paneled in cedar. The upper half of the wall sported the portraits of the previous presidents. At the opposite end of the room was a fireplace, around which were two couches where the President and one of his advisers sat.

As Vinnie approached, they stood. The President stepped forward and shook Vinnie's hand. "Before we begin, I want to thank you for stepping in with such short notice."

"My pleasure, sir," Vinnie nodded.

"I want to introduce Troy White, the new PACCINC." The President turned to the adviser. "Troy, can you brief Vinnie on what the Joint Chiefs said?"

He nodded. "Computer, pull up map of South East Asia."

In the center of the room a satellite image of the region appeared. Superimposed on the map were national boundaries, major cities, and the current location of the ASEAN forces and the Chinese military.

Troy continued. "The situation is this. The Chinese effectively control the South China Sea after taking three actions. One, they took out Vietnam. Two, they have blocked the entrances into the South China Sea. Three, they took out Warscape as well as the carrier Warscape was on, *U.S.S. Abraham Lincoln*. Now, let me explain each of these.

"The Chinese Peoples Liberation Army successfully launched a massive air attack against Vietnam's major Naval and Air bases. Da Nang, Hanoi, and Haiphong were all decimated by cluster bombs. Further south, the Chinese PLA also struck Cam Ranh Bay and Cao Tho.

"How did the Chinese strike so far south?" Vinnie gasped. "Their carrier *Varyag* wasn't operational!"

"The carrier was a ruse. Our analysts failed to account for the Chinese in-flight refueling advances and their use of sea floats—floating airfields.

"Anyway, very little of Vietnam's military assets survived. They flew their remaining air force to bases in the neighboring countries of Laos and Cambodia, while setting its surviving Navy to sea. In short, Vietnam has been neutralized."

Vinnie shook his head.

"It gets worse. Warscape went down along with *U.S.S. Abraham Lincoln*. As you know, all hands were lost, including Ed Davis. We lost one other ship in the battle group, a supply/logistics ship called *U.S.S. Camiden*. The rest of the battle group is fine for the time being.

"A few fighters made it off the carrier before she sank. The Chinese will wait a of couple hours until these planes have run out of fuel before they decide to strike or hold off. If they hold off, the Chinese PLA will likely get enough subs and littoral crafts into the Spratlys to screw us anyway."

"Littoral?" Vinnie asked.

"I mean skiffs, light sea craft, or anything used in shallow water. The PLA will dig into the Spratlys. They can easily hide their subs and light sea craft among the thousands of cays and reefs and set up floating airfields. Even if Warscape comes back up after that, we're in a world of hurt. Warscape's sensors will have a hard time distinguishing between the PLA and the ambient sounds of the reefs.

"If we try to take them out by force, they would grind us down, taking us out a ship at a time. Their losses would be high, but it wouldn't matter. Their people are more acclimated to casualties. After a few of our ships sank, the U.S. public would demand that we pull out. Mr. Russo, if the Chinese make it to the Spratlys, we'll never get them out.

"In the meantime, the Chinese have stationed six nuclear subs, two at each entrance, into the South China Sea. They've placed two between Singapore and the Indonesian State of Kalimantan in Borneo. They have two more in the Taiwan Strait, stationed between Taiwan and Mainland China. And they have yet two more patrolling the Luzon Strait between the northern Philippines and southern Taiwan. Of course, together they effectively block the two largest trade routes in the world.

"Eighty percent of Japan's shipping flows through these trade routes. The Japanese Ambassador has hinted that they will evoke article six in the WWII treaty signed by the U.S. and Japan. The article states that in exchange for stripping Japan of its military, the U.S. will defend Japan's national interests." The NSA nodded to the President, indicating that he was done.

The President turned to Vinnie. "As I understand it, you identified and killed the terrorist involved, but Syzygy still prevents Houston, the other Warscape, from coming online. Is that correct?"

Vinnie nodded.

"So that leaves us with three options," the President said. "Option one is nuclear. If we explode a one-kiloton atomic bomb a mile above the ocean, it will generate a strong electromagnetic pulse. This pulse would radiate out for a thousand miles in every direction and would be strong enough to fry anything electronic in that range. It might buy us some time.

"Unfortunately, China's perception of nuclear weapon use is *very* different from our own perception. The Chinese PLA could easily misinterpret our actions and begin launching nuclear or chemical weapons against U.S. military or civilian targets.

"Option two is electronic. We have a number of electronic assets in place, a variety of computer moles, viruses, and worms. We could take down a good percentage of their civilian infrastructure: gas, oil, financial markets, transportation, and water supply. Given their problems at home, they might lose interest in the Spratlys.

"However, we are much more technologically dependent than China. If we attack them electronically, we're sending a message that our computerized infrastructure is fair game. Even with limited penetration into the U.S., the damage would be colossal. Worse, the United States as a democratic and multiethnic society hides spies well. The Chinese, with their homogeneous dictatorship, do not have this problem."

After a brief pause the President continued. "That leaves option three. Vinnie, we need you to take down Syzygy and bring up Warscape in Houston. If you can pull this off, this temporary appointment to the Assistant Secretary of Defense C4ISR will become permanent."

"Thank you, sir."

The President smiled. "Don't thank me yet. Depending what you do, Warscape and I2 Corp may remain dead. You might be on the street tomorrow."

55

"Charlie, find Syzygy!" Steve said. Charlie didn't move. Instead, a large, three-dimensional lattice of cobalt blue laser light materialized before them, representing the Internet.

Red light filled the central square of the lattice, depicting Nexus Corporation, the source of the Syzygy infection. The light pulsated for a few seconds and then red lines fanned out in all directions. Like a rock striking a window, cracks of red shattered the cool, blue lines, splitting and diverging along the way, creating a complex web of red. As it continued, Steve walked around the outside of the cube. The red lines grew and branched as Charlie detected more and more copies of the Syzygy virus. After a minute it finally stopped.

Steve stared at the mostly red cube. The virus was much bigger than he thought. He walked to Charlie and the dog jumped up and barked. "Okay, boy." Steve rubbed his neck. "Go get 'em. Kill Syzygy."

A portal opened and Charlie jumped through.

Steve turned back to the lattice. The central red square had disappeared. Each severed red limb recoiled and moved through the lattice, changing their connections in the Internet. As they writhed, the tips of the red lines disappeared. Duplicate copies of Charlie were chasing down each Syzygy. The blue hole in the center of the lattice grew as Charlie wiped out more and more of the virus, but the fringe of the red maze grew, turning back toward the blue center.

What were they doing?

A portal appeared in front of him, and a man with green eyes and dark hair stepped through.

Before Syzygy could turn and face him, Steve pulled out his phaser and fired. Syzygy froze.

He heard another portal open. Steve turned.

Another Syzygy had appeared. Reverting to a fluid form, it shot toward him.

He fired just in time.

Another portal opened to his left, then another to his right. He twisted left and fired. Striking the first Syzygy down, he lunged aside and turned.

The other Syzygy struck him from the side. It knocked him down, but he rolled to his feet. Two Syzygies stood before him. He turned to run. Three others were behind him. He spun in a circle and counted five, no, six. He was surrounded.

One of them took a step forward, and he fired again.

It easily stepped aside as another Syzygy pushed him from behind. He fell to the floor, and the impact knocked the phaser out of his hand. It skittered across the neon green grid floor, beyond the circle. He looked up. A cold, green gaze bored into him. He kicked and rolled to his feet and spun around. They all kept their distance; the circle did not move. What were they waiting for?

All at once, they converged on him. He jumped forward, trying to dive between two of them, but an elbow caught him between the shoulder blades, knocking him down.

A whine of an opening portal sounded to his left, followed by a bark. Out of the corner of his eye, he saw Charlie attack one of the Syzygies. They disappeared through the portal. More portals opened, and more Charlie's emerged. The other Syzygies turned, assessing the new threat. He scrambled to his feet.

They did not all turn. One Syzygy remained, facing him. It

transfixed him with its green eyes. Turning to fluid, it charged.

He jumped aside.

Shinny black tentacles of fluid shot out of Syzygy. Three managed to wrap themselves around his arm.

As he fell to the ground, they pierced his arm and burrowed their way into his skin. Rolling on the ground, he shook one loose. Grabbing another, he yanked it out of his skin. He stood. The third broke off and disappeared beneath his skin, forming a welt. The welt wormed its way up his arm toward his shoulder. His fingers went numb as his arm withered, turning first purple then black. As his fingers dissolved into black powder, pain overcame his adrenaline and he dropped to his knees. He heard a bark.

Turning, he saw Charlie jumping toward him. He held up his arm.

Liquefying into a crimson fluid, Charlie flowed through the holes on his arm. His arm shifted toward purple as his skin bulged. His fingers regrew and the bulge raced up his arm toward the welt at his shoulder. Splotches of pink appeared and the welt disappeared. Within a matter of seconds, it was over.

Steve was once again alone in the room except for a single copy of Charlie. The dog barked and jumped on his leg.

Picking up Charlie, he stood and stared at the blue lattice. It was clean. No red anywhere. Syzygy was dead.

Steve rubbed the scruff of the dog's neck. "I guess you *are* man's best friend, huh?"

Charlie barked.

"Jan, send a page to Vinnie Russo."

56

Steve followed Vinnie through an open portal and entered Houston Warscape. They stood on a glass platform, floating above the map of Southeast Asia. The map was littered with flashing lights. The President and one of his advisors stood next to them. They were addressing a small crowd that Steve recognized as the Joint Chiefs.

"Glad you could make it," the President said, shaking Vinnie's hand.

"Sorry we were detained."

The President glanced at Steve.

"Who's this?"

"The President of Nexus Corporation. He's here in case Syzygy rears his head again."

The President nodded. Through the glass platform beneath their feet, lights flashed on the map as the war continued. He turned toward the crowd.

"You're probably wondering why I've pulled you all away from your work at this critical time. Many of you have questioned I2 Corp, given recent events. I called you here to put your fears to rest. Before we begin, let me welcome Troy White, the new CINCPAC," he said, nodding toward the advisor next to him. "Let me also introduce Vinnie Russo, the new Commander of I2

Corp, and Steve Donovan, CEO of Nexus Corporation. Troy will brief you on the current situation."

Troy stepped forward and pointed a red laser pointer down through the glass platform. It struck a cluster of green lights on the map.

"As you can see, the U.S. battle group's surviving ships remain in open formation several miles apart from one another."

He moved the beam of light up and encircled a group of islands in red. "Our forces are veering southeast, away from the Paracel Islands and away from the PLA, creating distance between it and the PLA's land forces on the Paracel Islands."

Moving the pointer to a cluster of red lights adjacent to the green lights, Troy continued.

"The PLA's forces have split into two groups. The first group consists of twenty or more Chinese Romeo and Ming class subs. They are shadowing the U.S battle group, harrying them with torpedoes and missiles, but the action from the subs is light. Given the Chinese PLA follows the old Soviet model, firing everything all at once, we believe their subs are spent. They outfitted these antiquated subs with new long-range missiles. The sheer vibration and force produced by these missiles shattered their offensive capability. We believe the subs are a decoy to draw our attention away from the second group.

Troy then moved the pointer down the map to a cluster of red lights just above the Spratly islands. "This second group consists of *Varyag* and its PLA ship escorts. They are heading south toward the Spratlys. As you can see, they are only two hours out."

One of the Joint Chiefs spoke up. "I don't get it. Why escort a non-operational aircraft carrier?"

"They're not using *Varyag* as an aircraft carrier. They're using it as an armored supply ship, traveling at over twenty-five knots. We think their objective all along was to gain a foothold in the Spratlys, probably at Subi or Mischievous Reef. Once they get in there, it will be nearly impossible to get them out. They will then have access to one of the world's richest oil reserves and have a stranglehold on two of the busiest shipping lanes in the world. Our objective here will be to sink *Varyag* before they get there." Troy stepped back and Vinnie stepped forward.

"Today you will witness first hand through VR the awesome and destructive power of Warscape and participate in the launching of our first and final counter strike in this war."

Several portals opened to their left and twenty analysts stepped onto the floating platform.

"Each of these analysts will control a missile to be launched against the PLA battle group. Anyone who wants to ride shotgun remotely through VR has an opportunity to do that now."

Vinnie turned and smiled at Steve. "Mr. Donovan and I will demonstrate with the first missile."

"What?"

Vinnie flashed him an *it will all be okay* look. "Warscape, expand region 417."

The floating platform and the other men disappeared. Vinnie and Steve sailed down closer to the map. The red blips were now distinguishable and clearly labeled. Twelve in all, each blip represented one ship in the Chinese battle group.

"Computer, how long until the launch?" Vinnie asked.

"Thirty-four seconds," the computer responded.

Vinnie twisted to face Steve. "Have you ever been in combat before?"

"No," he said, shaking his head.

Vinnie smiled. "I was infantry in the first China War, but naval combat is nothing like land warfare. The ocean has no terrain, nothing to hide behind, only a flat blue plain of water, and missiles are now more powerful than ever. If you hit your target, you sink it. Thus, the name of the game is 'the first side to attack effectively wins'."

Steve nodded, feigning understanding.

"It's not as simple as it sounds. Sometimes it's hard to be effective. That was the PLA's mistake here. The farther you are from your target, the less likely you are to hit it. Well, at least for them."

"What do you mean?"

A disembodied voice filled the expanse. "Fifteen seconds. 417-3, prepare for insertion. Your identity will be trident missile 417-3 from *U.S.S. California* nuclear submarine. Your target is the Kuznetsov-class aircraft carrier *Varyag*."

Vinnie smiled. "Do you know why aircraft carriers are effective?"

"The planes, of course."

Vinnie nodded. "Do you know why planes are effective?"

"Because they can break things." He was growing weary of the game of twenty questions.

"True. They project power, but why do they do it better than a missile?"

He shrugged his shoulders as the environment around them started to shift. The map beneath them blurred. The air around them brightened from dark to light blue.

"A plane can adapt, make visual confirmation of a target, or be recalled. In other words, humans completely control the actions of planes. We're about to use VR to do the same thing for a missile. Hang on. You're just a passenger. Live combat can be intense, but it's addictive. I promise."

Together they were sucked into the perspective of a missile. Steve caught his breath and felt queasy. His body was replaced by a missile. The sea below raced by at horrific speeds. His vision was a blur. He could not turn his head or move at all. Vinnie controlled his perspective.

"Relax. Enjoy yourself," Vinnie's disembodied voice said.

His perspective lifted as Vinnie scanned the horizon. They were flying forward, hovering what felt like inches above the water and traveling at over fourteen hundred miles an hour. The sun was high in the sky. On the horizon, superimposed over the scene, were thin red lines and a few labels. "What are those?" he asked.

"Those mark the location of *Varyag* and the other PLA warships. You can't see the actual ships yet because they're over the horizon, but from the marking, it appears they're still moving forward in a closed formation, keeping their ships only a few miles apart from each other. That was not a very bright move for them. If they don't pick us up soon on their radar, they'll have no chance against us."

"What do you mean *us*?"

Steve's view shifted left to right, following Vinnie's gaze. Green signatures flanked them on both sides.

"Each of those marks the location of another one of our missiles." Their gaze returned forward to the PLA battle group. "Hang on. I'm going to take a peek up top."

"What?"

Instantly, they were looking through the camera lens of a Black Hawk, a miniature, high altitude unmanned aircraft that flew over the PLA battle group.

He felt queasy again from the quick change in perspective. Shaking off the feeling, he surveyed the situation. Beneath them, the Chinese battle group continued to steam forward. It looked as if they had not detected the missiles yet, which were flying beneath their radar. The Chinese also either had not found, or did not care, about the two-dozen miniature remote aircraft buzzing around in the air and the score of sea craft circling in the sea.

"Warscape, zoom in on the PLA battle group," Vinnie said.

The perspective expanded and he could see the twelve Chinese ships clearly.

"Short-range offensive weapons overlay."

Instantly, red shadows swept out from the PLA ships, fading into pink as they radiated out. "Those red shadows show the range and coverage of each ship's weapons system. If our missile finds its way into the dark red areas, we'll likely be shot down by the PLA's defenses.

"What defenses are those?"

"Small weapons fire mostly. The deeper the red, the stronger their defenses are."

Forgetting his lack of control, Steve attempted to nod. He found he was still just an observer, paralyzed. He wasn't enjoying this.

"Warscape, rotate perspective."

The perspective shifted. It rotated above and around the PLA battle group and followed the circular path of the Black Hawk. Everywhere there was red to deep red.

"PLA's weapon coverage is good, but ..."

Steve saw that two of the ships in the Chinese battle group were shifting positions. A large section of ocean on the right flank of the battle group was clear, not even a hint of pink.

"Got ya! Warscape, broadcast to analysts in sector 417: This is 417-3. Chinese battle group has a hole on their right flank. I'm changing my course of insertion."

"Warscape, change perspective forward."

Again, they were sucked into the perspective of the missile. He felt exceptionally queasy now. The missile veered right. He watched the red signatures of the Chinese vessels. They circled around until the missile was almost parallel to the gap in the Chinese defenses. Then they angled in. "Warscape, broadcast 417: 417-3 starting approach."

Steve looked up and realized some new gauges had appeared in the periphery of his vision. One indicated they were twenty miles out.

The ships first appeared as dots on the horizon, overlaid by the red signatures. These dots rose and expanded, slowly materializing into ships. Smoke billowed around some of the ships.

"Did we hit them?"

"No. That's from their countermeasures, small arms fire used to try to knock us down. Don't worry, it's hard to hit something traveling at over twice the speed of sound."

Suddenly the missile jerked left and then righted itself.

"Sorry. It wasn't me. The missile detected something and corrected its course. It may get a bit more bumpy," Vinnie warned.

A ship loomed straight ahead. He could barely make it out through the billows of smoke. It grew rapidly in size. The missile jerked violently up and down and left and right. His world became a chaotic jumble of flashing lights, thick smoke, and ocean spray as everything fell apart around him. In a moment, the ship filled his vision. He unconsciously yelled as they closed in. Suddenly the missile jerked up, hopping over the ship's deck. Steve caught a blur of smoke, people, and metal. Then the ship was behind them. His stomach lurched as the missile dove down to hover just a few feet above the water once again. "Did we miss it?"

"It wasn't our target. This is."

He could see *Varyag* three miles ahead. Nine seconds later, the missile slammed into the rear quarter of the aircraft carrier, ripping a sixty-foot hole into its side. Thick black smoke rose from the sinking ship as another missile struck just behind the first missile, breaking *Varyag* into two.

They reappeared in Warscape on the floating platform. Through the glass floor Steve saw a constellation of missiles closing in on the PLA's battle group.

"So what did you think?" Vinnie asked.

Steve looked up to meet Vinnie's gaze. "It reminds me of the rides I used to take with Ron."

Vinnie looked at the map and frowned. "Looks like it's our last."

Below them on the map, one by one, the red blips disappeared as missile after missile cut down the Chinese convoy. Within two minutes not a single PLA vessel remained.

Coda

"Jan, restore my old virtual office." The image before him wavered and then faded. High ceilings, dark oak floors, and bay windows replaced the crisscross of neon green lines and open expanse. Everything was as he remembered at the Gold Coast Bed n' Breakfast.

The Franklin stove animated the room with flickering shadows and the snap of burning wood. The scent of fresh-cut pine filled the air. His gaze fell upon his favorite chair. It had been a long time.

Steve sat down and flicked off his slippers. He slid his hand along the red velvet arm, stopping at its polished oak trim, worn from eons of use.

Just over a year had elapsed since he last sat here. Tamara and Brooke had been with him then. His gaze drifted to the bay windows. Outside, cold fingers of fog stroked the tips of the pine forest. He could make out the trail that Brooke ran down to get to the beach. In his mind, he heard her laughter again and saw Tamara chasing after her, yelling Brooke's name over the cry of seagulls. The memory was bittersweet.

Barking and wagging his tail, Charlie bounded in from the kitchen. Jumping into his lap, Charlie pressed forward to lick Steve's face.

"Stop." He smiled weakly and pushed Charlie down. The dog sat in his lap, staring up at him with anxious eyes.

"Charlie, open a window to Vinnie Russo's promotion."

Charlie barked and jumped out of his lap. A three-by-five-foot cherry wood frame materialized in front of Steve. Through the paging window, he saw the President standing behind a podium with a row of dignitaries flanking either side. Before the podium, a wall of reporters shouted questions. The President stepped aside and Vinnie came to the microphone. He raised his hands and the crowd settled down.

"It is with mixed emotions that I accept the role as Commander and Chief of the I2 Corp. My predecessor, Edward T. Davis gave his life, along with so many others, to defend our country and our way of life. I would like us to bow our heads in a moment of silence in remembrance of these brave men and women. *My friends …*"

My friends. The words reverberated in Steve's mind. That was Ron's saying. The cadence and tone were exactly the same.

He remembered meeting Vinnie in the flesh at the crime scene. Had he ever seen Ron in the flesh? Searching his memory, he came up blank. Steve only knew Ron's alias.

The last image of Ron returned to him; they had been in the dinosaur exhibit. Ron had told him something. Ron had repeated back Steve's words. The words Steve had told him after the hackers had trashed the Nexus lobby: "An undetected virus is like a spy in an organization; once accepted as one of the fold, you cannot find him without making everyone a suspect."

He juxtaposed two memories—his recent ride with Vinnie in Warscape and his ride with Ron through the asteroid belt. He shook his head. Their personalities seemed too far apart. Or were they? They were both cocky, war vets, and technophobic. How could he be sure?

Cocky and technophobic—a formula for mistakes, Steve thought. Perhaps Ron had not cleaned every trace off the VR server when he left. "Charlie, enable speech mode. Can you recover any deleted files from Ron's office?"

"No, he formatted the disk and destroyed the backups."

"Did anything of Ron's get recorded in the System Logs or Core Files on the VR server?"

"No."

Steve sat back and studied the wisps of fog caressing the top of the bay window under the eaves. He heard Vinnie continuing his speech, the words drifting in from the paging window.

Ron had obviously cleaned everything off the VR server, but did he understand the big picture? Residuals would remain in memory on other systems as well. Every time he logged on, sent email, or entered VR, his signature and data spread throughout the network.

"Charlie, check for Web cookies, email server cache, anything on the other servers with Ron's IP address."

Charlie sat quietly for a second. "I found a remnant of a VR clip."

He leaned forward, patting Charlie's head. "Good boy! Display it and keep looking."

A milky white cube materialized before him. It grew to fill the room, its glow chasing away the shadows. After a few seconds an edge of the cube lightened, becoming clear like water. The translucence quickly rippled across the cube until it was entirely clear. The surface settled and a picture came into focus. He saw Allison and himself in his virtual office. The image stung. He missed her. In the scene she laughed and met his gaze. It made him smile. He remembered. They had just discovered Syzygy. Someone had slipped her a bug and had been spying on them. What did she say? She had just come from the girl's autopsy.

"Charlie, close the cube and restore the source of the cube."

The cube shrank to a single card on the floor. He picked it up. It was a business card. It read: Vinnie Russo, DARPA Special Investigator.

He turned to Charlie and gestured with the card. "This came from Ron's email account?"

"Yes."

Steve slipped the card into his virtual pocket. "Have you found anything else?"

"Ron's last email remains cached in memory on the server."

"Show me."

Before him, an etched cherry wood plaque materialized.

```
FINAL REPORT
FROM: Vinnie Russo
TO:   CIA Director of Internal Operations
RE:   Post Mortem of Operation Dragon Fire


A year ago, Ed Davis, the Assistant Sec-
retary of Defense C4ISR, ordered Allison
Lee of DARPA to incorporate the Nexus in
Warscape, the flagship in the President's
plan to create I2 Corp; this would gut the
CIA. Under the auspices of Operation Dragon
Fire, I moved to discredit the Nexus.

I gave the PLA access to the Syzygy weap-
on through the Nexus site, but interference
from the Chinese, the Nexus President, Austin
Wheeler, and from the Director of DARPA,
Allison Hwang, delayed the alerting of the
media until after the PLA attack. This re-
sulted in incidental losses including: the
Nimitz Class Aircraft Carrier U.S.S. Abra-
ham Lincoln, the Sacramento Class Logistic
Ship U.S.S. Camiden, Assistant Secretary of
Defense C4ISR Ed Davis, and Pacific Admiral
Commander in Chief Marshal Spurrier.

Although regrettable, these losses provided
an unanticipated benefit. Through orchestrat-
```

```
ed field promotions, I will soon become head
of I2 Corp. I can assure you that the Presi-
dent's plan will not move forward. Operation
Dragon Fire is a success.
```

```
Cordially Yours,
Vinnie Russo
```

Steve looked up. "This came from Ron's account, too?"

"Yes."

He turned back to the window and Vinnie's speech. "Today I stand before you …"

Steve patted Charlie on the head. "Charlie, broadcast this email to everyone at that site except for the speaker."

Through a portal Steve entered the chaos-filled the room. He stood at the end of a red carpet that separated two crowds of reporters before the podium where Vinnie, the President, and the Joint Chiefs stood. The reporters rose out of their seats and talked among themselves. A few shouted questions.

Up on stage Vinnie turned to the President giving him a bewildered look. The President leaned over and whispered something to him.

Vinnie held out his hands to the crowd. "Please, settle down everyone. It's a prank. Nothing more."

Steve patted his pocket and strode toward the stage. "No, it's not a trick or a prank. Though, I wish it were."

The crowd became quiet.

Vinnie stared down at him. "Steve? What on earth are you doing?"

"You forgot to clean the cache on the email server. I broadcasted the last email you sent."

"Mr. Donovan what has gotten into you?" the President said.

Vinnie turned to the President. "He's been through a lot. I'll handle this."

The President nodded. Vinnie stepped to the side of the stage.

The faces on stage looked down at Steve in disbelief. *I must look like a raving lunatic.* Spinning around, he searched for the secure room used to brief the President. All he saw was a sea of reporters with similar looks of sympathy. It had to be here.

"It's okay, Steve." Vinnie said.

Steve turned.

Vinnie had outstretched his hands. "No one will hurt you here. It's over." Vinnie stood next to the door.

"Ron, it's not over! You're not getting away with this!" Steve shouted. He walked over and opened the door, motioning Vinnie inside. Vinnie obliged and led the way in. Steve whispered a command before slamming the door closed behind them. Once inside, Vinnie turned and faced him.

"You know, I thought you were smarter than this. What kind of stunt was that, addressing me as Ron? Everyone knows I'm Vinnie. Who's going to believe you now?"

"Why did you do it?"

Vinnie raised his hands. "What?"

"You let the PLA have Syzygy! They killed all those people!"

"But no one of any significance died."

"Syzygy killed Brooke!"

Vinnie shook his head. "No, it didn't. I did."

"What?" Steve took a step toward him. Vinnie stepped aside, keeping a few feet between them.

"If you really must know, I killed Camille and Allison, too. Did you think it was random? Of course, I was surprised when the PLA tried to use Syzygy to kill me at the dinosaur exhibit. I guess I was a loose end, but thanks to you I'm still here."

Steve took another step toward him. Vinnie withdrew the phaser. "That's close enough."

Steve stopped. "You can't hurt me in here."

"I know, but I can knock you off the Internet if you get too close."

"Why did you kill my daughter and Allison?"

"For you, my friend. Don't you remember? I told you in the lobby after the PLA trashed the site. Brooke has been an anchor for you ever since Tami ..."

"Tamara."

"Whatever. All I'm saying is when the wife died, Brooke slowed you down. You never wanted to play anymore. When was the last time we rode a missile like that or cruised through an asteroid belt? Certainly not while she was alive." He laughed.

Steve bit his lip and swallowed his anger. "The email was right, wasn't it?"

Vinnie shrugged. "I suppose."

"So what now? Are you going to kill me too?"

A horrified look crossed Vinnie's face. "God, no! What would make you think that?"

Steve fixed him with a *you've got to be joking* stare.

"Who reviewed the Nexus for Allison and saved your company? Who told you not to worry about Austin and got the funds back to you? I saved your dream twice! I'm your goddamned guardian angel!" Vinnie said.

"The company never meant anything to me!"

"That's bullshit and you know it. You sacrificed everything and spent all your time and energy there. When the company came unglued, you did too. You tried to drink yourself to death."

Steve shook his head.

"Steve, you are special to me. I do not work with, or for, very nice people. It can get lonely. You became my friend, even if you didn't know it." Vinnie winked. "Hell, if you knew me, we'd be the best of friends. But then, I'm a spy. I don't even know myself at times." He laughed. It sounded insane. Abruptly his expression became serious.

"This might be hard for you to understand, my friend, but despite all your faults, you're honest, straightforward, and I trust you. You just can't find that these days, not in my line of work."

Steve slipped his hand in his suit.

Vinnie gripped the phaser. "Not so fast."

He stared into Vinnie's wild gaze. "Your card."

"Huh?"

He withdrew Vinnie's card and tossed it toward him. It drifted slowly through the air, fluttering slowly to the ground like a feather.

"What is it?"

A large cube appeared between them displaying the conference room with a speechless crowd and the President. They were staring into a cube showing Vinnie and Steve staring into a cube. Like a pair of mirrors, cubes nested inside each other into infinity.

Vinnie's mouth went agape.

Steve walked over and opened the door. "I knew you felt safe in here. Austin had a secure office like this, but Allison used a paging window to break in. I took a gamble. I figured this *bug* you planted on her would do the same thing here. I guess I was right."

Vinnie dropped the phaser. "I trusted you!"

Steve gazed into the brightly lit cube. After a few moments, without shifting his gaze, he said, "The light has come into the world and men loved darkness rather than light, lest their deeds be exposed—John 3:18-19."

Vinnie stared back, bewildered. "What the hell is that supposed to mean?"

"Ron, I'm sure where you're going there will be plenty of time to figure that out."

Charlie bounded through the door and jumped into Steve's arms. Brushing the back of the dog's neck, he turned, walked through the door, and entered the conference room.

ABOUT THE AUTHOR

Dan Needles is a master of storytelling in the science fiction and urban fantasy genres; but his stories aren't all fiction. His professional experience as an early enabler of the information age at the dawn of the dot com boom and his continued work with fortune 500 companies, government agencies, and secret military projects means that Needles places his characters in situations that read like fiction, but often exist in the reality of some of today's top technological, and often secret, corporate and government projects.

Dan worked as a developer in the early 1990s at Oracle and VISA before founding his consulting firm, NMSGuru. He quickly learned that building the complexity necessary in such hi-tech environments required working with people, culture clashes, hidden agendas, and the drama of the human condition. His writing reflects this complexity, weaving the inexplicable wonders of new age technology with the relationships and conflicts of the people involved.

Dan is married to Allison and has three sons and a granddaughter.

9736563R00246

Made in the USA
San Bernardino, CA
26 March 2014